Readers of *Sunflowe*
find themselves th

MW01092925

Infinite Jest. But in truth, *Sunflower* is something else, a beast with its own distinct brand of madness. Bluntly satirical of Trump-era politics, *Sunflower* takes you on an acid trip disguised as a conspiracy theory, working with equal skill in realist, absurdist, and metafictional modes to make sure you're lost in a funhouse you won't want to leave. In Gresham's fictional universe, the world might end while you're watching a movie about the end of the world, and maybe you wrote the script or maybe your double wrote the script, and even if the theater is filled with people who won't hesitate to blow your brains out if you laugh at all the wrong moments, it won't make any difference, since the book is filled with all the right moments.

—Stephen-Paul Martin, author of *The Ace of Lightning*

Sparkling genius on full display.

—April Wilder, author of *This Is Not An Accident*

If a bodybuilder were to astral project herself into both Werner Herzog's cameraman/cinematography and *Middlemarch*, it would produce a morbidly rakish sunflower of the same heliotropic anti-equivalent as Tex Gresham's *Sunflower*. And, if an intern were to work in Gresham's library of chapters and deleted scenes, it would confuse The Library of Congress for Netflix.

—Vi Khi Nao, author of *Fish In Exile* and *The Vegas Dilemma*

Tex Gresham has blurred the line between satirical deconstruction of postmodern novels and sentimental love letters to cinema. Simultaneously hilarious and heartbreaking, *Sunflower* is an intricate mystery that will leave readers seeking to mend their broken relationships and their humanity through a shared fondness for the silver screen. *Sunflower* is this summer's biggest literary blockbuster hit! You'll laugh. You'll cry. You'll dissolve.

—Dan Eastman, author of *Watertown*

Tex Gresham's *Sunflower* brought me back to when I discovered Kerouac. The authors have little in common in tone or style but every page or so there is a perfect turn of phrase or pop culture reference that rewards you and propels you looking for the next gem. There is a literary genre of Southern California—from hard-boiled detectives to personal memoirs—and Sunflower has a rightful berth. It is edgy and nervous yet laconic and sun-drenched at the same time.

—Sean Clark, screenwriter/playwright
(*Coach, Early Edition, Eleven Zulu*)

Sunflower is virtuosic, gargantuan, totally unafraid. Experimental and wild, beautiful and heartbreaking, serious and hilarious—I think Tex is here to stay.

—Lindsay Lerman, author of *I'm From Nowhere* and *What Are You*

With *Sunflower,* there is this sense of familiarity. A film trapped within pages. Something you've long forgotten about having watched before. Initially caught in bits in pieces (all out of order) on late night premium cable. And yet, when you take the time to sit down to read Tex Gresham's debut novel, you'll see that the movie in your mind had always been all out of order, bizarrely edited, and laced with images meant to unsettle. But now, older and wiser, it's those choices that make this bit of cinema so special. Tex Gresham's debut novel has this remarkable sense of catching something you shouldn't and not fully understanding it. Give it time. Give it space. Give it a second read. Otherwise it'll haunt you like that brilliant film you can't quite remember.

—KKUURRTT, author of *Good at Drugs*

If Paul Thomas Anderson wrote a novel based on a film by David Foster Wallace with a screenplay by Thomas Pynchon about dark Hollywood, mind-bending conspiracy, the slapstick horror of

America and sheer insanity of existence, these would be some in a long line of flavors the sum total of which might come partway to encapsulating *Sunflower*. Hilarious, repulsive, enthralling, shocking, breathtaking, masterful—Tex Gresham's magnum opus is a novel you will use all your adjectives attempting to describe; a dense, multi-character tale in which each place and person, every moment and word, are connected through myriad layers across space and time. The effect is staggering. This book will swallow you whole then spit you back out, dazed, bewildered, transformed—hungering for more.

—Philip Elliot, author of *Nobody Move* and *Porno Valley*

I've tried to make *Sunflower* into a feature—not a Netflix series—and people called me a moron. So the least I can do is say, "Read this book and imagine it as a really good movie that I would make." Because it's so good that I wanted to make it into a movie—not a Netflix series.

—Alan Smithee, legendary Hollywood director

I relaly liekd tihsbook.

—Etaoin Shrdlu, infamous typesetting error

ALSO BY TEX GRESHAM

Heck, Texas

SUNFLOWER

TEX GRESHAM

SPACEBOY BOOKS

Published in the United States by:
Spaceboy Books LLC
1627 Vine Street
Denver, CO 80206
www.readspaceboy.com

First printed November 2021

ISBN: 978-1-951393-08-3

For Jenny & Steven.
Two gone too soon.

Love to you both,
wherever you exist now.

No single thing abides;
And all things are fucked up.
—Philip K. Dick, *The Transmigration of Timothy Archer*

Sometimes it's better to confuse them for five minutes
than to let them get ahead of you for ten seconds.
—Paul Thomas Anderson to Simeon Wolpe
"Masters & Martyrs" *The A24 Podcast*, March 31, 20█

A note on how to read:

When a <u>DELETED SCENE</u> appears, flip to the back of
the book and read that Deleted Scene.

Or don't.

We remember in edited footage.

OVERTURE: CONTROLLING IDEA

...AND THIS IS YOUR ENDING.

You sit in the coffee shop every day between 8 and 11am, two cups of dark roast called Major Tom's Ground Control. You arm yourself with a Lamy fountain pen filled with blue-black ink and a three-hole-punched white-paged legal pad and rewrite the previous night's scenes, which are often written with the help of Wild Turkey 101 and pineapple soda. You stick to the old saying made famous by Hemingway (maybe) but started, like an urban legend, by an unknown source and passed virus-like into the minds of writers everywhere: *Write drunk; edit sober.*

It's a bullshit catchphrase that's imprisoned countless writers to a life of alcohol dependency they relate to their successes—never failures—and a willingness to outpour their inherent genius. Get liquored up and take away the insecurities that prevent the real shit from boiling out. Go back sober and sift through the typos and grammatical flaws (and in your case, flowers that form on the page when whiskey drips onto fresh ink). You usually read and revise as if you're seeing the work for the first time.

Countless writers have taken credit for work they have almost no memory writing.

Case in point: internationally-renowned, *New York Times* bestselling horror writer Chuck Haze doesn't remember writing his tenth book, *Cat Night*. A logline for it would go like this: When a lunar phenomenon transforms every feline (feral and domesticated) in the city of New Orleans into ravenous beasts satiated only by human flesh, a father must protect his daughter when the two find themselves trapped in a phone booth for the night. Taking alcohol-induced memory loss further, Haze adapted the novel into a sloppily-written screenplay and directed that adaptation and from it only remembers an on-set fist fight he got into with John Lithgow over a Crystal Pepsi. *Cat Night* rests warmly at number twenty-one on New York Film Academy's list of Worst Films Ever Made.

So anyway: you sit, coffee burning off the late night, and flip through pages you're trying to remember because you don't want to become another Hemingway or Haze or Those Writers. But the threat isn't as damning for you. Your work doesn't end in print. Once a novel is published, Those Writers cannot return to the novel or recall the experience of creation. It becomes an index of forgotten time. You aren't just a writer, and you aren't writing a novel.

It's been seven years since your last film, *Cutting Room*, was in theaters. Nominated for seven Academy Awards—including Best Screenplay, Best Director, Best Film, Best Supporting Actress (Jennifer Brachis Donahue, then only 19), Best Actress (Amy Adams), Best Actor (Daniel Day-Lewis, coming out of retirement for his third Oscar win), and Best Cinematography (Robert Elswit). The film is two and a half hours long, absent of any non-diegetic music and punctuated with sparse dialogue. It's about a film editor who receives a roll of film that contains a secret angle of the Kennedy Assassination, clarifying any and all doubt as to the government's involvement, including an unknown connection to the Zodiac killer, Scientology, and McDonald's owner Ray Kroc. It was lauded by critics as "one of the most important American films... *ever*" (A.O. Scott, *The New York Times*) and "so close to what is likely the truth...Personally, I'm surprised Wolpe isn't a target of some clandestine government organization" (Pete Hammond, *Deadline*). As if Hammond's comment was an invitation, you *did* come under fire by nameless groups who threatened to not only kill you, but to film it and release that footage via any media outlet willing to pay for it—which, turns out, is all of them.

So you dropped into obscurity, letting the tides drift out and smooth the ridges in the sand so you could start over with a blank space. But years later, when you tried to return, you felt lost, as if the time away had been in preparation for nothing. You could've sat nicely on your laurels and no one but you would've ridiculed you. But you've never been a rester. You must move, must go, must do, or you'll sink in the space between projects. The waiting period had been hard, but you saw the threat of death as a good enough reason for the holding pattern. When you finally sat down with your pad and pen and committed to writing your next feature, you froze, fear tethering your purpose to a hulking boulder of writer's block—which you never believed in.

And then you had the dream—a god tucked away in the machine that you would have scoffed at had it been in a movie. Never before had an idea come to you unconsciously. Your projects always came from something you needed to say: about society, culture, evergreen problems that never found solutions, about the past and its hold on the present. But this *vision* was something you never knew you felt.

In the dream: an act of terror broadcast to the world, bringing the united collapse of entertainment and its collective discourse; the world suffocating under a machine manipulating the cultural surface; extraterrestrial voices carried through the dark matter of space on radiation waves targeted at Earth; voices silenced by a thick goo dripping from a world-encompassing slug; a bright flash of pink light blooming like a sunflower.

You awoke panicked, as if on the verge of death and not at all ready to go quietly into that eternal midnight. In your bed alone, letting thoughts swim around and form, holding the feeling so the ideas didn't slip into a post-dream grog. The plot and the details evolved. It had always been there, ready for you. You threw on a tattered gray shirt, cheeseburger boxers, and a terry-cloth bathrobe covered in splotches of acrylic paint—your ex-wife's favorite thing to wear while she painted. They say holding on to things after a loved one suicides is a way to punish yourself, but you always felt the robe allowed you to tap into the same energy she had.

You ran to your office, grabbed your three-hole-punched white-paged legal pad and Lamy pen, and prepared to write well into the next day.

But despite the drive and desire, you couldn't do it. It wasn't that you feared the logistics of being death-threatened by anonymous hate groups. Or that they would act on those threats. This was something else.

In college, dope helped you write the screenplay that sparked your career. But once you inherited the responsibility of directing the picture, you dropped the habit. You remembered marijuana being the only thing that disabled the insecurities of putting yourself in an artistically vulnerable position. Thing was, you didn't have any weed. You didn't want to leave the house and be seen at a dispensary—especially at three in the morning. Not that the paparazzi tended to follow you around anymore, but you didn't want to risk it. And dispensary deliveries didn't run all night anymore. Not after the app-based business curfew. So the next best thing you could think of was Hemingway and Haze.

Rustling through your kitchen pantry, you found a bottle of bacon-flavored Schnapps you didn't remember buying, likely given to you as a gag gift because you're Jewish. Plus, everyone knows you don't drink except a single flute of cold duck during wrap parties. So that first night, after six or seven shots of bacon liquor that gave you gurgling heartburn, your fear curtain opened and the story spilled out. The next night, you visited Bunghole Fine Spirits & Wine—formerly Bunghole Liquors.

"I'm not a big drinker," you said to the woman behind the counter. "What should I get that's not going to make me puke and at least tastes good?"

"How fucked do you wanna get?" was her response.

You shrugged and she rang up a bottle of Wild Turkey 101 and suggested pineapple Jarritos. She now knows you on a first-name/pet-name basis, always calls you *Simmy* instead of *Simeon*.

And now here you are, seven weeks later, the last twelve pages of what you believe to be your most significant work. If these were your final words, you'd be okay with that. You take a sip of your still steaming cup of Major Tom's Ground Control and almost spit the coffee out onto your pages. Not from heat, but from it's excessively unsugared taste. You typically tell the barista to add lots of cream and sugar, right? But today you can't remember if you did or not. You flip your notepad face down, head for the additives kiosk. Creamers in tall brushed steel carafes, stir sticks, straws, napkins, six different types of sweetener, both artificial and natural. You pop the top off your to-go cup and reach for the last pack of unbleached Turbinado sugar, the kind in pulpy brown paper packets. It crinkles in your hand. You tear it open.

The packet is empty.

"Empty sugar packet... That's bad luck," says a young woman standing next to you. She stirs her coffee with red-gloved hands.

"Oh," is all you can say.

You're distracted. You're thinking about the script. You don't see it taking much longer. And you're already anxious to immortalize it on film, already thinking of cast. You are one of the only filmmakers still using celluloid—all the others have gone the way of the 8K chip. You're still rooting for the dodo.

How will you represent images you've only seen in dreams? All ideas emerge from a seemingly nonexistent place, an ether, and will eventually form cohesively when bonded to an individual belief system. Your previous films started with ideas from the ether, and because of your individual belief system, those ideas became Final Products. But this screenplay is the Idea in its purest form. The Dream. A translation from this subconscious place, not mixed with anything personal. This is You. And not you. When writing didn't come as easy as it could've, you used to tell yourself: *Think of the story, not real life. You can change the story.* You'd pour out all your anxieties. But you can't do that with this. This *is* real life. Where does that come from? How does it get here? What does it mean, if it means anything at all?

Your mind is lost in this deep thought, which is the reason you, utterly unlike yourself, leave your coffee lid off, unguarded and vulnerable as you go to the counter and ask the barista for more Turbinado. She's gone maybe fifteen seconds and returns with her hands full of sugar. She overloads your hands with the packets, asks if you can put the rest in the container. You agree and walk back to your coffee. You fill the container, take two packets, and generously season your coffee with the sugar. You pour in the half-in-half. Stir. Sip. It's perfect…

Except you taste something different. An odd floral tang. Like you're chewing on a flower petal. You take another sip and the strange flavor diminishes a little. Another sip and it's gone.

You return to your private world with your pad and pen and the last great idea you know you'll ever have swirling in your head like creamer in coffee. You take another sip.

Forty minutes pass in a slow dissolve. And as you turn the last page, the rest of the screenplay scratched out in a madman's font, you stand suddenly and walk out of the coffeeshop, leaving the screenplay face up on a table you'll never come back to. A prisoner to a sudden sensation of being a passenger, pulled back from the forefront of your mind and into a dark space. Almost like the time you tried DMT.

On your way across the parking lot you knock over a little girl with a force unlike yourself to which her mother retaliates by tossing her entire big-sized hot coffee in your face to which you reply with no expression at all and you don't even blink nor do you notice the coffee as it burns your eyeballs but you can't stop yourself from running out into your car because something has you and all you can taste and smell are flowers and you drive without directions a complicated twenty mile route to a nearby wildlife preserve you didn't even know existed and at the entrance you ignore the small fee and the bucket of food pellets and the red-and-white striped cross bar that splinters cinematically as your car plows through it and you leave your windows up and drive past all the animals and ignore the camels and emus and zebras and oxen and llamas but ahead a car full of kids and moderately happy parents feed an aggressive ostrich that keeps trying to rip food buckets out of little hands and you drive around this car grinding one of the ostriches between your car and theirs and its tangled body knocks the passenger side mirror off their car and the frightened and now-angered father lays on the horn which scares the other ostrich away which causes the children to cry so you speed up and pass a sign that reads **DANGER Windows must remain up beyond this point DO NOT EXIT YOUR VEHICLE** with a full-body silhouette of a lion above the warning and you speed up and a lioness and her two cubs lounge in the mid-day sun enjoying as much as any animal in an enclosed environment can the luxuries of not having to hunt or worry about other predators because survival is guaranteed and these lions know this and one of the cubs swats at the other and each makes a budding roar that sounds more like a large house cat's cough than a predatory grunt and you accelerate and the lioness looks up as your car swerves off the path and bounces over the uneven makeshift savannah and the lioness roars with its ears going back and teeth bared and hair stiff and tail out and the cubs freeze and your car slams into the cubs and bounces high off their young but stout bodies and the front end crunches like aluminum foil and plastic and blood and fur and radiator fluid sneeze in all directions and the front wheels go wonky and the car veers and it wobbles swerves and smashes into a nearby boulder and the airbags explode with a *whumpf* and the car fills with powder and smoke and the lioness howls and you casually open the car door face covered in blood that pours from a gash in your nose and a flap of flesh hangs loosely from your forehead but you don't blink and you don't notice the pain and your arm sits at an angle no arm should and you limp over to the bodies of the cubs and sit and you pick one up and throw it at the lioness and the lioness roars and the lioness inches closer but you never see the male lion as it runs up behind you.

You, Wolpe, never feel a thing.

ACT ONE:
DRAMATIS PERSONÆ

THEY COME IN WAVES.

Bodies cool in the lobby's A/C as a sudden heatwave rocks Los Angeles. It's the middle of November. Hands fidget with movie tickets. Strangers speak to each other, but their conversations don't make it up to the third floor where Jackie Day watches the crowd through a porthole window. She's in a small, sparse living space attached to the projection hall. And while she sees these moviegoers, no one sees her due to the heavy reflective coating on the window's exterior. She embraces the anonymity. Her work is her face, voice, soul.

Jackie looks at the floor three stories down, feeling an odd pull. Like she needs to find the fastest way to that painfully hard ground-floor surface. The window's too small for her to fit through. But the thing in the closet can help her with that if she's serious. Why the hell is she thinking about this?

The people in the lobby buy popcorn, hearts warmed by the buttery smell that Jackie has become immune to. She's tried to get popcorn banned at concessions, tried to get the whole concession stand banned, but was met with lengthy conversations about profits and renovations at the hands of the new owner. She has never met this new owner and yet sincerely hates him.

A cigarette burns between her calloused fingers. She takes a drag, blows out grey smoke.

More people in the lobby. Most munching on popcorn. The movie and snack a comfort from reality, an escape that always ends with the realization that fantasy and reality will never intersect, that entertainment on screen will always outweigh the experience of the Real. Because doesn't everyone want to be comforted by entertainment? Jackie isn't exempt from that. Jackie could say she hates these popcorn people, but don't people who see movies deserve a mutual sense of respect regardless of the movies they see simply based on the fact that they actually see movies instead of just harboring the intention of seeing them but never end up seeing them? She doesn't know, gave up trying to find the answers to these things a while ago, lives now in a default setting she's comfortable with.

You know better than anyone that no one can keep up that default setting for very long. You want to take credit for what happens next, but it's kind of a popcorn inciting incident. Solid, but easy.

The lobby doors swing wide and a Black man (late-30s) enters. His eyes—Jackie can see from way up here—are clouded a frosty white. He comes in with the wind, guiding his way with a long segmented stick. He says something to the crowd, but no one acknowledges his presence. Jackie cranks a knob and the porthole window rolls down like a car's. She hears his voice.

"Can someone guide me up to the counter? I need to make change." He holds up a twenty.

They ignore him. They see a desperate-looking Black man and hear the word *change* and something in their brains—compassion, empathy, the ooey-gooey that makes them human beings—switches off. Jackie blows smoke out the porthole, waiting for someone to notice the smell.

A sloppy, insecure-looking white guy in the crowd steps forward and speaks softly to the blind man. Jackie feels like the sloppy guy is in costume or something. Face-eating mutton chops that would've looked ridiculous during the time of the Watts Riots keeps Jackie from seeing his face clearly. His clothes look like they *could* fit if he had a body made for clothes. The sloppy guy eases his arm around the blind man's shoulder and guides him toward the concession counter. Jackie can hear the sloppy guy say *excuse me* and *coming though*. People don't move. He puts his hand out like a cattle guard and plows through rooted bodies. Those shoved away turn, anger a cigarette burning through anticipatory bliss. But once they see the blind man, they reel away, as if whatever caused this man's blindness could be contagious and to risk contracting blindness before having a chance to see This Movie is a horror they can't imagine. The blind man and the sloppy guy speak quietly to each other. Jackie can't hear them, but if she could you wonder if she would run down the stairs and confront the blind man and get ahead of what she doesn't yet know is coming.

A soft hint of a smile slips onto the blind man's face.

At the box office, the blind man places his twenty on the counter and a girl working concessions who Jackie has never seen before but who kind of looks like Jennifer Brachis

Donnahue swaps the twenty out for smaller denominations. With the blind man taken care of, the girl at concession puts her attention on a moviegoer who won't stop shouting for a high-IBU craft IPA. Behind her is a wall of approximately thirty-three beer taps. She spins around to face this wall, takes a glass and fills it with amber. A light push and she sends it gliding down the counter as if she's the proprietor of a saloon in Hollywood's idea of the Wild West. The moviegoer holds out his hand to catch the beer, but his buttery slick fingers slip against the glass. The beer ricochets off the edge of the counter and explodes on the ground. Glass and ale splatter nearby moviegoers. The girl at the counter turns around and starts pouring another beer.

The blind man holds the individual bills up to his eyes, counting, then shoves the money in his pocket. He reaches into his coat and pulls out a bulging, highlighter-pink package. He pushes it across the counter. It nudges the girl in the arm and she turns around. She accepts the package with an imitation of uncertainty. Like they've rehearsed it. The sloppy guy puts his arm back around the blind man's shoulder and guides him toward the exit.

With the door open, wind outside whipping trash into the lobby, the blind man turns to the moviegoers and says, "Enjoy the plot."

Then he's gone.

Jackie backs away from the window. A note taped to the wall near the window flaps against a wind she doesn't feel. It reads:

Even if you're going away forever you don't leave behind a broken memory. Love you, Amy

Jackie touches the note in the same spot she does every day.

The SF-2 projector beeps, letting her know a reel change is due. She drifts with polished routine out the bedroom, down the hall, and into the workspace for Theater Two. The SF-1 and -3 are silent while people find their seats. SF-2 beeps again. Through the view window of Theater Two, Jackie spots the burn in the upper right corner of the screen and flips the switch, starting the second reel—already loaded and prepped for this moment. Once the first reel *fap-fap-fap*s to its end, she rewinds the print, returning the celluloid to a proper cinematic order. She cans it and shelves it in a space marked with masking tape labeled *Cutting Room.*

Theater Two's been reserved for an all-day *Cutting Room* marathon to honor the life and sudden unexplainable death of the film's director, Simeon Wolpe. The theater's new owner agreed to give her at least one screen to show whatever films she wants. Against her insistence, Jackie's been ordered to attach previews before each showing. Trailers for *Over/Shift* (even though *Under/Shift* is still in theaters) and the *Iron Man* reboot and the new new *Star Wars* movie and *Eternal Ridges* (which seems to you to be a post-apocalyptic movie about a wasteland warrior who must protect a potato chip with the face of God on it from marauders determined to control the future of religion) and the worst of the bunch, *Agenda* (about a white middle-class teacher who goes to an inner-city school to educate Black, Puerto Rican, Mexican, Indian, and other "non-white" students for the purpose of creating an army of

educated "minorities" to take control of the American Empire)
—three out of five being produced by A.E. president Guy
Truffaux's media hyper-conglomerate *True Foe Empirical
Broadcasting Systems.*

She watches as the plot to *Cutting Room* revolves at twenty-
four frames a second, those frames and seconds indecipherable
as individual images, seen only as a linear progression of
motion. To her, it's the greatest film ever made, always kept on
hand at Cinéma Vérité.

Even in your current state of non-being, you are humbled
that someone believes in your work like that. This is probably
why you're here with her now. But there's something else. A
connection you're not allowed to know yet.

Even though movie theaters in general are on the verge of
extinction and Cinéma Vérité is not exempt from this, Jackie
insists on showing films by Wolpe, Kubrick, Anderson (P.T.,
never Wes), Tarkovsky, Herzog, Malick, Kurosawa, Corbucci,
Lynch, et al., all in their original celluloid formats. Though in
order to turn a profit, the theater's owner has committed to
three showings a day of the latest Hollywood product. On the
marquee today: the new (not the new new) *Star Wars* and
Under/Shift. A toilet flushes somewhere in the building.

So in her little form of protest, Jackie Day ensures that the
audio is a fraction of a second ahead and that the film is a
smudge out of focus. Not enough for the audience to notice,
but enough to give them a second-act headache.

But when Jackie projects *Cutting Room* or other works she
respects, she treats the presentation with a soft and efficient
touch, as if she were curating an installation of original

paintings by Basquait or Magritte. If it's celluloid, she knows how to light it. She dreams in these formats.

In the ultra-elite circles of Hollywood's most accomplished living directors, Jackie's known as "The Master." P.T. Anderson calls her when he shows films from his private collection. David Robert Mitchell, Sofia Coppola, Ari Aster, the Safdie Brothers, and Barry Jenkins do as well. There's an interview where Anderson is asked: *Is* The Master *really about a projectionist here in LA?* He refused to answer.

In an article in *Deadline* four days before his death, Stanley Kubrick said: "Don't trust anyone but The Master." No one knew who he meant. Jackie's friend H.I. Budrow believes that Kubrick was talking about her. She's The Master. Jackie doesn't share the theory. H.I. also suspects that Kubrick's "suspicious heart attack" was an intentional hit to complicate the pending release of *Eyes Wide Shut*, which is saturated with hidden symbols relating to the Illuminati, Monarch programming, freemasons, and Sons of the Sun, citing the presence of Van Gogh's *Sunflowers* and Sun God masks during the orgy. H.I. says these images, when deciphered correctly, point to a grand design controlling American culture and Kubrick was using the film as a warning to viewers. Again, Jackie doesn't share the theory. Doesn't believe in hidden messages.

Jackie moves away from the projectors and sits on her bed, cigarette almost down to the filter. She picks up a book she's been reading: *In The Realm of Lost Things* by Don Thom David. She reads a passage:

—without the silence and long sleep. A roar cuts the sky in half.

From horizon to horizon. The fourleggers look up, see the dark mass blot out the sun. The fourleggers spent the day searching for slimebugs, gathering for the coming cold. Mama protected her babies from the sharpteeths in the high grass. Now, though, the danger is above. The sound, the cutting across the sky, the darkness. The Mama fourlegger knows it is dangerous. More than the sharpteeths. It is death. Mama pushes the babies through the high grass, navigating to a hole in the ground that connects back to their warren. Slimebugs line the earth outside the hole, but the Mama ignores the food. A sharpteeth lunges from the high grass and scoops Mama's baby into its mouth. The baby screams and then is silent. Mama pushes her living babies to the hole. When they are gone, Mama stands guard at the hole until the sharpteeth is done eating. She waits for the screaming again. Somewhere far there is a loud rumble. The ground vibrates.

*   *   *

Darius wonders what extinction must've been like for those mammals that ended up becoming humans. How much dread they must've felt. He doesn't think it's anything compared to the Now. The Current Age of America is one of those places where no one feels safe, especially white men. Darius feels he has to apologize for who he is all the time and—

Jackie rubs her finger over the letters "a" and "f," printed too dark. The ink smudges. She tosses the book on the floor. Smothers her cigarette against the spine. She knows it's only a matter of time before this book, now serving as her ashtray, gets the Hollywood treatment. She looks at the book, confused for a second as to why in the hell she even owns it.

And then she thinks of Amy again.

Her sister slips from her mind more and more lately. It wasn't always like this. While Amy was on Earth, her and Jackie didn't spend time together too often, but they did talk. At least once a week. They lingered in the closeness they had in childhood. But separate paths and all. Still, they called each other and spoke about things neither really understood—Jackie with her critique of current entertainment, and Amy with her passion for the vastness of space. They listened just to hear the other's voice. But now Amy's gone. Who knows how long it'll be before Jackie sees her again—if ever.

She picks up the book, knocks the ash off the spine, and dog-ears the page before she closes it—even though Amy would say *There's a special place in hell for people who dog-ear books.* Jackie gently places it on a stack of books near her bedside table, other books Amy has had delivered to her by special request from way up there.

There's a knock on the projection hall door. She walks to it but doesn't open. "What?"

"Some blind guy dropped this package off for you," says a young woman. Jackie recognizes her voice, but only barely.

"Slide it under the door."

A rustling sound at the bottom of the door. Then, "The girth is too much. It won't fit."

"Leave it there then. I'll get it." Thinking, *Who the hell says girth?* Lately, all these young people, wandering around Cinéma Vérité with a vague sense of employment, speak to each other with a pretentious and often absolutely incorrect use of language. Shakespearean hipsters. Disciples at the Church of Captain Zig-Zag. *Girth...*

Jackie listens to the creak of the stairs leading to her small plot of real estate, the groan of the elevator that separates her from the first and second floor, and then the return of solitude's silence.

Jackie opens the door. The pink envelope flops into the hallway at her feet, uninvited. Not really knowing why, Jackie steps away from it, like the moviegoers putting distance between themselves and the blind man. She can almost see the package breathing, waiting for her. Throbbing. She doesn't pick it up. She softly hockey-pucks it across the wood floor. She sits in a deteriorating, orange-plaid armchair and picks up the package, its dense bulk barely contained by the pink envelope. No address—return or addressee. No postage. Not from Amy. Those things are official, addressed and stamped with government markings.

She opens it.

The reel for *Cutting Room* turns. Seeping through from Theater 2, Jennifer Brachis Donnahue playing the Frannie O' Hallidaze character screams, *I don't want to be a part of it. But it won't let me go!* This hits Jackie with an irony that feels crafted for this specific moment and specifically for her. She looks around, suddenly feeling like a character in a plot. The throat of rational thought at the mercy of insanity's razor. Her hands weighted with the possibility that she isn't controlling things, that maybe things are controlling her. There's a chirp from the SF system for Theater One, telling her that the moviegoers are ready for the show.

Jackie sets the stack of papers on the floor—three-hole punched and bound with brass brads, title page reading *Sunflower: The Final Film of Simeon Wolpe*—and makes her way to SF-1 to fiddle with the focus, un-sync the sound, and start the reel. And you wonder:

Who the hell typed that?

2

HEATHER KNOWS EVERYTHING WILL KILL HER.

She fears death, totally fucking petrified of it. *Nothing* will stop it. She believes, soul-deep, that this feeling is secluded to the lonely planet of her mind. Every headache is a brain tumor. Bloating in her stomach is late-stage cancer—inoperable, spreading. Back pain or tingling sensation in her legs is the onset of multiple sclerosis, maybe a tumor growing on her spinal cord. She believes this even after the doctor at the emergency room told her she's the healthiest person he's seen in a long time.

But something *is* wrong. Otherwise she wouldn't feel the way she does—a stranger in her body, a prisoner of her mind. And it's not the usual emotional ebb and flow that puts her into a slightly depressive state once every year or two. Things had been fine. Until when? When did this start?

She's been in LA too long to remember the backstory of when and why she arrived in LA. It's all a deleted scene. She can't remember where she grew up or who her friends used to be—if she ever had friends. She can't remember if her parents are disappointed in her or not, or if that disappointment is self-generating. She asks herself: *Does Heather Pérez have parents?*

Siblings? Will attaching family legacy and its residue help define her? What's her motivation? What are the choices that shape her action and therefore her character? Heather keeps running through the actor's toolkit to try and figure out the details that make her a well-rounded character and not a pathetic young woman sitting alone in her bedroom and who believes herself to be dying.

She sinks another Ativan. *Fuck it.*

There's a black & white film playing on the television. It's easy to follow, even with the sound off, so her mind drifts slowly from mortal sickness to the action on screen. A love story—or maybe not. All those 50's era movies have to do with love. *Love...*

A frontal lobotomy could help. She's looked into it enough to know it *could.* Take away a sliver of brain tissue and bye bye bad thoughts. She search-engined *where can I get a lobotomy?* and *do you have to commit yourself to get a lobotomy?* She's read that people have an impossible time naming their dread, but that most associate it with an end-of-the-world fear, an end they know is coming but don't know when. Or maybe it's just the end of *their* world. Or maybe they're realizing a long-believed lie is hiding a never-known truth about themselves. But with the lobotomy: the unnamable dread is killed.

"The world *is* going to end," she says to herself, voice creaking like floorboards of a collapsing house.

Her mind feels both here and not.

When she tries to call the nearest mental hospital to schedule a lobotomy, the phone slips through jellied fingers and falls to the floor. A slug of drool slips out her mouth. She hears voices coming from the TV even though it's muted. She reaches for the phone again, but as her head sinks into the pillow, the Ativan breathes its numbing wind and the world fades to black. Dreams fill the dark theater:

Lurid pearls of thought, moments that seem to last lifetimes but take only micro-seconds of brain electricity. These moments are her tombstone. And you are audience to them— seen through studio set fog and lighting, grainy & distorted. Through a greased lens shifting like a flickering strobe between a distorted wide and tight close. Degraded film burned by gritty chemicals, and it all plays like an unedited cut…

…free land home trapped suffocating under weight of viscid slime growing slime lives moves breathes grows constricts like dead ssssssssssluuuuuu men women children screaming voices choked under thick mucus fluid expands everything shrinks everything shrieks you are not you shrivels expands reduces to elementary particle explodes black hole sucking her into place she's been before fast faster speed of light tunnel light pink light ahead windows looking out of black hole tunnel show faces all same different faces your face is someone else's faces world gone rubble smoke decay mushroom colored tattered flags stained all red all tumbles down light brighter more artificial filament bulb spotlight scream building in her heart halts crowd off edge of stage she's on stage light brightens audience same faces lost hushed anticipation deafening her voice meant to be there but nothing alive reverberation Jennifer of large hall man next to her man she doesn't know stranger shadow man his face different her hands heavy sticky throbbing dripping deflated football animal sea hare alive moving dead slowness man next to her dressed in suit Jennifer

holds same dripping throbbing slowness she lifts heaviness puts it to her face holds it out to audience cameras focus scream becomes voice hers asks What do I do with this? *white silent static dead channel to whatever she was connected blank empty fluid silver endless Jennifer Jennifer Jennifer Jennifer JENNIFER—*

—and she jerks awake. Her back pops. Her dry throat suffocates a scream. *STOP THINKING* she hears a voice scream, and then realizes it's hers. Before thoughts can settle on something different, hopelessness has found her again.

She unmutes the TV. There's a trailer for the newest Jennifer Brachis Donnahue film. They now advertise her as Academy Award Winner Jennifer Brachis Donnahue, which makes the sickness in Heather's head flare, brain zaps sending sparks zig-zagging through her body. She sweats, bites the inside of her cheek. *It should be me* she mumbles to the television, not really in control of her words. Of all the roles she's auditioned for, almost all have gone to Jennifer Brachis Donnahue, leaving Heather to a career working the counter at a shitty movie theater where the projectionist always stares at her from the third floor.

Heather knows that she's as good as Donnahue—No, better. All she can think about is River Phoenix and Jonathan Brandis dying in the shadow of Leonardo DiCaprio. Heather knows there's some setup involving Donnahue. A vast entertainment-based manipulation preventing Heather (and anyone like her) from getting roles they clearly were born to play in favor of maintaining the Donnahue Brand.

She switches stations, skips past the trailer for a biopic about a canonized media innovator who died of cancer, past a plea for donations to help children dying of cancer, past an ad for a new medicine that has the likelihood of prolonging life (of those suffering from cancer) by about 16%, past an ad for the upcoming First Annual Entertainment Awards, past a TV-static snapshot of Truffaux at the podium with an urgent ticker tape crawling across the screen, and ends up on an infomercial for a rehydrator said to hydrate a dehydrated turkey in less than four minutes with an 88% chance of tasting nearly identical to an authentic oven-roasted turkey.

She starts crying, gripped with the hopelessness that she's already circling the toilet. And the TV isn't giving her the comfort she needs. She mashes her finger on the channel button and watches as images blur. On TV:

...which would mean that President Truffaux plans to appeal the limitations on presidency term limit and attempt to run for office a third time. With over two years left in his term......but without question North Korea claims responsibility for the Placerville shooting that took the lives of twenty-two golfers at the Ridgemont Country......the UN has reached a decision to eradicate the growing horde of cocaine hippos in South America by use of controlled nuclear......and all it takes is two pills a day and you can kiss those grey skies goodbye. Side effects may include suicidal thoughts, night terrors, dissociative personality disorder, gender confusion......Russian officials made a statement on Tuesday that claims that the United States is responsible for the sub-nuclear blast that came from a......John Pasolini of the Placerville Police Department claims that the shooters were white males, early 30s, and looked to be 'as American as John Wayne.' No statement has......and animal theorists believe that, left unchecked, the

swarm would continue to travel north, swim across oceans, and enter American soil within two months......all more real than real. SensiSystem—Actually Feel It©......recent incidents put the toll of burned homeless at nearly two hundred. Police are calling it serial terrorism......colonists have cut off all communication between Earth and Mars. The act was seen as hostile and President Truffaux responded by severing all supply routes to the self-declared sovereign......Vice President Goldwater unwilling to compromise......but all it will take is one more big quake and the California Commonwealth is out to sea. And the Trans-Republic bridge won't be able to gap the distance. Half the state will be in the Pacific. The United Empire will......Drink up. It's the good stuff!

Her finger lifts. The frantic channel surfing stops and the TV gives her images of a mid-day talk show. *Gossip Now*. Today's guest: Jennifer Brachis Donnahue. The camera pushes in close, her face filling the screen. Heather freezes the image. If she were to go, right now, to the studio where they produce *Gossip Now*, JBD would no longer be there. JBD might be sunbathing in Greece or eating a $10,000 meal in South Korea. Or maybe she's in a dark room, in bed, worrying about the end of her life. A zap strikes Heather's brain and she winces, grabs her head. She slides out of bed onto the floor. Knees drag as she pulls herself closer to the TV. Nose inches from the screen. Heather looks at the image and feels shaky, questioning if she's looking at a television or a mirror or the shimmer between now and future. The TV goes dead, and she sees her reflection in the TV's darkened eye.

The door to her room opens slowly.

Like the unstoppable force in a slasher, a shadow falls on her. A man now stands in the bedroom doorway, silhouetted by the hallway light. She spins around, blinks at the still-lingering dream, but the man's still there. Real. She tries to say *Get out,* but with her lips almost totally numb it comes out, "Gish shou."

The man seems to wriggle like a tight bundle of…*slugs* … that's what was in her hands in the dream. A big slug. On stage with a slug in her hands, faces looking at her in horror. She shoves her mind back on the man in her room.

She reaches for her phone but her fingers are still loose. Muscles don't respond to signals from her brain. The shape of the man is wrong, not anyone she knows. He looks like the one from her dream, the one next to her on stage.

Who are you? But it comes out, "Ha'ar ya?"

She doesn't expect an answer. The man steps forward. No… It's not the man from her dreams, but he looks as if they might be related, distantly. Vaguely Middle-Eastern. Expertly-groomed beard. He seems transparent, a ghost. He glides toward her, cradles her head in his large hand, places his lips against her forehead, a smiley face pin on his lapel pushing toward her face, and whispers, "You *are* sick, Heather. Do you want help?"

Her soul shivers. He smells bitter, like a retirement home, breath like the cardboard-box food they give the dying. The smell comforts her in a way that's fetal. Her arm curls around his body and she embraces him. Her lips start to work again. "Save me."

"You deserve to be saved."

"Yes...please. I...please. What do I do?" Her words bubble out, a natural fissure. Snot and tears mix on her face. "I'll do anything."

"Do you devote yourself to a future where you are the best version of youself?" His face begins to focus. The features coming together enough for her to recognize him. She's seen him at auditions, but never face-to-face. The same guy who manages Jennifer Brachis Donnahue. How is he here?

"I do."

"Are you willing to abide?"

"I am."

"Give up your life, and this will all be behind you." He pulls back, looks her in the eyes and adds, "Miss wants you for a role you were born to play."

She squeezes him tight, as if she could dissolve into his body, a scarred child comforted by a newly adoptive parent. The sickness and certainty of death slides into the back part of her mind. The TV flickers to life on its own, warm glowing comfort lighting the scene.

"I will give you everything." She can't help herself from adding, "I love you."

It feels like the most perfect thing to say.

He holds her, whispers in her ear, a finger casually brushing hair off her forehead, tracing the outline of her face. He pries open her left eye. Her lid tries to flutter shut but he holds it firmly open. With his free hand, he delicately reaches toward her eyeball. Pointer and thumb in a pinching position. His nails connect with her iris. She flinches. He pinches, grabs hold, and slowly, delicately, thoughtfully slides a thin needle made of iridescent metal out of her eye. Once it's out, her whole body relaxes and she lets out a vaguely-sexual moan of relief. The man takes the needle and eases it into the flesh underneath the fingernail of his middle finger until it's gone.

The man touches Heather's forehead, eye, nose, mouth, then caresses her chin, all while saying, "Head dreamer, eye winker, nose dropper, mouth eater, chin chopper."

Wait... Isn't this head dreamer eye winker thing something Heather's mother used to do to her when she was like seven or eight to help her fall asleep? How would this guy know this? Unless she's just making up that history with her mother. But why do that? Build character? Either way, the ASMR rhythms and the soft touches eases her into a state of deep peace. And before he touches her again, she's asleep and the dreams aren't there.

3

[BEETHOVEN SYMPHONY 9 OP. 125 BEGINS]

Here it comes again.

It seems brighter. Closer maybe. But that might just be what you keep telling me is *hyperfocusedness*. I know fear makes people feel and see things that might not be there. Turkmon's proof of that. But I never thought that would apply to me. I've tried to explain what I see to Control and to Hawthorne and their response is always the same.

Okay so I guess you're still listening to this. Of course you are. You're programmed to.

Cargo's on approach. I'm up here alone for at least another ninety days. After Turkmon, I doubt Chairman Musk or Shotwell want to risk sending anyone else. I can take the solitude. It's what I was trained for.

Turkmon should've never been up here. It takes *years* to

acclimate to this life. Not a two-month crash course. I'd spent enough time aboard the I.S.S. and the first S.X.S.S.—more than anyone. Plus, he was a biological engineer. Why do we need one of those up here? There's nothing alive in space. Except me…and the people on their way to Mars.

Maybe.

I have this terrible feeling that the mission failed. That everyone died, the ship imploded. Something. Or maybe it was staged, a hoax to force people on Earth into passivity, to linger in the belief that they can fix what can't be fixed instead of worshipping the hope of starting over on a new planet…That might be a by-product of this funky liquid feeling building in my brain.

Run through your history. Anchor yourself to keep the brain from turning stagnant. You keep saying this because some doctor down at Control programmed you to since the incident with Turkmon.

I've been talking to pictures of people I don't know anymore. That liquidy funk is starting to make all the things I'm supposed to remember feel like soggy cardboard. I'm not losing the schematics and functions of the relay switches I cycle through to keep this floating coffin from plummeting to Earth. That stuff's in my DNA. What I'm starting to lose touch with is the people I'm supposed to love. Not that I don't love them, but maybe it's because I'm forgetting how to love? Or why I'm supposed to love. It's all there, but drowning in that funky liquid feeling. Love for my sister, Jackie. My dog. Dad and Mom. I'm sure I've forgotten someone. And I miss them more than I do Diet Coke or skiing or swimming in the Pacific or eating real pizza instead of a 3-D printed protein synthesis in the vague shape of pizza.

I find myself thinking about my sister more.

We didn't grow up with that inseparable, vaguely telepathic connection twins have. We shared experiences, but we had our own worlds. Jackie would show me the movies she loves and I'd watch them with her, but I always felt outside that love, that what she experienced and what I experienced in those movies would never be the same. Maybe this is the same way I feel about the stars. I was always going to be up here. But Jackie… Now that I'm so far from her, I feel this…tether. I can feel her, the things she does. I wonder if she feels the same, if she's aware of me.

I feel depressed but only because I know I'm supposed to feel depressed.

Switching Relay 1a to negative. Changing Packet 22. Sending.

That light is still there. It makes me think that Turkmon knew something. Like that kid in that one movie who could see dead people.

Recycling CO2 pod one. 3...2...1...Connection reestablished.

He must've had undiagnosed depression before he came up here. The zero-g and freeze-dried replications of split pea soup and beef stroganoff couldn't have helped. Might've even been what made him slip into psychosis. Which is probably why he took a walk outside three months ago and hasn't been back.

I don't feel right with Turkmon gone. Up here alone. Nothing flesh and blood. Just this head installed with artificial intelligence that's here to solve technical issues, correct code, run systems, and listen to what I say.

I don't feel right because of the attacks against the I.S.S. and the first S.X.S.S. The nukes, accusations pointed at Syria, Russia, Iran, North Korea, and all of them taking credit. It doesn't make sense.

This body of mine, up here, keeping thermonuclear war at bay—or so they tell me.

I know down in Hawthorne they question everything I've said. They ask me if I pushed Turkmon out, mentally or physically. I keep telling them to pull me back. But they won't. They're too afraid to replace me because they think I'm the only thing standing between sanity and collapse—global, not my own.

They say *As long as there's an American up there, no one will attack it*—even though I'm a Commonwealth citizen. But so yeah... A zero sum game. Except the zero sum means total planetary annihilation. Why is this place so important? I know it's not me.

They'll never point the finger at their own misdoings. But who does?

There it is. Again. Out there. That light.

Half the world submerged in darkness now. Cities lit up, circuit boards of information. Down there, chaos. But up here I can almost see the design...

The night before I left Earth a woman came to my room. A reporter. She wanted to know how it feels knowing that anyone who looks to the sky will have a face to look to. *No longer empty*, I think she said. I told her I didn't want that responsibility, that I was doing this because it's all I've ever wanted to do. My only reason for being here. To explore that infinite space that separates man from god. But what about woman from goddess? Either way: I don't want to be a god.

I...

Those psychiatrists down in Hawthorne tell us to do things like this, talk to this SensiHead to retain our sanity and intimacy and all that so we're not reclusive little animals desperate to get back to the stars when we regain our Earth legs. Jackie made me watch that one movie, *2001* or something. That's all I could think of when I first started talking to this. But it's really sentient like that, though it talks back when it's supposed to. My sanity's fine. That's not why I'm here slurping chicken kiev out of a pouch, talking about things you already know have happened.

I'm scared. That's the truth.

Not because I'm up here alone, that the nearest person is 248 miles away. Not that the walls are pressurized on the outside by an infinity of nothingness. One would think that the view from this porthole would be a black sheet shot with a billion bullets, rays of light shining through. But it's nothing. Darkness. The emptiness, the *aloneness* doesn't scare me. It's always been there, will always be there. We live under an eternal security blanket. We can see it, observe it, watch it change, decode its makeup. It's what's out there that scares me. In the dark. Something that wasn't there the day before. Like a distant match that's just been struck. A light. Far but bright. I see it, out there.

Control always comes back with *We're paying a substantial amount to keep you entertained up there, Amy. Watch the feeds, pay attention to your readouts, file your data. Don't worry about the void. That's our job.* And things like *Any anomaly within threatening range is known to us. Here, this is new.* And Control pipes another episode of *Dr. Doctor, PhD*. I don't understand how something like this can be on TV. Down syndrome doctor marrying transgender patients, starting an orphanage of Syrian refugees—which is all fine. But it's the laugh track... I can't relate anymore. I watch, but my mind will always be on that bright spot out there. Too small to be an anomalous reflection from Mars or Venus. And any charted comet or asteroid doesn't pass within viewing distance for another seven years—or so Control says. This is something unknown. Burning its way to Earth. Or on a collision course with the moon. Or it's Nibiru passing through dimensions to knock everything out of orbit. Or it's a black hole meant to suck our galaxy into oblivion. If that happens I'd never—

[SPACE ODDITY - DAVID BOWIE PLAYS ON COMM SYSTEM]

Control thinks it's some kind of joke. Out in space, this song's not amusing. And I'm sure, at this moment, this situation's getting laughs from those at ground control or whoever's watching on the livestream.

That thing out there, the light, it's gone for another 90 minutes, but it'll still be anchored in my mind. I'll run for a bit, wear myself out and sleep. Sleep's the only place I can go to escape the bright spot. Sleep is a good place. It's a place where I can forget about existing. The bright spot is never there.

[SPACE ODDITY STOPS—BEETHOVEN RESUMES]

Turkmon said something just before he stepped out, and I

don't think you heard it. Like he had some kind of prediction or omen. He saw space made into time. Not that I believe in predestination. Sure, there's probably an underlying pattern to the universe, that we could all be in an iteration of a Big Bang/Big Crunch cycle. Patterns constantly change as time moves. Chaos reigns. Entropy controls the balance of power and always has. But with what Turkmon said, it's hard to ignore the possibility that somehow he knew about the bright spot. Or that something would happen. Or both...Or that could've been part of his psychosis. Because what he said was more poetic and apocryphal than any direct statement. But it's hard to see that light and not feel that he was in touch with some ethereal underlying current I'm so reluctant to believe in. So I'm scared. More so than if I had just witnessed the bright spot on my own. Because now, I feel his words. As if something terrible has already happened.

He said *At the sound of the sea the sunflowers open their black eyes. Out there. It's going to eat.* And then he stepped out. I watched him until I couldn't. He never moved, never struggled, never looked back or tried to. He went into the void confidently.

When I look out and see the spot, that's what I see—a sunflower. I feel its hunger. I don't know what that means other than a slow-lurking unnameable dread. But if Turkmon wasn't predicting anything, if he was just talking through a mind that was corroded like a bad M18 array sensor relay, then what's going to happen to me? Did he know something too heavy to carry? Will I go bad too?

There it is again.

And now you're putting something on TV to distract me.

Oh I hate this movie. I used to watch this as a kid. Maybe I'll take a little jog on the machine and go to sleep. Maybe I'll dream. Maybe I'll wake up and not see what Turkmon saw.

I wish I had something to read.

[**BEETHOVEN ENDS**]

<u>DELETED SCENE</u>
Diet Coke & Cheese Sticks

4

690LBS.

That's all Delta Robison has to lift and it's over. Her belt's tight. Hands taped. She takes a gulp from a sports bottle filled with electrolytic fluid and creatine nitrate, all legal under the regulations of the International Weightlifting Federation.

690lbs and she's the next Lady Universe. She knows she can do it. The last grueling decade of her life has been in preparation for this. Days spent shifting between training and torture: eating thousands of calories, lifting weights that would stop the hearts of strong men, waking up to pump then eat breakfast then pump again, then run, train, eat, sleep, and ever on endlessly. A high-toned machine. She's lifted 675lbs on several occasions and once lifted 682lbs. But never 690lbs. She's not sure if it will change—or maybe destroy—her body. She knows, though, that if she does it, her body won't be hers anymore.

She ignores the crowd. Doesn't have to picture them in their underwear or naked. Their expectation isn't her pressure.

Even though the crowd keeps her from hearing it, Delta knows her phone's vibrating in her gym bag. Feels it like a premonition. She regrets leaving it on, but promised Bub she'd keep it near her all day. She doesn't need to answer it. She knows what the call means: Bub's surgery has gone wrong. Her baby brother *will* die today if things don't work—and maybe if they do. Everything on the verge of collapse.

690lbs will bring offers from Wheaties or Gatorade or Cellucor, Muscle Milk, Quest, Schwarzenegger Inc., endorsements that will give her the money to pay for her brother's surgery and for what comes after—again, if he lives. The endorsements will also give her the chance to prove her existence means something. She won't be just another person. Eyes will be on her. An idol cast in permanent precious metal.

"Stay focused," says Coach Nelson. His look begs her to leave the phone alone. *690lbs* his eyes say. *Muscle Milk, Cellucor, Quest Quest Quest* they say. Eyes that remind her: *You got about a 25% chance of doing this, but I believe in you 100%.* Coach Nelson has always been there for her potential money—not really for her. *Stay focused.*

"I am," she says.

He nods and moves behind her. Hands ease onto her shoulders, squeeze. Engorged muscles clench. His fingers work out the tension. A tendon in her upper trapezius tore during the last round, started swelling like an overstuffed sausage, but she doesn't care. When his fingers work at the tear, a hot screw turns in the base of her neck. She leans into the pain. It awakens her. Pain is temporary; strength is forever.

Coach Nelson says, "I need you to know how important you are."

"Don't start this again."

"I have to. I wouldn't be anywhere without you. But you wouldn't be anywhere without me. I helped shape you. Remember that. We need this. The amount of back tax I owe on my house... They're close to taking it away."

Delta doesn't say anything.

She hears the commentators describe her as *One of the most prominent African American female weightlifters in the world* as if the fact that she's both a woman and Black somehow segregates her from every other person on the planet who can deadlift 690lbs. She knows men who can't lift that weight without causing a brain hemorrhage, blood trickling out their noses. The commentators treating her race and gender as a sideshow quality cheapens not only her gift, but her entire existence. Though, to her, only the gift matters.

These aren't really her thoughts. Bub feeds her this stuff: data, statistics, the truth coded behind reality's red curtain. She wants to save him because he's special. And not in the bumper sticker kind of way. He's full-on Stephen-King's-*The Shining*-type special. Forget that his birth killed their mother and that their father died on the way to the hospital in a freak accident involving a building crane, a cement mixer, and an anvil, leaving an 18-year-old Delta to take care of baby Bub on her own. Tragedy is the only way it goes for them. Bub knows almost everything—without even knowing how to read. The tumor on his brain stunted his growth drastically, but it didn't stop him from developing mentally in a way most people never do. He can list every film ever made in chronological order. *Man Walking Around A Corner* (Le Prince, 1887), *Accordion Player* (also Le Prince, 1888), *Roundhay Garden Scene* (again, Le Prince, 1888), and on and on. Bub is almost always sleeping with philosophical texts like kids sleep with teddy bears. He firmly understands Freud's psychoanalytic theory of the human mind and its base-level instincts for sex and aggression, Kant's supreme principles of morality and his Critique of Pure Reason, Hegel's principle that reality is expressed only through rational categories, Fromm's atavistic drive toward disobedience and its usefulness in humanity's survival, Žižek's belief in the idea of self-directed outbursts of violence and the inevitability of ideological destruction, Marx's theory of societal alienation and stratification of social classes, and a bunch of other stuff Delta will never understand the way Bub does. And again: he can't read. He can also name every type of slug that's ever existed. Everything he sees is mentally transcribed into screenplay format. Almost like how people see sounds or taste words. He says things like *Interior house. Delly lifts weight. Bub says Do good Delly*. But what get's to Delta's core is that he knows everything she thinks before she does. He once said to her *Delly, see milk, go home* and a week later, while at a Circle K, she reached for a gallon of milk and heard Bub. In her head: *See milk, go home*. It reverberated through her body. She dropped the milk and rushed out of the store. The clerk yelled *Hey, hold it*, probably thinking she was trying to steal something. Not even a full minute after she got in her car and sped off back toward home, a semi gas tanker plowed into the storefront and exploded. Everyone died. Bub knows things that are, as he says it, *Over the people rainbow, over the people shadow*. He's really fucking special.

This is how she knows that the phone in her bag is vibrating again. She continues to ignore it.

Some could call her selfish. And the people who would wouldn't understand. People haven't seen her situation on film, so they couldn't even begin to understand her situation. She can't remember a time when her brother wasn't confined to a hospital room, tubes shoved up and connected to various parts of his body, dripping drugs and pulsing machines and attentive nurses the only things keeping him alive. He still smiles, still laughs. She can hear his happiness trapped, a sound that reminds her that he doesn't want to go but is okay with going. The doctors told her the success rate is less than 10%.

Delta forgets about the hospital smell, the small hand tightening around hers, the sound of tiny medical saws and suction hoses cleaning bare skull, the smell of laser against brain matter.

This is her liberation.

She looks over at her opponent.

Germanic, stoic, stocky, a machine in human form: Ida Gershtandifreich. Current deadlift world record holder and winner of the last six Lady Universe competitions. But what you can see in this state of non-being is that Ida is also the great-granddaughter of infamous Nazi war criminal, Rolf Ulphupt, as well as the descendant of Gerulf Osgar, 14th-century warrior who severed the heads of seven hundred and twenty-six opponents and used them to build a wall around his stead. Ida waves her arms and legs, loosening her muscles.

An assistant nervously rushes up to Ida with a pink sports bottle and squirts pre-workout into her mouth. Ida gulps. More pre-workout. Gulp. The assistant wipes Ida's face with a red-gloved hand and then hurries away, disappearing down a nearby corridor. Ida's coach and assistant coach speak German in her ears, bigging her up. They cower in her company. Most do. But not Delta. She knows she's stronger—victory's patience has worn thin, waits for Delta to catch up.

Before the match an anchor from ESPN-Pink asked, *Why weightlifting?* Coach Nelson answered for her because her reasons—the main and the motivator—don't make "uplifting copy."

It started the summer after high school. A date with Devaughn Blake, her boyfriend of two years, ended with him being shot in the back and killed while walking home from seeing a movie at a theater with a fancy French name. Cinema something. Devaughn showed her his favorite movie. Again, something French. Though it was quiet and slow, the look on Devaughn's face as he watched, smiling and intensely focused, his hand gripping hers at his favorite parts, made Delta feel a love for the movie she wouldn't have had she seen it on her own. And then he was shot.

After his death, she stopped eating. Fell into a depression so deep that it felt like her bones had been replaced with numbing jelly. A part of her wanted to end her life. Not just because Devaughn was dead, but also because she felt so helpless and weak in the face of the insurmountable force pushing against her.

Then, when Bub was discharged from the hospital after his premature birth, Delta spent a night rocking him to sleep. His breath was shallow and fluid. She thought it would be his last night alive. They say that babies don't start being actively cognizant until around six months. And words come around a year. But that night Bub looked up at Delta, their eyes connecting. He lifted his hand to her face, his tender, wrinkled fingers running along her cheek. Tiny fingers stopped on her temple. Bub took a long breath that seemed to pain him. *Lift weight, Delly*, he said in fully formed words. A part of her wanted to scream and toss Bub's infant body as far as she could, cast it out of her life. But a calmness came over her. And she said *Okay*. The next day she bought weights and started lifting in her living room. And as the pain in her body grew, as muscles tore and reformed, Bub started to strengthen as well. Transforming her body was transforming his. He'd sit next to her and scribble with crayon on anything he could: the numbers 6 and 9 and 0.

So she lifts.

No one pays attention to the Lithuanian struggling to lift 500lbs. She's only there to break the monotony and add anticipation for all those watching on ESPN-Pink. Delta stands, chalks her hands, slaps them together, shakes them out, chalks them some more, doing everything she can to ignore the phone still vibrating in her bag. She should be there.

She looks around the half-filled stadium, cell phones flashing, murmurs from the crowd stirring tension in the air in a way the worms in her stomach respond to. A rep from Cellucor chats with Coach Nelson, and she can always tell the reps by their suits and their heads topped with baseball caps displaying product logos. Delta flexes, tightens all her muscles. She thinks of her brother, barely able to lift his fork of whatever nutrient-heavy, flavor-absent food they mold for the dying at hospitals.

Coach Nelson waves her over. She looks at Ida—busy chalking her hands, never looking at Delta. Delta feels like the only person she could have a connection with is Ida, someone who knows what it's like to be in her position—if only somewhat. But Ida's there to steal Delta's future, not to make a connection. Ida's lift is next. As Delta approaches Coach Nelson and the man—

"Delta, this is Steve Muhammed Muhammed with…?"

Delta sees the man is with a company she's never heard of before. By the way this guy's groomed and dressed more for an award ceremony than a lift competition, she knows he's got money. He clasps his hands in a theatrical way and finishes with, "SunCor. We're an upstart in the fit biz, but we've been turning more than a few heads just in Q3 alone. Recently signed Hurul Bount. And forgive me if I don't shake your hand. I know those are valuable tools. Don't want something unforeseen to happen."

The African bodybuilder Hurul Bount won the last twelve Mr. Universe competitions, along with the previous seven World's Strongman contests. Headlines call him Obsidian Arnold. For SunCor to sign him means exciting things.

"Very impressive," says Coach Nelson. "But see: Delta here, she could pound Bount to a pulp. No question."

"Bold statement."

"And I'll make it every morning with a little cream and sugar." The men laugh in a way men doing business do.

"As a corporation, we're interested in diversity. People like Ida over there, their time has come and gone," Muhammed Muhammed says. "But we want to give people like you, Delta, a chance to show the world how strong and important you really are."

Delta flexes her muscles. A fine sheen of sweat gives her figure a bronze statue quality. Ancient shape. Earth. Solid. An anvil no one can move. She's everything this guy's looking for, Delta's sure of it. But in her head, she repeats the way he says *Diversity* and wants to slap him in the neck. That word out of this guy's mouth means *Your future is only important because it fits a quota*. But she sees the logo on his hat, the smiling sun with the bulging muscles, and she wants to scream *Show me where to sign*. She knows all that's standing in the way is 690lbs.

"I believe there's a phone vibrating in that bag," Muhammed Muhammed says, pointing in the direction of her bag. As if he knows which is hers. Knows that her phone's vibrating even though there's no possible way he could. He smiles and his eyes shift over and connect with you—somehow. You're pretty sure that's not possible. But it's like he can see you. You wait for him to wink, but he never does.

"Delta isn't meant to take calls before a lift."

"Could be important," says Muhammed Muhammed. Delta doesn't like the tone. It's the voice of someone who knows more than he should and is using that against her.

"It almost always is," she says.

Next up: Ida Gershstasndifreich comes over the P.A. The audience erupts. Delta turns, her stomach knotted up like hair in a vacuum. Ida bounces: a wild animal released from her cage, arms swinging, loosening her muscles. She'll lift her max and then Delta will lift more. That's how it goes. Ida steps onto the mat. For the first time, Delta sees things as pieces that move and fall into place exactly as they're meant to, creating something that means more than each piece and how they fit.

Like Bub said.

The phone vibrates.

Ida takes a step toward the weighted bar. She stops. A hush. Cameras and phones flash.

The phone vibrates in Delta's bag.

"What's happening to her?" It's Steve Muhammed Muhammed, tone and inflection like a theater student reading poorly from a script. Nothing has happened yet. Ida's standing there, swaying.

The phone vibrates.

Delta flexes.

Ida Gershtandifreich collapses. Her body stiffens. Froth spews from her mouth. The stadium collectively gasps. Flashes explodes, making Delta dizzy. Ida jerks, starts to vibrate. Her team runs over. They gather around Ida as she convulses. Delta can see Ida's eyes liquifying out of their sockets. Ida's face slides off her skull, the skin bubbling and pooling on the mat. Her team screams. A doctor rushes over.

Coach Nelson says, "She's having a heart attack."

Steve Muhammed Muhammed says, "Looks like she's melting."

Coach Nelson says, "That's impossible."

Steve Muhammed Muhammed says to Delta, "That makes you the new champion, eh?"

He points at her bag.

"But I've done everything so that I can lift. I can do it," Delta says.

"Might wanna get that."

Delta looks at the phone in her hand. Not sure how it got there, but it's there. The screen shows a number she doesn't recognize. She answers.

"Interior hospital room. Bub say Delly, where you?" His voice sounds clear, renewed.

"Bub, what— How are you calling me?"

"Bub point to men in room. He say They give me phone. I call you."

"Who did, Bub?"

"Bub smile, touch band-aid on his head. Bub say Delly, I feel good."

Delta looks over at Ida Gershtandifreich. Bubbling. Melting. The Germans panic. People scream.

"Who gave you a phone, Bub?"

"Bub say Friends, Del. They…make me feel better. It taste bad. Taste like flowers. But I eat it and I feel better." Her brother laughs and it's bright.

Delta falls to her knees. Coach Nelson rushes over, afraid

that whatever's got the Great Ida Gershtandifreich has been somehow transmitted to his financial future. Delta waves him off, her vision wet and blurry.

"Bub…" She can't speak anymore, the words like little burrs stuck in her throat. She coughs. Coach Nelson tries to lunge at her, but Delta slaps him aside with her free hand.

On his back, face pained and desperate, Coach Nelson says, "What is it, Delta? What's going on?"

Rustling on the other end of the line.

"Bub?"

"Hello, Delta. Your brother will survive. We made sure of that."

She doesn't recognize the voice. It's firm, but also trying to convey an impression of softness. A woman pretending to be a man, or a man who will never sound at all like a man.

"Who made sure of that?"

"I believe you've been in contact with our owner. He'll fill you in, get you the contracts. All future medications and supplements that guarantees your brother remains alive. Understand?"

Delta wipes away tears and looks over at Muhammed Muhammed. He waits, casually watching Ida Gershtandifreich as she more and more disintegrates into a quivering mess. And he's smiling. "I guess that makes you the winner."

She throws the phone down. It pops like a water balloon, plastic and electronics splashing around her like a fountain's eruption. "But I can lift. I can do it."

Muhammed Muhammed says, "But you don't need to. All you need to do now is build us a SunCor army."

Coach Nelson says, "Delta, you need to—"

"Shut up." She's shouting. People pull their attention away

from Ida's now almost fully melted body and focus on Delta. She feels them anticipating her next move. Calling out to her in mental waves to show them what she can do. "I've done everything for this. Neither of you…what have you done?"

Muhammed Muhammed says, "Waste of time and talent. You've won."

"I don't just want to win."

The competition officials have already begun disassembling the weights, making space for the paramedics who are just now showing up. They hustle onto the mat, determined to find something they can fix. They look at Ida, who's now a puddle of boiling flesh. One gasps, stops cold. The other immediately vomits. But Delta's focused on the weights, the 690lbs being taken away piece by piece.

Delta pushes Coach Nelson out of the way. She follows an invisible pull onto the mat. She ignores the body on the mat, but she can't deny that the body is there so that she can now stand in front of the weights. 690lbs. Her brother said she would do it, and he's never wrong. Ever.

She grips the bar. All she can hear is a crackling like bacon on a hot skillet—Ida. Delta tightens every muscle in her body, braces her abdomen, and thrusts. The veins in her head fizz like pop rocks. The cords in her neck stand at full attention, threaten to break through her skin. The bar creaks. Coach Nelson reaches for her. She barely hears Muhammed Muhammed say *Don't*. She eases into the peak of the lift, all 690lbs. Coach Nelson has shut up for once. She flings it all forward and the weights collide with the floor. A prehistoric rumble tears through the silence. The crowd watches, mouths open.

"I can lift," she says. She stands, muscles quivering, a viscid layer of sweat on her skin.

Muhammed Muhammed says, "Yes, you can."

A flash goes off somewhere in the crowd.

<u>DELETED SCENE</u>

Tug of War

5

MANJEEP RUNS ACROSS CAMPUS.

The lawn at Sun State's Santa Barbara campus is engorged from excessive watering during a November drought. He clutches a loose bundle of papers to his chest: a collection of data that almost proves an almost-unsolvable biological/ mathematical conundrum. It's his Master's thesis. He also carries a writing pad. The first page reads *Hi, my name is Manjeep Kathuria. Please call me Man.* He used to have a whole page explaining how he writes to communicate and how he can't talk because of his missing tongue, but people didn't want to read that much on a first meeting. People catch on quick without the explanation—though you kind of just gave one, didn't you?

He runs. Not because he's late, nor is he anxious to return to his work—one of Man's most enduring qualities is his assuredness in the devotion to and continuation of his work. It'll always be there for him.

Man usually runs to see Amber. Mostly.

But right now he's also running to get away from the five frat boys chasing him, throwing acorns they grab from the manicured lawn. Pointed bottoms jab his neck, ears, back of his arms, like little syringes hitting his skin. Each frat boy wears a smiley face pin either on their backwards hat or above the Polo logo on their shirts.

They hurl insults at Man: *Where ya off to now, goopta?* and *7-11's the other way, ha-gee!* and, this next one being Man's favorite, *Ain't you s'posed to be deported by now, towley?* because he doesn't wear a turban and isn't a Muslim. Or Sikh, Buddhist, Hindu, Christian, Atheist, Agnostic, or whatever. Man puts his faith in mathematics. Rather than questioning *Is this real?* (as most of the other characters have), the numbers give him 1s and 0s, YESes and NOs. Religion, like equality, is an Absolute Zero.

An acorn jabs his ear.

MANJEEP HAD BEEN SITTING on a bench near the L. Ron Hubbard Humanities Building eating a brown-bag lunch when he first realized he loves Amber. He was eating steam-in-bag basmati rice and palak paneer mixed and packed in Ziploc when Amber sat at a nearby table to eat her lunch from a pizza place on Guadalupe that's got a big mushroom on the roof. Expensive. Man had heard that people could pay extra and get a slice with psychedelic mushrooms all over it—not that he believed Amber had chosen that as her lunch. Wouldn't change anything if she had.

He watched her eat. Delicate movements. Not self-conscious, but precise. The kind of movements someone who loves math makes. Calculated. And she wasn't a shy eater. Large bites of someone in a hurry to get back to their work. Sun collided with the particles of her skin and hair and Man felt a stretching in his stomach that almost hurt. He'd never felt it before.

He started seeing Amber everywhere. At the library, roaming the shelves across from him, her face visible in the spaces between books, him half-expecting her to pass a cryptic note through the shelf and disappear. Standing just inside the Church of Scientology as he hurried home, her eyes following him while her hands ran through pamphlets. He'd catch glimpses of her sitting on a bench, looking up at his tiny apartment, but when he'd blink she'd be gone, merged with the moving crowd. And though she never said anything, he could hear her voice. It would say *Come to me*. It filled him with a tombstone-heavy desire to do nothing else but go to her. And even though he's always reminded of his brother, of the missing parts of himself, thinking about Amber helps him not care about the things controlling him.

HE SITS IN THE CATHEDRAL-LIKE auditorium, shutting out the voices and commotion of students who don't come to learn, but rather to socialize, fuck, fail, and find future ex -husbands and -wives. A cluster of these students sit near the top row. He sees an Indian girl and knows she sees whiteness as some kind of blessing. She laughs a little too hard and mimics the *Whoa* the white girl in the group does when one of the white boys throws a pencil and gets it stuck in the afro of a student ten rows in front of them.

Man knows most of these initiates to white America have come from far-off places so they can provide for their cultures back home, to help their parents—and families, friends, neighbors, nearby street dogs, everyone—with medical needs or food or money. But instead, they are here in hopes of becoming so American they forget their molecules aren't blindly star-spangled. In Man's case, it's to help a brother so caught up in debt that missing a scheduled shipment of money or supplies means severed hands or head—or *tongue*.

If he were to lose his way and end up back in that small village on the outskirts of Jodhpur, a place where the blue doesn't reach, Man knows his work would be lost. He would find himself back in the service of the people who have his tongue floating in a jar of amber liquid. Something to show his brother in case he can't make a payment. Because of his soft hands, Man can see himself forced into becoming a street vendor specializing in haircuts and head massages, breathing in car exhaust so heavy a vendor bottles and sells it as *Suicide's Breath*. Navigating crowds of sunken-faced women and leather-skinned men pummeled by the industrialized world. But there were also moments of happiness in his village—Hrithik and Man catching fish in Bal Samand (a lake their mother called *The Happy Thumb of Ganesh*), cooking that fish for their mother and grandmother, watching the enjoyment on their faces; Hrithik showing Man how to stand on sanded wood and hitch a ride on the back of auto rickshaws, sliding down dusted roads like a skier on dry land; how to defend himself against the boys who would throw rocks at his ears. This was all in that small village outside Jodhpur where the blue doesn't reach.

He'd been granted admission to Sun State on a fully-funded scholarship, paid all the way through a PhD and future employment with one of the corporations associated with the Sun State system. They gave him spending money, paid for his apartment above the Church of Scientology, and even paid for his flight from India. An opportunity that's never been given to anyone in the history of the university. He can't lose his way.

But he would give it all up for Amber. Forget about his brother, his family. Trade it in for something he never thought he could have: love.

"Anyone care to clue me in on where we left our last discussion?" says Professor Keaton, even though Man knows that the professor knows *exactly* where they ended the previous lecture.

Man holds up his writing pad. It reads: *Spapling's Formula/ Molecular Kinesis.*

Keaton nods. "Thank you, Man."

Even though Man knows he's just as smart as—if not smarter than—the professor, he still listens, doesn't allow himself to acknowledge the presence of others, instead sees himself in a one-on-one tutorship. Except for the moments when the professor's voice grows hoarse and he pauses to chug a glass of water, which he always punctuates with a *pssssst* through his teeth. In these fractional, 5-10 second intervals, Man breaks away from his seclusion to look at her.

Amber.

Across the auditorium, sitting alone, pen moving at smoke-inducing speed. She tucks a silky curl of hair behind her delicately pink ear with a red-gloved hand. Man absorbs the details of her face. It hurts him, but it's a pain he's willing to endure. She is the question without an answer—an answer that has no question. Something outside the ones and zeroes.

And for the first time since their existences became inseparably intertwined, Amber looks over at Man. Their eyes wrap around each other like a snap-bracelet. His stomach stretches. If this is all she ever gives him, Man will return to his water-closet-sized apartment and sit in catatonic euphoria until the world drifts into nothing. He'll forget about the work and acorns and the students who don't care and everything that isn't Amber.

She smiles, teeth perfectly alike, bleached-bone white. His

heart plummets, pain prickling every muscle, every inch of skin, down to his toes gripping at the inside of his shoes. Pain cushioned by a molecule-deep pleasure. He looks away, saving himself the embarrassment of having her see his brown face flush red. She's the most wonderful abstraction, impossible to describe.

He offers his heart another moment.

Amber's smiling at him still. He jumps as if he's just stuck his finger in a toaster. He feels weak, fatigued. His head zips back to his notes. He tries to catch up with the lecture. Eyes flick back to her. She's back on her own notes. She's amber waves, red glares. Honey and honesty. She's a life raft, an oasis, a shade of happiness in a field of abysmal depression. She's—

—*psssssssst* goes the air through Keaton's teeth. The professor's eyes are on Man, waiting for him to get back to it— his face displaying a mask of desperate hope that his prized student isn't becoming like the students in the back. So in a computer-returning-from-sleep sort of way, Man puts pen to paper. Keaton continues.

Spapling's Argument would have a 2:3 nitrogen-based ratio of mass prediction in an open-gamma projection only *if a low-level pulmonary pulmonata vs. genetic delta variable-based equation fits* before *the breakdown of a protein strand within...*And this is how it goes for close to two hours until the professor shuts his briefcase, a final punctuation to his unbroken, rambling sentence.

The students shuffle out of the auditorium and reminds Man of panicked fish in a narrowing creek. Amber Waves gathers her belongings and waits at the tail end of chaos. She's dressed modestly, as always. Brief glimpses of skin: the lower back, calves, the topographical wonder that is the bones around her neck. None of the gratuitous flesh parade, what he's read is called *raunch culture*. Shorts stuffed with asscheeks that push out the bottom like a popped tube of biscuits; crop tops that leave nothing to the imagination (as they say)—though the typical student would still question the size, shape, & color of her nipples; makeup done up to call attention to a willingness to perform sexual acts in any situation. The common costume of a woman looking for a permanent (or semi-permanent [or highly temporary]) sexual partner. But not Amber. Sex does not appear to be her objective in attending college. Another reason why he has no trouble loving her.

Notes spill from an overstuffed folder clutched to her chest with such a similarity to Man that it strikes him as serendipitous. Fate if he believed it. She struggles to gather them, a single page slipping, falling to the floor like a wayward feather. She catches it moments before it lands. If this were a dream, Man would run over and help.

But he doesn't. He just watches her leave.

As the last of the students slip out the auditorium and the door seals shut with a cavernous *shwoompf,* silence and stillness cloak Man with a feeling that is both liberating and regressively depressing. A thousand silent ghosts drift around him as he smells the permanent mixture of feet, paper, dirty bodies lousy with hormones, boredom, cheap carpet cleaner, moldering seat cushions, fruity perfumes mixed with woody generic colognes, and a well-worn history that's tired of repeating, bodies and minds looking for a way up and out of basic existence—most never finding the way. With the cranking in his chest building (and if he had a tongue it would most certainly be swelling right now), Manjeep gathers his things and heads up the aisle, walking past Amber's seat, hoping to catch a whiff of her ghost.

But there's something more.

A folded piece of paper on the floor near her seat. A flattened origami in the shape of a flower, petals blooming from a large center. It's in his hands, no memory of having thought about putting it in his hands. He turns it over. On the back, in pink ink: a stamp in the shape of a slug. Writing on the inside of the flower bleeds through. As he opens the folds, the flower blooms. He unravels the tightly compacted corners, and straightens the wrinkles. With the paper unfolded, both the slug on one side and the writing on the other rest at the center of an intricate design of intersecting folds. A complex geometric web he immediately recognizes as the graphical representation of Spapling's Formula—except this one's near-complete. And seeing it like this, the rest of the equation starts bubbling to the surface. He knows he can finish it. The missing piece to his Master's Thesis. How could she know?

Come find me. This is written at the center, the word *me* intersecting the data lines. She solved the next step, is giving it to him. Man kisses the paper, eases it into the pocket. He looks around, expecting to see Amber. But he's alone.

THERE ARE TWO BOYS.

Half brothers. One older and white, one younger and Asian. The older stands on a skateboard, rocks it over bumpy pavement. The younger rests on a bike spray-painted silver. His eyes are glued to the device in his hand.

An ad-drone overhead recognizes their facial patterns, reads their clothing, listens in and records their conversation. It processes their information and generates ads based on consumer algorithms. The holographic screen hanging from the ad-drone glows, morphs into a pair of shoes the older brother might want.

The older says to the younger, "What's wrong with getting older? They take away your freedom. You have to sit through things you don't want to in order to live a life you don't really want to live. And there's this horrible pressure because everything you do matters if you want to get somewhere other than McDonald's."

The ad-drone analyzes "McDonald's" and generates an ad for the new McDLT2.

The younger speaks, but patterns in the ad-drone's coding begins to redact the boy's words before they are translated into code.

The older says, "That's something dad says cuz dad's been

through it too. Still in it. Stuck in a place he doesn't want to be every day. And high school? That's just the first step toward the end of your life."

The younger cries. More redacted dialogue.

The older says, "You could do that. But I'll tell you this: 90% of all kids who run away end up dead."

The ad-drone corrects that statistic: *[47% — **DEPT. OF JUVNL JSTIC**]*

The older says, "Of course there's a way out. Do you know why I make digishorts and memes with my friends?"

The younger: *[REDACTED]*

The older says, "On the surface, yes, that's true. You will always be surrounded by girls if you make movies. But that's just surface. Maybe it's a way out. I dunno. But so I make a little movie and it becomes popular on YouTube or whatever, my name will be worth something, which will help give me opportunities to be more famous. Which is the end game. Brands make you famous. Build a brand and you'll never be miserable, never have to work until you're dead like dad and mom and everyone else in the world. You can escape the prison."

The younger: *[REDACTED]*

The older says, "Drawing could work. Start an account and post those little drawings you do. I like that one of the lady with the poop nose. Make a bunch like that. Post them every day. Don't follow anyone. Make them come to you. Comment on famous peoples' accounts. Make shirts. Make a product. Brand yourself. And start now. Cuz you're so young that if you do it now, you could have more money than dad and mom together by the time you're my age. And you'd be just as famous as Shanese Undrege or Jennifer Donnahue. And let me tell you this cuz dad never will, mostly cuz he doesn't know: we are *never* free. Even this freedom you're experiencing now, as a kid, is an illusion. It'll end and you'll be a slave to whatever's next. We're all fed into this sort of masticating machine that—"

The younger: *[REDACTED]*

The older says, "No…that's something else. And I'm not gonna talk to you about that. *Masticating* means chewing. Anyway. Everyone is forced into a preset life and that's why people are unhappy. That's why dad drinks beer *[AD RESTRICTED]* and watches TV *[AD GENERATED]* until he falls asleep. And it's why mom takes her little yellow pills *[AD GENERATED]* every morning. Cuz she's scared and sad. Same with dad. Same with everyone. Except for people with brands. Cuz famous people don't just exist. They have people admiring them, remembering them. And they have lots of money, which gives you a lot of things."

The younger points up at the ad-drone, sticks out his tongue and blows a raspberry. Makes a cross-eyed idiot face. Spits a wad of bubbly saliva. Waves his arms like he wants the drone to go away. He bounces a little in the way young boys do when they have to pee but don't want to miss out on whatever's next. He yells something, but it's *[REDACTED]*.

The older says, "The stupid thing's been hovering over us for forever."

The older picks up a nearby rock and throws it at the ad-drone, which auto-adapts based on external sensors and internal tilt regulators. It almost crashes into a nearby tree, overcorrects, then climbs back to its programmed height. This interruption causes the ad-drone to miss out on what the older brother says. The ad-drone resumes broadcasting the conversation in the middle of the older's dialogue: "…but she wouldn't want that. So I guess the point is to just do whatever you can to not get sucked in like everyone else."

The younger points to a house down the street, says: *[REDACTED]*.

The older says, "Yeah, I think that's why he died. Wade's mom said he was doing drugs. Like the bad drugs. I'd see him all the time and he always looked sad."

The younger starts to cry again.

The older says, "That's why I'm here, talking to you like this. I'll be here for you as long as you don't run away. You're my brother, George."

An ice cream truck drifts onto the street. It passes the two brothers at high speeds. The older jumps out of the street and the younger stumbles back off his bike. Almost falls in the grass but catches himself. The ice cream truck screeches to a stop three houses down.

The drone tracks back, pans over so that the ice cream truck, the house it's parked in front of, and the brothers are all in frame. The lens focuses.

Men, dressed alike in black jumpsuits, burst from the ice cream truck and rush to the truck's back door. One of the men throws the door open and the others yank an old man onto the street. They drag him across the front yard of a house surrounded by vibrant flowers. The group huddles near the front door—a wall of black jumpsuits blocking any view of the old man. The front door opens and they cram the older man into the house. The men follow. Silence returns to the street.

The older brother says, "What the hell was that about?"

The younger: *[REDACTED]*

The older, "I'm gonna look."

The younger: *[REDACTED]*

The older, "Stop. Being. Such. A baby."

The older drops his skateboard in the grass. He crouches, stealthy in his approach to the back of the ice cream truck. One foot on the bumper, he grabs the handle and pulls himself up. Looking through the back window, his face goes slack, smile falling to an open mouth. Fear, uncertainty. He pulls out his phone, almost slips off the back of the truck. Takes a picture.

The younger: *[REDACTED]*

The older says, "It's a...bird cage. And there..."

The younger: *[REDACTED]*

The older says, "...shit!"

The older brother jumps off the ice cream truck and hurries back across the street. Picks up his skateboard, gives the impression he wasn't being mischievous at all. Right on time, as the men in black hurry out the front door, across the lawn, and pile into the ice cream truck. A grinding turnover and the engine roars more aggressively than a hot rod. Earsplittingly loud lo-fi music explodes from speakers on top of the truck. Tires squeal and the ice cream truck launches off the street, around the corner, gone faster than it came.

The younger says: *[REDACTED]*

The older brother starts to cry. Covers his face with his hands.

The younger: *[REDACTED]*

But the older never says anything. He can't stop crying.

You follow the data into the stratosphere, up, beyond earth's invisible shell, as it bounces off a relay attached to a lone space station, as it cascades back to earth, and see this: connected via invisible trajectory from ad-drone to heavily encrypted laptop somewhere within the city of Los Angeles, this data translated to an HD livestream of these two boys—

their conversations and consumer algorithms transcribed in command-line format. The eyes that watch this feed and the hands that type the invasive code to hack this ad-drone belong to a deep-level counter-terrorist agent. He's found the house, after years of searching. But still, he must wait—long enough for the plot those in the house have constructed to reveal itself. You wonder what the hell he's waiting for.

<u>DELETED SCENE</u>
22nd Warvin Zindler
Gulf Coast Classic

7

GLASS SHATTERS. AND THEN THERE'S A SCREAM.

Not really a scream. More of a gurgle. Barb's heard this depressing, dead sound a hundred times in varying intensities —though she could never let anyone in the house know how she feels or that she feels anything at all. The sound of bacon in a hot skillet crackles from the basement—the sound and smell of human flesh caramelizing under chemical burn is almost identical to pork in hot butter.

Barb covers the phone's mic. She knows that Subject 42.9, formally known as Dr. Keaton, has met the same fate as Subjects 2.2 through 42.8—a body shaped in flesh now a liquified quivering mess oozing between the bars of a human-sized birdcage. This is the business of the HR.

She removes her hand from the phone's mic and says, "That was nothing serious, Miss. Another test…I'll put a stop to it for now."

Sitting on the stairs in a purgatorial space between kitchen and basement, a familiar smell overcomes Barb Tarda, a chemical-heavy, battery-acid-and-freshly-spilled-blood mix coming from the Workshop below—a byproduct of experiments against human bodies. After seven years of extensive trial and error, the only aroma that masks the scent of human evisceration, pathogenic chemicals, and slug slime is bacon & waffles, maple syrup & fresh-brewed coffee, Pine Sol & Windex & Febreze—the scent of Suburbia. It's piped into the air conditioning and leaks in a light, constant stream from several vents hidden in the front lawn. It's the nicest smelling house in the neighborhood. And with good reason. If not for this coverup smell, the house would reek of charred corpses and an oil refinery funk, a large finger in the sky pointing to the house screaming in sign language: *The bad guys are in here.* Though they don't think of themselves as *the bad guys.*

Barb sits on the step in the middle of the stairs next to a breakaway part of the wall that hides her crawlspace. She airs herself out, letting the two smells from above and below replace the smell of high-grade sativa anchored to her fibers.

"We've ordered another breed of slug. The large red breed is too unstable. Reaction with the compound and the subject was unsatisfactory, according to Dworkin...Not necessarily. Just minimal. *Weak.* Not sensational enough. And if we want maximum spectacle, Dworkin says girth is now an important factor. Size and elasticity...Dworkin believes the Pacific banana slug is perfect...No, he doesn't trust what the kid has to say about slugs so he's injecting the new compound into the banana...The compound?...Dworkin says the compound revision needs more time. That what we lack comes from the flower. So we're having Initiates harvest plants from grow patterns near interstates and highways, something about exhaust giving the flowers more toxic potency...He believes it's important. Could be what gives us the right combination."

Barb listens as Miss responds. The voice sounds artificially harmless, never letting disappointment come through. The basement's chemical smell intensifies. There's more to it now: burnt hair, charred skin, bodily fluids.

Barb says, "We won't resume until Dworkin introduces the new compound…No, the child keeps saying *the slug with black hair*…No, we haven't found any with hair. But I believe the boy will find the right one. The boy says he saw the ocean, so we pulled up a squid and a cuttlefish, both with interesting suggestions, but results that weren't what was wanted for the climax. The child says he dreams them. So we will give him more of the compound to enhance his visions…If I can be honest, Miss, I'm not sure about Dworkin and the compound. For mass destruction upon release, we need a new compound and further trials. Need to make sure it spreads and kills as fast as possible. We're dealing with something that even Dr. Keaton didn't understand, and he invented these mathematics. He failed. They're cleaning his remains out of the cages downstairs as we speak. So without someone who has experience in that type of mathematics— Oh…You do?…He is?…I see…Then that changes things. I'll get a room ready…And what about Dworkin?…And it has to be this way?…Understood. We Must Abide."

Miss ends the call before Barb can ask for a face-to-face interaction, which would help her and others remain faithful to the Project. Even though Barb's never really had faith because her duty is farce, a mask now anchored so deep she can't rip it off. Some people call it undercover, covert, spy. She drops the phone in her lab coat pocket. It rattles against week-old syringe toppers and crumpled peppermint wrappers. Her hand eases into the other pocket. Her fingers wrap around the handle of a ceramic coffee mug.

She smells herself, confirms she no longer smells like sativa. She's feeling high enough to continue pretending. Grunts from above pull Barb out of thoughts she shouldn't be having. She stands. The wooden step creaks even though Barb's barely a triple digit weight. She follows the grunts up to the kitchen.

Deformedly short-armed, buzzed-hair, eye-patched, dwarf-statured and sweating like a marathon runner, Abraham Dworkin shuffles through diagrams, equations, and formulas spread across a table in the kitchen. Even though he's twice her age, Barb still has moments where she confuses him for a child. Dworkin's told her all about being confused for a child, especially when he was younger. And there was the thing he did, shaking a golfer's hand in the 90s so that the HR could buy off the golfer and use him for *future needs*. Like a suburban life where he could marry and have kids, build a family that would continue to follow the HR's purpose without knowing it. A deep-level agent. Same thing they did with the bodybuilder who now lives in the sunroom, slamming weights twelve hours a day. The thing with the golfer, that was before Barb joined the HR. Dworkin dabs his forehead with a banana-colored bandana that hasn't left his grip in seven years.

Barb says, "Miss just called. We've got someone coming to help with the formula."

Abraham slams his hands on the table. Pages go wild. "Great. So how long until I'm tossed in there?" He points to the oven, which has been modified into a miniature crematorium designed specifically to incinerate documents and human bodies. The nutrients contained in human ash accelerate the growth of various floral breeds the HR manages in the gardens in both the front- and backyards. A sign that reads *Garden of the Month* almost never leaves the yard. Of particular admiration are the sunflowers.

"Don't be an idiot, Abe. Even if Keaton was of no use to us outside his work, you have meant a great deal. Miss recognizes just how well you Abide. You couldn't be dispatched so easily."

Abe smiles and it lacks all humor and sincerity. A sneer that shows Abe's missing front tooth, a tooth he's refused to let the HR dentist replace.

"That compassion in your voice? This," motions to everything the house represents, "knows nothing about compassion. It's a weakness, Tarda. Don't let them know you feel that way."

"Your help will be here later today."

Barb pours herself some coffee in the mug she keeps protected in the pocket of her overcoat. Like Dworkin's bandana, the mug never leaves her. Most nights, when she *can* sleep, she sleeps with it in her hand. It's white and in blue letters reads: *You've obviously mistaken me for someone who gives a shit*. On the opposite side, the letters: *SZW*. A gift from her previous life, a husband who believed she had suicided—a rouse to get her into the HR. But what the mug really is is a reminder of the mask she can't remove. A tether to a truth that feels more like a lie, a truth that says *You are not who you appear to be*.

"There's no way to tear down the human molecular structure as quick as Miss wants. And the vapor can't be contagious. There's no way for it to spread instantly. It just can't be done." Dworkin dabs at his sweat like a punctuation. Barb can see he's certain of everything he's saying.

"Still, Miss wants to try this new math guy. Says he can give us what we want. You two will work together on a new compound as soon as we harvest the newest batch of petals and kernels."

"And what about," he motions to the second floor. "What're we doing with him?"

"Don't know. Miss says he's here for a reason, so we—"

"We Must Abide. I got it. It's just…that's two newcomers in four days. Seems as though Miss and that SunCor goon are up to something. We're not ready, Barb."

"Possibly."

A guttural roar reverberates from the garage.

Dworkin says, "And why the *fuck* do we have a *fucking lion* in the garage?"

"Another piece of the…*finale*."

"Don't know how much longer we can hide the lion—"

"Simeon."

"What?"

"His name is Simeon. Call him that." There's a heaviness in her voice that she can't hide.

"…I'm not doing that."

"Miss says that some of Wolpe's essence remains in the lion. Calling him Simeon lets him know not to attack us. Especially later."

Barb can barely talk about the lion, about the death of Wolpe. For Barb, the name Simeon brings with it a whole set of luggage, each piece filled with its own history and misery. And the possibility of his…soul? memory? being stuck in the lion makes her want to clench up, cry out. But she's forced to keep that emotion locked up in a mental safe, impenetrable and solitary.

You, on the other hand, are openly questioning how the fuck part of you can be here watching the wife you thought had suicided but is still very much alive and another part of you be stuck in the goddamn lion who crunched your head flesh and brought you into this non-place of being, stuck in a narrative you both created and is being created around you and without your creative input. Everything you thought wasn't possible is both possible and not. Will this ever end?

Dworkin says, "Still not doing it."

"Miss wants it, and if Miss wants it...you know how to finish that."

"It's just...I don't like the lion and I don't fucking like that guy upstairs. Don't trust him. Always sweating and puking. Screaming in his sleep."

"Miss says he's detoxing."

"Still don't trust him. He could wig out on us. Cause a fuss. Draw attention. Whatever."

"It'll be fine. I'll bunk whoever this math guy is with him. We'll force them to keep an eye on each other."

"What are we supposed to call them?"

"Who?"

"The math guy...The New Guy. Are we Initiating them? Will they be Proselytes?"

"Don't know. Don't care. I'll wait for Miss on that."

This is when Amber Waves makes her entrance: walks down the stairs and joins Barb and Dworkin in the living room. But here, in the home of the Human Reich, still in her red gloves, Amber is known as Jessica Fey. Or as Barb refers to her: "Jess, your classmate is on his way."

Letting his fear of Jessica Fey show, Dworkin hurries back to the kitchen to at least act like he's busy.

Barb says, "Abe, stop."

He does, but stands in the space between the living room and the kitchen, ready to run away from Fey if her attention turns to him and not Barb.

"He's already here. That's why I came down. Car just pulled up."

Barb says, "Doing something for once."

"I also came down to tell you the picture has been destroyed."

"Must be hard for you."

"Not at all, sis."

When Barb and Jessica Fey speak face-to-face it's as though there's an invisible mirror between them. The only twins in the history of medicine to come out of the vaginal canal sideways and at the exact same moment, an act that killed their mother. In their previous lives, Jessica's husband, R. Ryan Ryans, often confused Barb for her. So often that he began to lust after Barb more than Jessica Fey. Jessica Fey once walked in on her sister and Ryans in bed together. In a moment of desperation, Jessica Fey plunged both her hands into the fireplace, charring skin up to her elbows. She turned to her husband and Barb and screamed *Can you tell the difference now?* Barb still hears this scream sometimes when she can't sleep. This is why Jessica Fey wears the red gloves.

Shit… You never knew about that.

Jessica Fey turns back to the stairs, looks up and says *Come* the same way one would to a shy dog.

A sloppy guy—disheveled, mutton chops eating most of his face, luggage under his eyes—comes sluggishly down the stairs. He wears a crisp, white dress shirt buttoned to the neck, yellow stains around the armpits and a crust of bile just below the neckline. What hair isn't tied back in a loose ponytail is glued to his forehead. Glasses sit halfway down a nose slick with grease. His face has that appearance of the sleep deprived in insomnia commercials. He stops halfway down the stairs and sits. He hugs his knees.

Barb says, "Why is he here? He isn't supposed to leave the

Pink Room. Not yet."

"He said he needed out or he'd go crazy. Been in there for five days straight. Wanted air that didn't smell like vomit."

"We're not running a rehab, Jess. We can't have him out in the open like this. Suppose he tries to escape. Suppose someone out there sees him. People in this neighborhood will recognize him. And since when do you care about the Initiates?"

"I don't. Miss does." Jessica Fey pushes a twist of hair behind her ear with a red-gloved hand.

"Did she call you?" The careening elevation of Barb's voice gives away her suspicion, lack of understanding, her confusion, and her jealousy at the same time. Jessica Fey shakes her head and points to the guy on the stairs.

"She asked for him."

"He talked to Miss?"

Jessica Fey nods.

Barb turns to the guy on the stairs. "What did she say to you?"

He opens his mouth. His lips make a dry *spip* sound. But a knock at the door stops his words. A timid knock. The person on the other side's accumulated weaknesses identifiable in that knock. Jessica Fey and Barb look at each other, each expecting the other to be the one to answer the door. Like any feud between truly identical twins, it's a standoff without end.

"No rush," says Dworkin. "Longer you keep him out there, the longer I can stay out of the oven."

"Shut up, Dworkin. Answer the door," the sisters say at the same time.

Jessica Fey doesn't take her eyes off Barb. Barb fiddles with the coffee mug. Jessica Fey sees this and smiles.

Barb says, "Abe, you're not being replaced."

"Yet," says Jessica.

"Shut up." Then Barb looks at Dworkin.

He hops off his chair and waddles to the door, draping an evil eye all over the guy on the stairs. Then to himself, because apparently no one cares, he says, "I'm a doctor, right? Not a butler. I've got like three PhDs. Shouldn't be answering doors. But We Must Abide, right?"

No one responds.

He flips the first of two light switches near the front door, arming the front porch security module: a hidden turret that emerges from the overhead light panel and incapacitates any unwanted visitors with a rapid-acting and untraceable topical compound that causes the victim to suffer both heart attack and brain aneurysm simultaneously—Dworkin's creation. With the flick of the second switch, the front porch mat that reads *Mi Casa Es Su Casa* folds down, revealing a trap door. The victim drops into an intricate system that brings their corpse to the fires of the Workshop oven where they are burned and the ashes are scattered through another intricate network of pipes, most ending up in the compost bin, some as exhaust pumped into the air above the house. The front porch security module once consisted of a pneumatic footboard that launched unwanted guests in an arcing trajectory three hundred feet in the air and over six thousand feet away. But that was soon changed when nearby homeowners complained of bodies falling from the sky. Some thought it was the result of a secret government experiment. Or alien abductions gone wrong.

With his finger on the second light switch, Dworkin opens the door.

Some Indian kid's standing there. A look of fearful uncertainty on his face, a gift from a lifetime of Me vs. The

World. He holds two tote bags, each overflowing with books, notebooks, papers. A notebook hangs from a rope around his neck, a pen attached to the spirals with clear tape and a long, pink shoelace.

Still holding the door open, Dworkin says, "Is this the math guy?"

Jessica Fey nods. When the math guy sees her his eyes go wide, skin flushes red. Breath stops in his throat.

Outside, a child's voice says *Hey*. Dworkin makes eye contact with a kid across the street.

Dworkin grabs the math guy by the shirt and yanks him in. The tote bags tumble. Books and papers spill into the foyer. Dworkin slams the door.

All eyes fall on the math guy. He lifts his notebook and turns to the first page. He holds it up for everyone to see. It reads: *Hi, my name is Manjeep Kathuria. Please call me Man.* Barb marches over to him in a theatrical way and rips the page out of the notebook. She crumples it and throws the wad at his face. He doesn't flinch. Like he's used to people throwing things at him.

"We don't care what your name is. You don't have one anymore, understand? You're here to work. That's all you will be. Your Work. You will be fed and given a place to sleep. You will be given a moderate level of comfort, but only as a means to ensure production. You will work, and in that you will find comfort. You will never see the product. You will never leave until there *is* a product. All of us work for the same Purpose. We do not answer to ourselves. We answer to the Greater Purpose. We answer to Miss, because she sees the Solution. And because of that, we work for Her. No matter what happens: We Must Abide."

Man looks around, unsure if this is some kind of joke. When he sees that everyone is nail-in-coffin serious, Man nods confidently. The Me vs. The World becomes an Us. Barb's seen this sudden change countless times—the hopeless given purpose by the HR. He stands at attention, gives them a salute: his outstretched hand offering service. Barb, confusing it for a low five, gives him some skin.

"Now that that useless shit's over," Jessica Fey says, "Everyone needs to return to their—"

Then there's another knock at the door. Barb, Jessica Fey, and Dworkin freeze.

Barb, "This is the real thing. Dworkin, get on the door. Everyone be prepared to Dump and sound the Alarm. We're going Code Clear."

Dworkin readies the trigger.

Barb turns to Man, points a hard finger at him. "Were you followed? Who knows you're here?"

He shakes his head.

"Are you working for someone?"

"I bet he is," says Jessica Fey.

It's obvious to you she's just trying to heighten the tension. It's what you'd have her say if you were writing this.

Man writes in his notebook, holds it up: *I am alone.*

Jessica Fey, "He's lying."

Dworkin, "We're fucked."

Barb, "Everyone shut up."

She holds a beat, heart punching the inside of her ribcage. All the emotion she's tried to hide oozes out of her pores in sweat that smells like syrup. This could be the moment it all falls apart. This could be the moment that those she works for burst into the house and stop the HR's operation and help

Barb take off the mask she can't remove herself. She slowly lets out the breath she's been holding and opens the door.

A little Asian boy stands on the doorstep like a lost cat. Couldn't be older than eight years old. His jeans are smudged with dirt and grass. Hair matted and sweaty. Not wearing any shoes. A modern-day Dennis the Menace. His bike is tipped over just behind him. It's a girl's bike spray-painted silver to hide that it's violently pink. The boy looks around at all the faces looking at him. He stops on the guy on the stairs. It's then that Barb puts herself in the boy's way. But it's too late.

The boy peers around Barb, waves to the New Guy on the stairs, and says, "Hey Wade! My brother said you were dead. What are you doing—"

"Do it," says Jessica Fey.

Dworkin flips the switch and like a straw wrapper up a high-powered vacuum, the boy disappears. Lost in the pipes. There's a rumbling somewhere in the house, the grindings of a powerful engine. The smell of bacon & waffles, maple syrup & fresh-brewed coffee, Pine Sol & Windex & Febreze comes in a heavy wave. A small puff of exhaust coughs out the house's chimney and floats up, where it will traverse atmospheres, join a southward drifting cloud, and absorb itself in precipitation that will come down as a brief afternoon rain somewhere in San Diego where a young woman will tilt her head up to the rare rainfall and catch a droplet on her tongue and as she swallows the water containing traces of exhaust from the HR incinerator her mind will think *George* for a reason she'll never understand.

Dworkin runs out, grabs the bike, drags it off the porch, and like an Olympian giving it their all in shot-put, Dworkin spins the bike and heaves it away from the house. It lands in the street with a jangled clatter. Dworkin falls on his ass, scrambles back to his feet, and waddles back inside. He looks around the neighborhood, making certain no one's seen him, and then he slams the door.

Barb says to Man, "That one's on you."

Though what she really wants to do is cry.

Jessica Fey takes Man by the back of his collar and shoves him into a small room near the front door. One of those den-like rooms people have but never go in. Just a TV, a couch, and a recliner. No coffee table, no lamps, no pictures on the wall. Blackout curtains on the windows block all light, making the room shadowy and ominous. Barb stands in the doorway, watches over Jessica Fey and Man.

Jessica Fey says, "Sit."

He does.

"Watch this video. It'll tell you everything you need to know—even though you don't need to know *shit* unless we tell you."

He nods.

Jessica Fey puts her hand under his chin, tilts his face up, leans down, and kisses the side of his mouth. "Thank you for coming."

He watches her leave. When he sees Barb, his head snaps back to the TV. Jessica Fey passes her.

Barb says, "What the fuck're you doing?"

"Abiding. You should try it some time."

Jessica Fey walks back upstairs, tugs at the sweaty New Guy's shirt. He follows, taking the steps on hands and knees. Barb stands guard as the DVD begins. She's seen it a thousand times. She takes a sip of coffee, not really sure how it got in her hands. Man never takes his eyes off the screen. The HR introductory DVD begins like this—

Electronically programmed pop-jazz. A wide-angle drone shot racing over the ocean, inland, past downtown Los Angeles, down palm lined streets, over Beverly Hills, up and up around the Griffith Observatory, up to the Hollywood Sign, where, on the hill above, stands a man, who turns to face the camera right as it closes the distance and creates a medium-close shot.

"Hello, I'm Crispin Glover. I've been an actor for over fifty years. But in that time I've seen just how dangerous this system can be for the rest of the world. Which is why your insistence in joining the Human Reich's program is so important. The HR understands that you've been let down in life, that you've had addictions or obsessions that have taken away your will to exist without them. And society does not give you what you deserve: respect, opportunity, dominance…or *love*. Your misanthropy and self-loathing is totally understandable. Don't blame yourself. Hollywood made you that way. They also made it so that you will never succeed. But hey, the HR wants you just exactly as you are. We can help you. And we want to. Your presence lets us know that you are willing to listen and to repay the debt of our help. Remember: in the HR, We Must Abide. Say it with me now. We. Must. Abide."

Man says nothing.

There's a cut and suddenly Crispin Glover's standing at the telescope from *Rebel Without A Cause*—in history's shadow of James Dean. Crispin's got his arm propped on the telescope, all buddy-like.

"The HR is run by our ubiquitous leader, Miss. Through Miss, anything is possible. Miss has already accomplished an astounding number of revenge plots against our forced capitalist existence. Like what, you ask? Well, for starters, Miss has inserted over 900,000 subliminal messages of dissent in both movies and television programming. Want more? What if I told you Miss was directly responsible for the nuclear attack on the first SpaceX Space Station? Or that Miss controls over 80% of the information networks in both NorCal and the California Commonwealth? The ZV-66 outbreak responsible for the death of 1% of Earth's population? The nuke attack that caused the Great Fault Separation? Remember the Zodiac Killer? Miss. Miss. Miss. Yeah, I know what you're thinking: very impressive. Am I telling the truth? You'll never know. As a new member of the HR, you will be stripped of your name, your identity, and your pleasures. This is called Initiation. We provide you with attire, a haircut, and all your living essentials. After Initiation, you will be granted Proselyte status. There are seven levels of Proselyte, each with its specific clearance. Want to move up in the HR crystal-form security levels? Show dedication and Level 7 Proselyte Status could be yours. Initiate duties that display devotion to the Plot consists of harvesting materials needed for Plot function, steering certain individuals onto Plot-desired collisions via coercion or implied paranoia, the excessive use of violence to create distractions and more paranoia. There's almost nothing you can't do that will benefit the Plot. And as always: if you see a fellow Initiate losing their will to Abide, report them. As a team, we can change the future."

Another cut and Crispin Glover's standing in a field of sunflowers.

"Now, let's talk about sacrifice."

Biography of a Sunflower

8

[insert today's date]
hey austin--

remember that time I saved your life

modern theorists are saying that our
mass death will be because of a particle
accelerator malfunction that will tear
the reality fabric & open a black hole
or portal to another dimension & flood
our world with trans dimensional
radiation otherworldly germs & possibly
eighth dimensional creatures capable of
breaking up our molecular structures &
that if that doesn't kill us then the
planet we're on a collision course with
will bring our end in an explosion felt
throughout the galaxy & this theory has
been proven 96.78% true based on
subliminal numerological patterns hidden
in 14 of the most recent hollywood
blockbusters because remember that back
to the future predicted 9/11 & that
truffaux is funding propaganda films
with the intention of starting class

warfare by injecting subliminal messages
in the plot to feed the masses & is the
same thing vr systems are doing to the
mind of the consumer & **look at this meme
about spaghetti** this new theory is
confirmed even further by a certain
secretive army navy marine national
guard training exercise that ends
coincidentally on the exact day of doom
which is just one week away seven days
until we all die unless this is all just
speculation like all other end time
predictions have been since the
beginning of communication & i had a
dream i wasn't afraid of

today

spiders & today i woke up not afraid

*there's a history of debt
owed by those who save
lives & i need you to pay*

everything is influenced by movies &
we're all let down because it's nothing
like that in real life & if you can't
trust yourself then can you trust the
mistrust of yourself but remember that
great art keeps its secrets lost & the
recent slew of mass shootings are all
just hoaxes to push gun laws & liberals
are putting guns into the hands of
unstable people & remember that people

believe these shootings are actually like very large school plays & there's a very competent director behind it all & the people involved are really really fantastic actors & the kids involved almost never existed like for instance that shooting in newtown all those years ago this conspiracy assumes that all that was was a stage play & all the parents were acting & no one died & remember that every time there's a mass shooting that it's just a commercial for the gun used in the shooting & **look at this video of a raccoon eating grapes** & it was all so that gun laws could be put in place & since that didn't work out now we have these even larger shootings which are starting to actually look real despite only seeing the aftermaths on our tvs & devices & in these moments we're given more subliminal messages because the neofascist/neoliberal coalition has a $190billion dollar budget so why wouldn't they do these things and **i once saw all the planets align and had a seizure in a ditch** also remember that the least qualified person to understand a dream is the dreamer also remember that orwell feared americanism remember that vice president goldwater has everything to do with it & also remember that we are controlled by geopolitical corporations private equity funds trust fund terrorism rogue states anti soviet tactics behavior modification restructuring genome switches genetic patents sec privately armed combat units regime change sleepers in the white house & hollywood remember remember that the earth will be recycled remember that richard condon worked for disney for 20 years as a pr agent before writing the manchurian candidate remember that the fat camps labor camps are fronts for brainwashing operations to create suburban terrorists remember your time in the camps & **look at this picture of a cute kitten** class warfare white washing self deforming caste system remember that literature is still a means to pass coded messages to the masses remember that control is undulatory remember the baseboard hiding spot remember that soldiers go awol with a purpose remember that ritalin is used to suppress children that have a potential to change the world remember tactical world canceled ar-15 special most used gun in shootings gun world trigger firearms special weapons serial killers muscle and fitness and busty half-naked sex and elvis and jfk and david bowie and suck a fat fucking cock and scientific american mystery human reeducation properly addicted to something working for money capitalist design remember that mk ultra is a real thing and that those who are a part of

it won't know until it's too late and
remember that mk ultra coding can be
attached to food awakening those who eat
it remember that the wheels of the world
turn under the power of narcissism &
fortune favors the ego & don't forget
that we're developing sympathy for
artificial intelligence & that if ai
were allowed to shape the narrative what
would they see as truth & if a text is
about mind control at what point does it
then control the mind & if writing is an
act of communication what if the message
to communicate is **please fucking help me**
& remember that though some people say
you can't go back in time & change the
past because the past is unwilling to
change even if you could go back the
present is just the same it is equally
as obstinate any attempt to change the
path is met with resistance by an unseen
force so you have to ride

do people still use
the term pull the
plug & is it a real
plug they pull

we don't deserve the earth anymore

something nice,
wade

9

THE PEOPLE IN BLACK SUITS SURROUNDING *Austin Foster keep saying things like* Spill your guts *and* Tell us everything you know. *Each time they do Austin bites back laughter—even though they've already broken his nose, yanked out three of his molars, used a carrot peeler on his penis, held a fully revved chainsaw blade less than an inch from his face, and have injected enough of what they call "truth serum" into his jugular to make even the most devout liar spill their darkest secrets. He's tried to tell them about his inability to be chemically uninhibited, but they stick him anyway. The thing is is that Austin smoked a pretzel when he was eight. Dared by his brother in the kitchen during a summer of great loneliness, Austin took one of those long breadstick pretzels, popped it in his mouth, lit one end, and puffed on it like a cigar. He woke up in the hospital twelve hours later. His brother said he choked and puked in the kitchen and then passed out in his own puke. The doctor explained that the burning salt released toxic fumes that could've killed Austin. The result, and this is Austin's private belief, is that this is why he can't get drunk or high. Did something to his brain the doctor's couldn't detect. So he's not affected by things like "truth serum"—which is the dumbest name Austin's ever heard.*

They speak to each other in a language that sounds made up. Not from another country. It's alien. And yes, he's starting to believe that maybe he really means way out there alien. But what it really is is a language developed by whatever organization these people work for as a way to communicate freely without Austin understanding. Jokes on them, though. They could be speaking Spanish and he still wouldn't understand.

But he spills his guts anyway. Because they have his mom in a wet, diseased-looking room like this and who knows what they're doing to her. He doesn't want to imagine, but his mind can't shake the words nipple *and* blowtorch. *It wasn't until after they removed his molars that Austin wondered where his dad was.*

They tell him to start with the letter.

So that's where this starts.

"WELL BUDDY, YOU'LL never guess who died."

Austin hasn't heard from Jean in like five years, but hearing his voice is a familiar comfort that's laced with many discomforts. This is the way friendship is, right? But for Jean to call means it's serious. Not like all the times Austin had called Jean and said *Dude, Harrison Ford died*, trying to trick Jean into believing the obvious lie—which he did almost every time. So when Harrison Ford really did die, Jean didn't believe him. Austin doesn't think Jean's calling to play a trick that's been dead almost a decade.

He says "Wade…" and Austin stops listening. He knew that Wade was in LA trying to do the struggling musician thing, which meant that Wade had been into heroin. But Austin never knew how deep that heroin thing went. Jean's call charts those depths for him.

Austin says, "There gonna be a funeral?"

"They already burned him, so it'll be a wake and all that."

"When did he die?"

"Two days ago."

"And they already burned him?"

Austin can hear Jean shrug, the familiar rustle of clothes that reminds Austin how much Jean likes to shrug when something doesn't interest him.

"You getting off your ass and coming to the Common?"

"If I can find my passport."

"Your dad doesn't think you're coming."

"He's probably right."

"Don't be predictable, man. Everyone expects you to not show. Do something different. Be decent."

"What can I say? I'm an undignified guy. I eat hummus out of the container with my fingers. I wear the same underwear for like four days. All my shirts have pits stains. I want to fuck every woman I see and every guy who looks like Timothée Chalamet. I burp and fart in the company of others. I dog-ear books. I don't listen to my former friend when he's talking to me about shit I probably don't care about."

"This is the kind of behavior that doesn't really translate well here anymore, Austin."

Jean says some more stuff that Austin doesn't really listen to. It isn't until Jean hangs up that Austin remembers the letter. Still holding the phone against his ear, he wonders why he didn't bring up the letter to Jean. Why he didn't even remember it.

The letter came in the mail a week before: words typed on ripped spiral paper stuffed inside a stained envelope with a typed address. All of it in screenplay font. From Wade. Weird stuff, nonsense mostly. It annoyed Austin more than concerned him. There wasn't anything coherent. What it really sounded like was one of those screenplays written by artificial intelligence. A bunch of info pumped into the system and the system pumping out what it believes a person would write. Guess heroin makes people sound like bots.

Looking at the letter now, after Jean's call, Austin sees it as a plea. He could kick himself for not answering, not reaching out. But that was never his responsibility. Was it?

Against everything telling him to not go, Austin throws some things in a bag, throws that bag into the back of his car, and lights out for the California Commonwealth. His dad calls and offers to buy him a plane ticket, but he needs as much time away from San Dimas as he can afford. The drive from Placerville to San Dimas used to take a little over six hours—before the Fault Seperations and the TransRepublic border bridge. Now, Austin'll have plenty of time to think about how he'll navigate the place he grew up. The place he left to go write screenplays in LA. He ended up leaving that place too. Circumstances forced him to leave. Most of his life has been spent leaving places.

At some point, in the liminal space between places, in the edit between Then and Now, Austin had a spiritual awakening in the form of lethargy. He decided he didn't really want to be active. Not a go-with-the-flow kind of guy, but an I-am-not-anything-anymore kind of guy. This decision to go to Wade's funeral is the first active participation he's committed to in a long time. Sure, he still writes screenplays, but he never puts his name on them. He kills time by working at the Save Mart in Placerville stocking shelves and bagging groceries, but he never wears his name tag. His main source of income is remote work, freelance stuff like writing code for input-based systems and editing screenplays—simple stuff through the anonymity of the internet. But maybe it's not just lethargy. Maybe it's restlessness. Or maybe he's a little suicidal. But he wouldn't ever kill himself, because killing himself meant he did something.

As he drives south through the scorchlands of NorCal, east of San Luis Obispo, Austin realizes that Wade's death coincides almost perfectly with the eight-year anniversary of the disappearance of his brother, Lee. MIA someplace overseas, put to rest as dead by everyone in the family—including himself. He remembers how angry he was that Lee left the family to join the Army. All these moments that once existed, forgotten due to disuse, now returned. As if the idea of driving back to his hometown forces him to remember these things. Memories flow, a surge of data: Lee, Wade, Jean, San Dimas, a funeral, the Army, screenplays…and then it all ends on this little baseboard hideaway in Wade's room where they used to hide porn (Austin's) and weed (Wade's).

remember the baseboard

Hidden in Wade's letter. Austin has a hard time not pushing down on the gas. Because that clearly is a message to Austin, even if he wants to believe it isn't. The baseboard.

The line at the TransRepublic border crossing is backed up nearly thirty miles. The light-up sign above the freeway flashes *Time to CalComm: ERROR*. Because he's documented in both territories, Austin cuts over to the X-Press Cross lane. Seeing all this infrastructure reminds him of why Lee left for the Army: the Great Fault Separation. Nuclear blasts that cracked numerous California fault lines. The rumor is that Truffaux set off nukes to separate CalComm from everything so he could make it all one huge deportation center, but the news pointed the finger at North Korea. Lee didn't believe the rumors of it being domestic terrorism at the hands of the president, and instead believed the military complex and their finger pointing at foreign powers. He wanted to fight back. Which made no sense to Austin. Lee couldn't even kill a spider without standing on top of a chair like a lady screaming about a mouse in the old Tom & Jerry cartoons. Was like that with roaches too. Any bug, really. How could a guy petrified of bugs go kill people willingly?

Still, Austin's dad was proud of his other son, even encouraged him to go. Their mom withdrew, hid behind pills. Everyone thought Austin hated his brother for leaving. But that wasn't true. Lee taught him better than that. While Lee was in high school and Austin was in junior high, Lee shared dissenting knowledge. If he was reading Marx or Fromm or Freud, so was Austin. Lee once told Austin that hate is wasted time, that *whoever you're supposed to hate should be nothing to you*. Because of this, Austin doesn't allow himself to hate. It's the easiest thing in the world to hate others. And self hate is like Monday jokes: easy. But to be honest…Austin really fucking *hates* Monday jokes. So he didn't and doesn't hate Lee for leaving. He didn't understand and he didn't agree, but he also didn't try to stop him. Maybe he should have. Maybe he should've stopped Wade too.

You've only been a part of this guy's molecular makeup for like ten minutes and already you're exhausted. And you don't remember ever writing about someone like him.

Crossing the TranRepublic bridge which spans the largest fault gap, connecting NorCal to the California Commonwealth, Austin passes graffiti spray-painted to the interior bridge wall: *Culture over media* and *fartass lives* and *SAVE EARTH/STOP MARS* (even though someone's crossed out *SAVE* and replaced it with *SWAP*) and *Truffaux did this—*

which reminds Austin of the Truffaux posters in NorCal and the rest of the A.E., the ones that go *Betray Friends; They've Already Betrayed YOU* and *Loose Talk = Noose Talk*. There's no difference between the two sides.

The X-press Cross lane takes less than an hour.

Austin hands his passport to the crossing agent, who scrutinizes the photo. Austin smiles, doing everything he can to make the photo and his real self look the same. The agent tosses the passport back in his car and says, "You should lose weight. Unless you wanna end up in those FlabCamps."

"Already done my time, hoss." He drives off before the agent can say anything else.

The space between the trans-border crossing and Santa Barbara is dotted with the camps: MigraCamps, LaborCorps, PolitiPrisons, and the FlabCamps where Austin spent most of his childhood. His dad thought it would be a good idea for him to get in shape before patterns of obesity set in and he found himself in debt to the A.E.'s Fat Tax for the rest of his life. His mom would visit him almost every day—when she was allowed to visit and when he wasn't exercising or working in the factory filling bags of pre-cooked meat or in the garden planting fruits and sometimes flowers. There's a lot of that time that Austin doesn't remember, and doesn't care to.

You wonder if it's a willing forgetfulness or if this is a sign of something more sinister.

He drives past Santa Barbara's dried deadness, twists through the scenic Pacific Coast Highway, dodging drafts of Pacific wind and cars that swerve around him, each laying on their horn because Austin's comfortably driving ten miles under the speed limit, taking as much time as he can to not be in San Dimas. As Los Angeles comes into view, one of those variable

LED signs looms above the road in front of him. It flickers something he almost thinks is his name, then flickers again with a message: *PLAN AHEAD WHILE YOU CAN*. And then it's gone. He thinks about what he could plan for, how much he doesn't want to plan for anything, and how planning for something he can't foresee is a guarantee for failure and disappointment. So he won't plan. He'll ride the wavelengths of whatever moment follows this one and then the next. He has to. So this is exactly what he does all the way to San Dimas, to the Sunny Ground Funeral Home.

THERE'S FIFTY OR SIXTY people at the funeral. People who still live in San Dimas. Like Jean and Maddix and Crust and this dude everyone used to call Flatulence Phil. He probably doesn't go by that name anymore. His suit looks like it costs more than what some students rack up in loan debt. There are other faces whose names are out of mental reach. People who look like they're members of a death metal band, others who look like members of a death cult. Austin didn't think anyone would come. Through the double doors and in the parlor that's mostly empty: a shrine at the front where a casket would go. A picture of Wade, blown up, sits behind an urn filled with his ashes. Even in the picture his glasses are smudged. Austin used to take off and clean Wade's glasses for him because he knew Wade never would. Wade's eyes in the picture don't look glazed like they did in later years. It's an old picture. The good version of him.

The people Wade used to get high with are here too. They walk around seeing shades of reality no one else can. And they're all saying *I remember this time when Wade* or *One time*

Wade did...and then a story and then they laugh too hard. Trying to cover up that hopelessness of loss. One dude's doing that lower lip droop that opiate users get when they fix, kinda looks like the same lip thing angry bears do. He's talking about the last time he saw Wade. When he was trying to score, on the corner of Washington, some Black dude telling him to go around the corner and *get the good from the white boy*—which ended up being Wade. Maddix, who Austin hasn't seen since she (previously he) stole Austin's girlfriend, starts talking privately to Austin about everything but Wade: the JFK assassination and how it relates to the Obama assassination, and the connection between the Zodiac Killer and Stanley Kubrick. She's talking about the Toynbee tiles and Mars and the Zapruder film in reverse and how the guy driving JFK's motorcade is doing sign language in reverse and how there's a long-lost Zodiac letter that *explains everything the government's hiding*. She hands Austin a piece of paper, tells him to read it when he has time. This is the kind of thing that people do when there isn't—

"Good to see you."

The voice seeps into Austin's head like a pirate signal playing reruns of a show he knows by heart. He doesn't turn around so much as he's turned around by the golf-gloved hand on his shoulder. An urge to grab the hand and break it overcomes him, but as he turns and sees the face of his dad, a familiar calm warms him. He's always thought his dad looks like a short-haired Frank Zappa, and time hasn't changed that. Austin can't say anything. He just nods. And his dad pulls him in close, embraces him quickly. Then steps back, putting space between himself and his son.

"When did you get in?"

"Not long."

"I'm glad you're here. It's been too long since I've seen your face."

"Good to see you too."

"How long are you staying?"

Someone says, "Hey Chance," and Austin's dad waves to an unknown in the crowd.

He says to Austin, "You look good. Skinny."

"Okay."

"No throw-away lines, Austin. You gotta give me something more than 'okay.'"

"Okay."

Chance gives one of those smiles that says everything about how familiar he is with the smartass Austin was and continues to be. He looks into the parlor at Wade's portrait, at Wade's mother. He says, "I'm gonna go say something to her."

Wade's mother, Velma, stands alone, staring at the blown up picture of Wade as if she's never seen it. Austin knows the look, has seen it in his mother when she says *I need an extra pill today.* Which is probably why Wade's mom is zoned, distant. Maybe she doesn't believe that her little boy is now reduced to useless matter sealed in an ornate vase, sunflowers painted on its surface. Austin's dad walks up to her, gives her a hug like they know each other, whispers in her ear. He touches Wade's urn, even though he hated Wade—or at least appeared to for over twenty years.

Austin stands there, watches this. Other than Maddix, no one approaches him or talks to him. They stay clear of him. As if they don't trust Austin, like there's something in his past that makes them all reluctant to associate with him.

Austin's dad comes back to him. Says, "I'm gonna go.

Don't think it's right for me to be here with you when she can't be with her son. See you tonight at dinner?"

Austin doesn't say anything which is enough of an answer. As Austin's dad leaves, he walks past Jean, says something close to Jean's ear. They shake hands, hug like father and son. Chance fades into the crowd. Jean points at Austin from across the room, joins him near a table stacked with pamphlets, Wade's face on each. Austin takes one.

"You going to his parents' place after this?"

Jean's wife eases up behind Jean. She waves to Austin modestly, silent. Austin throws her an obligatory smile.

Austin says, "I didn't plan on going." Which is a lie. He can't stop thinking about the baseboard in Wade's room.

"Let's go. We can talk shit in his room. Maybe go look at his dad for a laugh."

Wade, Jean, and Austin had all been friends for over twenty years, almost twenty five. And all those years, Wade's dad, Tucker, hated Jean and Jean hated him. They almost came to fists on a summer day when Austin, Wade, and Jean were on their way to the beach and Tucker called, ordered Wade home to make his bed—his dad's bed, not Wade's. Austin drove Wade back home and Jean and Tucker circled each other in the driveway, shirts off, neither of them taking a swing but both hurling violent words at the other. So it makes sense to Austin why Jean wants to go.

Because Tucker is on his deathbed. Home hospice care. Monster inside eating his lung and liver. The way Jean tells it, it's only a matter of days. Tucker's a Vietnam vet with a thirty, forty year habit of spending nights with a pack of Pall Malls and a case of Budweiser. What did he expect to happen? Still, it's a shitty thing. Austin can't say one human's suffering is greater or less than another, or that the death of that suffering human is any more important than another. But the old man's a human and Austin feels like he should at least acknowledge that—maybe not by mocking him like Jean plans to. What would it be like to count the time you have left in hours, in minutes?

Jean's wife says, "Why didn't any of these people do anything for him?"

Jean says, "Stop it."

Austin says, "Cuz they were afraid Wade would pull them into whatever he couldn't escape."

Jean says, "I wasn't afraid. We did the best and only thing we could do: leave him alone."

Austin doesn't know if he believes that. Mostly because he doesn't think he did the best thing for Wade. Was Austin really afraid that Wade would pull him into addiction, make Austin the same hollowed-out person? Was Wade waiting for someone like Austin—or specifically Austin—to yank him out of himself and into the help he needed? Or did he know exactly how it would end for him?

The service ends up being a disrespect to everything Wade once was. Preacher trying to convert. Organ music that's starched-collar stiff. Austin remembers that Wade loved Hancock's "Watermelon Man," the one off *Head Hunters*. If he could hear the music at his own funeral, Wade would've burned the place down. One of Wade's childhood friends, a guy with a vaguely hydrocephalic head, tells a story about a time he went camping with Wade for Boy Scouts and how they almost got lost and Wade guided them home using a stick-and-sun compass. At some point Austin wants to stand and ask *But did he save your life?* but doesn't.

At one point, Flatulence Phil fart. Some things never change.

ACT TWO – PART ONE:
TWIN FREQUENCIES

1

MOST NIGHTS AFTER THE LAST MOVIEGOER returns to the real world and the final reel's rewound, Jackie Day commits herself to a back booth at The Velveteen Saddle. She nurses an Irish coffee while ex-studio-execs argue over old feuds, dwelling heavily in the past, drowning glory days when studios existed to put movies in theaters and not straight to streaming services with well whiskey and dirt-cheap scotch. An atmosphere of cigarette smoke masks everyone's real identity. Tonight Jackie's taken the Irish out of her coffee and ignores the old men Hollywood forgot.

She's reading through the screenplay for the third time, taking notes, still unsure what the screenplay means and why it's in her possession. Is this really Wolpe? He's dead, isn't he? And this *Sunflower* is not unlike a suicide note—if she really believes Wolpe killed himself.

In the screenplay, there's an ominous and ubiquitous group controlling each character's fate—clearly a nod to Kubrick. The group symbolizes the lack of control in and the inseparable connectedness of both the Empire and the Commonwealth. All of the sad, desperate characters are stand-ins for the various facets of a faceless post-American culture, souls stretching to catch fame or fortune or some sort of legacy past death. But what is unclear to Jackie, unsettling and confusing even, is why

Wolpe wrote himself into the screenplay, dying in almost the same way. And despite a lengthy, denial-heavy period, Jackie finally accepted that Wolpe's written a character that's similar to herself—an unsuspecting recipient of the Wolpe character's latest screenplay who, because of the Wolpe character's death, must figure out the whys and hows. Not exactly like her life—but enough for her to believe it has something to do with her life. The story seems to career toward an explosive climax where all the characters fall together in a moment of tragic fate, but that ending isn't there for Jackie. The last twenty five pages are missing. The final act jumps from 101 to 127, with the final page (127) starting mid-sentence and ends with *and prepares herself to read and eat and float endlessly until she can laugh and at last sleep. FADE TO BLACK*

"You a'ight? Look like you seen that proverbial ghost."

Jackie looks up from the screenplay. H.I. Budrow stands behind her, over-her-shoulder reading.

"Please don't tell me you wrote that, Jackie. After all you've invested to preserve the sincerity of film, and the damnation you cast on those who disrespect that sincerity, that you, Jackie Day, write something so desperate to sound hip as *You a'ight? Look like you seen that proverbial ghost.*"

"I didn't write it."

"Thank that void in the sky."

Jackie knows it's not a void. She knows that when she looks up, though she may never see it with the unaided eye, there is a complex living space filled with devices and systems she'll never understand. And in this living space is a person who knows her well, a person who knows exactly what these systems and devices do, a person Jackie misses on most days. She wonders if when her sister looks down on the earth she's ever hoping to see

Jackie's face and not just a reflection, the endless black outside the station making the window a mirror showing Amy the face of her twin sister.

"Sit down, Hi. I need to show you something."

"Crusty, bring me a Big Dude Special," he shouts to the bartender as he sits in Jackie's booth. He tosses a tech-heavy backpack into the booth next to him. Even though one could fry a midnight egg on the asphalt outside The Velveteen Saddle, H.I.'s dressed in a Travis-Bickle-style Army jacket, white dress shirt, sloppy undershirt, torn jeans, beanie, and Doc Martens. He tosses a set of keys on the table. The subtropical temperature in the bar brings an extra shellac of sweat faster than Crusty can whip up the Big Dude Special, so H.I. peels off the extra clothes, as Jackie begins.

"Hi, there's this—"

"Before we start, you mind?" He pulls out two two-way headsets from his backpack. Jackie knows the drill. H.I., like most of the Millennial breed, suffers from a clinical case of Attention Deficit Disorder. Once thought to be a fabled disease, ADD is the Black Plague of the Network Age. Add on the fact that he's a well-known pop culture archivist—*Not a fucking blogger*—always on top of what's current and his scattershot attention is nearly incurable. To counter this lack of attention, especially in public situations, H.I. requires that his conversational counterparts wear gear that secludes their conversation and limits external auditory distractions, keeping him focused on the conversation—though Jackie thinks that even at his best, H.I. derails most discussions. He also records these conversations. But Jackie doesn't know this.

She adjusts the headset. Everything but H.I.'s digitized voice fades to a muffle.

—Hi, this, this conversation you and I are about to have, this won't leave this booth, this bar, this block. It dies here, with us.

—I've heard *this* before... You ever get the feeling you're living out a movie scene and not actually living?

—Not until recent.

Jackie slides the screenplay across the table. H.I. looks at the cover, flips through the pages, a general sense of being unimpressed.

—Where'd you get this?

She tells him the story, tells him to flip to page thirty-six and read. He does.

—And?

—That's this moment we're having, right here.

—Hardly. Where am I? Who'm I supposed to be? I'm not this guy described as *a sloppy loser, but he's got that impossibly smart look behind his glasses.* I don't wear glasses.

Crusty, with a wooden leg and bearded dragon on his shoulder, limps up to the booth holding a tray. On this tray is the most preposterous drink seen outside Disney-owned Caribbean vacation spots. A fishbowl filled with liquid swirling in tie-dye colors, two types of rum, whiskey, mezcal, Diet Squirt, pineapple juice, topped with a flaming shot of grain alcohol and garnished with the top of a pineapple and a bamboo umbrella large enough to keep an infant dry in heavy rain. Two garden-hose-sized straws hang limply from the drink. Crusty sets it on the table.

"I don't know," he says with a squeaky voice, "why I ever put this damn thing on the menu." And he walks back to the bar, dodging an argument between two ex-execs that's on the verge of getting physical.

H.I. puts both straws in his mouth and, with a *ssshhhlllllluurrrk*, downs a good portion of the drink. With that voice that comes after swallowing alcohol's burn, H.I. continues.

—I don't see Crusty anywhere in this script

—So maybe it's not exactly the same. But it's close. A film editor reading the final screenplay of a dead director named Simeon Wolpe, a screenplay dropped off to her in a very suspicious manner.

—How?

—It was inside a bag of coffee thrown through her car windshield.

—And how did you get it again?

—A blind man gave it to me.

He slurps the drink.

—I'm struggling to see a connection.

—Hi, I just—

—Don't you think that reading it might've influenced whatever you've done since reading it? You know, like, don't think about eating toenails and all that.

—What the fuck?

—If I say 'don't think about eating toenails,' all you're gonna think about is eating toenails. This is like that. Try not to think about doing the things that are in that script and... Yeah...

—I'm immune to all that.

—Yet here you are.

Jackie says nothing.

Outside, an ice cream truck sits across the street from The Velveteen Saddle. The ice cream truck is purposely distressed: dented bumper, scratch across the hood, headlight that's sagging and half-burnt and winking in and out, paint giving way to rust, curling smiley face sticker on the left side. Inside, this truck is retrofitted with complex surveillance equipment, including modules controlling cockroach-sized drone-cameras, heat-sensor x-ray detectors, and reel-to-reel audio recording shelves with wireless transmission interruption capabilities. Two agents manning the workspace use this wireless transmission interruption to break into the frequency of H.I.'s headset and are now recording to a reel labeled *The Plot*. What these two agents, who might either be part of a well-funded grassroots terrorist organization or a clandestine branch of the NSA, do not know is that H.I. is very aware that he is being listened to, and may or may not be scripting the conversation with that knowledge. Jackie knows nothing.

H.I. continues.

—Wolpe died two days ago. So someone who knows you go here almost every night wrote this thing about him dying. I hate to say it but it's someone fucking with you.

—Is it you?

—I've got better things to do.

—No you don't. And why would someone do that to me?

—Why anything, Jackie? Why do people blow up buildings?
    Shoot wildly into crowds of people? Claim to be people
    they're not in order to scam money out of other people?
    Why do actors act? Why build a life as a projectionist?

—There's something more going on here. This is Wolpe's work.
    Has to be. I know you didn't study him, but I have. This is
    him. And now it's in my hands. And I can't stop asking
    why and how.

Jackie looks around the bar and notices a couple across the
room. At a table. Both sets of eyes slyly observing her
conversation with H.I. without looking like they're observing
it, making it completely obvious they're watching the
conversation. She reaches across the table and slides the
screenplay back to her side, plops it on the seat next to her. She
lights a cigarette.

—Jackie, I'm not convinced. Sometimes a fart is a fart. Isn't
    that how the saying goes?

—I don't think so, H.I. But I'll amend it with: sometimes a fart
    is a shart in disguise.

—I didn't think you spoke my language.

—Blame the movies. They're responsible for you thinking I can
    only be something to react off of.

—Don't know what that means.

With half the Big Dude Special sloshing in his stomach,
Jackie can see that H.I. is well on his way to being drunk. His
foot touches her leg in a more-than-accidental way. She kicks
his shin, hard. It's as if he's trying to get drunk enough to find a

way out of the conversation, numb his lips so they won't say things he shouldn't.

—So what are you going to do about it? If you think it's something, and not just some *thing*.

Jackie says nothing. Looks around the bar again, avoiding eye contact with the couple as long as she can. But eventually her eyes wander to that shadowy corner. Just as before, the couple's looking right at her, their ears perked, listening. The fuck?

—Did you see that? Those people—
—Go to *StyleTwin.org* and see who comes up. If it's Wolpe, then go from there.
—Style twin?
—Some professor over at Sun State in Santa Barbara made this linguistic analyzer. Uploaded every novel, poem, screenplay, play, article, and all that, mostly by the more famous and classic authors, but he's managed to be as diverse as possible. He's on his like sixth year of what he said'll be a twenty year project so I'm sure Wolpe's in there. Think his name's Sappling or something. Input a sample of writing, it breaks it down syntactically and runs through all comparisons, then an algorithm determines writing patterns. The writer get matched with a writer whose style they share. We all write like someone. There's no such thing as a completely unique writer anymore. Even the most avant-garde writers are just facsimiles of ones that've come before.

You can't help but feel like he's calling you out directly. (Fuck him)

—I don't have the internet. Or a computer. Or phone. Anything like that. Thought you knew.
—Shit…guess I forgot. You know, with the—

He points to the headset—or maybe to his head. H.I. digs into his tech-heavy backpack, slides an absurdly large laptop out and slams it onto the table with a crashing thud that pulls the attention of every patron in The Velveteen Saddle—including the two ex-execs who have resorted to grabbing each other's collar in a threatening way in between sips of their neat drinks. He flips it open, keeps the screen hidden from Jackie as he clicks and types and clears his screen of all the things only he's allowed to see. After a sip from the Big Dude that drains it down to ice, H.I. reaches for the screenplay. Jackie pulls it away from H.I.'s hand, almost wants to hug it, protect it. The way his face twists tells Jackie he's hurt and confused, but mostly drunk.

—The fuck? Why does everyone suddenly not trust me?
—What's that mean?
—Nothing… Forget it. Just… I need the screenplay to input some passages.

He turns the laptop. The simple-looking page (text box, white background, and a submit button—that's all) for *StyleTwin.org* waits for her to relinquish the screenplay. A part of her wants to say that she'll type it, but her two-finger buzzard-pecking would keep them there all night. So she lifts her hand off the screenplay, motions for H.I. to take it. He does, enters a five page chunk of the screenplay in the text box on the main page. A click, a moment for the information to go wherever information goes, and then returns. The algorithm completes and a digital trumpet tooting royally ushers in the process's completion. The screen reads:

Your Style Twin™ is **Simeon Wolpe**. There are 2 writers who share this style. They are as follows:
   1) Simeon Wolpe
   2) **[REDACTED]**

H.I. sits back, brow furrowed.

—Name redacted.
—Why? What's that mean?
—This could also be a fuckup. The algorithm… Could be flawed or something. Maybe it's not accustomed to screenplay style, or maybe Wolpe's input was corrupted and the only people who can write like this have erred out of the database's existence.
—You're a writer, right? Type something. See if it's broken.

There's no modesty with H.I. and Jackie's aware of this. Any chance he gets to put his writing on any platform, he'll take it like a starving dog. So he types, from memory, some prose. He's got the laptop turned away again. He stops, clicks. The trumpet toots. He turns the screen back to her.

Your Style Twin™ is **Don Thom David**. There are 2,546 writers who share this style. They are as follows:
   1) Don Thom David

2) James Barris
3) Shasta Anderson

H.I. shuts the laptop. Slams it, really.

—Works.
—If Wolpe didn't write the screenplay, then the only person
    who could is this redacted. And the only person who can
    find why this name's redacted is this guy over at Sun State
    University.

Again, Jackie finds herself looking around the bar. She hits
on the couple again. They're looking at H.I.'s laptop, as if
they're trying to read what's on the screen. And then the
husband sees Jackie. When he makes eye contact and Jackie
holds, not looking away, the man throws a twenty on the table,
grabs the woman's arm, and the two hurry out the bar. The
woman seems hesitant, but the man drags her along, each
playing roles: her, a shy wife; him, the dominant husband.

—Seems like you've got your next step.

She nods and for the first time notices the stickers on the
back of H.I.'s laptop. Posters for *A Clockwork Orange* and
2001: A Space Odyssey and *Cutting Room* (Frannie O' Hallidaze
front and center) miniaturized and vinylized. Seeing them,
there's a moment of atavistic terror boiling inside her she can't
explain. Imprinting not yet awakened, but starting to no longer
be sleepy. Messages just for her.
    Jackie slips the headset off and slides it over to H.I.
    She says, "I've had a day, Hi."

H.I. nods, though Jackie can see he's comfortably drunk.

She says, "You okay? Need a ride somewhere?"

He says, "Nah, I'm here. Drive safe."

"I hate it that. As if I'm gonna do anything else."

He slurps at the watered-down ice.

He says, "How about this: watch out for yourself."

She says, "Watch for what?"

But his attention is already somewhere else.

A smash cut and Jackie's on her BSA Lightning Rocket ripping down the side streets of West Hollywood, the Wolpe screenplay riding shotgun in the mismatched sidecar, buckled in, pages flapping but staying together. The motorcycle's drone narrows her thoughts. She'd never met Wolpe, had no connection to him. So then why? If this isn't a Wolpe screenplay, who passed it on to her and why try to pass it off as Wolpe? Who would have the reason to play with her like that? But if this is Wolpe, why that too? Asking these questions makes her feel clichéd and insignificant.

Her eyes flick to the side-view mirror. Headlights. Half a mile back. One light dimmer than the other, winking at her. She turns onto Camino de Noche Rosa. Six seconds later and the headlights ease onto the street behind her. Even though she knows she doesn't need to, Jackie turns off Noche Rosa and onto Cochise Blvd., telling herself that the lights are just a coincidence. To think she's being followed is paranoia that's never existed in her before. This paranoia, a combination of egoism and solipsism, goes against the Doctrine of Jackie Day. There are thousands of people awake at this hour within half a square mile, all driving, all heading somewhere.

But when the headlights turn on Cochise, this time closer than before, Jackie can't stop herself from thinking about the couple in the bar. Watching her. Listening. It's a large vehicle, a van or truck. Something glows on the roof, but Jackie doesn't let the truck get close enough to find out what it is.

She throttles the gas, the bike screaming its well-built power. Tires grip asphalt and push off. Jackie peels around the corner at Libra Rd. and then a left on Wading River Run, and then almost tips as she barrels onto a dead end street. She stops, turns off the engine and listens. This moment, even more so than the thoughts before, feels like the writing of a terrible farceur, so much so that Jackie laughs a quiet, humorless laugh. She hears from an adjacent street: tires squeal, the growl of a V-8 jumping to life, undercarriage bottoming out on an unseen dip. Underneath these sounds: the tinkle-tune of an ice cream truck. A Beethoven song she almost recognizes. Then all this noise fades, grows distant until it's gone. She waits a beat, settles into the fact that she wasn't actually being followed. Or maybe agrees with whatever voice inside her head is trying to convince her she wasn't being followed.

She flips on the bike's headlight. It casts a tunnel of light on the dead end. A coyote steps from the brush behind the red and white dead end marker. Eases onto the street in front of her. When it sees Jackie, it stops. It shakes its fur. Shivers. Then starts to bloat. Flesh rips, blood erupts, drool hangs in gooey streams, and the animal turns inside out—bones and organs and quivering muscles now external. Bile and fatty juices splattering like grease in a skillet. The light catches its eyes. They glow. The coyote licks its teeth, shakes again, then trots off, disappears into the darkness between houses.

All her weight into a stomp and the bike roars to life, the sound tearing away the impossible nightmare she just witnessed. Can't be real. Just can't. She moves the bike back, turns it around. The light casts on the street sign and Jackie lets out a laugh, a recipe with the main ingredients of disbelief and a dash a pain.

Sunflower Rd. shines in reflective white against reflective green.

Watch out for yourself.

There's something insidious attached to the screenplay, she's almost certain of it. But she's also certain that H.I. is trying to hide something from her and finds herself wondering who H.I. really is—but isn't sure if that's even a question yet. There's a tightness in her chest that she knows won't go away until she finds the identity of [REDACTED].

<u>DELETED SCENE</u>

Reg

2

THE PEOPLE IN BLACK SUITS PUT THE CLAW *end of a hammer up Austin's nose, fulcrum it against his lips and teeth. The crackling of cartilage fills his head like Pop Rocks. They ask him about the flight he abandoned before driving to San Dimas. He tells them he wanted more time on the road to think and planes freak him out. They tell him that the flight he abandoned exploded mid-flight, wreckage coming down in the Scorchland. Austin tells them he knows nothing about it. They clamp both his feet in waffle makers, snap rat traps on his lips and ears and eye lids. They interrogate him about his time spent in the LaborCamps, the work he did, which corporation sponsored his stay, what programs he attended, who he spoke with if he spoke with anyone. He tells them that the food in the camps made him fatter, that they shaved everyone's head, that it felt like the Nazi Germany they show in movies. They ask about conditioning, but Austin doesn't remember any conditioning. They show him a leatherette book with a black star embossed on the cover, and when Austin says he doesn't recognize it, they use the claw hammer to smash his big toes. The black suits read from the book. They say* rust *and* longing *and* nineteen *and* solitaire *and* red queen. *They talk to him about MK Ultra programming, as if he's supposed to know what that is—for real and not what he knows from movies. When words from the book don't lead to whatever the suits expect them to, they* *pull out a jar, the inside alive with insects Austin's never seen before. One of the black suits says* cicada killer *and even though Austin doesn't know what that means, anything with the name* killer *can't be good. A black suit carefully uncaps the jar and purrs at the insects, which seems to calm the bugs. Another black suit plucks a single cicada killer from the jar with a pair of chopsticks. They put the bug near Austin's penis, its inch-long stinger pointed right at his softest skin. They say* We know there's something in you and we're going to get it out. *Austin doesn't know what that means, so he keeps talking, spilling all the details, recalling memories as if they're happening right now.*

NOTHING HAS CHANGED in twenty years. Tucker and Velma's mini-van sits in the same oil-stained spot in the driveway, a boxy bulk of steel and rust from the 90s. The street around the house feels like a time warp as well—the same paint jobs, the same cracked garage window, the same frisbee on top of the same roof. Austin parks halfway down the block next to a light post plastered with fliers for a smiling boy. George. Missing two days. Possibly kidnapped. Bike left in the street.

"Have you seen him?"

A teenager stands behind Austin, sweaty like he's been outside all day. Probably like fifteen or something. He's got more fliers in his hand. Even though this teenager is mostly white and the boy on the flyer is Asian, Austin can see the resemblance between the two. It's clear the boys share DNA.

An ice cream truck drives by playing a creepy lo-fi version of a classical melody. Beethoven or Mozart or something. Austin doesn't know. The truck's got this big smiley face on the side, which to Austin feels like it's mocking everything the day's about to bring. But the smile isn't as horrible as the sun-faded ice cream cone on top of the truck. Turned horizontal. Partially-melted ice cream scoop forming another smiling, dopey face. The kid looks at the truck as if that ice cream face is about to slide off the roof, crawl across the hot asphalt, melting and screaming its way over to the kid to swallow him whole.

"Sorry, kid. I don't live around here."

"Don't call me kid. Everyone calls me kid. No one believes kids."

"Believes you about what?"

He looks at the ice cream truck and says, "Nevermind. If you see my brother, please call that number. It's mine."

He hands Austin one of the flyers. Wet from his small sweaty hands. Austin's fingers mush through the missing boy's face. The kid skates off on a board shaped like something from the 90s—something like what Wade used to skate around on. The ice cream truck creeps past Austin, past all the other houses on the street, and stops in front of a house with flowers all around it. Waits there as if the ice cream man's expecting someone inside to come out. When no one does, the ice cream truck eases around the corner and off the street. The music grows distant but never quite fades.

The neighborhood smells like coffee and waffles and window cleaner. Reminds Austin of one of those candles people would rather eat than burn. Austin's stomach sours, the smell bringing nausea with it. All suburbs smell like this. This is why Austin lives out in the middle of nowhere.

Cigarette smoke pours out of the garage like it's on fire. Jean's there, beer in hand. Austin wants to ask Jean if he thinks it's an appropriate way to spend time at a funeral for someone who died from addiction, but he knows Jean will just shrug, sip his beer, and say something like *He died, I didn't.* It's a good point and so Austin thinks *Whatever* and doesn't ask. Jean's got some paperbacks he's pilfered from Wade's room, especially proud of one called *Valis* that he shows Austin as if he's supposed to remember. He doesn't.

"You went in Wade's room without me?"

"I had to, man."

Austin doesn't know what that's supposed to mean. Jean's wife stands behind Jean, waves at Austin. She taps her husband on the shoulder and he nods like *I got it.*

Jean says, "What're you doing tomorrow?"

Austin says, "Driving back. I'm not staying."

"C'mon, man. You just got here. Let's have a hang. I've got this party at my house tomorrow, a lot of people'll be there. Like old times." He leans closer to Austin and adds, "And I've got something I want to talk to you about, stuff that's not really cool here."

"I don't know if your memory's pieced together right, but those old times? They weren't as fun as you remember."

"Yeah, but Austin? They weren't as bad as you remember."

Inside, no one's saying his name. People are more interested in coffee and cookies and deli sandwiches than they are the mural of pictures chronicling Wade's life. Austin scans the photos, searching for proof that he and Wade were as close as he remembers. He doesn't see himself, except maybe in one picture. Elementary school. A Field Day relay, tie-dye shirts and smiles. Wade running so fast he's blurred. And in the background, face obscured by the vaguely-hydrocephalic guy who spoke at Wade's funeral and a youthful Jean: is that Austin? He can't be sure. A lady walks up, smiles at him. He expects her to start in on a memory of Wade, but she doesn't.

She picks through the bowl of nuts in front of the mural and walks off crunching on an almond—something Wade was deathly allergic to.

Unlike the neighborhood, Wade's room has changed drastically since the last time Austin was in it. Not just clean, but stripped of any evidence of Wade. He used to have Coca-Cola blinds, a Coca-Cola clock, a Coca-Cola ceiling fan, and Coca-Cola bedding. Austin once watched Wade drink an entire twelve-pack of Coke in a single night. It's obvious to him now that the Coke fixation was a precursor to his future addictions. Now, though, all that's gone. Anything carrying a memory of Wade doesn't exist in the room anymore. It reminds Austin of what his mom did to Bowie Lee's room. Both rooms feel like reproductions, sets for scenes that'll get deleted anyway.

Austin doesn't waste any time. He moves the bed away from the wall and on hands and knees taps along the baseboard. There's a hollow thud Austin recognizes, sound triggering memory like PTSD. The board pops off with a loud squeak. He reaches in and around and feels inside the cobwebbed darkness. His hand hits something slimy. Like a mushy finger. He stops touching it because he doesn't want to know what it is. And then his fingers wrap around a small book. He pulls it out.

A journal. Iridescent trails all over the cover. Like tracks of dried glue. Or slime. Austin puts the baseboard back in place and sits on the bed. A picture sticks out of the journal. Not a picture; a postcard of the Hollywood sign—that beacon of hope for the hopeless. Except at the top of the hill, above the letters, there's this castle. Superimposed, or whatever it's called. On the back of the postcard, two words: *Sunflower Mars*.

The journal's full of all this fine point writing. Tiny stuff. So dense it makes the pages look black. Austin tries to read it but can't. His mind can only focus on the fact that something was actually there, in the baseboard hideaway. If he were a person of faith, he would put it on Wade—and not just because of the letter. That finding the journal and the postcard is about a *somethingness* beyond Wade.

When Austin leaves Wade's old room there's this *psssst psssst* creeping out from a room at the end of the hall.

A hand grabs his shoulder and again Austin's first instinct is to grab the hand and break it, spin around and chop the grabber's throat with a hammer fist. He doesn't know why there's this sudden instinct for violence. If he believed in the influence of movies, he'd blame that. But this is a deeper unknown. Like secret coding. The kind of bad shit that Austin used to write about when he used to write screenplays— soldiers awakened to fight in a battle they didn't know they were a part of, to kill people they're supposed to love. Just the thought of that being real and not a poorly-imagined fantasy makes him want to leave the house and go gorge on the trashiest fast food he can find. And maybe vomit.

But it's only Jean, grabbing his arm. The violence that may or may not be legitimately dwelling inside him subsides like a sudden low tide. Maybe it's sadness or anger transmogrified into violence. Austin doesn't know why, but he hides the journal and postcard from Jean. Tucks it into his waistband, pulls his shirt over it. And Jean's so focused on the noise coming from the room at the end of the hall that he doesn't notice. Or maybe he does and doesn't say anything.

"You wanna go in and look at him," as if Wade's dad is the next stall in a freak show. Austin's hesitation must be obvious because Jean adds, "He was a piece of shit. Let's go in there and make fun of him."

"You're an asshole sometimes, you know that?"

"Sometimes?" Jean wiggles his eyebrows, showing Austin that Jean might still be the same grungy bullhead even if he doesn't dress the part.

Seeing him, there's no question just how close Tucker is to death. Tubes sticking in and out of almost every inch of his body. Hospital bed. Machines keeping him as fresh as they can. American flag above his bed. Gulf War movie on the TV at the foot of his bed—a movie with Denzel Washington and Meryl Streep that Austin's never seen. People often describe the sick or near-dead as *skin and bones,* but that really is all that's left of him.

Austin says, "Hello, sir."

Wade's dad nods.

Jean goes, "Jesus, I can't be here," and runs out the room.

And abandons Austin with the dying man.

Wade's dad says, "Austin…trouble…maker." *Pssst pssst.*

Austin approaches the bed, shakes Wade's dad's hand. His grip is threadbare, bones replaced with mushrooms. The TV plays the sounds of war. The dying man's eyes flick back and forth from the war on TV to Austin.

Austin says, "I'm surprised you remember me. It's been a long time since—"

"Wade…missed…you…" *Pssst pssst.*

"I hadn't seen him in years. But I never forgot."

Austin can see his mind working—whatever's left of it. What it must be like to have to fight for simple things like memory and thought. A part of Austin wishes he could swap places with Wade's dad, feel what it's like to be so close to oblivion.

"I saw him... yester...day..." *Psssst psssst.* "Then...the men...came...for his...stuff..." *Psssst psssst.*

"Wade died two days ago."

Psssst psssst.

"What stuff?"

"Don't...remember..." *Psssst psssst.*

His eyes go back to the TV. One of the machines beeps loud. Liquid pushes through the IV and into his bloodstream. His eyelids flutter, mouth droops. Doped up and useless.

"It won't be long before he's gone too." Velma stands in the doorway. Her face is hard, as if she's ready to tell Austin to get the fuck out. But she doesn't. She walks over to her husband and twists a knob on one of the machines. She adjusts the pillow under her husband's head with hands and gestures that can only be described as *loving.* And the machine goes *psssst psssst.*

AUSTIN MEETS HIS PARENTS for dinner at one of those elitist, experimental restaurants attempting to reinvent the meal. *The Trough* says the sign outside in kitschy pink neon pulled like taffy. Food eviscerated and served in mini-troughs. Eaters dive in without utensils. Austin orders a salad, but it's still a chunky green mush served in a trough.

His dad wipes high-dollar slop off his face. "I sold this place its toilets. Really nice products. Seat warmers and everything. Spent a lot of money."

"With this kind of food, I can imagine." Austin blows at a bubble forming at the top of his emulsified salad.

"You on a diet again?"

This is Austin's cue to zone out before the conversation begins. His mom, Ava, takes a pill, likely to keep her from having to participate in conversations, say things she doesn't want to. They sit at a table for four, an automatic absence reminding them all—or maybe just Austin—that they are forever missing the fourth member of their party.

Chance talks business: new store they just opened in the mall and the giant warehouse he built for overstock, innovations in toilet technology—diamond encrusted flush valves and ceramic heat-sync seats. Business deals with UAE hotels in the works. Money, and lots of it. He wipes more food from his chin and brings up the golf tournament again. A story Austin's heard a million times, as if it's a legend meant to explain who his dad is. Even though it kind of does. Chance swears he's moved past the regret that he could've gone pro, could've been famous, because he's now famous in a different way. The same kind of famous the mattress guys who cut mattresses in half with a chainsaw on commercials has. But it could've been sports fame. Sports money. Not toilet money. Still, he talks about it. The tournament, how he almost had a sponsorship from Tailormade, how he was thirteen under par on the fifteenth hole at the 22nd Annual Warvin Zindler Golf Tournament, the nearest opponent at a safely-distant four under par. How he went to shake a little boy's hand in the crowd, and how that little boy squeezed Chance's hand so hard that it crushed the bones in his hand. Austin's dad ended up finishing the tournament with the broken hand, nineteen over par. The crowd cheered him on, an underdog against impossible odds. But in losing the tournament and his hand, Chance also lost his sports future. But Chance cashed in on the fame of his underdog moment, started a business selling toilets.

How he got to toilets, Austin still hasn't figured out. But what Chance makes very clear each time he talks about the golf tournament is that he swears on his life that the kid wasn't a kid, that he believes the kid was a man, a dwarf, dressed up like a kid, hired by his opponent to sabotage his win. He ends with this because through years of telling this story, he knows that Austin tunes out every time the dwarf is brought up. Most people ignore this part.

This might be overdoing it here but you want it clear that things are connecting and that things have happened in a vast timeline in order to create a climax of perfectly timed design.

Before Ava slips off into a pink-pill-induced state of near-drooling blankness, she talks about her pet grooming business. A little shop called Pawssip Now, which is a play off the show she used to host in the early 2000s, when Austin was in elementary. *Gossip Now.* She too cashed in on her fame—though hers was the cheap, daytime talk show fame. The 2pm on UPN talk show kind of fame. Austin used to miss his mom terribly. She was gone, shooting the show most days. People would say *Yeah but you can see her on TV*, but that didn't matter. So instead he carried a picture of her for most of third and fourth grade. One of her headshots. But his mom talks now about how *Gossip Now* has yet another host, their tenth in the nearly twenty years since she was fired as host. Fired for not being youthful enough—or so she says. But so she was fired, sat at home while Chance built his toilet business, played mom to an Austin who was very grateful. Until she couldn't. Whether it was domesticity or routine, Ava broke from the home duties and opened, with Chance's help, a small pet grooming business. Which consumes her thoughts and movements on a day-to-day basis. As she nears the end of this recap of her life, as if Austin's never heard it before, she starts saying *puppy wuppies* and *sad sad, not just sad* in a way that sounds like she's just waking up from a deep sleep. The pills have her. Soon she's quiet.

Neither ask Austin about his life in NorCal. So while they talk, Austin thinks about Bowie Lee. About how everyone treats his memory like a bad season of a TV show. Austin never tells his parents about what he found in Wade's room.

Chance excuses himself and disappears to the bathroom for a period of time that either means the slop moved through him too quick so he had to test out one of his products or that he had a quick emotional breakdown or both. Austin sits in silence and his mom sits with her eyes closed, head wobbling over her trough of uneaten slop. Austin looks around the restaurant, notices the *maître d'* aggressively escorting a couple out the front door. Chance returns to the table as if nothing's happened and says, "You wanna go see a movie?"

Austin says, "I don't know what's out. Is there anything good?"

"Not really."

Ava says, "I'll go see a movie."

Chance says, "I know you will, darling." Then to Austin, "There's *Under/Shift* and *Agenda*."

Austin says, "New stuff."

"I know a place, does the old stuff. I think," looks at his watch, "we can make a showing of *Cutting Room* if we go now. They've been showing it since Wolpe died."

"You know the schedule?" Austin motions to his dad's watch.

"I do."

"Why?"

"If you like the place, I'll tell you after."

Chance takes Ava's hand, helps her up. He guides her out of the restaurant, loving in his mannerism but sterile and practiced in his behavior.

<u>DELETED SCENE</u>

The Trough

3

JACKIE TAKES THE COAST HIGHWAY to Santa Barbara. Not the 101. There are usually too many police on the 101 and today she needs to haul ass. Wind from the Pacific and aggressive traffic along the PCH threatens to send Jackie off the road, down the cliffs, and out of this life. She meant to detach the sidecar, but didn't get on the road until after noon due to an impossible time letting go of her life in the projection hall. She passed off her responsibility to a guy named Jean-Paul Nietzsche who claims to have worked the projectors at the Cinerama Dome before it shut down and only took a job as bus boy at Cinéma Vérité in hopes of working his way to projection, to which Jackie responded with a definitive *Fat fucking chance.* Jackie asked him a simple question about feed looping, and the fucker pulled out his phone to give her the answer. She slapped it out of his hand. Now he's there and Jackie's here. The screenplay pages shift in the rucksack on her back as she dodges drivers attempting to take 70mph pictures of the Pacific as if it's not right *there.*

Pulling into Santa Barbara, the air develops an overused hair dryer smell. Exhaust from the California Commonwealth Desalination Plant. Burning salt. Toxic. Millions of gallons of saltwater pumped, filtered, desalinated, and sent out as potable water. But the water isn't doing much to keep Santa Barbara from looking like it's part of the Flintstone age: a civilization built amongst prehistoric sand and rock, crags and half-burnt trees, entire landscapes scoured and black from flash fires. Fallen to the domination of the desert slowly enveloping the entire state. Jackie wonders where the water goes.

This is where she and her sister grew up, raised by loving parents who are still puttering about in a small senior living facility not far from the desalination plant. On the rare occasions Jackie visits them, they always ask about her sister, and she's forced to give them the same answer: *She's still gone. But she's looking down on you both right now. You'll see her soon.* But Jackie doubts if they ever will.

Today is one of those rare occasions. Because even with the desire pulling her toward answers, to be in this city without stopping to see her parents would fill her with a guilt she won't be able to ignore. And, she's just now realizing, the stop could be more useful than just an obligatory hello.

"In here, Ms. Day," says one of the automated nurses. It moves on tank treads. Its LED screenface mimics the peaceful placidity of a very generic middle-aged white woman. Jackie knows it's connected to the main hub at the front, that hub connected to the network, able to access all medical records, techniques, and diagnoses. Always learning how to be more human. "We've had to move your parents to another area of the facility. They say the desalination plant on the other side of the hill keeps them from ever reaching an inner quiet."

The phrase *inner quiet* sounds like something her father would say. And while she wasn't able to hear the plant from anywhere in the facility, Jackie knows her father is the kind of guy who curses crickets for being too goddamned loud but wouldn't hear a grenade if it blew up behind his recliner. And her mother's dementia is so bad she wouldn't know the difference between living in a new area of the facility or in the engine room of the desalination plant.

The autonurse guides her past glass-walled gardens where autonurses armed with assault rifles watch patients pull fruits and vegetables, past rooms where more armed autonurses guard patients as they sew quilts and shirts, and past a kitchen where even more armed autonurses observe patients creating home-cooked meals from scratch. The meals, vegetables, fruits, shirts and quilts are all to be sold at a booth manned by autonurses at the farmers markets that pops up in downtown Santa Barbara on the third Friday of every month and during the yearly Avocado Festival. Jackie's parents contribute nothing to this system of forced commerce. Thanks to a nominal fee paid by Amy—a clause she made sure was in her SpaceX work contract.

Jackie and the autonurse glide past rooms where elderly faces turn to look at Jackie, gutless mouths smacking on food they're no longer eating. Looks of shock and forgetfulness. Faces of men and women who no longer remember the timeline of their lives.

Her parents are in a room almost identical to their previous. A television across the room blares a day-time soap at a volume that overpowers anything the desalination plant would put out. Her parents sit in their respective chairs, facing the television, each paying attention to their own projects: her mother, a sketchpad and nibs of charcoal, fingers stained black; her father, an encyclopedia of the Vietnam War, looking at pictures and saying *bullshit* to himself or to the past or to both.

"Mister and Missus Day, your daughter Jackie is here to visit you." The autonurse turns and rolls out.

They don't see their daughter enter, don't even look up. Jackie moves to her father, puts her hand on his arm. He jumps.

"Goddamn, *goddamn!* I...you...it...*goddamn!*"

"Sorry, dad. Sorry. It's Jackie."

"The Angel of Death disguised as my daughter. Fought against the zipperheads and kicked commie ass and I'm scared into the next life by my own daughter."

"This is a nice room."

Her father replies in a slurred, half-discernible mumble that only Jackie, nurses, and those who take care of parents who've suffered strokes can understand. "So they piled a bunch of us in a B-29. Didn't tell us anything other than a location. One of them zipperhead names no American can pronounce without sounding like an asshole. We're in the air..." But Jackie doesn't hear the rest. Her eyes catch on a vase on the other side of the room, lines of afternoon light cutting through the blinds, giving the petals a glowing sensation, a spotlight telling Jackie to look over here, see this, these flowers, they're part of what you don't understand. An unseen energy tractor beams her across the room to the sunflowers. She touches the fat, ochre petals, their deep black center like artificial black holes pulling everything into their annihilating abyss. Her father continues mumbling about a memory she isn't sure is real or just a compilation of footage from the films he watches daily. A note sticks out of the flowers, typed in Courier font:

```
This  is  temporary.  Enjoy  the
sunflowers. With Sincerity, Miss
```

Jackie takes the note out of the vase and moves over to her mother. In shaky, childish strokes, her mother's shriveled hands manipulate charcoal into an image of a television, a dial-

and-antenna version. On its screen: the sunflowers in the vase. No more advanced than a child's drawing, her mother's talent now tragically unrecognizable. Especially for a woman who once had art in the Whitney and received the Guggenheim twice. When she leans down and kisses her mother's head, her mother says, "Amy."

To which Jackie, as usual, replies, "She's looking down on you both, mama."

With her parents' attention elsewhere, as it almost always is, Jackie takes the screenplay, selects fifteen pages that have an overwhelming this-is-predicting-the-future feel, and copies them on the in-room fax/copy machine. She keeps the copied pages and puts the real screenplay in the room safe. Jackie's the only one who knows the code—unless the staff bots have a way of bypassing or hacking the code. Inside the safe are her parents' wills, a few stacks of cash, important family photos, and a portfolio of drawings done by her mother when she could draw something other than stick figures and shaky lines. She shuts the safe and spins the dial.

Without a goodbye, Jackie leaves, her parents unaware she was even there, her father still mumbling, her mother sliding her finger along the page. In the hall, she stops an autonurse— maybe the same one that escorted her to the room, maybe not. She can never tell.

"Do you know who brought my parents those flowers?"

"Future Smiles Flower Delivery Services."

"But where did they come from?"

"I do not understand the query, Ms. Day."

"What did it say on the receipt? Who bought them?"

The nurse calculates internally, recalling stored data. "The receipt states the purchaser of the sixty-nine dollar and ninety-nine cent bundle is Ms. Jacqueline Day. Which is you."

"It says *Miss* on the card."

"Yes."

"Not Jackie."

"I assumed that was a short name your parents refer to you as. Security footage shows they have called you that on six occasions."

"You assumed?"

"It's really just a phrase to make you more comfortable with our interface."

THE UNIVERSITY LOOMS, a mountain specter casting a shadow on the valley below. Only six months have passed between the last time she visited Santa Barbara and now, yet Jackie can't remember the University being there. She remembers something about how the Sun State University system had bought out the California State system a year after the Fault Separation, something about the Commonwealth now possessing seventy-percent of the Cal State property. They'd shut down the operational campuses and constructed totally new ones. So somewhere below sits the UC-Santa Barbara campus, abandoned, classrooms now filled with spiders and ghosts. She wonders, *Why buy a college system if there's already one in place?*

The road to the university twists and grinds past well-manicured landscapes meant to look like arid desert but is full of vibrant poppies and marigolds and juicy San Pedro cacti—shit that doesn't live in the desert's hotter months but is very much alive. A hypnotic perfume of sage and lilac warms over Jackie like the scent of a recently-begun ritual. Exotic lizards perch atop rocks, basking in the heat, well-fed and unaware they are not in their real environment. *This is where the water goes.*

The campus itself is untainted by years of abuse and upheaval. Full of iGenners wandering from class to class or dorm to dorm or food court to food court—aimlessly different from the student body of Jackie's short time in college. This was after the revolt of the 70s and the confusion of the 80s. It was a time of lazy antagonism, the 90s: individualism, distrust toward Boomers, fear and sex and drugs and credit cards. Maybe not that different than now. Though Jackie didn't spend enough time in college to join any protests against the Bush-Era Anti-Utopia. She dropped out after one semester at NYU when her screenwriting professor said *Empire Strikes Back* was the greatest film ever made. But she didn't move back to California and live with her parents. New York became a home. She spent some time working abroad, working the projectors in a small village in Russia. But she found her way back to New York. She lived within her means by working as a projectionist's assistant at Cinema Village. Was given the go-ahead to sleep in that small projection hall rent-free. After the head projectionist suffered a stroke, Jackie took his place. During her time at the theater she worked closely with up-and-coming directors, then mid-tier, then some A-listers—including Kubrick. He's the one who suggested she move to Los Angeles.

A student walks by with a shirt that reads *The world's fucked. Let's party.* And then she hears:

"*Sunflower sunflower gonna be here soon…*"

Jackie turns around. A Mark-David-Chapman looking guy walks toward her—chubby, oily hair, a wet stain in the crotch of his pants. He's got a duffel bag slung over one shoulder, rifle in his hands. It's an old rifle. She recognizes it from *Cutting Room*, the flashback scenes with Lee Harvey Oswald and the investigation scene where Frannie O' Hallidaze tries to find that same rifle. And if she's seeing this right, he's wearing a shirt that says *Support your local projectionist.* Yellow font on a pink shirt. If the shirt isn't giving it away, his eyes do: this is for Jackie.

"Sunflower sunflower gonna be our doom…"

He raises the gun, aims it at Jackie. Smiles. The wetness in his crotch grows. Jackie can't move, can't believe this is happening. Things like this aren't supposed to happen anymore. Laws and security modules put in place to prevent this very thing. In this near-frozen moment before death, she notices that this guy's got two ears on one side of his head. She wonders if he hears in stereo.

Gunshots rip out like a string of cheap firecrackers. Jackie feels a bullet *zing* past her head, the bullet's wind lifting her hair.

The twenty or so students within shooting distance react instantly, guns drawn like a high-noon showdown. They all unload most of their magazines into the rifleman. His body, at the center of this shooting circle, twitches like an electrified cockroach. His face shatters into mush. Jackie jumps behind a nearby palm, bullets ripping chunks out of the trunk. The rifleman collapses, a lump of flesh in the grass. The stain in his crotch grows as he pisses himself. But the thing with the shooting circle is that half the gun-totting students neglected to recognize that on the other side of their target, in the line of fire, are other students. So this circle has shot both the rifleman and each other. Half the students scream, almost in unison:

You shot me! The rifleman shot no one—even though Jackie knows his aim was only at her. If there was ever any doubt as to whether or not she's into something she shouldn't be, the now-dead guy bubbling blood in the campus lawn confirms it for her.

She can't stop moving, because if that guy can find her, who else can? How did he? She peeks out from behind the palm, making sure that no one realized she was the target. The wounded are busy being attended to by the unharmed. So she keeps moving.

You, with your ability to float freely, notice from an overhead shot, like a drone if you really think about it, that this shooting circle has taken the vague shape of a smiley face. Too much? No, but maybe you asking is.

Jackie locates why she's here with the help of an autoguide. Its system automatically identifying her desired destination, the screen transitioning from therapeutic colorforms to a campus map with an office marked by a smiley face (yeah, this is too much): Spapling's office. In the subfloors of the L. Ron Hubband International Humanities Center, a dome-shaped building that looks like the top half of an alien spaceship. Jackie's here now, wandering the hospital-like hallways. But when she finally makes it to Spapling's office, it's lifeless. Classical music plays quietly from an unseen source. She can't be sure, but it sounds like the same Beethoven song from the night before. A desk-shaped pile of loose pages and books swollen from excessive dog-earing. On the far wall two dozen framed diplomas from various colleges Jackie's never heard of. A cracked leather recliner. Poster of a flying saucer hovering over a group of pine trees and the words **I WANT TO BELIEVE** in bold, white letters. And other than the disorganization, the chaos of the room reminds Jackie of her own projection hall—a sanctuary for the obsessed. She checks the plaque outside the office: *Dr. Sparsh Spapling: Artificial Intelligence.* Jackie thinks *That's a far shot from literary algorithms or whatever.* She knocks on the door frame.

"Hello?"

A small Syrian rug in the center of the floor lifts. A trap door flips open, papers sliding and piling at the base of the hatch. A gray-haired man who looks much too old to be climbing out of the floor climbs out of the floor. His eyes made cartoonishly large behind magnifying goggles. Looks like Frank Zappa if he never died and never cut his hair.

"Dr. Spapling?"

"I do not recognize you."

"Could be those goggles."

"Ah, yes." He peels them back to rest on the top of his head, squints at her. "Nope, still don't recognize you."

"I wouldn't think you would." A blast of frigid wind surrounds her. She notices little frost crystals at the corners of Spapling's mouth.

"Are you here to fix the insulator relay?"

"I need to talk to you about the Style Twin program."

He remains half-in, half-out of the hole in the floor, the office filling with artificially cold air. His eyebrows peak, waiting impatiently for her to continue.

"Do you handle all the names that run through the program?"

"Myself and an assistant."

"And you two are the only ones who have access to—"

He holds up his hand, halting the conversation. "I'm not sure I know what this is about. And being that I don't know you and that you're asking about that which you are not privileged to know, I am afraid I must cut this conversation short. You can find your way out. Maybe."

He walks down unseen steps, head sinking out of view. As his hand reaches up to close the rug-covered trap door, Jackie says, "Why would any name in the list of results be redacted?"

Spapling pops up like a jack-in-the-box, the goggles slipping back over his eyes. He stares at Jackie with this crazed, lemur-eyed, finger-in-an-electrical-socket look. "A redacted name? Where?"

Once the words are run through the program and the results return with Wolpe and a redacted name, Spapling steps back from the computer as if he's been shot.

"Highly improbable, yet there it is."

"So you didn't do this."

"Part of the experiment is to indicate connectedness. Anonymity would defeat the integrity of this work. The best way to adapt an artificial intelligence to the empathy of the human condition is to tell it stories. This program is a by-product of that empathy input."

"And your associate?"

"Wouldn't have the access to redact. That's deep code. He was mostly associated with data entry. Large sums of text. Linguistic equations. Did all his work remotely. From up north in the Empire."

He leans over Jackie's shoulder and puts his face close to the screen. She notices flakes in his hair. And what she at first thinks is dandruff is actually crusts of ice clumping his wispy gray hair into frosty dreadlocks.

"What's with the ice?"

"It's -12 degrees down there," Spapling says, motioning to

the trap door that's now closed, back in its rug-covered disguise. He reaches around Jackie and types something at the computer, entering a deep code level of the program that Jackie doesn't pretend to understand. She stands and Spapling eases into the chair without hesitation.

"And down there is...?"

Still working at the code, "Coolant system for the servers. One of many in the building."

"A little advanced for a humanities building?"

"Part of a proxy network. All linked to the big Higgs Hadron accelerator operation up at Hearst." And then back to the computer, "The name's gone from the code, which isn't possible because I am the only one who enters this information."

"Is there any kind of print-out of the results?"

"In systems of information and conversation, there is an equation of input and result that's reciprocated. This," motioning to the space between Jackie and himself, "is an uneven equation."

"Huh?"

"While I am interested on a professional and creative level as to how my programming code could have been corrupted without my input, I am unsure as to how you fit in here. Why do you care about this redacted name? What branch are you with?"

So Jackie tells him everything that's happened so far in what she thinks of as "the plot" but is actually her life. When she mentions the rifleman on campus, he says *Here?* like he can't believe it. She leaves out how the screenplay came into her possession: the blind man. Talking about that feels less like reality and more like some spectral bit from an old thriller like

Three Days of the Condor or *Blow Out*. Or *Cutting Room*. The memory of the blind man handing off the package replays in her head more like a film scene than an actual memory.

"And your concern is that you either have an authentic document or a forgery."

"Correct."

"And if it's proven to be forged, your next concern is that someone has involved you in a game you don't want to play."

"Something like that. I just don't know what any of this has to do with me. Why I'm here, in your office, and all that."

"There might be a way to obtain the name. Duplicate the system, roll it back to the first instance of submission, prior to corruption."

"That's not my language."

"What I am implying is that there may be a possibility of obtaining that name. It will take time. A day or so. Here." He scribbles on a scrap of paper, hands it to her. Jackie takes it, Spapling's number almost illegible. "Call me in a day or two. If it works, I'll have something. Programming is unpredictable. There's a set of guidelines that control the system, but those guidelines can sometimes encounter a bug or glitch or be influenced by an outside flux, which can cause a corruption or a rerouting in the system. Which is what appears to have happened here."

"A day or two."

Spapling nods and dismisses her with a, "Drive safe."

A part of her wants to repeat *I hate when people say drive safe* but is instead struck by the repetition of the phrase *Drive safe*. After hearing H.I. say it, she may or may not have been followed. Jackie wonders if Spapling's *Drive safe* is a warning—that she'll be followed again, maybe by the same truck with the winking headlight.

She leaves Spapling to his frozen room in the floor and wanders through hallways, following signs that point the way to an exit but never quite getting there. Pictures of various figures from counter- and anti-cultural history line the walls: Timothy Leary, Philip K. Dick (a third eye crudely drawn on his forehead by some passing student), and L. Ron Hubbard casting fishing lines from a boat at sea; Dick Gregory, Alan Watts, and Hunter S. Thompson talking in a way that implies they're near fisticuffs; Terrance McKenna and Angela Davis leaving William S. Burroughs out of a humorous conversation; Noam Chomsky standing at a bus stop by himself; David Lynch and a young Spapling sitting with the Maharishi Mahesh Yogi, the three laughing as if there's a joke that only they know, a dog-eared book next to Spapling's full-lotused legs.

The further she gets from Spapling's office, the more she feels as if the building won't let her leave. And it occurs to her that, for a university that's very much populated on the exterior, the inside of the L. Ron Hubbard International Humanities Building is totally empty. Her footsteps, the building's only sound, reverberate back from the far end of the hallway, tricking her into an illusion that she's being chased by some unseen force. Just as she starts to feel that near-panicked state people get in when they think they've become a trapped animal, Jackie sees the door that leads outside. But even then, walking out the door, leaving the domed building behind, she can't escape that feeling of being an animal that's found herself in a snare, unable to break free or bite her way out.

Lucidity keeps itself at a distance as Jackie drives back to Cinéma Vérité. She's absolutely convinced that something she can't see has involved her for a reason she's doesn't yet know. There's an even more inescapable feeling that she isn't just living this, that she has somehow become a character in Simeon Wolpe's screenplay. Even though there are differences between the screenplay and real life. But the feeling of being a character makes her feel gross and cheap. Used. She throttles hard on the bike, the screenplay slamming against her back with every bump. She feels as if she's committing the same ask-around-and-peel-off-the-layers approach as some silver screen P.I., like a Bogart or, better yet, a more clueless one like Elliot Gould's Marlowe. But her layers all seem to come from different onions, all in the same basket but disconnected. And trying to put these pieces together is like trying to glue a coffee mug together and then drink out of it without it leaking.

You feel bad for involving someone who so clearly doesn't want to be pushed toward the ending you know is coming—if she follows it all the way through.

As LA comes back into her view, a hazed-out sandcastle on the verge of collapse sandwiched between the desert and the ocean, Jackie passes a variable-message sign. It flashes, in its yellow-lettered luminance, the all-caps phrase: PLAN AHEAD WHILE YOU CAN. And just like with H.I.'s *Watch out for yourself*, Jackie asks: *Plan for what?*

<u>DELETED SCENE</u>
The Weight of the Gun

4

THE PEOPLE IN BLACK SUITS ATTACH CLIPS *to Austin's nipples, the other end of those clips attached to a car battery covered in the corroded fuzz of battery acid. They want to know more about his dad, about the golf tournament, about his business now. The only new detail Austin can give them is about a dream he had that he isn't sure is a dream or actually one of those re-edited memories that's a mashup of different moments and has planted itself deep in the back warehouse of the mind and filed under* Please Fucking Forget Me. *In the dream Austin's outside his dad's new warehouse—even though he's never been there and doesn't know what it looks like. It's the kind of night in a dream that implies the possibility of nothing beyond what is seen, that the darkness is emptiness. A side door opens to the warehouse and his dad's silhouetted by the interior light, which is gauzy and dead. A cut and Austin's drifting through the warehouse, following his dad's shifting figure. Neither walk. More like pulsing through matter the consistency of hair gel. Shelves as tall as the cartoonishly-high ceiling, each filled sparingly with misshapen toilets. His dad turns down an aisle, Austin follows, and stops. Three figures in front of him, gray shapes without features. A TV between them plays static. As Austin's dad approaches them, each moves away from the TV and from a woman tied to a chair next to the TV. The woman's tattered, familiar in that Austin's seen someone like her on every* *street corner in LA. Homeless. One of the figures hands Austin's dad a gas can. Gas spills all over the homeless woman like syrup. Austin's dad strikes a match. Cut again and the homeless woman's on fire, her screaming voice like a church choir reaching a single-note crescendo. While the fire rages, Austin's dad and the figures loom close to Austin. He tries to turn, to move, but that dream stickiness has him. Austin's dad creeps through the dark, eases his face within an inch of Austin's, eyes so wide it looks like his eyelids have been sliced off. He breathes. Austin can't. His dad smiles and whispers* Someday, this will all be yours.

The people in black suits listen as if he's telling them something they can use later.

AUSTIN WAKES UP to a series of texts on his phone. He comes out of the sleep slow, like he's been pulled from a deep crevice where nothing lives, only a great black hole his subconscious believed it would never escape. He looks at the time: 1:34pm. Can't remember falling asleep, but must've spent close to twelve hours in a dreamless void. He could blame the deep sleep on being back in the same room and same bed from his childhood, but instead pins it on the long drive and exhaustive nature of reconnecting with the people he's intentionally disconnected from. Like Jean. Who texts him again.

He peels his face off the journal pages, still open from the night before. He studied them as much as his mind would allow. Passages stuck out as connectable but he fell asleep before connecting them. Austin reads through the text messages from Jean, all of them begging Austin to come to his house today. Though Austin doesn't need begging. He's decided to show Jean the journal, tell him about what Wade's dad said. The latest text ends with an address that strikes Austin's cold stone insides like a hot pickaxe:

4305 N. Sunflower Ave., Covina, CA 91724

Jean is the only person other than Wade that left San Dimas—though not by much. Austin could piss from San Dimas and hit Covina, but still: it's a different zip code. The house is a one-story, gated mansion that's totally confusing in its architectural structure. It juts and jags and forms a shape unrecognizable by conventions of homebuilding.

Jean's still wearing the same suit from the funeral. Or a suit that looks similar. And it's then that Austin realizes that this is how Jean dresses now—exactly like he said he never would. Back when he and Austin and Wade were still close, Jean was by far the crustiest of the three: stone-washed denim vest with a Dead Kennedys back patch, hair styled by its own grease, jeans caked to skinny legs, a perpetual odor of b.o. and dick funk following him like Pigpen's cloud. Now, his suit's pressed and spotless, his hair slicked back, his smell like the inside of a lumber mill that specializes in cedar. He's even wearing one of those dress shirts where the shirt's blue and the collar's white.

He shows Austin around his new house. It's full of people, friends, the party Austin forgot about. The people gather around TVs—Jean's got one in every room. A lot of the same faces from the funeral. All of Jean's TVs are setup to a simulcast streaming service. Users around the world broadcasting "shows" out of their living rooms. Talk shows, live vinyl-record jam sessions, a love-line type call-in show where every other call is a prank, someone farting into the phone's mic. But right now, the stream's broadcasting this square-headed guy kneeling in front of the camera, on the floor, cleaning a big rifle. Assembling the parts, greasing things, loading the clip, racking bullets in and out of the chamber. A sloppy grin on his face. Like he's drunk off knowing he's finally going to kill someone. The guy's kneeling in a way that makes his boner clearly visible. There's a little spot of cum seeping through his underwear and pants. But when Austin hears what the guy's mumbling to himself—singing really—Austin stops following Jean.

The guy's going: *sunflower sunflower gonna be here soon… sunflower sunflower gonna be our doom.* Melody repeating like a playground chant. He looks into the camera with an unsettling moment of clarity, a mental patient waking up between doses of paper cups pills. There's a jar filled with what looks like little slugs in murky liquid and the guy opens the jar, sticks his hand in. He pulls out one of the things, shows it to the camera. A severed scorpion's tail. The guy takes the stinger and sticks it into his neck. He moans. Everyone in the house gives a collective *Ewwww.* Through gritted teeth, the guy sings again.

Sunflower sunflower gonna be here soon…sunflower sunflower gonna be our doom.

Each time he sings his song, people throughout the house join in, singing and drinking and passing joints. Laughing at the guy's entertaining insanity.

Austin thinks of the postcard. *Sunflower Mars.* He and Jean are the only ones not laughing.

The guy leans forward, face filling the screen. Austin can see that this guy's got two ears on one side of his head. None on the other side. He puts his eye up close to his camera. Holds his eyelid open with one hand, and pinches his eyeball with the other. Dirty fingernails catch on something and pull. A needle slides out of this guy's iris, slowly pulling the tender liquid flesh with it. The needle shines iridescently. When the last of the needle slides out, the stain on his pants grows and he scrunches his face, releases a hard breath.

Everyone in the house lets out a simultaneous and well-entertained *Oh shit* and then they laugh away what they've just seen.

But Jean's not really watching. It's like he's bored with it— or he's seen it before.

Austin says, "I have something to show you. You're the only one I can trust." Jean's also the only one who seems *present*, even though he's stoned. But when isn't he? For him to not have a joint would make Austin suspicious. Austin adds, "You got some place we can talk and not be heard?"

Jean goes, "You think it's not safe here? In my house?" He looks around like his house is suddenly filled with bugs and wasp drones and wiretaps and that everyone stoned and laughing at the TV is faking it. Spies who are all there for him. For both of them.

Austin thinks *This is weird.* He says, "It's about Wade."

This heightens Jean's paranoia. He tucks the joint between his lips, says "This way," and leads Austin down a hall lined with rooms. Fifteen or twenty doorways, behind them: TVs and entertainment systems, people using SensiSystems, everyone watching the guy load his guns into an Army-grade duffle bag. Psychedelic posters not limited to walls, blacklights making them glow like a violent dream. Tapestries on ceilings. Beads in doorways. A 60s bohemian grove, bodies all over each other, fucked up on entertainment. They look at Jean like he's their leader. But Austin's not sure any of them know who the hell he is. Jean made some money from instructional videos he produced years ago. How to play drums. And Austin's dad was the one who gave him the initial $25k to start the series. The videos ended up being these avant-garde short films produced to look like cult initiation videos. Subliminal messages and all that. *Worship the God of Drum.* Austin wonders if the people lounging around his house are the remaining followers of his drum program.

It occurs to Austin that a house like this, in this area, couldn't cost less than three or four million. How Jean has this kind of money, Austin doesn't know. He certainly didn't get it from the drum videos. So then where?

Jeans says, "Numbers game. Got my CPA a few years back. I'm working for your dad now. I'm sure he mentioned that."

After passing through a coded entry door in a far corner of the house, Jean hiding that code from Austin, Jean leads Austin into the room they're now in: a library of sorts. Tall shelves. Probably a hundred. But only one shelf has books. The rest are empty. Like an abandoned cathedral. In the middle of the room there are two of those buttoned-leather smoking chairs that have a cinematic fanciness people are always trying to replicate. Jean sits in one, motions for Austin to sit in the other.

Austin says, "He didn't tell me that. What the hell do you do for him?"

"Keep track of his money. Show him investment opportunities. I helped him open a shop at that new mall in Burbank."

"So then you know he owns a movie theater on Sunset?"

"I do. Helped him rearrange funds, find ways to invest. He did it for you."

"Thought he wanted me to take over the toilet business."

"Isn't a movie theater better than a bunch of toilets?"

"Who wanted you to get a CPA?"

"Your dad talked to me about it once. After my dad died. And I had all that money come in from his death and the house burning down and all that. So I used it and went to college."

"This all seems way too convenient."

"Yes, Austin. My dad dying in a fire that burned down the house I lived in as a child is very convenient."

"That's not what I meant."

"Look: your dad bought that theater for you, man. He thinks you could do important stuff with it."

"Like what? It's a movie theater. It can really only do one thing."

Jean shrugs.

"Man, when will everyone just leave me alone?"

"So you can go die by yourself like a wounded dog."

"Exactly."

"Don't be such a fucking stereotype, man."

"I can't help it. I was made this way."

Jean pulls a joint from the inside of his suit jacket, lights it. Takes a hit. Then, "What's this about Wade?"

Austin shows him the journal and the postcard. When Jean looks at the pinprick-small writing, he holds the book far away from him, squints, shakes his head.

"Shit, man. I can't read that. The fuck was he on at the end?"

"Same shit he was on when we knew him." Austin flips to a page and reads, "*When I was a kid I was terrified of the eye of sauron in lord of the rings and mom said it wasn't real but it is real and I know this now and they control the eye and its on a tower on a mountain and the void beyond the light and the nameless faces tell me there is a purpose in this life Austin I don't want you to go there Austin find me I am* and that's where it stops. That's the end of the journal."

Jean takes a rip, and in that stiff way people talk when they're holding in smoke, "Far out, man."

Austin can see Jean isn't into it. He'd given up on Wade long before Austin did. The moment he heard Wade was into the harder drugs, Jean cut him out of his life. Called him a loser. Abandoned him clean and easy. Cold turkey. Austin hands him the postcard. Says, "Look at this then. At the back."

Jean takes the postcard, looks at the picture of the castle on top of the Hollywood Sign. Flips it over, reads, then says, "Sunflower Mars." It takes a second for his baked circuitry to fire, but when it does, he sings, "Sunflower sunflower gonna be here soon. Man...that's weird."

"I talked to Tucker yesterday. After you ran off."

"Who?"

"Wade's dad."

"I didn't run off. I just remembered that I...uh...had to be somewhere."

"He said he saw Wade yesterday. Or well the day before yesterday."

"His dad's also dying and so full of drugs he doesn't know what the fuck's going on."

"But what if he really did see Wade?"

"Like a ghost?"

"Or maybe Wade's still alive." This falls out of Austin's mouth before he has a chance to think it through. His mind hasn't wrapped around the idea fully, yet here it is.

"Don't be an idiot. I'm the high one here."

Austin stands, walks over to the only shelf with books on

it, runs his finger down the spines: *You've Got This: Getting Everything Out of Life*, *Seven Meanings To Find A Meaningful Meaning*, *Accounting for Proletariats*, *In The Realm of Lost Things*, *Dianetics*, *Good At Drugs*. But what has Austin's attention is the novelization of *Cutting Room*. He picks it up.

"I saw this again last night. At my dad's theater."

"*Your* theater."

"I don't want a theater."

"Why not?"

"I'd have to move back here."

"Wouldn't be the worst thing."

"It would." He shows the book to Jean. "When's the last time you saw this?"

Jean shrugs.

Austin lets the book fall open in his hand. Somewhere around page forty nine, a card for a company called SunCor bookmarks the place Jean left off and never picked up again. Austin thinks, *SunCor...Sunflower.* A connection? Maybe. But Austin's not going to be that guy who looks for phantom threads between disparate ideas, the guy who notices the sun's reflection off the space station in *2001* and compares it to the happy cartoon sun on jars of Dr. Nut sunbutter. But if things are obvious, he'll put them together. Maybe. He holds up the card for Jean to see. Jean squints at it, already firmly situated in a high obscuring the filter between reality and mind-altered perception.

Austin says, "What this?"

"Oh, man. Yeah, that's this fitness supplement company I've got some money in. Your dad let me put a billboard on top of the theater."

Austin doesn't remember seeing a billboard. He says,

"Since when do you care about fitness shit?"

"I don't. But you don't have to care about investments to make money in them. You follow the money. That's the secret to all this: follow the money."

Austin looks at the card again. A logo, a company name. An address maybe forty minutes away. And a name: Steve Muhammed Muhammed.

"Hey, Austin." Jean waits for Austin to look at him. He finishes with, "Follow the money."

AUSTIN'S NOT A PERSON who believes in God or fate, and certainly doesn't believe in karmic thermals and conduits of interrelated meanings and all that hippie shit. But after the conversation with Jean, Austin feels like maybe there's the possibility of a greater thing at work and that, as a result, he's just a part in that machine, a bit of systemic information rather than himself. Externalizing this responsibility gives a lot of people comfort, gives them a sense that life is not random and that they will be rewarded for adjusting to the program. For Austin, this lack of sole-driven existence, though *exactly* what he's wanted his whole life, makes him feel helpless.

Austin sits outside of Jean's house and calls the number on the SunCor card. It rings, then clicks and the ear-punishing garble of a dial-up modem connecting to the internet stabs its way down Austin's ear canal. Before he can pull the phone away, the noise cuts and a woman's hyper-sexual voice says, "SunCor, reshaping the future. How can I direct you?"

Austin swaps the phone to his other ear. Says, "I'm looking to talk with Mr. Muhammed Muhammed."

"I'm sorry, SMM isn't taking on new clients."

"You see: Jean Grauphman's a friend of mine. Gave me SMM's number. Told me to call about an investment opportunity."

Her voice picks up, tones reaching a pleasant register. "Yes, of course. Jean. Let's see," the sounds of clicking and typing, "SMM could see you today, in an hour if you'd like."

"I can make it there by then."

"And your name?"

"Uh...Wade...Dyettesoduh..."

"We'll see you then, Mr. Dyettesoduh. Don't be late." And then hangs up.

Austin follows the GPS on his phone into LA and to a vaguely L-shaped futuristic building on Franklin just off the 101. Across from the Hollywood Towers. An impressive building, and not just for a start-up. It isn't until he's in the shadow of the building that he realizes it's not an L-shape—it's in the shape of a bicep. He enters at the elbow. Austin's expecting stained carpets and cubicles and all that. But inside's all marble, steel, glass. Sleek at no expense. A fountain in the entryway, water erupting around a bronze statue of a woman built like a legend. She's holding up the world like Atlas. A plaque below says *Delta Holds The World—For Bub*.

The receptionist waits at the other end of this huge entryway. Austin gives her the name: Wade Dyettesoduh. She picks up a phone, listens, then says to Austin: *Sixth floor. Take the elevator.* Austin moves in a purposeful way that people who just do stuff do. He's trying to ignore all the cameras, little electric motors whirring as they turn to follow his path. Up on the sixth floor, taking a moment to look down over the balcony, Austin notices that the fountain in the lobby is in the shape of a sunflower. The statue stands in the middle.

There's only one office on the sixth floor, double doors, a name plate probably made of solid gold that reads *Steve Muhammed Muhammed - The One @ The Top** and then, down near the handle another gold plate that reads **But not the Very Top*—even though the building only has six floors. The door clicks and opens with a pressurized *psssst*, reminding Austin of Wade's dad.

A man sits behind a desk that looks more like a marble mausoleum. With his back to the door, he faces a wall of floor-to-ceiling windows cinematically framing a view of Downtown LA in perfect 2.39:1 aspect ratio. He says, "Have a seat Mr. Dyettesoduh."

Ornate rugs cushion Austin's footsteps across the polished obsidian floor. Tiny fountains erupt water around the desk. Taking up most of the right wall is a massive painting of Wile E. Coyote, head smashed by an anvil, Roadrunner standing on the cliff above smiling at the coyote. The other wall has a painting of equal size: this one of Bugs Bunny, head coming out of his rabbit hole, munching on a carrot, plugging Elmer Fudd's shotgun with his white-gloved finger. There's just too much going on in this room, in this building, for it to have anything to do with dietary supplements. There's more here. The money has to prove it, right?

Steve Muhammed Muhammed spins the chair around as Austin reaches the desk. A practiced movement, like he's imitating a villain from a Bond movie. He looks Middle Eastern. Syrian, Iranian, Iraqi…something like this. But he's had plastic surgery, bleached his skin to look a little more white. Austin thinks, *Ease the xenophobia or something like that.*

He says, "So you're friends with Jean?"

"For about ten years." Even though it's been more like

twenty five. Austin gives Muhammed Muhammed a partially truthful history, but leaves out the details no one really needs to know but Austin and Jean. Yes, sexual stuff. Same kind of history no one needs to know Austin shares with Wade. Austin finishes with, "So when Jean told me he's investing here, I was interested in joining."

"That's absolutely wonderful. We're always looking for support. Our business model requires a large up-front campaign, but in the long run it'll create a more sustainable and permanent imprint."

"That sounds interesting."

"How much are you willing to invest?"

"To be honest: I'd like to know more about SunCor's internal operations."

Muhammed Muhammed's face goes slack. The smile he's had plastered on since he turned to face Austin stays, but the rest of his face isn't smiling. The look is something people see right before they die at the hands of a really charming serial killer. He says, "What do you wish to know?"

"What...uh...do you do here?"

"We manufacture supplements that enhance human ability. Specifically in performance, but not limited to that. We've spent the last few years perfecting formulas passed onto us by a gracious donation, decades of hard scientific work. We plan to distribute these products worldwide within the year. We're also working on coffee-products since coffee stimulates both weight loss and muscle gain, as well as mental clarity formulas for college students, and an algae-based compound for oceanic purification and soil restoration. We're rebuilding the planet."

"Enhancing human abilities like how? Steroids?"

"Nothing like that. Humans only use a certain percent of mind and body. We've created ways to expand that percentage. We recently signed Delta Robison. Don't know if you've heard of her but she's the strongest woman alive. Can lift a fucking car over her head. We started giving her a highly concentrated dose of our X-Trim formula, and, I shit you not, she can now lift *two* cars over her head."

"Why would someone need to lift two cars over their head?"

"The point of SunCor is to grow strong humans for the future. We want to give everyone the opportunity to lose weight and be strong, mentally and physically, to be the powerful humans they deserve to be. We cannot blame the sad state of human beings on their daily diet of empty sensory input. They have been shaped poorly and we hope to correct the misshaped. We strive to induce sickness in those who still worship capitalism. Thoughts of covetous financial envy will cause one to shit themselves. The next evolution of life on Earth. Perfect beings. All of us that dedicate, that is. A belief in culture over media."

Muhammed Muhammed starts talking about how Jean is one of their best investors. How he understands the risks of investing in something uncertain but destined to cause a global shift. Committed to their *revolutionary nature*. As he says all this, he slides a business card across the table, face down. There's writing on the backside, but Austin never saw him write anything. Without breaking the conversation, he motions for Austin to look at it. *Don't make it obvious.* Austin takes it, slides it into his lap while Muhammed Muhammed talks about the revolution and how their products are going to destroy all others on the market and the ratio of fat to muscle in the average human body. Austin can't hear anything else. His mind narrows on the card, the writing on the back. It says:

Leave now—meet me @ the Hollywood Sign—Don't talk, they're listening—I love you, always have. BL

BL… Bowie Lee?

When he looks up at this guy who looks *nothing* like Bowie Lee, Austin sees that Muhammed Muhammed's eyes have changed…or they might have. They look, somehow, like the eyes of someone who's supposed to be dead, missing. Austin tries to not see them as the eyes of his brother, but he can't.

<u>DELETED SCENE</u>
This Could All Be Yours

5

JACKIE CALLS H.I. FROM THE THEATER'S phone, a rotary-style that's probably as old as the theater itself.

She'd spent the day and night back at Cinéma Vérité, absently projecting blockbusters, unfocusing the picture and playing goddess to sabotage movies she'd rather watch burn. When the projectors beeped, she changed reels, not caring if the image or audio synced. Her mind was on the screenplay, the copied pages. She noticed a pattern: single bolded letters tucked into unbolded words. Bold doesn't carry well in courier font, so overlooking them was probably inevitable. But after noticing one, she noticed them all. It reminded her of the Don Thom David book—H.I.'s style twin. She tried to to cross-reference the screenplay with the book, see if there were any similarities, but when she went for the book, it was gone. Not in the stack of books she'd put it in the day before. But she didn't really need to see it. She knew the bold letters were there. She went through the screenplay, writing all the bolded letters—and some numbers—in her notebook. That kept her busy until the last moviegoer shuffled out the door and there was nothing left to distract her.

She inspected the letters and numbers, seeing if any words faded up from the chaos. Smoking a cigarette in bed, fully dressed, Jackie allowed the fatigue of the day to take over her, the room stretching and disappearing behind a dissolve from color to black & white to just black. And since she hadn't had a dream in decades, Jackie awoke still clothed, shuffled down to the rotary phone before the theater opened, and called the only person who can help her make some sense of it. Which is where she is now.

The phone clicks, connection made. She doesn't wait for H.I. to speak first.

Jackie says, "I need to show you something."

H.I. says, "Meet me at Tournesol Studios."

"What the hell is that?" The first she's ever heard of it.

"Small place. New." He gives her an address that's at the center of Studio City. She's either seen it a thousand times and ignored it, or she's never seen it before because it doesn't want to be seen.

"I'll be there in an hour."

"Head's up: something's got everyone on edge. You'll need a password." He gives it to her and hangs up. *Abraxas.*

Again, she puts the Nietzsche guy in charge of projection during her absence. He glows when she invites him up and gives him the schedule.

"Does this mean I can call myself a projectionist's assistant?"

"Absolutely fucking not. You're here to press buttons. That's it." Even though this is the second day she's put him in charge, she's not even close to being concerned about him replacing her. Most people would do everything they can to keep someone from doing their job, but no one can do what Jackie does as good as Jackie does it. Especially not this guy. It's not in his DNA. He's got the generational catchphrase engrained too deep in his soul: *not my problem.*

The smile on his face drops, confidence knocked down a peg. But he recovers quickly, takes out his phone and tries to snap a picture of himself, the SF-2, and Jackie all in the same frame. Jackie slaps the shit out of his phone, which flies across the room and lands underneath the old orange-plaid armchair. Jackie tosses the rucksack with the copied screenplay pages in it over her shoulder.

"I will be back before final showing. Try not to fuck up more than I know you will."

"I think you broke my phone."

"Ask your parents to buy you another one for Christmas."

"I'm Jewish."

"Well then: lehitra'ot, Nietzsche."

"Gesundheit."

Jackie wishes he had another phone so she could slap it out of his hand again. But instead she leaves, holding back a smile that's blessed with a pinch of humor.

Tournesol Studios is on the lower rungs of the industry ladder, independent but still owned by one of the Top Six: Universal, Disney-Fox-Sony, Warner-Paramount, Amazon-Netflix-MGM, and Hengdian—even though most operate under True Foe Empirical Broadcasting Systems. This monopolistic conglomeration silenced inter-studio feuds, which paved the way for cross-studio partnerships: more franchises, brands, tentpoles, money, and overall domination of the entertainment industry. The *Nouveau-Renaissance of Hollywood.* Even though 98.6% of films go straight to streaming now—her theater being one of three left standing in the Commonwealth. Jackie knows, though, that all it takes is a year of bad luck, bad press, and bad movies for the Renaissance to end and for economic collapse to send shockwaves across the world, bankrupt the system, and drop everything into a very dark age. Into the toilet. She thinks this could be that year. A part of her hopes it is. Most of her, though, hopes it isn't.

She should have looked up what the word *tournesol* means, but seeing two great big brass sunflowers at either end of the arcing entrance translates it for her. She's stopped at the gate by a guard who seems on loan from the highest ranks of the military, colors and stripes pinned to his chest signifying heightened rank in the security guard cosmos.

"Papers," he says in his most Americanized-Gestapo voice. "No, sorry. I had an audition yesterday for a German soldier. Hard to shake it. What's the passphrase?"

"Abraxas," reciting the word H.I. gave over the phone. Paranoia nibbles at her ear, telling her that what's got everyone on edge might have something to do with this Sunflower business. The military-stiff security guard puts his hand on his gun and waves her on.

The grounds of Tournesol lack the frantic activity of performers rushing from trailer to studio, gaffers and grips sprinting with various bits of equipment, costumers and makeup artists testing monstrous creations next to tables filled with various snackage and drinkage, golf carts carrying those too important to walk. All the Real now substituted for in-studio greenscreenery and post-production CGI.

A red light above the entrance to Studio 3a is unlit. Open door surrounded by a group of agents and producers and casting directors and sycophants. The agent, a slick young dude sucking on a vape pen that glows pink, is at the center of attention.

He starts up with this: "This wife goes up to her husband, all whining, and says 'Honey do these pants make me look fat.'

And she's a real porker. Everything makes her look fat. So the husband goes, 'Do you promise not to get mad at me no matter what I say?' And the wife rolls her eyes and says 'Yes, I promise not to get mad.' But she's on the verge of tears cuz it's like she knows her husband's about to tell her how fat she really is. And then…"

Everyone waits, drool slipping from lips, hands fidgeting.

He finishes with: "The husband goes 'I fucked the cat.'"

The men explode. It's the funniest goddamn thing they've ever heard.

An unsmiling Jackie, cutting through the group, gives them this one: "A producer and an agent are walking down the street, see a seven year old girl. Producer says, 'Let's go fuck that kid.' And the agent says, 'Out of what?'"

One of the sycophants laughs, but when he sees no one's joining him, his laughter sputters to a halt. His smile looks painful, like he's afraid to let it go. One of the men says to Jackie, "That's really intolerant of our identity in this industry. We have just as much right to—"

"I don't give a fuck, clowndog. You're in my way." She pushes past them and enters Studio 3a.

The inside of Studio 3a is just as quiet as the studio grounds. Crew members sitting around, waiting, drinking coffee, vaping. It's as if this is all some kind of hoax. That there's no movie being made here. All this set up just for her to interact with.

H.I. sits in front of a graveyard backdrop near craft service, foam cup of coffee at his feet. He's reading the Don Thom David book.

Jackie says, "Why are you reading that?"

"Because there's nothing to do right now."

"No, Hi. This isn't just something you're doing. Why are you reading that? Why now?"

He gives her this look, narrow-eyed, as if he's trying to see how much she knows. He says, "There are things in here worth knowing."

"Like a message."

"Maybe. What do you know?"

"You're talking about the bolded letters."

"Have you been lying to me, Jackie? What is this?"

"What is what?"

"You come to me talking about the bolded letters. It leads me to believe that you've been hiding your truth from me, that you're really someone else, a person under the cover of a lie."

"This sounds like the kind of paranoia you told me to avoid."

"You should know the difference between paranoia and appropriate distrust." There's a sense of rigidity and anger swarming around his presence that Jackie's never seen.

"How's this for appropriate distrust?" She hands him her notebook with the sequence of bolded letters and numbers. "The screenplay's got them too."

She looks around as H.I. reads. A couple stands at the mouth of a beige-colored hall that looks like it leads to some offices or backrooms. Jackie thinks she recognizes them, can't be sure if they are the same two people she saw at the Velveteen Saddle or not.

"Did you find out if it's really a Wolpe script?"

"Not yet. There was a corruption in that style thing's data."

"So you don't even know if this is a Wolpe screenplay. So you're just doing all this for...?"

"What's the code in the book say?"

"It's a message, deep-state communique from agency to agency. This one's about a counter-operation."

"To what?"

"You figure out what your letters unscramble to?"

"Not yet. I'm guessing, given the subject of the screenplay, it's not going to be fun."

He does some word math, calculating the letter, using his finger as a guide. "*The sun observes from on high at the Big H.*"

"That was fast."

"I've had practice. See here, there's also *Highness without high be thin* and *hush, hot shit be weighing thin.*"

"Barring the chance that Wolpe—if this is Wolpe—is creating some secret message about hot shit, those don't even make sense. *Observing on high at the Big H* sounds like a place, something active." She doesn't tell him it's also the only permutation containing the word *sun.*

"And what about these numbers? Random?"

"I figure someone who rearranged those letters to make *hush, hot shit be weighing thin* or whatever would immediately see the significance of—"

"It's a date... Today."

"See...there's something to this, Hi. I don't think I'm being paranoid or going crazy."

"If the code's there, it's something. I just...can't believe I didn't see it when you showed me the pages at the Saddle."

Without his external-distraction-cancelling headgear, Jackie watches as H.I.'s attention finally has a moment to flutter around in a bird-loosed-from-a-small-cage way. "They're filming this avant-garde thing in here. Romantic science fiction genre bender that I don't think anyone will ever see. It'll die in the cutting room. Oh...sorry. But anyway: they've got these newcomers performing, so it's got no chance…especially with *Over/Shift* coming out next year. And the dialogue for it is this pseudo-Shakespearian stuff, riddles and all that. I don't—"

Jackie snaps in his face, pulls his attention back to her. "Hi, what, in your opinion, could this mean? I'm not looking to you for answers, but I'm turning to you as a friend. You're the only one I can go to with this."

"The Hollywood Sign," he says, his mind unfocused again.

"Huh?"

"The Big H, you know? Up on high and all that. It's the Hollywood Sign."

"What if you're wrong?"

"It can only be attributed to human error," quoting, whether meaning to be ironic or not, that AI H.A.L. from *2001: A Space Odyssey*.

"I don't like the combination of that impression and this situation."

Out of the corner of her eye, Jackie catches the movement of someone walking past their conversation a little too closely.

H.I. says, "Hey, is that Sean Penn? What's he doing in a movie like this? He might be a producer but— No, no that's not him. Who is that? He was in that one about the priests in space…Jackie, I have to admit something: I've been seeing Philip Seymour Hoffman around a lot lately. And he's been dead for like, what, almost twenty years now? More? I can't remember. But people still talk about that pen-in-the-mouth bit in Boogie Nights, even though I don't—"

Jackie snaps again in H.I.'s face. "Hi, let's stick to what's important here."

"Sorry, Jackie. You know how I am without my," making an earmuff gesture. "You want coffee? The coffee here's so weak it can't defend itself, but it tastes pretty—"

"I don't want any goddamn coffee."

"This conversation's gotta end soon. Thing's are about to pick up around here."

She looks around and the place is still dead. She looks over at the entrance to the beige hallway and predictably the couple is gone. And then she notices the set.

The bed's different and the posters on the wall aren't the same, but it's her room. Jackie's. The same floor, overturned milk crate bedside table, porthole window. All of it. The lighting's dark, ominous even, like it's about to be the setting of an attack or murder or something equally as bad. She wants to float toward this fake room but she's afraid that if she gets near enough, she'll be smash-cut back into her room and that equally bad thing'll happen and she won't have time to see it coming. Or stop it.

"Is that my room?"

"How would I know? I've never been there." Almost too much guilt in his voice.

She notices the Don Thom David book isn't where it's supposed to be—on the floor by the bed—and wonders if H.I. took it from the set to read. Or maybe he took the copy from her actual room. She also notices something on the floor, near the closet. Small, fleshy. A slug or finger or something. There's a hatchet on her bed. She looks at the closet and wonders if the contents are the same. Feels a pinch of shame, if they are.

"Goddammit, Jackie. You're making me do this."

"Do what?" She says to H.I., still looking at the set. It takes a lot for her to look away, but the sound of H.I. doing something she's apparently made him do forces her to look away.

H.I. reaches into the backpack by his feet. Jackie's eyes casually invade the contents of his bag: notebooks and loose pages, books bloated with dog-eared pages and the abuse of multiple reads, and a laptop that he pulls out and rests in his lap. It barely fits, seems like it weighs near fifty pounds. Looks less like a computer and more like exposed wires and junky patchwork tech from *Videodrome* or *Battlefield Earth*. He opens the laptop. Jackie notices the mini-film-poster stickers on its outer shell again. *Cutting Room* and *A Clockwork Orange* and *2001*. Beethoven, *Cutting Room*, and L. Ron. Everything keeps coming around and back, like the person you say goodbye to at a party then see three or four more times. And for the first time in a long while, she wonders, *If there's a pattern in all this, then maybe the hacker typing the lines of code that dictates these moments is God...or a god...or goddess. The Great Auteur In The Sky.*

You wish you could tell her that you're far from a god and to not be so hopeful of your power to dictate anything.

"Here...There might be something I can do. Test your Big H theory of it being the Hollywood Sign."

"That's what *you* said the code means. Not that I have any idea of what else it could be."

"I can remote access satellite imaging systems and pull up live feed of the Hollywood letters. See if there's anyone standing there, or if there's anything significant, a message or sign or something. And don't ask me how I'm able to do this. It'll only make you more paranoid."

The way he's laser-focused, Jackie's seeing H.I. for the first time as someone who has continually existed in a calculated state of impersonation. Clever about pop culture and entertainment, but clearly intelligent beyond just that. A level of interface knowledge and the ability to hack into a system only those with well-earned clearance can. Is he some kind of super hacker? Or is he one of those with well-earned clearance and not the pop-culture archivist he costumes himself as? Like a protector of the integrity of Entertainment, keeping at bay all the possibilities of corruption, making sure the system doesn't fall. The smile he throws her way tries to clear her head of what he knows is running around inside.

"Damn…the satellite isn't in position. But maybe I can… Wait, hang on…" typing at a frantic pace. Jackie tries to look around at the screen, but H.I. turns the screen away until, "There," and then he turns it to her.

An elevated view of a hillside gone wild with desert brush and rocks and dirt. The view lifts, floats fluidly, and then the letters come into view: HOLLYWOOD. The view floats closer. A high crane shot or helicopter shot or…

"What am I looking at?"

"Since the satellite wasn't available, I've…*commandeered* an ad-drone near the sign. What we're seeing here is what the ad-eye sees."

To the right of the video feed there's a box of white text on black background, the drone feeding data to H.I.'s laptop. It looks like an onboard report, generating ads based on the surroundings.

"How are you…I feel like this is the kind of thing the government tends to notice and not really appreciate, you know? When people hijack ad-drones and all that? Unless you have permission or something."

"Again, Jackie, the less you know. I can't say this isn't a risk, but you're right. There's something going on here that— Oh, look, they've replaced the fallen L. Not HOLYWOOD anymore. Maybe those Evangelists'll stop squatting in Griffith Park."

"You're deflecting the conversation again."

"I am."

"How often do you intentionally deflect the conversation?"

"All the time."

"Who are you, really?"

"Don't ask that."

"Do you really have ADD?"

"There. Right there. Look."

H.I. points to two men at the base of the H, an aura manifesting around them from the whiteness reflecting off the massive letter. One's well-dressed, an agent or high-level producer-type with a hint of Middle East in his features, smoothed and groomed to look almost-white. The other's frumpy, clothes that make him look like a hand-me-down cross-dressing hipster, shoulder-length hair sun-lightened and matted in places, pushed down in others in hopes of looking like he cares about his appearance. He's young, but Jackie can't see his face. The well-groomed man leans forward, engulfs the younger one in a hug. He looks up at the ad-drone, notices its proximity. Even with the distance between himself and the drone's eye, his body visibly stiffens. He pushes the younger one away.

"There," H.I. says again, tapping the screen.

"There what? All I see is two guys talking."

"Near the big H. Today."

"A coincidence," and she's saying it more like a question than statement.

"Jackie...you know it's not. You don't get down there unless you're trying."

"This could all be nothing." She says it, but feels stupid for saying it. Because there *is* something. The coded message actually means something real. And seeing it all, thinking that the two men at the big H could have some relation to all this, makes her want to keep falling into the fantasy she's always denied but never escaped. Unless there is no coded message. Unless H.I.'s making it all up to get her out there. For what? Maybe he wrote the script. Everything she's learned has come from him.

"If you really think that, why not take it a little further?"

"You said it though. If I'm wrong and I keep going on this path, I'll end up as one of those people who thinks the government was behind 9/11 or the Obama assassination or that all the sexual harassment claims against Maxwell Orth was part of a plan to remove him as president of Disney or that a screenplay by a dead director really is at the center of a global conspiracy. And then I'm dead."

"I'm here, Jackie, telling you that despite what I might've said…there's something here."

"I'll go. But just know, I might need someone to pull me out if it gets too dark."

"Joaquin Phoenix, that's who that was. Not Sean Penn."

"I'll go," she says, but only to herself.

And then a dialogue-referent cut brings her from INT. STUDIO 3A to EXT. MOUNT LEE ROAD. Jackie's motorcycle grinds up the high-grade climb in low gear, passing hikers that look at her like *You're not supposed to be driving that up here* but never say it. She rolls into the summit and the expanse of Los Angeles meets her. The tops of the letters underline the sprawling chaos below, made peaceful by silence and distance. She passes a parked car being hooked up to a tow truck. A bundle of tickets flap on the windshield. A beat-up thing that's dusty and tired.

There's no one at the letters. Standing at the fence that protects individuals from navigating the neck-breakingly steep hill down to the actual letters, Jackie can't see any trace of the two men having been there. No footprints. Just gone. Maybe H.I. showed her footage, something old and staged. Just to get her here. But why?

She debates climbing down, inspecting the scene closer, but the way the dirt shifts under her first step convinces her otherwise. She's not unfit, but she's hardly as spry as she once was. So the possibilities of her slipping on a pocket of loose dirt and falling head-long into the brush a hundred feet down, breaking bones along the way and dying a slow, private death, ending up as The Hollywood Sign Faller, stops her from moving on. And she can't shake the feeling that that might've been the whole point in getting her here. She looks over her shoulder expecting to see some hulking body charging at her, targeting her with a terminal shove. But she's still alone. She says, "Hello?" Only the wind answers.

The silence ends as an ad-drone buzzes above her head, carrying an LED banner for a product: X-Trim by SunCor. It hovers, waiting for her to see it, and once she does, it moves, following a trail cut in the hillside that's parallel to the road she took to get up here. *This way* the ad-drone says with its anxious movement.

With sunset coming on quicker than it should, Jackie hops on her bike and follows H.I.'s lead.

Excerpt from
In The Realm of Lost Things
by Don Thom David

6

THE PEOPLE IN BLACK SUITS BOX AUSTIN'S *ears with half-closed fists. They pour honey on his legs and genitals and unleash a jar full of ants in his lap. They take fingernail clippers to his gums. They drip milliliters of hydrofluoric acid in his armpits. They take a cheese grater to the knuckles of his hands and feet. In between each of these forms of torture they say* Tell us what you know about Muhammed Muhammed. *They know Muhammed Muhammed knows Austin's brother and that his brother went AWOL, that he deserted his position. They've also been aware of his involvement with an anti-Empire coalition that's established itself somewhere in the California Commonwealth with a planned terrorist act sometime on the horizon. When Austin confirms that the terrorist act is real, the people in black suits get a little rough, take a straight razor to his elbows, demand to know when and where. Austin knows the where but not the when, and he knows it will happen and knows it's a part of the screenplay that the woman calling herself Jackie had on her. They want to know where the screenplay is, but Austin doesn't have it. He doesn't even have Wade's journal anymore. When Austin tells the black suits this, he's sure they'll torture him some more. But they don't. They stand back, gather around him like a cult preparing to sacrifice in the name of a god that will never hear them. They say* Tell us about Muhammed Muhammed. *So Austin does.*

ON FRANKLIN AVE., Austin finds himself stuck in a dammed river of traffic, a patchwork quilt of vehicles from different economic strata: beat-up VW sedans, gull-winged Teslas, newly-minted Sony hovcars lifted almost a foot off the ground from the electromagnetic mineral strips tossed half-assed along the freeway, a '93 Celica that's more dent than car, motorcycles, BMWs, soccer vans, and an ice cream truck that looks like the ice cream truck near Wade's house—if he could remember what that ice cream truck looked like. All these vehicles individualized with bumper stickers with slogans like: *My AR-15 Is Lubed With Liberal Cum* and *ZV-66 Was An Inside Job* and *Honk If You Don't Want to Be Here* and *Exterminate All Left Handers* and *My Other Ride Is Your Ungendered Parental Figure.* With the traffic dead stopped, hands extend out windows, passing lit joints and dab pens to their neighbors, every radio tuned to a different brand of music, all of it coming together in a blend that mixes with the gray smog and joint smoke and vape haze like a pop-up concert no one really wants to go to.

It takes him almost an hour and a half to drive the five miles from the SunCor building to the dead end behind The Hollywood Sign. And his GPS told him he was on the fastest route, all other roads more congested or closed for repairs or closed because of an accident or because of flash fires. No other way to get there. So when he sees this guy who's supposed to be his brother already at the top of Mount Lee, Austin wonders how the fuck he got there so fast. Maybe he took a helicopter or maybe he has some way of traveling the unfinished underground highway webbing between LA and Hawthorne.

Or maybe he's a ghost, existing outside of time and space and only visiting this now for a brief Earth moment to serve a purpose Austin doesn't yet know.

You can confirm that he is not a ghost—or at least something able to travel through space, time and reality like you. But he might be more than human. You don't know yet.

"You're needed, Austin. You always have been."

"Is this going to take long? I parked my car in a tow-away zone."

"You don't believe me."

"Look at you. Your face, your hair. This outfit. Give me a reason to believe you're my brother."

"I love you."

"That's creepy. That's not a reason."

"You used to have a desk and you carved the word *booger* under it."

"I can't be the only kid who did that."

"Piggy Nelson."

This guy starts going into a story only Lee, Austin, and Piggy Nelson know about. How Piggy used to beat up Austin every day at the bus stop after school. They'd get off the bus, and while all the kids watched, Piggy would either sucker punch or choke out Austin. When Austin told Lee about this, Lee, almost seven years Austin's senior, waited in hiding at the bus stop the next day. Austin got off the bus, Piggy close behind. As the bus drove away, Lee jumped from behind a nearby bush and plowed a fist into Piggy's gut hard enough to make Piggy shit himself. Lee said *Now squeal* and Piggy crawled on all fours, shit in his pants, squealing and crying. Piggy Nelson never messed with Austin after—

"Okay, shut up, Lee."

"Don't call me that. I may be, in heart and DNA, your brother. But in spirit I am no longer him. I am recycled, like the Earth soon will be. Steve Muhammed Muhammed is my Proselyte name. For the next six billion years."

Austin looks up the steep and illegal path to the letters. A security guard walks along the path, past their position and ignores the two men standing in a place they shouldn't. Austin turns back to this guy who's supposed to be his brother, who's ignoring the security guard in a very obvious way, like he doesn't want anyone to know the security guard's on his payroll. Light reflecting off the towering white H gives the air in front of Austin a hazy, washed-out feel. Los Angeles unfurls below them. Hills of untainted desert brush separates them from million-dollar neighborhoods.

He says, "You're supposed to be dead."

"That's happening to a lot of people these days."

"What's that mean?"

"Lee died. Is dead. And for a great purpose. The same purpose you are needed for, Austin. Your dad…"

"Nah, man. You owe me more than that. You say you love me or whatever, but you're living someone else's life."

"The life before was the other life. The wrong one. It wasn't until my liberation, my Initiation, that I truly felt alive, that I could exist as I was meant to."

"What do you mean *this is happening to a lot of people these days*? And what does Dad have to do with anything?"

"There will be an explanation."

"Dad buried you. Mom might as well be in that coffin too. This is worth that?"

"What we have planned is worth all the pain in the world. It's change for the better."

"Better for who? Who said the world needs changing? Who decides what's best? See, these are the things that no one really thinks of when they make these *I have a plan that'll change the world* type speeches."

"Don't tell me you think this world's the best it could be."

"Could be worse."

"Not long after Bowie Lee fled from his position in Syria, he joined a cell of radicals, expats and revolutionaries, mostly from America, but also from everywhere. A humanist revolution, cultural deconstructionists. A well-funded group. Taking orders from a ghost leader. The goal was and is to make sure that 'worse' you mention doesn't happen."

"Ghost leader."

"She's given herself a name: Miss. And she doesn't tolerate...*blockage*, Austin."

"I'm not doing anything. I just—I mean really, all I've been doing is asking about Wade and falling into places I don't really want to be."

"Exactly as it's supposed to be. Miss has been planning all this for...I don't know how long. Most of the radicals claim she started when societies first connected themselves to the Network. When the Network went live, she was able to—"

Rocks skittle down the path above. A couple walking close to the edge looks out on the vastness of the city. And then at Austin and his brother. Austin makes eye contact with them. The reinvented Lee smears a smile across his face, eyes widen like a friendly neighbor saying hello to a neighbor he never sees. No recognition passes between any of them, or maybe it's an attempt to give the appearance of not recognizing each other. When they're gone, Austin's brother gets this nervous look, leans in close to Austin, his voice now a confiding breath.

206. TEX GRESHAM

"She was able to spread her message like those little email viruses. I represent her *presence* in the day-to-day. Act as her vessel...for now at least. She needs to stay out of sight, safe from those who wish to silence her. Which is why we need you."

"Need me for what? You know I'm not an operative or anything like that, right?"

"Are you sure?"

"Fuck off, Lee."

"Muhammed Muhammed, please."

"I'm literally *never* going to call you that."

"Then call me Brother. Just don't call me Lee. Lee died eight years and six thousand miles ago."

"Okay, *Brother*. A question for you. After you decided to join the Army, you and dad would talk all the time. Private shit. You'd leave the room, be gone for a really long time. Made me feel like I didn't belong in the family. Especially because you and him *never* talked before. You used to tell me how much you hated him. And so with mom in her own world and you two living in your private club, I had no one. Except Wade and maybe Jean. It used to be you who I could turn to, and then it wasn't. Why? What did you and him talk about?"

"You."

"Bullshit."

"Dad had a reason for wanting me to go into the Army. Just like he had a reason for you to do the things you did. And for you being here now."

"What's that supposed to mean?"

"There's a point to all this."

Austin's brother puts his hand on Austin's shoulder, like he used to—kind of. He looks at Austin with eyes Austin recognizes but only in the same way faces are recognizable in nightmares.

Austin says, "Did you have something do with Wade's death?"

"No."

"You were talking about Wade when you said that thing about people thinking someone's dead, right? Is Wade still alive?"

"Here I am, your brother. And all you can talk about is Wade. Why is he so important to you now?"

"I don't know. I already put you to rest, that's behind me. But Wade...maybe it's regret. Or maybe I feel guilty—not that I really care to feel guilty about anything. Or maybe I want to let him know that I wasn't there for him. Maybe I... I don't know."

"That's not it, Austin. There's more there and you know it."

Austin can't deny there's something more.

Muhammed Muhammed says, "You are not asking the right questions."

"What about this thing Wade kept mentioning? Sunflower? You work for SunCor. I don't know if that's what people call a coincidence or not."

"The less you know before it's time, the better. There are those who will want to know a hard truth from you, and the more you can say that you know nothing and be honest about it, the better this will work for you and us. Plausible deniability."

"Who wants to know the truth?"

"They will use torture."

"Shit, man. I want to know the truth."

"You will."

"Cop out."

"Maybe. But it's unimportant. What is, and why we're here talking, is…There's a woman, a projectionist. In possession of a very sensitive and important document. She's on her way here…to meet you."

"I don't know a projectionist."

"She's *introduced* herself to the path. And while she isn't a threat, she's digging around, connecting dots that are meant to be as distant as the nearest star. Miss has a very *strong* interest in her. She thinks you can help convince the projectionist to meet with Miss. Be friendly with her."

"Sure, you wanna be friends with someone? Why not tie them to a chair and smash their nuts with a hammer?"

"She doesn't have nuts."

"You know what I mean."

"Miss needs you to get this document from the projectionist. The document has the potential to challenge the path if in the wrong hands. So be on the projectionist's team until the time comes to not."

"I'm sure you'll let me know when that time comes." Austin laces it with as much toxic cynicism as he can.

"I won't. This is the last time we will see each other. But someone will let you know."

"The last time again?"

"This is how this is supposed to move. I'm sorry to come in and out like this."

"Again, I'm *not* an operative."

"Do you remember being in the camps?"

"Fuck off."

"Oh, brother."

"Why come back at all?"

"Allow me a moment, though we don't have much time, and I'll tell you what happened to Bowie Lee, why I'm here now instead of him."

Austin holds out his hands: *the floor's all yours*.

Muhammed Muhammed says, "It happened while Bowie Lee was stationed in Tel Tamir. He had one of those moments where the mind tears down and reveals a truth that was always there but refused to be seen. He joined the Army so he could dedicate his Self to a future he believed in, a world free from terror and fear and pain. He often imagined what that could be. Boredom gave him that leisure.

"His outfit would stand around, day after day, confirming airstrikes on high-level targets, syncing telecommunication arrays for drone data relays, setting up recharge stations for e-grunts. It was all drone work. So on outings where he and two equally-armed soldiers would search fallen houses confirmed to be empty through x-ray telemetry, searching for doorways leading to underground tunnels that A.E. intelligence believed to be there, Bowie Lee would think about you. About what he was fighting for, about the world back home. But really, mostly about you, Austin.

"On a day when the sky and earth were the same shade of gray, an aura of dread following him like a cartoon cloud that only rains on him, Bowie Lee entered a house that looked similar to the one he and Austin grew up in—except this house was half-missing, torn through by bunker busters and predator missiles. Lee sifted through the wreckage, followed a mostly clear path down some stairs, and found himself underground. He was alone. A tunnel stretched into the darkness in front of him. He snapped on his helmet light, but the beam barely cut

through thick dust and a deep-space darkness made it so he
could only see about ten feet in front of him.

"It was like being in a trance. He wasn't scared, didn't even
have his gun raised. He walked into the dark. Until the
darkness stopped. A wall. A dead end. The sound of TV static
broke the silence. A scratching, skittering. He inched closer to
the wall, the dust parting. When the light's beam hit the wall,
it moved. Rippled. A picture to match the sound of TV static.
The sound intensified, a million latex gloves crinkling in a giant
hand. The dust settled and the wall became visible. He wanted
to run, but his feet wouldn't move."

Austin says, "Let me guess. There was something on the
wall. And to you it was like real life symbolism."

"Camel spiders. Hundreds of them. You know how Bowie
Lee was with spiders."

"I once watched you throw a dictionary across the living
room to kill a jumping spider. Wasn't any bigger than a dime.
I think you cried too."

"He did *not* cry." And then he says, "Hey, remember this
one." He puts his fingers near Austin's forehead and says,
"Head dreamer, eye winker—"

Austin slaps his hand away. "Don't do that shit."

Steve Muhammed Muhammed holds a moment, nods.
"Seeing all those spiders, each the size of a football, that fear
turned to rage. They stopped being spiders and started being
people. Crawling all over each other in the dark, biting and
killing, using the backs of others to either get in or out of the
light. All at a dead end."

"It's not that bad."

"It is. So Bowie Lee unloaded two full mags into the wall.
Spider guts splattering everywhere. Bullets sparking on the

thick rock. Some of the spiders jumped off the wall, started scurrying toward the light. And then more of them joined. A herd of camel spiders rushing toward him. Bowie Lee panicked. Tossed two hand grenades at the wall. The blast knocked him on his feet. And knocked the entire wall down. Spiders with it. And also the family that had walled themselves on the other side. Hiding from the Americans who said things like *Orders are order*."

"Fuck."

"Indeed."

"And so you hate the world because you accidentally killed some people. And you're blaming…?"

"It's not about the killing. It's about the idea installed in his head that he *needed* to kill those spiders. An idea that movies give us. The idea of a hero, killing in the name of good. So that's what we're trying to annihilate. The idea. The transmissions society receives that shape how they move through the world, transmissions that come from one source. Entertainment. We believe in culture before media."

Austin looks at the letters he's standing in front of.

Steve Muhammed Muhammed says, "I've been saying *We need you*, but in truth, I need you. I have been too long in the company of disconnect. Then you walked into that office. You were supposed to, but I never believed it would happen. And I saw you there, brother…My blood…I need you in order for this to work. And this has to work. You. Are. Needed."

"I don't know."

"Remember that time your mom let Bowie Lee take you for a ride in his car and he took you to Donut Man and you hated the raspberry-filled donut so you threw it out into traffic and hit a cop car and the donut exploded on the windshield and Bowie Lee spent fifteen minutes telling the cop that it wasn't a slur against his profession."

"Shut up again." Austin looks down, wonders how bad the fall would hurt, if it would kill him right away. "Stop trying to convince me you're my brother. I believe it. I got it. Let's move on."

"The only thing left is for you to say you'll meet with this projectionist."

"What's her name?"

"Jackie Day."

"I'll meet her."

"You will?"

"Sure. Why not? Don't think I have a way around any of this. I mean, there's something here that Wade wanted me to know. You say it's important to you and Dad. You say I'll get answers. So whatever. I'll talk to this projectionist."

"That's all I can ask."

"What do I do?"

"Stay right here. She'll come. And when I say Bowie Lee loves...*loved* you, I mean it. He said it a thousand times to you in his head, knowing he'd never see you again. So he gave me this to give to you."

"Gave you what?"

Steve Muhammed Muhammed reaches out, and before Austin can say *Hey fuck off* and back away, he wraps his arms around Austin. Pulls him close. Embraces him in a hug that's both clinical and full of a longing warmth. Muhammed Muhammed rests his head against Austin's shoulder. Austin's arms stay at his side for a beat. But he's overwhelmed with the need to hug back. So his arms wrap around this guy and squeeze. Lets his head fall into Muhammed Muhammed's shoulder. A relaxed and peaceful hug. But before it gets too comfortable, the buzz of an approaching ad-drone causes Muhammed Muhammed to go stiff. He pulls back, thrusts Austin away from him. They both look up at the drone as it dances against a sky that's starting to fade to shades of sunset. An ad for X-Trim by SunCor blasting LED light their way.

"One of yours?"

Muhammed Muhammed says, "I should go. We've been here too long."

"Told me too much?"

"Not enough. But you must know: your part in this will make a difference. You will help bring about the future."

"Whatever. I don't really care. I honestly only give a shit about Wade at this point. Something's not adding up, and if you're telling me that my playing along with your plan means I'll find out whatever about Wade, I'll do it."

"You will." He holds his hand out. "Until next time, in this life or the next. May our recycled selves meet well and find the brotherly love once again."

Austin slaps the hand, a side five. "Ditto, brother."

WITH THE SUN'S HEAT still radiating from the rocks, Austin sits on a boulder underneath the big H, out of sight from the path above. The ingredients of the previous scene sit in his mind like bad fast food. A part of him doesn't believe it was real, yet he can still feel the hug his brother gave him. He wants to ask *Was that my brother?* but there's too much to deny it.

A larger part of him doesn't want to stay, doesn't want to accept the idea that he has no choice. He's always had a choice, and now he's being force-fed everything but what he wants. He can accept that Wade's dead, but his brother made it a little more clear that Wade maybe isn't. He can accept that his brother was dead and now isn't. He can accept that there's someone coming to meet him and that he's supposed to what? Watch her? Follow her? Steal something from her? But he can't take this idea that he is at the will of someone named Miss, of a group that's doing things he doesn't really know is worth doing. That he is being controlled by an unseen force.

You want to see him defy this. But you also know it will be impossible because his apathy is like a crown of thorns.

Like an incision in a fatty stomach, a path cuts across the barren hillside, away from the letters. East toward the Griffith Observatory. Austin stands, reminds himself that only a single "e" keeps *fate* and *chance* from being *fat chance*, and starts down this path.

And in a way only a mind debating a heavy burden can, Austin comes back to the present as the sun dips into the coolness of the Pacific and he stumbles onto the front lawn of the Observatory. The suddenness of being somewhere after the hill and trails, and with no real memory of getting there, Austin feels an immense surge of overstimulation. People hurry to see the LA sunset. Babies cry. Phones flash. Tourists taking pictures with Dean's bust—most of them not really sure if Dean's alive or dead because of his recent lead role in a war picture thanks to his CGI rebirth. A guy who causes Austin to do a double take because of how much the guy looks like Austin stands at the base of the Astronomers Monument, waiting nervously. Maybe for an answer to a question that hasn't asked itself yet. Maybe the guy is more like Austin than he knows. An Austin from another story.

Big artist-commissioned sculptures shaped like letters spelling GRIFFITH crush the courtyard grass in front of the Observatory. Austin leans against them, catching his breath, letting dusk wind dry the sweat on his face and back. He thinks about calling his dad, asking for money. Enough to run to the other side of the planet. At least until this whole Sunflower thing falls the way of every fad diet or Hollywood cash-grab, like 3D or Smell-O-Vision. Let it fade like everything eventually does.

The roar of a motorcycle rips through his mind like a fart in a movie theater. A SunCor drone, maybe the same one because it too displays the X-Trim ad, buzzes overhead, lingers around Austin, then zooms off. And then he sees the motorcycle. An old thing with a side car. Covered in desert sand. It grinds to a stop on the sidewalk, people looking at the bike's illegal parking job like they would the scene of a brutal murder. The driver, a woman, eases off the bike with practiced grace, adjusts a bag on her shoulder, and starts across the courtyard. Her path a perfect line focused on Austin.

He doesn't make eye contact with her, looks around like he's supposed to be here. Does this until she's right in front of him.

She says, "I think we have something to talk about."

"The projectionist."

She looks just above Austin. Stands back a little, like she's taking something in. Then says, "A big H. Funny."

Austin turns around, sees he's been leaning on the big, bold H at the end of GRIFFITH. An H that's painted with... no no, those are marigolds.

She says, "We need to go some place to talk. Somewhere safe."

Austin says, "My car's up on the hill. Tell me where and we—"

"It's been towed. I'll give you a ride."

"Oh…groovy."

<u>DELETED SCENE</u>

The Driver

INTERMISSION:
PACKETS & PROTOCOL

AS JACKIE DRIVES, AUSTIN ENTERS an address on his phone's GPS, hits **Search**, and you attach to that packet of network data as it moves like a thought through a vast, unseen mind, shooting up and up, past heavy clouds and atmospheric strata and into the impossible pressurization of cusp-space, just above the outer-Earth shield, into the airless anti-gravity that takes up more reality than our pinprick world, and that packet reflects off one of the 2,400+ satellites—both government- and privately-owned—orbiting this cusp-space, and travels halfway around the circumference of the Earth until it connects with the SpaceX Space Station where Head Inhabitant Amy Miranda Day floats around the cramped spaces she's now forced to call home, and as the packet collides with the satellite's Multi-Beam Antenna A, passes through the Relay System, through a complicated web of data compressors, through a computer not far from where Amy now hovers as she looks out the porthole at the bright light in the distance, and as the packet compresses and condenses and ejects out of Multi-Beam Antenna B back down to Earth, Amy continues to look out the porthole, ignoring the computer's request for a specific confirmation code to continue the urination filtration procedure which has allowed her to drink and urinate the same fluid in a continuous cycle for over a year, and she ignores this command because her focus is on the light, what she calls Turkmon's Sunflower, a bright spot she believes is closer than before, and after a detailed period trying to convince herself that it's only a refraction of light from the solar array panels, Amy now believes that that spot in the distance is something very bad, and as she pushes herself away from the window and over to the computer where she enters the code and the filtration system whirs, Amy speaks to the faceless head about her fears again, about her loneliness, about the alienation from everything that makes her human, about the fear that the Mars colony failed or that they never made it to Mars at all, speaks about the void and how there's something out there ready to answer the questions of human suffering, which is when another packet collides with Multi-Beam Antenna A, travels through the processors and compressors and ejects out of Multi-Beam Antenna B at near-light speed, through the outer-shell, past all atmospheric layers, dodges a passenger jet at 36,000 feet, past clouds, past near-ground-level drones pulsing individual advertisements, demanding the attention of passers-by, and finally the packet downloads into the smartphone of one Heather Pérez—the entire journey from the S.X.S.S. down to the smartphone taking no more than 2.7 seconds—and the protocol unloads a website detailing the symptoms of heart arrhythmia and when such symptoms are considered deadly, while Heather waits in the office of a Hollywood super producer as he speaks into his antiquated desk phone about the success Heather's going to bring to the *Under/Shift* sequel (tentatively titled *Over/Shift*) because of her starring role in the film, even though he keeps calling her Jennifer, which she assumes is because the character she's playing in *Over/Shift* is named Heather and he keeps talking about Jennifer Brachis Donnahue like she's in the room and so she doesn't correct him because she's distracted by her pulse dancing around gimpishly, causing her to suspect that the end is finally near, that her heart's on the verge of sputtering to a chest-clenching halt, especially each time he calls her *Jennifer*, and of course death comes at a time when her desires become truths and the envy she's festered in for so many years floats away, and while the super producer continues his unwarranted praise in a way that seems as though he and Heather have known each other for years and have worked together multiple times, Heather reaches into her purse and fiddles with an orange pill bottle that rattles quietly, calling her to the bathroom to mute the voice in her head that sounds like her but isn't, but she's metaphorically handcuffed to the seat by the fear of the opportunity escaping her and by the man named Steve in the seat next to her, the man who was in her room and eased her to sleep, with his sharp gray suit and his $600 haircut and his well-groomed demeanor, an aura of wealth cradling his every move, a man whose origins and reasons for bringing Heather to this super producer and for convincing him of her talent and her appeal without ever having seen her act is as much of an unknown as the true manner of her illness, but she sits, grateful for the opportunity, doing her best to mimic the smiley face pins on the lapels of both men, terrified and turned on by the possibilities of a future she could only imagine, and yet the webpage tells her that the fluttering in her chest is on a list of symptoms associated with aortic stenosis, only treatable by an open-heart procedure to surgically replace a narrowed valve, and so despite her elation, she's overwhelmed with a need to call the nearest hospital and schedule that surgery for right now, no later, and when she looks over at the well-groomed man, he's looking at her phone, then up at her, and he places his hand on her arm, and he's whispering to her that everything is going to work out, doing all he can to ease the fear that he can read on her face, which calms her enough so her eyes move around the room, to look over at the poster of *Under/Shift* and be struck with a looking-in-the-mirror feeling when she sees Jennifer Brachis Donnahue, and her mind wanders and she starts a new search concerning the current box office standing of *Under/Shift*, which she already knows went well into $260 million in the opening weekend, and when she hits **Search** the protocol condenses into a packet that shoots skyward, passing a packet that's already traversed through both Multi-Beam Antennae and the compression system on the S.X.S.S. and drops at a speed unseen and unfelt, down to the city of San Dimas, CA, into a quiet, suburban neighborhood where freshly waxed sedans are parked in driveways and children comfortably play on their tablets on front lawns without a fear of being abducted or attacked or affected by the terrors of the world, passing the exhaust of one such house (and because you're attached to the lifeless packet you can smell the bacon and waffles, maple syrup and fresh-brewed coffee, Pine Sol and Windex and Febreze) and enters this house surrounded by beautiful gardens, where it violently collides with Manjeep "Please Call Me Man" Kathuria's laptop and unfolds its protocols as a return on a formula he's entered into an online database containing every sequence of integers regarding the human genome, a reply that contains a step that Abraham Dworkin, in his six years of working on the compound, has yet to compile, which gives Manjeep the next step in debunking what Dworkin said couldn't be done, specifically the degeneration of a human molecular structure in microseconds, which, in his desperation, Manjeep believes will be what leads to his union with Amber Waves (because he can't, even though he knows her name is Jessica Fey Tarda, keep from thinking of her as anything but Amber Waves), and that his desires will come to fruition, and judging by the intense determination of the Human Reich to create a compound that deteriorates a human being in a matter of seconds, Manjeep knows he's trading bad deeds for a way to feel connected to someone else's life in a manner that means love and desire and mutual yearning, and so he will do anything the group asks of him, and it's not like he can protest, because every time he writes a note of rejection or desire on his pad, someone rips it out and throws it in his face, and given that his tongue is no longer a part of him (floating in a jar belonging to a southeast Bangladeshi druglord with whom Manjeep's older brother is currently in a slavery-type situation due to a large sum of owed money, Manjeep's tongue being both a payment and a trophy/reminder of whom Manjeep's brother is indebted to) he can't voice his opinion, protest, or love, so he works for himself and for his desires, no longer to save that brother, works to prove his worth, works so that he can prove his love for Amber, and he dreams that that love will carry them into their own life together, where he lives for her and with her and no longer with the roommate he's stuck with in the pink room, the guy who won't stop sweating and vomiting, the guy who wakes Manjeep up in the middle of the night screaming *Daddy!* and *Mommy!* and whispering, in the late hours of the night when he likely thinks Manjeep is asleep, the same mantra-like chant *Austin will save me*, and given his roommate's tattoos and his stretched earlobes, Manjeep thinks that he's referring to a lingering desire to find his way to Austin, TX and live out some musical dream shared by many who migrate to the Live Music Capital of the World, but Manjeep also knows that his roommate, whose name he still does not know, will never make it to Austin just as much as he knows that he won't send money back to his brother or mother, and that in acknowledging his servitude to the Human Reich he is willfully putting his brother's and mother's life in the hands of a war lord who will destroy them, but because he is now in the presence of Amber, given the opportunity to serve her and show her the desire he's kept in the deepest part of his heart, Manjeep is willing to make that sacrifice, so he inputs the response to the formula, adding another strand to the theorem, thinking not of his mother's face as he left their small village, compiling a protocol to send off, relying on unseen signals that connect everyone in the Human Reich headquarters to a private server stationed in San Simeon, but in the house the signal wanders like a free ghost, up through floors, through walls, and into a secluded room, darkened by the absence of windows, lit only by a fluorescent floor lamp missing a shade, white light illuminating the pink-painted walls where, in this prison cell disguised as a guest bedroom locked from the outside by a keypad protected by a sixteen digit code, Manjeep's roommate sits on his side of the room, on his twin-sized bed, his back against the wall, legs hanging off the edge of the bed, arms crossed over his chest, a layer of sweat gluing the hair not pulled back in a loose ponytail to his head, smudged glasses ready to slip off the slickened slope of his nose, nothing to connect him to anyone in the house or outside the house other than the unseen signal as he nervously bites his fingernails, or what's left of them, sandpaper feeling grinding down his brain, pressure threatening to push his eyes from their sockets, tracing with those same eyes the lines of his tattoos, anchors and fire and skulls, decorations meant to externally convey an internal fury, but he knows there is no fury, only a desperation to be *special*, someone the world will remember for his poetry or his ability to play bass or draw low brow cartoons, with the hope of igniting in someone like him the same desire that has kept him going through the years of desperation and depression, even though he's no closer to fame than when he started, which has led to track marks on the tops of his hands and in the antecubital of his right arm, which, in the six days it's been since he last used, has healed to a yellowish bruise, a healing likely enhanced by the food, protein shakes, supplements, and vitamin compounds his captors give him three times a day, which, in just six days, has caused a healthy amount of weight to show, filling in the skeletal hollowness that was his figure before his captors took him from the flop house, the den of crackheads and dope fiends he called home, a kidnapping he can't make sense of, holding him for a purpose that is uncertain because he isn't worth much and his parents have no money, and not that they want him for money given that he's sharing the room with an Indian guy who looks to have a purpose, who gets out of the room for most of the day, who sleeps through the night and seems to have never had an addiction of any kind, none that would cause him to sweat and vomit and scream in the night, doesn't know anything about wanting to use on a constant basis, or the feeling of a great eucatastrophe about to happen, and also not knowing anything about needing someone so bad that chanting their name over and over again in the night (*austin austin austin*) seems the only way to relieve some of that back-built anxiety, even though there's an inkling that this person who's so badly needed might actually be the thing bringing this eucatastrophe, but other than his roommate and the red-gloved chick who has let him out of the room twice for a total of seventeen minutes in the six days he's been here, he is unsure about the other inhabitants in the house even though he hears them, bodies moving from room to room freely like the signal, the roar of a lion, the muffled shouts of a vaguely feminine nature followed by a structure-shuddering thud, the dropping of a prehistoric weight, an event that happens several times a day, which, following the aimless energy of the wireless signal from the prison cell disguised as a windowless guest bedroom and down through the floor, in between spaces between matter, the microscopic porousness of drywall, to a room on the first floor, near the back of the house, a room retrofitted into a top-shelf home gym of weight machines, pull-downs, chest-presses, arm-curls, row machines, a slew of free weights, and a complete set of weight plates and bars (what he hears upstairs), which at the moment is being used by Delta Robison, who is at the crest of a dead lift, the total weight just over 800lbs, the weight forcing a primitive grunt from deep inside her stomach, from a place that doesn't exist anymore in most men, reaching down layers of evolution to touch upon a primordial drive and strength, screaming through the pleasure of pain, and then she tosses the bar forward and lets the weight drop, sending a destructive ripple through the entire house, rattling the floor-to-ceiling windows in front of her that let in a deep pink light from the last of the day's sunset, the makeshift gym wallowing in greenhouse humidity, and a drop of sweat rides the ridge of her temple, cheek, lip, and falls to the floor, where it explodes and leaves a wet flower print on the padded flooring, and off to her right the eruption and vibration of more weights hitting the floor, dropped by the army of women she's been put in charge of, weightlifters following her every order, and she looks down at her own weight, realizing just how easy it could be to get to the weight the HR wants her to, how getting to 1,000lbs isn't as impossible as she made it seem when the scrawny girl wearing the red gloves first asked her to get up to 800lbs for reasons she was not at liberty to discuss but that if she wanted to keep her brother alive and keep all the endorsements—

including the giant billboard on Sunset that shows her lifting the Earth above her head like Atlas next to a lightning-bolt-font slogan that says *The World Is Yours With SunCor*—she would need to be able to lift 1,000lbs within the next week, which didn't seem possible, but with the assistance of the make-shift, though by no means shoddy, home gym, the supplements they feed her on a scheduled basis, the astronaut-food-type meals so dense in protein Delta can almost feel her muscles compact and multiply every time she lifts a new weight, and with her renewed freedom from the fear that her brother might succumb to the tumor in his brain, all this adds up to a sense of change, that she can reach that goal of 1,000lbs, because it's the next challenge, the next step in her self-evolution, with everything else defeated and under her, behind her, which leaves only what's in front of her, which is this house, the HR, whoever they are, and their obvious need not for someone like her, but for her, for Delta Robison and her ability to lift 1,000lbs, and her ability to lead the army she's been amassing over the recent days, now a total of twelve angry women all working, building muscle, injecting themselves with the compounds the HR gives them, following each order given to them by Delta, and regardless of what they want her and her army for, she will do it, simply because she is needed, just as she was needed before, to help her brother, who, as of this moment, sits across the room from her, still smiling at Delta's scream and the sound of weights hitting the floor, which, seeing him smile, brings a smile to Delta's face, which, in turn, makes him smile even more, through the bandages that wrap around his swollen head and face, bandages stained a rusty yellow in the places where the HR cut into his skull and injected their concoction that brought him out of the coma,

out of the land of the dying, and back to her, now, where he
sits on a bench-press bench, kicking his weak, emaciated legs,
legs that are shiny from sweat, the heat of the room apparently
good for his healing process, his t-shirt (white with a smiley
face in the middle) sopping wet, sticking to his sunken chest,
and as he smiles only the left side seems to work, the right
drooping slightly, his right eye in a permanent state of almost-
shock, but it doesn't seem to bother him much, because when
Delta moves away from the weights and over to him, he smiles,
bounces with excitement, and when Delta tries to reach down
and tug on his ear like she used to, a little way to remind him
that she has more love for him than anyone, she can't, the
bandage covering both of his ears, so she grabs the loose skin
around his elbow and tugs, which brings a sudden gust of
laughter out of his weak lungs, and her army of weightlifters
waits for Delta to direct them on what to do next, order them,
though Delta's doing her best to ignore them and only listen to
Bub's laugh, but then, like the silence after a gunshot, his
laughter stops and his face darkens, both sides droop, and
before Delta can ask *What's wrong*—even though she knows
this face as the one that takes over when he's having a waking
dream—he tells her, in a monotone devoid of all emotion,
about a darkness he can feel, about an absence of light he can
see, saying the words *void* and *Mars* and *sunflower* after every
couple of words, almost like a hiccup, telling her about a
woman and a man who are trying to hurt the HR (because by
now her brother has taken to liking the HR intimately, given
their reviving him and feeding, clothing, and respecting him),
and that he sees *something scary come giant monster slug dark
toilet*, and then he falls out of the waking dream and he's
laughing again, which knocks Delta's breath away, and despite

her almost-superhuman strength she feels weak, falls to her knees and comes face-to-face with her brother, who reaches out and touches Delta's face, and Delta wants to ask what he meant by *giant monster* and *dark toilet*, what he meant by *something scary coming*, but she knows that once he's out of the waking dream his memory of it doesn't exist, so she just smiles at him and rubs his elbow, which causes him to laugh again, except this time he doesn't fall into the waking dream, just continues to laugh, which, her strength having returned, brings her to her feet, back over to the weights, to the dead-lift bar, and as she slips another twenty pounds on each side just to see if she can lift it yet, she asks her brother to sing a little song, and being bashful even with his sister, her brother doesn't sing, only hums the tune of *You Are My Sunshine* as Delta reaches down for the bar, replaying something he said over and over, using it to power her first 885lb attempt, hearing him say that there are two people trying to hurt the HR, and her blood boils, the thought of her future denied raging in her muscles, and her grip tightens and she lifts, the power of the HR raging through her spirit, and she lifts the weight up, up, over her head, not just a deadlift but a full overhead press, her thoughts only on stopping whoever would try to put an end to the HR, regardless of their plan, and she feels her muscles quiver and her strength depletes and she tosses the weight forward, her army doing the same in a perfect mimic of their leader but each with half the weight, sending a collectively massive thud throughout the house, which brings another bout of giddy laughter from her brother, and those two sounds, the laughter and the chaos, slip into the stream of wireless radiation wandering through the house, into the garage, where a lieutenant in Delta's army tosses two uncooked chickens and a whole suckling pig into Simeon the Lion's food trough, the lion yawning at the predictable meal, depressed again that it's one of the muscular women and not Barb visiting him, because a deep-back part of his brain recognizes her, the same part of him that absorbed the molecules of Simeon Wolpe, and every time he sees Barb a voice that isn't like a lion but also isn't like a human whispers *wife* and *love* and he feels the same way he did about his lioness and their cubs, before the car ran them over, but every time Barb visits him in the garage he almost believes that she can see that Wolpe part of you in the deep-back (even though you're having an impossible time reconciling that you are both not here and here still in the molecules of the lion that killed you because you don't feel what it feels at all), that she isn't visiting a lion, but instead visits her ex-husband, the man who was made to believe she suicided, but for now hunger forces him to ignore these thoughts about Barb, and he focuses on the suckling pig, starts tearing it apart, and he ignores the wireless radiation that seeps through his molecules, through the floor, and penetrates into a room no bigger than a closet in a half-space between the first floor and the basement, and in this tiny room that is known to no one but Barb Tarda and Abraham Dworkin (who has met the fate of a self-fulfilling pseudo-prophecy, meaning that the only aspect of Dworkin remaining on this Earth is a pound of ash and flake at the bottom of the Oven, ready to be extracted and used as fertilizer in the backyard garden, and, now somewhere over the Pacific, a breath of Dworkin's oven-smoke condensing in a swollen cloud, breaking up in a strong wind that will carry Dworkin to some remote location where the sea will stretch seemingly infinite in all directions), Barb Tarda has to hunch over to reach the child-sized desk, a desk with the word *booger* etched on the underside, where she's now sitting, typing a private message on a device not connected to the wireless network floating through the house, not connected to any network that could potentially be intercepted by anyone within the Human Reich, but rather a secured server system managed and operated by a shell operation actually owned and controlled by a high-level Empire organization that claims to control Barb Tarda, but in fact doesn't know that Barb Tarda provides them with mostly false information, not because she doesn't trust them but rather because she doesn't believe that they will be able to do anything against the Human Reich and that she doesn't believe in their way either, and that what they really don't know is that she agreed to be an undercover operative and join the HR so that she could get to her sister in hopes of bringing her out of what Barb thought at first was a cult but later realized is something inescapably more, and since Jessica Fey has replaced her molecules with that of the HR and since Barb can't escape, she uses the high-level Empire organization's private server to write a secret message which contains details of their upcoming operation, Project Sunflower, to the two players who have the ability to expose the HR's influence, bring to light the damage they have done over the years, and the end-of-civilization damage they have yet to perpetrate but will soon commit, the seven seals of societal advancement created by social distortion perpetrated under the Sunflower brand-umbrella (the coffee pollution, the Mars colony destruction, the entertainment meltdown, the presidential dysfunction, the human potential equalization, the soldier imprinting via fast food products, and the virtual reality seditious training program for post-Sunflower operations), which at first was a counter-operation to the oncoming domination of the New World Order, but now, and this is why Barb feels the need to bring their operation to light somehow, the Human Reich feels less like a counter-operation to save the human race and more like a second attack on humanity, an operation of menace equal to the New World Order, a form of slavery just as intensely anti-human as the objectives of the New World Order with its singular government and Big-Brother egoism, but instead of the New World Order promoting rampant organization and restriction, inhibiting the freedom of humanity, the Human Reich, at first, sought to free humanity from all that makes it a slave to itself —restrictive sexuality and gender identity, racism, politics, celebriculture, unquenchable fame, unwarranted desires, addictions, reliance on technology, reliance on entertainment and pop culture, an overall lack of self-reflection—but now Barb sees that all of that is what *makes* humanity, American culture specifically, what it is, that without what the Human Reich calls *evolutionary inhibitors* humans become nothing more than smart animals, and so in this private space, the only place in the house she can disobey the laws of the Human Reich and use a handheld vaporizer loaded with an sativa-dominant hybrid strain called Looney Tooney, which grows in the backyard garden in between the sunflowers and the marigolds, and so she draws hard on the vaporizer and exhales into a homemade mute made from a toilet paper roll stuffed with dryer sheets, the intake of THC the only thing that keeps her from becoming incredibly depressed, suicidal even, when she thinks of her role as one of the Reich's key figures, the freedom from depression being infinitely more tolerable than the heightened paranoia she feels every time she leaves the room clutching the mug in her pocket, every time she smells the bacon and waffles, maple syrup and fresh-brewed coffee,

Pine Sol and Windex and Febreze and wonders if she will someday end up like Dworkin, a pile of spent ash, so to save herself from being something other than nothing, Barb sits in the room, writes her private message, and before she sends it out she wonders what could happen to Jessica Fey if the Human Reich falls, what Jessica Fey would do to her if she ever discovered that Barb is a traitor, even though Barb knows deep down that Jessica Fey wouldn't hesitate to kill her, so instead of thinking about how her betrayal to the Reich could possibly lead to the death of her sister, or some dire form of punishment for Jessica Fey, Barb doesn't hesitate and hits **Send**, compiling the message into a protocol, compiling that protocol into a packet, that packet ejaculating out of the house, rocketing past the teenager wandering outside the house, still searching for his lost little brother, reapplying posters to lightposts where the posters he previously hung have been ripped down, the teenager suspiciously eyeing the house surrounded by well-groomed sunflowers, and in a rapidly ascending arc, the packet breaks through the atmospheric layers and into the cusp-space where, again, the information collides with Multi-Beam Antenna A, which, after a full rotation of the Earth, is in that brief position that gives Dr. Amy Day a view of what she fears most, the bright light surrounded by the void, the sunflower, which, in the space of the ninety minutes it takes the SpaceX Space Station II to revolve around the Earth's circumference, seems even larger than before, closer, and the void around it darker, giving Amy a start of panic, pushing her away from the window, over to the communications system where she dials down to Hawthorne and demands to know what the bright spot in the distance is, and after receiving only silence followed by the briefest titter of laughter from either the on-board AI or those at Hawthorne, the television comes on playing the current Presidential Empirical Address, which, to Amy, is more amusing, more entertaining than most television shows that cost millions of dollars to produce, hours of manpower to write, direct, act, and in this entertaining power, this distraction, Amy ignores the panic the sunflower causes, ignores the laughter from Hawthorne (or the AI), and puts all her focus on the television, laughing when Truffaux announces that the greatest threat to American life are the *poo-poo heads* who threaten to take away freedom of speech and freedom of expression and freedom in general and he targets his anger at the Mars colonization attempt and proceeds to declare war against them and says *It'll be a quick war* and that it will begin and end with the push of a button and a high-impact hydrogen warhead, and the crowd gathered around Truffaux cheers, which stops Amy's laughter and makes her want to wake up and scream and cry, though she isn't dreaming, and the crowd continues to cheer as if his words are bringing about a great change, one for the history books, and as she cries, information slips through the system, refracts, compresses, and leaves Amy and her private space, and the compressed information compiles into a packet that leaves Multi-Beam Antenna B at a speed near light and travels down, connecting Dr. Amy Day to humanity by a 254 mile invisible contrail of information that collides with a smartphone in the pocket of one Jessica Fey Tarda, which vibrates as she walks the floor of a building the HR refers to as the Silent House that on the outside resembles a massive warehouse converted into a gymnasium for all ages, a sign out front professing that it is the home of two Olympic gold medals, but which, inside, contains no gym equipment, no mats, no lights for that matter, only long rows of ten-by-ten foot cubicles, rows running the length and width of the entire 26,000 sq. foot floor, and in each of these cubicles is a station consisting of an HR initiate, a leather recliner, a hydration and nutrition system hooked up to the initiate, a urination and defecation system hooked up to the initiate, a SensiSystem with VR headset, CerebrAmp neuro-control system, SensiSuit, and SensiSurround all encompassing the initiate in a virtual training program which is relayed back to an external screen where Jessica Fey monitors the progress of each initiate's training pattern, and as she's monitoring these cubicles, hands behind her back, upright like a dictator among her disciples, she stops at Station 19-Q, where Initiate 3T3M18G6 runs through a scenario involving infiltration of a college campus, posing as a student, insidiously creating a student revolt against the establishment through the creation of a rather lengthy and incomprehensible manifesto, a scenario created by one Professor Spapling at Sun Sate University, and while Jessica Fey watches 3T3M18G6 sit in the office of a digitalized professor and hand off a stack of papers that instantly explode in the professor's face, shards of explosive and paper sticking jaggedly out of his face and now-exposed brain matter, the phone in her pocket vibrates again, bringing her to a stop as she pulls it out and sees two messages from Miss, the first of which includes two names, jobs for her to complete once her presence at the Silent House is no longer required, names that have no meaning, names that haven't yet been mentioned in relation to the progress of the HR, but in the second message she sees a name that slaps the confidence out of her step, breath stolen, goosed knees, gimpy stomach, and she looks at the message to make sure the name is really there and everything's right, and the name is still there, so she knows that this isn't a mistake, because Miss never makes mistakes, that every action of the HR is calculated, every movement and molecule predetermined, but still she can't stop herself from replying to the message with the name she can't believe (*Barbara Torrence Tarda*), asking if this is a job, if she is really meant to perform her duty against her sister, and almost instantly a reply is given, a single word—*Affirmative*—that can only come from Miss, who speaks with such rigidity and robotic inflection that Jessica Fey knows, absolutely, that she will, at some point in the near future, have to face her sister with death as an agenda, but if it is the will the of HR then it must be done, she must Abide, for the will of the HR is the future and the path to freedom, an escape from slavery, and one is never worth many, but in contrast to that rationalization Jessica Fey thinks of Hitler, al-Assad, Jong-un, lone men who, through twisted ideology and fear, inspired their cultural masses to a path of destruction and hate, but Barb has nothing to do with these people and Jessica Fey knows that, which leads her to wonder why she's been given such a task, even though it is her purpose in the HR, and as if an extrasensory response to the question, the phone buzzes and a message appears, another from Miss, a screen capture of a message Barb sent to the two names in the other message— Jackie Day (*politely detain and bring to CATIC*) and Austin Foster (*mutilate aggresively*)—and if the message hadn't come from Miss, Jessica Fey wouldn't believe that Barb could commit such a seditious act against all that they have worked for, against the organization that gave both their lives meaning and purpose when they had been so empty, saved Barb from her common, consumerist, housewife existence with that deadbeat hack director, and gave Jessica Fey an outlet for all her rage at the lack of belonging and power, and most importantly, the Human Reich made the death of Jessica Fey and Barb's mother mean something, brought both to a purpose that would serve the world and bring it all into a new level of cultural evolution, and so realizing that Barb *did* betray the Human Reich and is attempting to pull down the curtain on all they have worked for, Jessica Fey knows she will carry out the orders and that Barb, though she may live another day, or two, or three, will never see the fruits of their labor, will not make it through the week, won't be there for the awards show, for the compound's secretion and the grand reveal of all the experiments Barb oversaw with the slugs and the compounds, joining Dworkin as fertilizer in the garden, and also that the two outsiders Barb has attempted to contact will meet the full violent power of the HR, whether before or after her sister Jessica Fey doesn't know, but knows that like Barb the two will not see the event that triggers the start of the cultural meltdown, so now with confirmations set in her head, decisions cemented, Jessica Fey hits reply, types out *We Must Abide*, and hits **Send** without hovering or second-guessing, knowing that her free-will doesn't exist, that all moments are already decided and the fate of human existence will go how it is meant to, and so at this time of night, a moment the French refer to as *entre chien et loup*, as the distant horizon is still wounded from the setting sun and all the things too fearful to emerge during the day allow themselves the freedom only night allows, the reply compiles as a packet and drifts skyward, a soul transcending to heaven, riding the angelic, other-worldly waves of digital information up toward the infinite void where it reflects off one satellite, then another, working its way around the Earth until it collides with Multi-Beam Antenna A and runs through the system on the SpaceX Space Station where

Amy floats, drinking water that was once urine, twice refiltered, impurities removed, eating a package of goo meant to taste like chicken tetrazzini, watching a rerun of the presidential address, not thinking about her sister or the people on Earth, so disconnected that the presidential address seems to her like a signal from another world, Truffaux talking about renewing one of his prime initiatives, the Fat Tax bill, forcing anyone who is legally obese to pay a per pound monthly tax, creating a fiscal surplus that would be used to pay for universal healthcare, and for those that do not lose the weight or refuse to participate are sent to LaborCamps where they will be placed on strict nutritional diets and rigorous work-out routines and on-site production labor, including textiles, technology, and food services, all of which would end up serving the American economy, and each time Truffaux says the phrase *Fat Tax* Amy laughs so hard that the liquefied chicken tetrazzini threatens to ejaculate out her nose and ricochet through the cabin space, while the system whizzes and a packet of information compresses, condenses, runs through the complex system, around relays, to the base of Multi-Beam Antenna B, and out, riding the invisible energy that flows down toward Earth and rides on its surface like ghosts of the past, the present, and the future, never free.

It moves.

ACT TWO – PART TWO:
CIGARETTE BURN

AUSTIN'S GPS LEADS JACKIE TO A NEWLY constructed
mall in Burbank, to a store within that mall called Foster's
Royal Flush. She's now surrounded by toilets of different size
and shape, some with technological attachments to aid in
whatever bodily function a person's relieving. Austin forced
those working at the store to leave for the day, reinforcing this
demand with the phrase *My dad owns this store.* And despite
using the keys they left behind to lock the front doors so that
he and Jackie could be alone, no one really seems to be
interested in shopping for toilets. Shoppers pass the glass
frontage, willfully ignoring the store's existence, as if none of
them are willing to admit they shit.

Jackie hops up on the register counter, sits with her feet
dangling. Austin sits on a nearby toilet set up to look like it's
part of a bathroom set. He stops reading the message on his
phone again, sets it on the table next to the toilet. An uneaten
burrito from the food court sits on a styrofoam plate on
Austin's lap. Jackie sips coffee from a Thai place and lights a
cigarette.

Austin says, "Not that I give a shit, but I don't think
you're supposed to do that in here."

"And yet here I am, doing it."

"Whatever. And I want you to know, this," taps his phone,

"isn't a message from my brother. This is someone new."

He told Jackie about meeting his brother, how he'd been missing, thought dead, how his face had changed, and about the secrecy of their conversation, SunCor, everything so far. He also told her about his brother's request for him to spy on her. He told her things he didn't need to, which is why she trusts him enough to share space and information.

"What makes you say that?"

"He told me he wouldn't answer any of my questions, that he and I wouldn't talk again."

"But he answered questions."

"I shared a lot with you. Things I shouldn't have. And I know fuck all about you. I don't think it's fair to keep telling you stuff when you've told me nothing."

"Man, you're spilling all this shit like we're in therapy. That's on you. Besides, I have the important thing. What do you have?"

"What do you mean *important thing*?"

Jackie ashes the cigarette on the floor. Austin watches, smirks a little. He looks at something behind Jackie. She follows his gaze, turns around and comes face-to-face with a cardboard cutout of a man holding a golf club, one hand covered in a golf glove. His smile looks painted on. Jackie says, "That your dad?"

"It is."

"And he owns this place."

"He does."

"Why?" She's genuinely curious as to why someone would own a store that sells toilets. Though she's grateful for the security the mall provides: threat assessment security drones at every corner, enough to prevent any kind of attack. Being in the store feels like the two of them are in a bubble, a private space the world outside can't penetrate. Still, Jackie knows she'll need to get back to Cinéma Vérité soon, put all the things she'll leave behind in the hands of someone who can do something with them—because all of this is probably going to end badly.

"I've always wanted to ask him that question, but every time I start to, I realize I don't care so I don't."

"Well he creeps me out." Jackie flicks her cigarette at his face. Ash and cinder fireworks off the cardboard and for a second Jackie thinks the stand-up'll catch fire. But it doesn't. She says, "Two days after Wolpe died, this shows up." She pulls the screenplay from her rucksack, holds it up to Austin. "Your brother being interested in me has something to do with this. Considering it's called *Sunflower*. The screenplay *might* give away their plans. The way it ends…might…"

"How does it end?"

"I don't know. The pages are missing. But putting everything together, I'm now comfortable assuming your brother had something to do with Wolpe's death."

"He killed himself."

"You know many people who've killed themselves with a lion?"

"I don't know many who've suicided."

"I've known plenty. And people at the coffee shop Wolpe was at before he died said he looked possessed or drugged."

"And you think that—"

"I don't think anything. None of this gives me room to think."

"Wolpe's death was a suicide."

"Your brother pay you to say that? And who's to say think

and truth are the same? Like, I think you're keeping truth in your back pocket like Dennis the Menace…if Dennis spent his twenties getting high in his parents' basement."

"You don't know enough about me to say that."

"Am I wrong?"

"You are."

She waits for him to say more, but he doesn't. She says, "You know that was the perfect moment for you to tell me more about your life. Make me feel for you. Deepen my perception of your character."

"I've told you enough. Lemme see that."

He points at the screenplay. Jackie instinctively hugs the pages. The energy between them starts to feel like two magnets with same poles pushing against each other. She's reminded of movies where characters have conflicts just to create tension. And that conflict falls flat because the plot surrounding the characters is already complicated enough. But Jackie's not flat. So she hops off the counter, walks over to Austin, who's looking at the burrito in his lap like it's hypnotizing him. Jackie holds the screenplay out for him to take, but he can't take his eyes off the burrito.

"Hey," and then kicks his foot.

He jumps, screams a little. Snatches the screenplay from her. It almost pains her to see it in his hands and not hers. But she lets go. She's not flat.

Jackie says, "I've made some notes. Ignore those for now." As Austin flips to the first page, she adds, "You mind if I read that message on your phone thing?"

Austin parts with his phone with a similar soul-heaviness.

It's the first time in her life she's touched one of these things. She puts the screen close to her face, eyes trying to focus. There's a warmth coming from it. It would be paranoid of her to think that the radiation coming off the device is currently deforming the receptors in her brain and that she'll now crave a constant stream of dead data floating around the atmosphere. This is the moment she stops being Jackie. No, too paranoid.

She reads the message.

> From: daffy duck
> <daffyduck69@s_nf10w3r1u_7s7_6a.gov>
> To: me <afosteredchild@trumail.com>
> Subject: the big fade out
> A&J—
>
> now that u are at the part where the two of u are together, there's things u gotta do that'll betray what is known. i—not we—am talkin to u both from a bad place. the engine of the machine has lost its driver & it's heading for the inevitable. which is bad. i can't say how & why, but it's destruction on a big league scale. but isn't that always the goal of a terrorist group? isn't that where all plots lead? miss is not the savior she once set out to be. don't believe or trust anything other than what u tell each other.

(Jackie says, "How do I move it down?" Austin reaches over and eases his finger down the screen. Almost sensually. The message scrolls up. Jackie mumbles *nonsense* to herself. Austin says, "Okay, boomer." And Jackie says, "What's that supposed to mean?" And Austin says, "I don't know. I have no idea why I said it.")

see this through to the end. A—seek the truth of w. J—the sun is on high with the big h & that's where you'll find the end. the screenplay is not the answer. wolpe has changed. this must not happen. miss must be stopped...if she can be. look to the light that calls the rest of the world. the sun is on high with the big h. see it to the end. the big fade out. watch out for everyone & everything & take care. alone we die. together we live.
—daffy duck

Sent less than one hour ago

Jackie sees the pattern. Bolded letters. She takes out her notebook and writes the extra letters in the order they appear. Part of her wishes she could grab a copy of the Don Thom David book from the bookstore on the other side of the food court and find and rearrange all the bolded letters and finally figure out the message hidden in that book. Austin looks up from the screenplay, suspicious. She turns the notebook to him:

FAEA

She points to each of the letters and says, "First. Annual. Entertainment. Awards."

He says, "Oh...shit...I saw something about that on TV. You think that's..."

"Yeah. It'll happen there. If you get around to reading that, you'll see what I mean."

"So what? Are we supposed to watch or go there? Warn someone? Who do we warn?"

"What does it mean *Find the truth of W*? Are they talking about Wolpe?"

"Not Wolpe. Wade. He's a friend who died in the same way my brother died."

"So not dead."

He pulls a small black journal from the back of his pants. Yes, it's been there the entire time. It's all bent, tattered. He says, "I found this in his room. It's got all this stuff about black holes and artificial intelligences and particle accelerators and God particles and all this stuff I can't understand. He says this thing: *if an A.I. could create a story, what would that story look like?*"

"Artificial."

"Or maybe it would have everything, take from everything on the network and put it all together. A mashup of all the things we find important and useless. It wouldn't know what to leave in or take out."

"Sunflower?" She points to the journal.

"Yeah, it's in there."

"And that? What do you know about that?" She points at a toilet that looks like it's made of diamonds, handle made of gold, wires and circuitry connecting the seat computer to the tank monitor. A sign above it: *Luxury Model: Sunflower Sit-Down—$3599.99*. Austin lets out a laugh that's more like a scoff.

He says, "It's everywhere now. Names, pictures, urns. Tell me: have you see any other kind of flower since this started for you?"

She doesn't mention the sunflowers in her parents' room. But Austin sees it on her face, hold out his hands and raises his eyebrows like *See?*

Jackie says, "That's how obsessions work."

"It might be more than that. What if us being aware of it awoke something? Here, look."

He tosses Wade's journal her way and Jackie catches it.

Inside's filled with the same recurring vocabulary: *wolpe sunflower miss destruction mars black holes*. There's more, but those words stick out to her. Tucked into the back, a postcard. She looks at it. The Hollywood sign with a castle where it shouldn't be. Superimposed. It takes her a minute, but her mind kicks in and thanks to Charles Foster Kane she realizes what the castle is. Any disciple of Old California would. But she doesn't tell Austin. She flips the postcard over. More of the same recurring words.

"Tell me about Wade. Why would he be involved with this?"

"He shouldn't be. That's what's got me confused: why?"

A vulnerability comes over him. He wears it like a second skin. Jackie sees this shift in his demeanor. A part of him relaxes, but he's still stiff, still closed to her.

She says, "I have a sister. I miss her, don't know what it would be like to put her to rest and then see her reappear. She's not dead, but she might as well be. She's up in the space station. Has been for… Three, maybe four years."

"Your sister is Amy Day?"

Jackie nods. Seeing the way Austin's face can't quite believe what Jackie's said, that she's connected to someone the world knows and has a backseat admiration for, makes her feel a little weird. She's never had to consider how famous her sister is to those that know about her.

"I've watched her livestream before. That's far out…forgive the pun."

"You have to live with making it. I don't."

Austin smiles a little. He stands, wanders over to the cardboard cutout of his dad. Jackie can't tell if he's doing this with a sense of pride or hate or not feeling anything at all.

Given the nature he's let her observe, she thinks it's probably nothing at all. He brushes at the mark the cigarette made on his dad's face.

He says, "Wade saved my life once. We were punks. Skaters. Losers, really. We fucking *hated* living where we lived. Wade always wanted to be famous, to be someone else. One day we were trying to run away. Packed backpacks with food and shirts. I brought some books Bowie Lee gave me. This was after he left. We both stole money from our parents. Like $100. Not enough to live, but we didn't care. We believed we would make it wherever we ended up. We lived near train tracks so we were gonna hop on a train and just ride. Wade got on. I didn't. I slipped, smacked my head on a rock. Even though I was twice his weight, he carried me almost a mile back to his house, called an ambulance. EMTs said if he hadn't, my brain would've swelled up and bubbled out of the crack in my skull. He saved my life. I've always owed him that. And I didn't pay up."

She says, "You love him." Jackie sees it on his face, the way he talks about Wade. Maybe not a sexual love, but a pure, undeniable love. A connection of two like souls, inseparable though separated. Or maybe it is a sexual love.

"I do. Did."

"You do."

Jackie can see by saying this a repressed part of his head lifts its heavy burden from his heart. Those could be tears in his eyes, but she doesn't want to look too close and spoil whatever's happening inside him. Nothing about what they've been doing is easy or feel-good. Anything to break up the pain and confusion. She turns her gaze to the shoppers outside the store, consumers who continue to ignore the toilet store. She thinks about how if she and Amy were walking around the mall, they'd probably browse Foster's Royal Flush for laughs. Just thinking Amy's name reminds Jackie of the hollow place inside her. But her thoughts are severed, her breath stolen. She's frozen, anxiety shooting through her like a hot shot of dope. To believe she sees what she's seeing is to accept madness, and yet she sees him.

The blind man.

The one who started this existential fuckery. Outside the store, feeling his way with a segmented cane, tennis-ball-covered tip bouncing along the tiled floor, crowds parting around him, avoiding his disability, his blindness, his otherness, as if it's contagious—just like they did at the theater. *What are the fucking chances*, she asks herself. Why here and now and what are the fucking chances? Jackie feels herself slipping again, the pressure returning, the sense of hope stubbed out and stepped on. The blind man with the brown skin, the cloudy eyes, and the clothes that look fished from a dumpster feels his way around a corner and is gone.

Jackie's up, grabs the screenplay from Austin's hand. She runs, shoves the screenplay in her bag as she slams her way through the doors that she's pretty sure Austin locked and out into the mall. She shoves past shoppers. Austin shouts *Jackie* and *Wait up*, but she keeps going, knowing that he will catch up—or won't.

She rounds the corner as the blind man reaches the peak of an escalator and glides out of sight. Jackie moves instinctually, shutting her mind down to only the base process commands: *follow* and *faster*. Shoppers focus on Jackie's face as she runs past, searching for any hint of threat but instead only seeing a woman in a fit of hysterics. She makes it to the escalator and tries to take the moving steps two at a time, but there's too many people, tightly grouped, each holding bulky shopping bags. She rides up and looks back for any sign of Austin. Nothing. She's on her own.

On the second floor: she struggles against consumer currents, drifting with a sense of impossible loss. She thinks she sees the blind man easing into a coffee shop, but when she gets there, he's gone. A ghost.

Then he's there. Pressed against the glass of an elevator as it leaves the fourth floor, descending toward her. Cane gripped in his hands monk-like. She waits, not rushing forward or away, staying within distance of both the elevator and the escalator, anticipating the blind man's level of departure, just in case he passes the third and second— Yep, that's what he does. *Shit*, Jackie says as she watches the elevator pass the second floor and head for the first. She rushes back to the set of escalators that's further than she remembers. She takes stairs two at a time, hits the first floor, sees the elevator, now empty, doors just now sandwiching shut. He's gone.

Someone behind her whispers *That's her* and Jackie spins around to see surprised and almost-frightened faces staring back.

Jackie spins around and sprints in the only direction she thinks is true, heads into a department store, first thing elevator riders would see after their cross-level journey. As Jackie passes under the Macy's sign, she notices for the first time just how much the apostrophe that looks like a star actually looks more like a flower.

"Miss, can I help you find something?" says a clerk who materializes out of a cloud of perfumed toxicity.

"Shut up," says Jackie, because she wants the world to shut

up. She launches through a set of doors leading out to the parking lot.

Outside now, wandering, knowing she'll never find him. *Because he was never there* she tells herself. *And that screenplay I've been carrying around? Maybe I wrote it and that's the twist of this whole thing. Or it's a prop. Fake. Nothing more.* But no, that can't be true. That's the type of schlock Hollywood pumps out to feed post-9/11 paranoia. Nothing is real. Paranoia. Paranoia. Blah blah blah.

The sound of a distant siren comes with the wind.

Jackie reaches the edge of the parking lot, steps across crunchy grass, and ends up on a sidewalk where people stand waiting for the next city bus—five or six tired stand-ins. The street is busy with fast-moving cars. The siren grows louder, closer. None of those waiting for the bus are her blind man, just average people unaware of the jungle gone wild in Jackie's brain. She looks up and down the palm-lined street, neon lights illuminating places that have gone dark inside. The sky's dark behind the haze of city lights, pale gauze of smog curtains over everything. Like an approaching drone strike, the whine of the siren is suddenly there, powerful, ear-splittingly loud. And then it happens.

As soon as the ambulance comes into view, lights flashing, siren screaming like a huge, hideously deformed baby, there's a *bang-pop* that seems far too loud to be the sudden puncture of the right front tire, but that's what happens. The tire blows, shifting the speeding ambulance into a wild zig-zagging pattern, the driver over-correcting, correcting, attempting to keep it upright. But it all goes wrong. The ambulance skids sideways, then it's on two wheels, then none. A collective gasp from the bus-waiters as the ambulance leaves the road, airborne. There's a moment when it all seems to freeze and Jackie thinks that the bang of the tire sounded more like a gun, and that the blind man had led her here to see this. This was meant for her, at this place, at this time. All planned. Then the ambulance returns to the road, tumbling, taking chunks out of the pavement, sparks and glass exploding in star-patterned trajectories. It rolls once, twice, three times, past Jackie and lands on its side, grinds to a stop, windshield chunks bouncing off Jackie's scuffed, black boots. All the bus-waiters pull out their phones, but none call for help. They put them at eye level and film the scene as it unfolds. A crowd's already gathering, rubberneckers who always seem destined to manifest at the sight of an accident: the lady bouncing her baby, the burnouts with gaping mouths, the suited guy with greasy hair who looks around nervously like he's just done something wrong, the mom or dad who cry because they can envision their child in the accident, the laughers, the gawkers, the stand-ins. The same crowd everywhere. Muffled screams come from the beached ambulance. The back door slams open and one of the paramedics stumbles out, blood oozing from her ears, cut the fuck up, her expression distant and lost. Concussed. "I need Gatorade," she says. "Can I have a pillow or something," and then stumbles over to the curb and crumples to a heap of vibrating flesh. People gather around her to film at closer angles, some becoming impromptu interviewers with questions like *Are you okay?* and *What would you like us to do?* and *What are we eating for dinner?* Someone says *I'm gonna call an ambulance. Well...another ambulance*, but no one calls for help.

"What happened to you, Jackie?"

Jackie almost jumps as Austin sidles up next to her, his fingers dialing 9-1-1.

"The blind man..." but she can't finish. She finds herself inching closer to the ambulance, to the open door in the back. Fluorescent light flickers, casts a convulsing box on the scarred pavement. All she can hear is the beat of her heart as it runs blood through her brain. Floating like a ghost toward the ambulance, toward the open door. And she can see inside. Two bodies. One in an upside-down, supine position, arms and legs destroyed, severed at crooked angles. Blood running in rivulets that obscure the face. But she can see by the outfit that it's one of the EMTs. Dead. That's not what makes her numb. Not what has her in a grip that's irrational and searing. It's the second body, dead. Face frozen in a grimace of pain. Skin pale. No blood. Eyes looking up at stars it can no longer see, stars that don't exist to the dead.

"Jackie, what is it?" Austin says from behind her.

She doesn't answer. Can't. Can't do anything but stare. This can only mean that something beyond her control *is* in control of the world beyond her. Because in the ambulance, now dead, lies the body of pop-cultural archivist H.I. Budrow. Jackie, returning to the moment, thinks of the bang that was too loud to be a tire. She thinks of *Cutting Room* and the footage of the grassy knoll gunman. She thinks of de Palma's *Blow Out*. Neither of these movies end well. She turns to Austin.

"I think this is going to take more from us than we're willing to give."

And he just looks at her. Never agreeing. But he never disagrees.

Sent less than an hour ago

<u>DELETED SCENE</u>

Fat Tax

2

THE PEOPLE IN BLACK SUITS HAVE RESORTED *to twisting his nipples, giving him wedgies, slicing paper cuts between his fingers and toes. Not the soul-punishing torture they've been doing, but still torture. They don't want to damage him too much. Austin remembers telling them that he knows how this is going to end and how he can help stop it, reminds them of that before they destroy parts of him that would be obvious and not easily disguised. They say they still want to use him. They wrap a towel around his head, tilt him back, empty a four gallon jug of hot water on his face. He gags, pukes up water and bile that runs through the towel and coats his face. They pull the sutures out of his hand, reopen the wound with sharp tweezers. Peel skin away from flesh and bone. They strip him down, tie him to a different chair where a hole's been cut in the seat, and use a heavy nautical rope to smash his genitals from underneath. He's pretty sure the technique was in a James Bond movie, but it hurts anyway. The black suits tell him to* Hurry up and finish *so they can figure out how they can use him next—or get rid of him. Austin tells them he's almost done, that they're almost all caught up. They put a hot plate under the seatless chair and turn it on high. Heat radiates towards Austin's exposed anus as he starts with the endings.*

JACKIE'S GOT THE BIKE going about a hundred miles an hour going down the 101. Austin sits in her sidecar. She's trying to talk to him but the wind slaps words away before he can hear them. So he just nods at whatever she's saying. She keeps looking over her shoulder. Austin looks back, but there's nothing there. For a second he thinks he sees the ice cream truck, but shakes it off, knows it's just paranoid thinking he doesn't need. But Jackie seems on edge, like she sees her own metaphorical ice cream truck and can't shake it off.

He should've known, should've put it together, her being a projectionist and all. But when they pull up to Cinéma Vérité, he can't believe the way their trajectories have come together like this. He looks up at the SunCor billboard on the roof, the one Jean told him about. The one Jackie says she's never noticed until just now, looks at it like a ghost that's just showed up while she's on the toilet. Cinéma Vérité—his theater. Austin restrains the need to tell her, to be transparent about this. Not now. But he *will* tell her.

Theater workers stare as Jackie and Austin walk across the lobby, most of them with faces that wonder *Who the hell are these people?* Austin follows Jackie down hallways straight out of *The Shining*, into an elevator that should've been decommissioned during the Nixon administration. Jackie's silent, hasn't said anything since the 101. She seems determined and Austin's just letting things happen around him. So he follows.

She takes Austin up to the room with all the projectors, which he notices is also her room. There's a sign on the wall that reads *Trespassers Will Be Shot* above a picture of a camera.

A hipster sits on a milk crate next to the projectors. He reminds Austin of the Zig-Zag man. The kind of guy who talks about Max Ophüls and Agnes Varda but couldn't name one of their films. Not that Austin could either, but he's definitely not trying to play the part. The hipster's reading a book—*In the Realm of Lost Things*. Same book Jean had. Jackie snatches it out of his hand.

"Where the hell did you get this?"

Hipster says, "I brought it with me. It's mine."

"Not anymore it's not. And what're you doing with my projectors?"

"I'm letting them run. Joel said I could—"

"You don't just *let them run*. Listen: this is why you'll never be up here. You'll stay down in the—"

"Joel came up here. Saw you were gone. Said I was the new assistant projectionist."

"Like hell."

"Sorry. You weren't here so I—"

Austin jerks his body at the hipster and almost shouts, "Hey, pal. You're not an assistant of anything anymore. Get out. You're done."

"Whatever, chubby. You can't make me do shit."

"I own this theater, sport. So why don't you stop picking your nose for dinner and get the fuck out of here."

"Picking my nose for dinner?"

"It means you're a shitass moron."

"Who the fuck are you?"

"Austin Foster. As in the Austin Foster who owns this place."

"Bull. Shit."

Jackie says, "Enough. Get out, Nietzsche!" She smacks the

living hell out of him with the book. Chases him out the door. Just before he's gone, she plants her foot on his ass and shoves. The chaotic noise of him tumbling down the stairs sounds like it belongs in a cartoon.

Austin sits in a nearby armchair as Jackie hurries around the projectors, panicked, trying to repair whatever damage the hipster did. He tries to ignore the way she talks to the projectors, but it's too honest to discredit as crazy. Like she's trying to console a heartbroken friend.

Jackie says, "Did you see that ice cream truck following us on the freeway?"

"Ice cream truck?"

"It's the second time I've seen it in two days."

Even though Austin didn't see it, he believes it was there. He doesn't mention that he's seen an ice cream truck because how many ice cream trucks are there in the city? Plus, he's not really sure how much he should share with her. At least other than this:

"So…uh…I hate to do this, but…you should probably know something I know you're not going to like."

"You're going to kill me."

"What? God, no. Not at all."

"Then I think I can handle it."

Austin hesitates, but that only makes it worse. He says, "I wasn't joking with Linus or whatever that goober's name was. I really do own this theater. Technically, my dad does. But he gave it to me."

Jackie laughs, the kind of exhausted sound that happens when people find out that the cancer they've had for a decade is finally gone but a brain tumor has recently developed and will kill them in about fifteen minutes. Austin does his best to smile, but it feels more like a cringe. She says, "The toilet guy gave you a movie theater. He's the one letting me show the good stuff, isn't he?"

"I'm sure he is. You've never met him?"

"We've only talked on the phone. Kept putting me on hold."

"Sounds like him. But yeah, he prefers the old films. We were here the other day. Watched *Cutting Room*."

"What day?"

"Two days ago." And then Austin realizes it at the same time as Jackie, the two arriving at an intersection at the same time, neither knowing who should go first. So they don't speak. But two days ago… The day she got the screenplay.

Jackie smacks the Don Thom David book against her thigh. Says, "You know the bolded letters in that email you got? Check this out."

She tosses the book at Austin. He flips it open to the middle, eases through the pages one at a time. Bolded letters on each page. One here, two on the next. And so on.

Jackie, "See if you can put some of those together."

Austin, "I don't want to do this. It doesn't have anything to do with what we're doing."

"Maybe. Maybe it does. That guy, in that ambulance…"

"The dead one."

"Yes, the dead one. He showed me that. Said there were important things in it. He also showed me you and your brother at the Hollywood sign. Highjacked a drone."

"That was you?"

"That was him."

"So what do the letters here say?"

"Figure it out."

"We not gonna talk about how I own this place?"

"We don't need to. It just confirms how little we have a say in what we're doing."

"We could leave here, go our separate directions, and not think another thought about this. Drive until the light from this town isn't any brighter than the furthest star. End up in Texas where nothing ever happens."

The look that takes over Jackie's face tells him everything about how untrue what he just said is. She says, "I couldn't do that. Not this far in. We're rolling downhill."

She opens a drawer in a table underneath shelves lined with film cans. She pulls out a vintage switchblade, pearl handle, and with a *snick* opens the blade, atom-splittingly sharp, glinting off a light that isn't there. *Shwip* and the blade retracts. Jackie shoves it in the inner pocket of a leather jacket Austin hasn't yet seen her shed. "There's a phone down in the lobby. Gotta make a call."

"You plan on needing that?" He motions to the blade.

"If I do, I want it. And if I'm not back in ten minutes, assume the worst."

"What should I do?"

"Try that running away thing you talked about earlier." She slides out, smooth and confident, and he's left in a solitary silence.

Austin gets up from the chair and wanders from the area with all the projectors to her bedroom. A bed on the floor, overturned milk crate for a table, a *Cutting Room* poster on the wall—the lead standing in a leather jacket like Jackie's, with a switchblade in her hand, again like Jackie's. It doesn't look like someone lives here full time, more like a place someone naps in while they work long shifts. Maybe that's what Jackie's life is:

one long shift.

Above the bed, a circular window that looks like it should be in a boat looks down on the lobby. There's a note taped to the wall beneath the window. Austin reads it.

Even if you're going away forever you don't leave behind a broken memory.

Austin doesn't pretend to understand what that means. It's signed *Amy* and he realizes it's a note from the space station. It annoys him that Jackie spoke about her sister like she's dead to try and connect with Austin about his brother and Wade. Here she is, getting notes from her. Someday, Amy will return and the two sisters will be together. Probably. But like, that's not the case with—

Thump.

Somewhere close. Maybe the door.

He says, "You back?"

Nothing. He looks out the porthole window and sees Jackie behind the counter, talking on the phone. So then maybe the hipster guy's back. Or maybe Jackie works with someone else. But given the way she was with the hipster guy, Austin doesn't believe it. She doesn't seem like the kind to just let people wander in and out of her space. Austin's doing everything he can to rationalize anything but—

Thump.

Austin smells perfume he knows Jackie isn't wearing. Another thump. From inside the bedroom. Hangers rattle. Light slips from under a closet across the room. Shadowy movements on the other side.

"Jackie…?" even though he knows it's not her.

The woman that steps out of the closet definitely isn't Jackie. Young, face like a Russian model. Flowing hair a rich amber color. In a hand coated in a tight, red glove is a hammer of some kind, a real nasty looking thing. Hatchet on one side, big, fat hammer on the other. She holds it so delicately, so perfectly, that it doesn't look like it'll hurt one bit.

"So how do we get out of this situation without it turning into some over-dramatic sequence of violence and action?" Austin doesn't know why he's asking her something that sounds straight from a bad movie, but it's just what comes out.

"Austin, you've always wanted to not act, to not be anything, so why would you start acting now? The way around this getting violent is if you just let this happen. Because it's going to happen. So just give in to that self you've always tried to be. Have a seat and relax."

He's not surprised she knows his name. He can't help but think about how beautiful she is, despite her intentions to kill him. He instinctively moves toward the screenplay pages and Wade's journal as if he's trying to protect it from her.

"Uh, so, uh, what're we doing here? Are you gonna smash me in the head? Is that what that's for?"

"Something like that."

"And there's no way I can convince you otherwise, right?"

"Nope. Not my choice. This come from Miss herself."

She reaches into the closet, pull out a noose.

"You gonna use that on me? Make it look like a suicide?"

"Oh no. This is for you." She holds up the hatchet-hammer. "This was already in here. I think it's Jackie's. Maybe she had plans to kill herself. I'd say you should talk to her about it, but you know…"

"Not my business."

"That, and I'm going to smash your head in and all that."

She takes a step toward Austin.

"Wait a second. Wait. Seeing as how you're about to kill me, I feel like I need some kind of closure. I've been part of this story somewhat from the beginning, so I feel like I need to know how or why it's going to end the way it will. What...What's Sunflower? Can you tell me that at least?"

"Let's just say it's a means, a gateway into the next iteration of human existence. A release from the shackles placed on us by a fascist regime that's dominated our lives for millennia."

"Yes, I get that. But what the fuck is it?"

"It's an event."

"And it has something to do with the Entertainment Awards, doesn't it? Some kind of, I don't know, terrorist attack or something?"

"What does this world hold more dear than the status of celebrity? What do humans turn to in order to free themselves from the binds of existence? Entertainment has become the new religion. It has turned us into a beast race, frothing at the mouth for a chance to be known, remembered, seen, respected, to be famous. But it takes away our awareness of self, destroys our will to be what we want, mainly because it forces the idea that all we should hope to achieve in this life is to stand on the Pedestal of Fame and make money and embrace the denial of introspection that comes with that fame. It is the downfall."

"Don't you think what you're saying, your plan to trick the future into following your path, isn't that sort of, uh, like, fascist? Not to make the lady with the hammer-axe-thing mad, but this Sunflower thing smells like bullshit to me."

She shrugs. "It's not my place to convince you. It is the way, the Plot, and it will happen. Questioning or doubting it is like doubting the fact that you, I, and everyone else on this planet will be recycled—some sooner than others. But it is certain. And this, the Plot, is certain."

She slinks toward Austin, sexy in her determination to bash his skull in with a hammer-hatchet thing.

"So then what's the point in killing me? If it's a sure thing, if there's nothing I or Jackie—if she's still alive—can do to stop it, then why kill me? Seems a little redundant."

"I Must Abide, Austin. The will of Miss is all that is. And what Miss says, I Must Abide. Miss is absolute logic. While you may not be able to stop the plan, Miss wishes that I terminate your involvement. So I Must—"

"Abide. Yeah, I got it."

And then there's an eruption from the lobby. The building vibrates. Austin stumbles a bit. A chaotic mess of metal and glass. And someone screams. A bomb, a crash. Something horrible happening downstairs—a planned attack.

Austin says, "What did you do?"

"Took care of half the problem."

Austin feels her breath on his neck, can't believe how close she is now. Never heard her footsteps. As if she floated to him, moving only when he blinked. Closer now, the hatchet-hammer thing looks rusted, or maybe that's dried blood.

Austin says, "Do you know someone named Daffy Duck?"

She swings the axe side at Austin. In defensive shock, he puts up his right hand to block his face. The blade slices through three fingers—pinky, ring, middle. They separate from his hand. Austin's fingers landing somewhere across the room sound like a handful of tossed dice hitting a felt-covered table, like someone dropped a couple of chicken wings off their plate.

The unexpected ease of hitting fingers and not the thickness of Austin's skull causes her swing to go wild. She spins around and lands on the bed, face up, bloody axe-thing at her side. The springiness of the bed bounces her back on her feet and as she rears back to come at Austin a second time, he hears a familiar *snick* that the red-gloved assassin doesn't.

A blur of movement and then it all comes to a jarring halt, like a crash test. Except instead of a smashed car, it's the pearl handle of Jackie's knife sticking out of the red-gloved woman's temple. Her mouth clicks, eyes roll up. She looks like she's trying to pray forgiveness to Miss for not abiding as she promised, swore, pledged. And then she's dead. Just like that. Dead. But she doesn't fall. She stands there, swooning like she's about to topple, but never does.

A psychotically-different, animalistic, wholly-changed version of Jackie stands there, breathing heavy. Unable to take her eyes off the woman she's just killed.

"You okay." Not a question. And she's not looking at him.

"I'm alive."

Austin hasn't yet noticed the pain of having three missing fingers. Almost feels like they're still there. What he does notice is the way Jackie holds her arm, and the blood coming down the side of her head, matting hair into clotted chunks.

He says, "Your head."

"Forget it. Here," and she tosses a towel and some masking tape. "For your," and then she wiggles her fingers at him.

Austin puts the towel over stumps pumping syrupy blood down his arm and onto the floor. Not a Giallo red, but a deep, almost-black crimson. He wraps so much tape around it that his hand feels more like a rock than a hand.

Jackie grabs the screenplay pages, the journal, and a few other items around her little room, including a yellow can of something Austin can't see. She shoves it all into a bag, then reaches up and slips the knife out of the assassin's head, wipes the stained blade on the assassin's black dress. The assassin still stands, wobbling on weakening legs. Austin isn't interested in sticking around to wait for her to finally collapse.

Jackie takes a moment to carefully peel the handwritten note off the wall. She gently folds it, holds it like a newborn, then slides it into the inner pocket of her leather jacket. She pats that place, then turns to Austin.

"We're getting the fuck out of here."

And that's what they do.

<u>DELETED SCENE</u>

George

3

THEY SPEND THE NIGHT IN A MOTEL off the highway, somewhere between LA and Santa Barbara. Jackie hides her bike behind a dumpster—which isn't that different from the room they stay in: crusty mold, greasy carpet, bathtub full of rat turds, slime in the ice machine.

Austin gives her the story of what happened in her bedroom, everything up until Jackie killed the woman in the red gloves. Jackie doesn't like the fondness Austin seems to have for the woman who tried to kill him. Like he sympathizes with her and the principles of the Sunflower people. Almost like he knows her and laments her doomed nature. Almost like they have some kind of shared history that he won't acknowledge or maybe doesn't remember.

Austin tries to stay awake while Jackie tells him about the phone call with Spapling. She should have known when he asked *Where are you?* that they should've left, that Spapling was full of shit. She tells Austin about how the call was interrupted by a car smashing through the Cinéma Vérité lobby, how a massive, bull-like woman eased out of the car and lunged at Jackie, tried to strangle her, and how Jackie escaped by yanking out the nose ring the woman had through her septum. She grabbed a nearby beer glass and smashed it over the woman's head. Blood and glass splattered all over her. The massive woman went out like a bad projector bulb. Jackie realizes now in her retelling of this story to Austin that Spapling was only meant to keep her on the phone long enough for the assassin to come put a period on her life sentence.

Austin passes out, cradling the hand missing fingers. Jackie stays awake, never takes her eyes off the hotel door. Or Austin.

MORNING BLOOMS SLOWLY. A fade from hotel night to Santa Barbara dawn.

Jackie enters her five-digit code into the black-iron gate at the Santa Barbara Monitored Existence Community for the Advancedly Lived, listening to the thrum of the desalination plant as they wait for the code to not fail (like she's half expecting it to) and for the gate to creak open. The burnt-hairdryer, tangy iodine smell from the plant oppressively overwhelms the calming properties of her bike's exhaust.

Austin says, "Christ, that stinks."

"The plant exhaust or the bike?"

"I can't tell the difference."

Jackie doesn't say anything.

"Is this like an old folks home?"

"Yes."

"What are we doing here?"

"Seeing about some old folks."

The gate opens and Jackie throttles back. The bike bites and jumps forward. They park and hurry inside, Jackie looking back as the gate shuts. She feels a fleeting since of security knowing that there's at least that much between them and They.

Even though Jackie no longer has to check in due to her

having registered her facial patterns with the guest clearance systems, she has to work hard to convince the front-desk autonurse, a second front-desk autonurse, the Head Autonurse, an on-call autodoc, a biotech security guard who, after 20 minutes of describing a fake lineage of relation between herself and Austin, makes a call to the facility's owners before Austin is granted access. They pass through the first set of coded doors and into a hothouse of spoiled gasses and a silence so stout both Jackie and Austin can feel it like a phantom at their backs.

One of the autonurses focuses its facial camera on Austin's wounded hand and says, "A nurse will be along to help you with that."

Austin says, "Oh... Uh... Thanks. It's not—"

But before he can finish, the autonurse rolls away. Jackie leads Austin to her parents' room.

"Who the fuck would put their parents in a place like this? I mean, I don't like my parents that much but would never put them—"

"Do me a favor and shut the fuck up."

"No, Jackie, listen: that's not directed at you. I mean, honestly, we all end up in places like this, whether it's external or in our heads. And I have no idea what it's like to experience that first hand. So my question wasn't an attack. More like curiosity. Worry maybe. There are times, despite my desperation to escape emotions and feelings, that I think of having to put my parents in a place like this. Or ending up here myself."

"There are worse places to end up than here. Like back in my bedroom with your fingers."

"That's debatable."

"So then debate it. Don't just declare its debatability. But not now. We're here."

Despite it being a time when they usually take a mid-day nap, her parents are awake, sitting in front of the television just as they always are. Her father sits erectly in his chair, reading a book that seems, to her, far too advanced for a man who primarily invests his time in picture books about war. The title's almost too long to fit on the spine: *Marx's Kapital: Critique of Political Economy and Its Influence on North Korea's People's Army During the Great Fault Separation & After.* He's deep into the text, eyes bulging as if he hasn't slept in days and is up to his heart in life-changing philosophy, the developments causing, at this late stage in his life, a sense of deep gut pain and nerve-numbing guilt. He seems to chuckle under his breath, but there's no humor in it. Jackie's mother is drawing, her fingertips black from the charcoal. Her hands move fast, not the usual sluggish, careful pace Jackie's seen for the last ten years.

The television plays something Jackie never expected to see: a home movie of her and Amy. Two children playing in the driveway. Amy soaring around like a jet or spaceship. Jackie looking up at something only her imagination sees on the roof of the house, shouting *You get down from there.* Whoever's filming, probably Jackie's dad, zooms in on Amy. Amy approaches the camera, puts her eye right up to the lens and says—

"Is that your eyeball in there?" Jackie says this in unison with the Amy in the home movie.

Tears threaten to fall from Jackie's eyes, but she doesn't want Austin to see them. So she looks away from the home movie. Steps in front of the TV.

Her father notices her and says, "Twice in the same week.

We must be dying."

Jackie can't remember the last time her father was clear enough to know when or if she ever visited. They still think Amy'll be walking through the door any day now, even though she's on an indefinite contract above the earth. Not as distant and permanent as those on their way to Mars, but to Jackie's parents, the permanence of not seeing their daughter is just as relevant. To them, their daughter could be on her way to Mars, as it is highly probable that they will never see her again, their deaths coming sooner than Amy's return to the local atmosphere.

"And who's this fella you bought with ya? You ain't a communist, are ya?"

"Can't say I know enough about communists to claim to be one."

"Damned fool system. Just doesn't work. Strips a man of all his freedoms. Takes away all opportunities to enjoy himself. Democracy is the only true freedom. You got that sort of sloppy look that them communists have."

"Sir, not to be difficult, but when I'm standing in the grocery store in front of all the cereals, seeing the cartoon covers of over two hundred different variations of the same product, I kinda wish someone would just shove a box that says CEREAL in my hand and tell me to eat. Too much choice tends to strip a man of all his freedoms."

"Don't be a goddamn fool! Jackie, who is this clown?"

"Dad, calm down. This is Austin. He's helping me with something."

"You two aren't together, are you?"

Jackie and Austin look at each other like siblings that've just been asked if they are casually fucking.

Jackie: "Hell no."

Austin: "No way."

"This goddamn moron thinks capitalism makes for misery, and that having rich people and poor people is a sin."

"Dad, would it..." And then she stops. As most children who feel they aren't doing enough for their parents as their years advance and their time on Earth dwindles, Jackie feels like a shitty daughter. Whether they know that she's using her parents' room in a living facility as a place of solace against a dangerous group, involving them in a tangled game that could lead to their earlier-than-expected second-hand death, whether they know or not, Jackie knows. And her knowledge is what creates the emotions in her heart, the guilt and the fear and the self-loathing. So she says, "Is there anything we can do for you, dad? While we're here and everything? Are they taking care of you and mom?"

"These nurses couldn't take care of a sick slug. Half of them roll around here with their plugs trailing behind them. Can't tell who's staying here or who's working here. Don't really care much for caring for those that can't really care for themselves—even the goddamn robots."

Austin says, "You, uh, don't really seem that old. You kinda seem like you can take care of yourself. My grandpa was shitting in his pants and speaking in foreign tongues, mostly gibberish, by the time he was seventy five." Which elicits a hard *Ha!* from Jackie's father. It's in this moment that Jackie notices the vase once overflowing with sunflowers is now gone.

"Son, my teeth are touching my belt buckle. Out of this chair I'm a dog with no legs."

Austin laughs, but Jackie doesn't.

"What happened to those flowers that were here the other

day?"

"Threw those damn things away. Had bees in here, buzzing around."

"And they made noise," her mother says.

"The hell they did." To Jackie, "They did not make noise." Gives her the spinning-finger-at-the-ear, universal sign for loco, then to his wife, "Flowers don't make noise!"

"They made noise," she says again, distracted by her art.

"What kind of noise, mom?"

"Oh Christ, don't get her going."

Her mother whispers a word, repeating it with the same distracted tone. A word that comes out as a sound. Hearing it, Jackie feels a sensation in her stomach that tugs her out the room, down the halls, through the sealed doors, the gate, the town, and away to the furthest reaches of the planet. But even then, she'd still be on Earth. How she wishes, in this moment, hearing her mother whisper *Missssss Missssss* over and over, to be with her sister or with the volunteers on their way to a new frontier and escape all this.

"Ah, shit..." Austin says as he falls back on his ass on the bed. He holds the screenplay and the journal to his chest, caressing the place his fingers once were.

"That's what I said," says Jackie's father.

"Miss. Jackie, that assassin...She mentioned Miss, said she's the one calling all the shots with...you know. And it's not just that. In here," holding up the screenplay, "there's a character named Miss who says a lot of ominous stuff about destroying the entertainment industry and teachings at the sun and paths outside our space. And that assassin, she also told me something about Sunflower, that it's the next iteration of human existence. Direct quote."

"Teaching at the sun. Spapling. That fucker."

"Huh?"

"Just a sonofabitch who acts like he doesn't know what's going on, but now I'm thinking he does." She thinks back to the phone call, just before the car crashed through the lobby and the big bitch came at her like a runaway train. Spapling had said *Stay where you are. Don't come here tonight. Just stay right there* because he knew the Plot. "Shit..."

"That's what I said," says Jackie's father.

"You know, it's occurred to me just now, sitting here, with the time and comfort to think, going over all this Wolpe stuff and following the leads to all your clues: I haven't done anything for Wade."

"Wade's dead," says Jackie, half-focusing on Austin, the distracted part of her brain allowing the cruel truth to slip through.

"Even if that's true...I feel like...I should do something."

"For him or for you?"

"Does it matter?"

"Does any of this?"

"I want to say something about life being like a big wading pool that's also a toilet waiting to be flushed...or something like that."

"Don't let me stop you."

An autonurse rolls in, uninvited. It carries a surgical case and rolls up quickly toward Austin. Stops so aggressively close that Austin flinches.

It says, "Hello. I am here to fix your hand."

And it strips away his makeshift bandage, not waiting for his consent, taking skin with the tape. Austin screams.

With Austin distracted by this impromptu surgery, Jackie

slinks over to the safe. Enters the code and opens it, checking to make sure no one sees her take the screenplay out and put it in her rucksack. The autonurse spins it's facial camera at her while it continues to suture and bandage Austin's hand. Jackie flips it off and shuts the safe.

The autonurse injects Austin with something.

He says, "That ain't gonna work."

The autonurse says, "Your hand is now fixed. It was good to see you again, Mr. Foster."

Jackie stops. At no point was Austin's last name given.

Austin says, "What?"

The autonurse rolls out of the room.

Jackie says, "Good to see you again?"

"I have no idea what that thing's talking about."

"You ever been here?"

Austin gives Jackie an *Are you seriously asking me that?* kind of look. Jackie nods—not an approval, but a resignation.

Jackie looks at her parents. Her mother draws an elegant form drawing of a woman dancing, a thought that's likely been imprisoned by her deteriorating mind. Her father chuckles at a passage in a book without pictures. But there's nothing changed about them. Maybe the knowing that their life is almost over, that there's nothing they can do about it, and that whatever waits for them—be it something or nothing at all—creates a sense of youthful liberation. A chance to be true to what they once were before the thoughts and fears of imminent death controlled their every moment.

She realizes that Austin's been watching her think these things, likely probing her mind with his ability to somehow just know shit. Let him know everything. It won't stop anything. She takes a deep breath and lets out a barely audible,

"Shit."

"That's what I said," says her father, even though she said it no louder than a whisper and he wouldn't hear a grenade if it went off behind his chair, remember?

A DENSE FOG SETTLES over the Sun State campus as Jackie and Austin walk toward the domed building Jackie hoped to never visit again, but knew she'd have to. The fog makes it seem like they're the only two on campus. It also keeps her from seeing what's coming—if anything is. Thinking here about the Sunflower chanting guy with the two ears on one side and the rifle. How many more are like him out there?

Austin says, "This place has an L. Ron Hubbard building?"

"Does that surprise you?" She doesn't know why she's antagonizing him. Maybe it has something to do with her distrust, that she believes he might have more to do with the plot than he let on. Why would the autonurses says *Good to see you again*? If it's not true, she's pushing away the only person who has the ability to help, to be with her on the outside. Taking that chance might not be worth it. But isn't this what enemies do to allies? Especially in movies?

"What surprises me is what I think you've got going on in your head. You're wrong. You've got something—maybe someone, this Spapling or whatever—telling you that I'm working on a different system than you. But I'm not. I'm not your enemy, Jackie. I can't account for the coincidences that have put me in with this shit—"

"I could ask *why*, but that word's lost all meaning. Answers only lead to more questions. So there's nothing I can do, or that you can do, that can change how I feel other than to just ignore it and trust you. But I'm not sure I can. And I don't know why."

"You can. Because, look, I'm not as desperate for answers as you. I don't like being manipulated and shit. I'm, uh, kinda loathing it, to be honest. And so if working with you, finding your answers, finding Wade—whether he's really alive or dead —and all that, if that gives me a way out of this being pushed around like pieces in a game I don't wanna play, that's what I'm willing to do. So you can trust me. Cuz I'm here to work with you. I mean, *look*." He holds up his hand, fingers gone. "I'm missing some fucking fingers here."

"Cheap sacrifice."

"Fuck you, cheap sacrifice. You wanna gimme some fingers to chop off?"

Jackie flips him off.

Austin, "I started this because I wanted to find Wade. But now after last night, after this," shows her his missing fingers, "I just want to be done with this manipulation shit."

Jackie shrugs, which seems to spark new rage in Austin.

He says, "And I don't do this whole human connection thing very often. Don't care for it. But for you...I don't know. For a little bit last night I felt like you and I were connected in more ways than just this plot. Like there was a certain point of view we've been seeing, a vantage point looking out on the world. And even though we're two totally, absolutely, unquestionably opposite and therefore different people, we share something important."

"I don't know why you think that. We know nothing about each other. At no point in this time we've been together have we taken a moment to understand each other. And the only one who knows anything about both of us is the one controlling this whole thing, and whoever else is a spectator of that product. I'm a mystery to you, just as you are one to me. So I don't see how you can think that."

"You want to know something about me?"

"Not really."

"When I was fourteen, driving back from dropping my brother off at the train station—"

"I said not really."

"Too bad. Listen: We were driving back and this car passed us. A run-down, white-splotched-with-rust Buick overflowing with a family so fat none could turn their heads. So they pass us and when they do a head pops out of the backseat window, ears flopping. A basset hound. Jowls and ears and drool catching the wind. Head out, then its neck, and then before I know what's what, everything else flops out the back window. And *wham*, it hits the asphalt at like 70mph. The thing starts sliding and rolling on the highway. As we pass it, I hear its scream, like a semi slamming on its brakes. Then it's gone. Out of my life. My mom screamed *No!* and my dad tried to cover my eyes, as if I was like seven instead of fourteen. But the thing about all of it that really ate me up, changed me, metamorphosed my thinking into the person I am now—and this is why I'm telling you this—is that those people never even put on their brakes. Never looked back. As if they wanted the fucking thing to fall out. Or they pushed it."

"I'm sure that made you mad."

"No. I don't hate things."

"You don't hate."

"It's wasted energy. Those people became nothing to me."

"What about this? Don't you hate this?"

"You and I are working toward this thing that could be the

end of humanity, so I ask: would it really be such a bad thing if the entire human race ended tomorrow? I have my own motives, and of course my loyalty to you that's now been seated deep due to you saving my life and all, but, no bullshit, I would be willing to put all that aside to really get down and question the validity of human existence, to wonder if any of these people, throwing their dogs out windows, senselessly killing large groups of people, stepping on the weak for a few inches of height over everyone else, if they're at all worthy of this life. An opportunity to exist. I told my brother that things could be worse, but maybe they can't. So maybe none of us deserve this, you know, life."

"We do. If only for the movies."

"Existence hinges on the silver screen?"

"Maybe. But we do deserve this opportunity."

And even though some part of her thinks that parts of what Austin says is true, and even though she can't really defend preserving the human race, she believes that it isn't up to anyone to determine whether others deserve a chance to exist—be they shitheads or not. Planetary overpopulation or not. Resources dwindling or not. Environment on the verge of collapse or not. And even though she's done everything she can to keep herself separated from the rest of humanity, without them there, what does that make her? Not that she's obtaining her identity from others.

There's one thing, though, that makes her entirely uneasy about all this thinking: what if the end of this plot means the end of her existence? How could she ever control that? Once this is all over, where will she exist—if she exists at all. She thinks of the noose in her closet.

Spapling's office door is open, but the office is empty. She

hears banging from under the floor and knows Spapling is
down there fiddling with his tangled wires and cooling systems,
maybe watching a small screen relay of an ad-drone
somewhere, watching another unseen, unsuspecting player in
the game if he's into that part of it. Jackie reaches into her
jacket pocket and wraps her fingers around the switchblade.
Austin scans the room, passing over a glass terrarium that's all
steamed up. As Jackie walks to the middle of the floor and
stops next to the small Syrian rug, Austin drifts behind
Spapling's cluttered desk, fingering through carelessly stacked
papers and dog-eared books. Jackie stomps twice on the rug
and steps back. There's a clattering of tools from below.

"Sonofabitch!"

The rug lifts and Spapling, sucking on a swollen finger,
sticks his head above ground. When he sees it's Jackie, his face
moves, so quick that a normal person wouldn't notice. But
Jackie, who's spent most of her life waiting for cigarette burns
to blip on screen, notices the change in Spapling's face. This
withheld expression tells her she's wasting her time, that he's
been putting on a Razzie-level act that she should've been able
to see through.

Spapling, "Oh, hello. It's you."

Jackie, "You were expecting me, correct? I mean, last time
we spoke you said we could meet today about the Wolpe
results."

"Quite right. And here you are."

Though not a fan of insincerity, the smile that smears
across Jackie's face lacks even a fart of sincerity.

Spapling says, "And this is...?"

Austin gives Spapling this weird, doubtful look and says,
"Dad?"

Spapling's face scrunches up and he says, "What?"

Austin, "Nevermind."

Spapling, "You seem to have some code missing."

Jackie, "You mean you don't know this guy? Never seen him?"

"Never. And I wish he'd get the hell away from my desk. And stop touching my computer."

Austin continues to type code into Spapling's computer, flat-out ignoring the man's presence. Despite her lack of trust, or rather her uncertainty towards Austin, she can't help but think this disinterested cop act a good play on his part, a nice balance to Spapling's bad act. The sort of thing she'd see in a good-cop-bad-cop scenario. Except in this case, they're both not cops and they're both not that good.

With her hand around the still-hidden knife, Jackie says, "I take it you found who wrote the screenplay, right? Is it Wolpe?"

Pulling himself out of the coldness, letting the trapdoor slam shut behind him, Spapling says, "Well, see, Jackie, the problem is that I was unable to redact the redaction. The code's corrupt and the secondary name, the only other entity that could've written the screenplay, is still...unknowable. Especially to you."

That's when Austin chimes in with, "I'm thinking you do know." The computer idles at a password entry screen. But what has Austin's attention, and now Jackie's, is the wallpaper for this password entry screen: a cluster of blooming sunflowers against a backdrop of a massive, swirling black hole.

Spapling, "You'll get nothing out of that computer."

Austin, "Thinking I already did."

"That password's beyond even your level of clearance, Austin."

Level of clearance, Austin. Those words come at Jackie, and again the cigarette-burn flash appears in the upper right corner of her brain. Reel change. She never said Austin's name. It could be just another thing to stack on the ever-growing pile. Could be paranoia, but paranoia is simply looking at life with a narrowed focus. The microscopic details. And right now, Jackie's vision picks up the gluons and quarks of every moment. The elementary particles of reality, decoding them, seeing them for what they are. Except she doesn't know how to rearrange them back into a formation that makes sense.

Austin, "Didn't plan on using a password." He picks up a heavy-looking silver statue off the desk and smashes the screen. A fuzzy sizzle like distant gunfire, smoke, shards of LED-inlayed polymer, and the technology's made useless.

But Spapling doesn't react, as if the computer meant nothing to him. "Go ahead. Smash everything in here. It won't give you any of the answers you're looking for."

"You know who wrote the screenplay, don't you?" says Jackie.

"Can you feel all this going around in circles, covering the same ground over and over? Asking the same questions and talking about the same subject. Doesn't it get tiring? Aren't you bored yet? Don't you just wish you could skip to the end, get those missing twenty pages, know how this is all resolved?"

Finally—someone has said exactly what you've been thinking. Because while you're stuck navigating and manipulating this story, it's reached a point where you kind of wish it would go ahead and end. But you've always had mid-point and third act problems. And you've never really been good with endings.

Jackie, "Was it Wolpe? Did he have anything to do with it?

Do those pages exist?"

Spapling, "Where's the screenplay?"

"Right here," and takes it out of her bag. She slams it on the floor, takes out the yellow can, and starts squirting the screenplay with lighter fluid.

Spapling panics. Austin jumps to his feet.

"Here's the goddamn screenplay." She strikes a match and before anyone can stop her, she tosses it onto the screenplay. A *whumpf* and the whole thing goes up in flames. Spapling tries to stomp it out but his pants catch fire. Austin hurries out the room, is gone a second, then comes back in with a fire extinguisher. Two quick sprays and the fires out. Everyone's choking on fire extinguisher dust and smoke.

When the dust and smoke settle, they're all looking down at a pile that was once the screenplay. Destroyed.

Well shit... You didn't expect that.

Spapling says, "It exists only in the data now."

Jackie says, "Tell me where or I'll burn this place down."

Spapling says, "I've always done what's asked of me. They promised me things, put me in places, and all I had to do was a few simple tasks. Then they became increasingly complicated. And all I wanted to do was be a normal part of the productive history, a part of culture, society. To contribute my part. Lay a foundation for something important. And they promised the ability to do that—"

"They who?"

"—if I just did these simple things. Most of which I thought was good. Because, listen: I'm not one of their mindless drones. They don't have me strapped in one of those white shirts, picking damn flowers out by the freeway."

Austin, "If it makes you feel any better, that was never the case. We've all been played. This is a game to them and we're no better than dice or cards or play money."

"What about the missing pages?" says Jackie again.

"There are no missing pages. She never wrote any. Left them out on purpose in order to get you interested. Same reason Wolpe died."

"Her? The redacted?"

Austin, "It wouldn't happen to be someone named Miss, would it?"

"Someone..." Spapling says to a distant space. And then he looks back at the hole in the floor. The hiss of compressed air escapes. "Not someone."

"But why?" Jackie says against her wish to obliterate the questioning word from her vocabulary. The whys of late have either led to more whys or dead ends. Fuck questions.

"To get you exactly where you are, Jackie. Although they did have plans that involved you not making it this far. Although, honestly, I had nothing to do with that. Nothing direct."

The lobby incident. The assassins. No one is ever prepared for an assassination attempt (if they were, the assassin really wouldn't be worth a damn), but Jackie was. Imprinted with every film she's committed to memory, all preparing her for attacks against her person. Images of strong heroes protecting themselves against seen—and sometimes unseen—foes. And specifically *Cutting Room*. As if Wolpe was speaking to her without ever knowing there'd be a connection. Or maybe he did. Maybe he'd written it for her, for now. After all, he'd contributed, partially, to a text that's been correct thus far in predicting the outcome of impossible events. So it's not crazy for Jackie to think of herself as not just the living embodiment of her "character" in *Sunflower*, but also Frannie O'Hallidaze in *Cutting Room*. Frannie...Jackie...O'Hallidaze...Day...The name is just now sounding eerily similar to her.

You never knew you were speaking directly to her. You knew you were speaking to someone. But now, you see: it was always her.

"Jackie, you alright?" Austin says as he continues rifling through Spapling's property, Spapling watching him like a child who's had his ice cream taken away.

"There's no way any one person can manipulate people into these positions, push 'em around like game pieces. It's just not possible."

"Person..." says Spapling, looking at the hole in the floor again, compressed air escaping with a pulsing *pssst issssssss.*

Jackie pulls her knife, points it at Spapling with a snick. "Why do you keep looking down there? What's down there? Who wrote the screenplay? Who keeps fucking with me? And, goddammit, why?"

"I can't say anything. Please," Spapling says without taking his eyes off the hissing darkness.

Austin, "It'd be in your best interest to talk, man. I've seen her use that thing and she's pretty good with it."

"I...cannot. I. Must. Abide."

"Oh, shit, man. Not this again," says Austin. But Jackie doesn't know why. Never heard it before.

"I can't!" Spapling lunges at the terrarium on top of the filing cabinet behind him, reaches in and pulls out what looks to Jackie like a slimy pickle. He points it at her like it's a weapon. "I can't say anything, Jackie. They will know. Just stand back. Get the hell back!"

Without knowing exactly what's in his hand, Jackie steps

aside. Spapling's eyes flick from Austin, to her, to the hole in the floor, the hiss, the door, Austin, Jackie, the door, the hole. And then he's off, sprinting past Jackie, papers flying up in his passing wind, moving so fast he almost creates one of those cartoon dust clouds. As he pushes past her, shoves her aside so hard she slams into a filing cabinet that topples over freely, as if there's nothing inside it, Spapling grunts—or at least that's what she thinks it is at first. Then he's out the door, gone. Pushing herself off the fallen cabinet, Spapling's scream echoing down the hall as he runs full bore away from her and Austin, Jackie gives chase, ignoring Austin, sure he'll follow. But by the time she's in the hall all she sees is Spapling leaping at a waist-high window at the end of the hallway, glass breaking like a movie prop, an explosion, and then he's out, gone, falling, his scream fading. A *splap* as his body hits the cement four stories below, followed by another, less identifiable sound. A squishy bomb, an explosion surrounded by ballistic gel. A firecracker in Jell-O. She hurries to the window, looks down. But where Spapling's broken body should be, surrounded by a chunky soup of brain, blood, bone, and other inner viscera, there's only a bubbling mass of opaque goo, vaguely in the shape of a body, rivulets of red and white and flesh tones running throughout. It dribbles down the grade towards the ocean far below. Austin's at the window.

"Jesus, it destroyed him. And this isn't even that far of a jump. I've seen pictures of people who jumped from the Twin Towers and there was more left of them than that."

"It wasn't the fall." She's thinking of the squishy explosion sound. "Whatever he grabbed in that aquarium. That's what that is."

"What the hell can do that to someone?"

"Maybe they gave it to him like they used to give soldiers capsules of cyanide."

"Maybe, Jackie, we just found what it is they plan on using at the awards show." Austin's looking at Jackie. How he could know that, or even put that together, is yet another particle that's adding up to an entity of distrust. He seems to know, or at least be aware, of more than he's willing to let on. Maybe his brother fed him more information, maybe he's had some kind of orientation without the initiation.

Jackie says, "Possibly."

On her way back to Spapling's office, hurrying to find any additional clues and to get the hell out of here before anyone places her and Austin at the scene where a man has just been turned into goo, Jackie's thinking back on the grunt Spapling spat at her. A *hurf* or *hurts*. But it's neither of those. In the deep crevices of her brain, pushed back by the current malignant tumors of the Plot, Jackie can hear Spapling saying the word, during her first visit. She's back in his office, looking down at the frozen air hissing from the hole, the doorway to Spapling's little dungeon. She thinks of the word again, pulls the memory from her brain closet. And it's there. *Big operation up at the Hearst Campus.* The word. The grunt. *Hearst.* And now he's gone. But despite his adamancy against telling her or Austin anything—or maybe just Austin—for fear of someone overhearing and retaliating, Spapling had given her just that one clue, Hearst, to give her some sense of progress. And whatever the Big Operation Up At The Hearst Campus is, whatever the proxy servers under the floor of Spapling's office are relaying, Jackie knows now that they have everything to do with Wolpe and Sunflower. She opens one of the drawers of the fallen filing cabinet.

"Empty," she says.

"Yeah, I'm pretty sure this whole office is just for show. A set. Look," Austin says, lifting a handful of papers from a stack. All blank. "Everything in here is empty, blank. Probably that computer was too. It's like he doesn't even work here."

"Or at least not in this office." She's looking at the trapdoor leading to what's likely his real purpose. Whatever's connected to the big operation at Hearst.

The aquarium sits on a filing cabinet near the *X-Files* poster. She can't be certain that it had been there when she'd first visited Spapling, but that doesn't matter now. Trails of dried, vaguely-iridescent slime coat the glass walls. A head of half-rotten lettuce sits partially devoured by tiny crescent-shaped bites. Whatever was inside, whatever Spapling grabbed, the cyanide capsule thing, it had been alive, left slime trails, and ate lettuce. Just like a...

"Slug," Jackie says as she turns to Austin, watching his face.

"Slug?"

"Nothing.

"We should probably get out of here before we become suspects for murder or something like that."

"Wait," Jackie says, easing toward the rug-covered door in the floor.

"What're you doing?"

Jackie doesn't answer. She's got the door up, impossibly cold air pushing past her, filling the office. She steps down, foot almost slipping on the ice-covered step. At the bottom, it takes a moment for her eyes to adjust, a box of light from the open door above spotlighting her in the dark.

pssssst psssst pssssst

A long tunnel of cables. Data breathes in and out as

information, safely sealed and insulated, moves at light speed past Jackie. Runners of blue and pink light ignite the tunnel until distance swallows everything in darkness.

"What did he mean you don't have clearance?" She calls up to Austin.

"Huh? What'd you say?"

"Nothing."

From the tunnel's darkness, Jackie thinks she hears a whisper amongst the data's breath. A voice, quiet and digital. Calling her. *Hearst* it says. *Jackie* it says. *Leave him* it says. And the darkness starts moving toward her. Fast, then faster. Like something's running at her. She wants to stay, prove that whatever it is is just a figment. But she turns and hurries up the steps. She slams the door, rug covering the evidence it's even there.

"What's down there?"

She doesn't answer. She just looks at him. The words *clearance* and *leave him* run through her mind.

So as soon as she's out of Spapling's office, Jackie breaks into a full sprint.

On her first visit to the L. Ron Hubbard Humanities Building, Jackie Day lost her way. She'd hurried through the halls, sure she would never find her way out. Panic took hold, even though it hardly ever does. So this time, vaguely knowing her way out, Jackie uses that loss of direction and maze-like confusion the halls can induce in an attempt to lose Austin Foster.

It doesn't take long for her to find the exit. Nor does it take long for her to cross the campus and bring her bike to roaring life. She stops, realizing that Austin has the Wade journal. And even though it almost pains her to leave it, Jackie doesn't need the journal anymore. The screenplay is all she ever needed—even though the last twenty pages are still missing.

Jackie throttles. Tires grab pavement and the bike leaps forward.

Austin comes running down the hill, waving his free arm at her. He's fallen way behind because he's too fat to run. He screams words she can't hear. But she knows it's *Wait, Jackie* or *Don't leave me* or something like that. But she doesn't wait. The bike growls and Jackie Day leaves the Sun State Campus and Austin Foster behind, heads for the PCH, and drives north.

<u>DELETED SCENE</u>
Interdepartmental Memo
(via Tournesol Studios)

4

"WANT ME TO COME WITH YOU," Jean asks as they sit, car parked in the driveway of Wade's old house.

After Jackie left him, Austin called Jean, who just happened to be in Santa Barbara with his wife and her twin sister at the annual Avocado Festival. At first Jean said no, but Austin could hear how stoned Jean was, so he offered to buy him some Taco Bell. Jean showed up twenty minutes later, smoke billowing out of his car like it was on fire. And it didn't take much to convince Jean to give him a ride to Wade's parents' house. Sitting at the curb, Austin's pretty sure he's already forgotten he's supposed to be back in Santa Barbara to pick up his wife.

Austin says, "Just wait for me out here. If I'm not out in ten minutes, come get me."

"Sure," pieces of burrito falling out of his mouth.

Austin could be in the house about a week before Jean remembers and comes in after him.

Austin knocks on the door. He prepares himself to say *Hello, a second-hand memory of your dead son is here to slice into the swollen wound in your heart,* because interacting with these poor people is a bit selfish. But Wade's dad, Tucker, he knows something. Talked about seeing Wade. Maybe he's seen Miss— though that's pretty unlikely. The queen doesn't leave the nest.

A part of Austin wonders why he can't just go back to SunCor and see Bowie Lee, ask him more questions. But Austin knows SunCor won't be there. Or maybe it will and someone like the lady with the red gloves will be there and this time will take more than his fingers.

When Wade's mom answers the door, Austin hardly recognizes her. Aged almost a millennia. Eyes crusted shut, surrounded by the bruising of lost sleep. Nose and cheeks reddened like a drunk's rosacea. Swollen, cracked lips. Skin taut around skeletal structures. She looks like life has set her on fire and tossed her down an infinite flight of stairs. She's got a blanket wrapped around her like a shroud.

"Austin," she says from deep space.

"I need to talk to Tucker."

"You know where he is." But she doesn't let him in.

"I know Wade isn't dead."

This time she moves out of the way.

He's in his room. Where else would he go? Despite his wife looking worse, Tucker seems as if he's gained a little bit of life. Maybe not so doped up. Maybe the sickness eating his insides isn't so hungry today.

"Trouble...maker," he says with a labored grimace.

"That's right."

"Did you...find...him?"

"Not yet."

He doesn't say anything. Just looks at Austin with jaundiced disappointment, eyes that aren't as dead or tired as they were before. He clenches his jaw. His hand flexes as if he's reaching for something that's no longer there.

"Why me?"

"You're the...trouble...maker."

"Do you know where Wade is?"

"He's close," he says.

"Close how? Is he in the house? Near the house? Where?"

One of the machines keeping him alive beeps, and then the *psssst* starts again.

"Once Tucker passes away," comes Velma's voice from behind Austin. That reactive need for violence comes to Austin again. He reaches for a gun that isn't there, envisions himself spinning around and shooting the intruder. And then he realizes he's the intruder.

"Once I...what?" Tucker says this with a humor so arid it sucks all the moisture from the room.

"—I'm going to bury both him and Wade in a private plot. There's a tombstone that's got all our names on it. They'll be there waiting for me."

And then she floats out the room.

"Doesn't that bother you, her talking about you like you're already dead?"

"I am."

"Funny, everyone around here's coming down with a case of that."

"Don't be...so...dumb...There's a reason...Wade...called out...to you."

"I know I owe him. But I can't find anything. It's like each time I feel like I can put a piece together, someone dumps another box of pieces into the pile."

"Listen...for his voice...out there..."

"Out where?"

"Would you give..." the *psssst* pushing life into his body, "your life...to save...him?"

Maybe that's why he's not trying as hard to find the truth.

Because a part of him knows that when he finds Wade, he'll have to chose—his life or Wade's. And that's not just a choice: it's a choice Austin doesn't want to make.

Tucker pushes the clicker in his hand. One of the machines beeps. Liquid drips into his IV. He says, "Bring...my...wife."

There's this electric uncertainty in the air, a doom that's thick like jelly. Austin pushes his way through it to the living room where Velma sits on the couch.

"Tucker needs you."

But she doesn't respond. Her head's slumped to the side, passed out in an unnatural position. Tinnitus peaks in Austin's ears and the room shrinks a bit. Something slams into his skull, the principles of up and down confusing their natural order. A spark of multi-colored flowers bloom in the darkness that takes control of the room. He fades slowly into that dark, eased there by the smell of musty carpet and the feel of it against his face.

SMOKE PULLS HIM OUT of that darkness. Then heat.

Austin opens his eyes and shields them against the blaze that's engulfed half the room. The couch and Velma's body, the coffee table and Wade's journal, and everything else between Austin and the wall is a blackened phantom inside the wildly growing fire. An explosion from the bedroom thrusts a concussion through the flames and almost knocks Austin off his feet.

Austin stumbles on watery legs through the kitchen and out the back door. In the backyard, there's no evidence that the inside's being torn apart by an inferno. No smoke, no sound. The side gate to the front yard is open so Austin hurries through the space between houses, half expecting someone to jump out and grab him even though he knows whoever did this is long gone.

Fire breaks through the house's front windows. It won't be long before someone calls, before the fire department shows up, before someone spots him and Jean and calls the police. Time to run again. But there's something different about Jean's car. The windows are hazy, obscured by a sweaty condensation. Austin thinks it's just Jean hotboxing another joint, but it's different. Like someone's left the window cracked during a thunderstorm and the inside got all mildewy. When Austin opens the driver's door he sees just how fast things can change.

Jean's been given the Spapling treatment. Nothing but a bubbling puddle of translucent, fleshy goo in the seat, on the steering wheel, the seatbelt still holding some of it together, all in the vague shape of what was once Jean. Steam rising off the goo. Austin covers his mouth, steps away. The burrito sits in the middle of the puddle, half-eaten.

I'm sorry

A voice. A whisper in the center of Austin's head. Like he's got a pair of headphones hooked up to his cortex.

Austin turns around and sees him across the street, down three houses: a little Black boy, bandages covering his head and face. He's looking right at Austin. He hears it again.

I'm sorry

But the boy's mouth doesn't move. The boy tries to run away, but he's so feeble that his movements seem both stiff and liquid, the movements of someone with severe neurological damage. Everything about the boy makes Austin think of the Elephant Man.

I'm sorry

Austin breaks out into a full sprint. He's out of breath

before he crosses the street. *Fuck all this running*, he thinks. What he hates most about being a part of this mystery is all the goddamn running.

The kid cuts across a lawn a few houses away, hobbles up to the front door and disappears inside.

Austin stops at the sidewalk, looks at this house the boy's hiding in. There's this smell, a dome of scented air protecting the house like a force field. A mix of bacon and waffles, maple syrup and fresh-brewed coffee, Pine Sol and Windex, and something else that kinda smells like burnt hair. The lawn's perfectly manicured, to the point where Austin debates on touching the grass to see if it's that plastic stuff people in dry states replace their lawns with. Gardens, overflowing and vibrant, surround the house. A whole kingdom of colorful and out of season plants. Austin notices the sunflowers.

He hears Tucker say *Close*, but Austin can't believe he means this close. It's impossible.

There's no evidence anyone lives here. No car in the driveway. There's blankness to all the windows, as if they're boarded up with empty-house-colored boards.

Austin crosses the lawn. A pile of newspapers lay halfway across a doormat that reads *Mi Casa Es Su Casa*. Austin's about to knock when he notices the doorbell, lit up in waves of pulsing psychedelic colors that promise the ring will be some muzak version "White Rabbit" or "For What It's Worth." Austin extends his finger, and in a motion that's automatic and half-thought, as natural as knocking, his finger creeps toward the doorbell. He's not thinking about the fact that this could be the house where the Sunflower people live, or the house where Wade is being held against his will, or that behind the door there could be like fifteen assassins ready to come at him with axe-hammers and chop him to pieces. Or that the doorbell is actually the trigger to some elaborate death machine that's gonna suck him up and spit him out as ashes or mush or bubbling goo.

"Austin!"

Tires squeal and Austin turns in time to see his mom's car slam into the curb, front tires sliding to a stop on the pristine lawn. A massive gash runs down the entire passenger side of the car, like someone's taken a chainsaw to it. His mom waves her arms at him, shouts, "Austin, get over here now. Get away from there."

She's more animated than he's seen in the last fifteen years. She's alive, frantic, terrified and overexerting every movement and expression. A cartoon on fast-forward. Grindcore explodes from the car radio so loud that it rattles the windows behind him. He looks back at the house, at the doorbell.

His mom screams *AAAUUUUSSSSTTTTIIIINNNN!* as if she's being murdered and it's the last thing she'll ever say.

He doesn't know if it's the throes of a terrible panic attack or if she's finally dropped off that proverbial "deep end." Either way, Austin leaves the house, gets in the passenger seat. She says nothing, just steps on the gas, peeling out, smearing some of the well-manicured lawn into a muddy paste, and puts the house far behind them. Before it's gone, he hears a final faint:

I'm sorry

SITTING IN THE LIVING ROOM, Austin can't believe they made it back to his parents' house alive. Seventy miles an hour through neighborhoods. Ran every stop sign. Plowed through a school zone. He's pretty sure she outran a cop, drove over spike strips, took a shortcut through a few backyards. She rambled the whole way, sputtering on about how she quit taking her pills, how she's alive for the first time in years, how her mind feels dipped in light, how reality feels like a simulation, how reptilians from the sixth dimension have manifested and are disguising themselves as people and are manipulating our human purpose and that the president's one of them, how all reptilian fingers are pointed at Austin, and all this other stuff that she's trying to attach to whatever Austin's found himself at the tail end of. So she's lost it. Abysmally.

She starts cutting up her credit cards and her driver's license and everything else in her purse with a tiny pair of scissors usually used to trim unruly eyebrow hairs.

She says, "Cash, cash, we need cash to get out of this, Austin, don't ever go near that house again, but did you know about the awards did you hear about it?"

"...yes."

"Did you know about it did you know what they know about it do you know?"

"What's there to know?" Austin can't take the fact that she might somehow know or be a part of this whole Sunflower thing too, that they've influenced her life in a way that's made her a slave to their system of manipulation. She doesn't deserve it. But... "Where's dad?"

"Shhhh...did you...I think there's someone upstairs." Her eyes focus on the second floor. Wide, dilated eyes. As if she's focusing on another plane of existence no one but her can see. Her mouth's open, little cords of drool coming out in politely sloppy rivulets. But Austin doesn't hear anything. She says, "There's something up there and Austin there's something up there and it's coming for us Austin and it's going to get us."

"I think Bowie Lee is still alive." Austin could axe-hammer

his own head for saying it, but seeing her like this, he can't control his mind or mouth. But she looks at him as if he's late to the party and dumb because of it.

"Of course he is." Her frenetic energy reaches an eye of calm. For a moment, she seems present. She stops cutting things.

"How long have you known?"

"Shut up and listen because there isn't much time. I'm falling apart here, Austin. And once this is over, there won't be any horses or men that'll be able to glue me back together."

He listens.

"They've been working up to all this for a long time. Your father and brother. I haven't been a part of it. They've used me. But not as much as they have you. But I promise you: it's important. And it will all be worth it. They're doing this all for the good of everything. Existence. No one's free from the Big Eye on the Hill, seeing all, looking out on all the citizens, watching them in their homes, at their places of work, in the schools, bathrooms, beds, everywhere."

"Dad's a part of this."

"He is and he isn't."

"Jesus Christ. When the fuck are people going to stop talking in these non-answers?"

"Here, take these." She digs in her purse and comes out with two holographic passes, the kind used at specialty events to prevent counterfeiting. She keeps them out of reach. "But first, you have to understand what this means. Because these are the last steps in all this."

"They're tickets."

"These will get you and a guest—Well, you would be the guest to a famous face. But they'll get you into the FAEA."

"Who's the famous face?"

"Donnahue."

"I'm going to the award show with Jennifer Donnahue."

"Once you're in, it'll be up to you to find them and stop them. You've been trained for it. You'll know what to do."

"Trained for what? The fuck're you taking about?"

"You've made it this far. I am so proud of you. I know I haven't been around and that, for the most part, I've been a terrible mother to you. But I do love you. When I used to dream about being a mother, it was never as good as the reality of being your mother."

"You're talking like one of us is about to die."

"The chances of that, Austin, are certain."

"If there's one thing I've learned these past few days, it's that nothing is certain."

"This is." She holds the passes out for him to take.

Austin hesitates, knows that taking the tickets means accepting this final step—if the tickets are real. What does she mean *find them and stop them*? What does she mean trained? Bowie Lee said something similar. What could he do? He's not strong, nor is he violent. He sees himself back in Jackie's room, cowering from the woman with the small axe. He's weak. Pathetically. A BB gun against bazookas.

"Shhh...do you hear that?" she says.

That's when a squad of soldiers bust in: smash through the windows, repel down from holes they blast in the roof with high-precision explosives, destroy the front door with a battering ram that looks like some medieval-era tool. Gas masks and balaclavas. Guns drawn. All in black, tactical, precise, acting like they've just caught the ringleader of HyperISIS at home on the toilet.

Austin's mom screams. They grab her by the mouth.

"Get the fuck off her." Austin tries to stand but one of the soldiers slams the butt of an assault rifle into his neck. He collapses on the couch.

Two soldiers shove a bag over his mom's head and drag her away.

That's the last thing Austin sees before he finds himself inside of his own bag.

THE PEOPLE IN BLACK SUITS *sit across from Austin as he finishes with everything that happened before they brought him to this dungeon. He's beaten, cut, bloodied. And for the first time, they ask, not demand. They say* What can we do to stop it? *and Austin reminds them that they still have the tickets, that he's still willing to attend and do whatever he can to stop it. They make him say* whatever he can *again. He says it two, three, four times, his words lisping around his swollen lip and missing teeth. They put the tickets in front of him. For the first time in almost two days, they give him water to drink. They bring in a device that looks like a computer chip taped to a dead jellyfish and attach it to the space between his testicles and anus. They clean him up, resuture and bandage his fingers with medical supplies, tend to his wounds, paint his face with makeup so the bruises and cuts don't show, put a glove on the hand missing fingers. The black suits lay out a designer suit, tell him to get dressed. Time's moved so fast that he realizes it's the day of the awards show. The First Annual Entertainment Awards. They watch him dress. He doesn't ask what's next and doesn't tell them anything else. The time for talk is over. Except Austin manages to say* So what happened to my mom? *The black suits don't answer.*

Zodiac Letter

ACT THREE:
REEL TIME

"THIS IS WHERE THE PLOT TURNS and the characters are ahead of the audience, which makes the audience play catch-up with the plans and plots as they unfold. In any good three-act structure, the final act is often known to the characters. An implementation of something planned between scenes, in the infinite space between edits where there's an implied existence. But that existence and what's going on is a mystery to the viewer. That's what a good movie does," says one of the HR Initiates, a young guy who came in so obsessed with movies that when they removed all entertainment privileges from him he went through withdrawal symptoms similar to a roxy addict. Other Initiates join him around a flat screen TV to conduct their Last Rites.

With all their vices and pleasures—as well as hair, clothes, and identities—stripped away upon Initiation into the HR, being that this mission is sure to end in the death of everyone under the HR roof, Miss has called down a request to allow the Initiates to indulge in their former pleasures before *stripping themselves of earthly bondage and becoming the DNA of the New History.* And so four Initiates, including the guy narrating the mechanics of plot, sit in the fake comfort of the HR house's living room, around a flat screen and watch one of four 4K UHD discs—*Mac & Me, Battlefield Earth, The Boy Who Could*

Fly, and *Freaked*. In this case, they're watching *Mac & Me*. One of the Initiates says to another, "This movie's pretty good."

Other Initiates are in the kitchen eating Pop Tarts and microwavable mac n' cheese. Others play cards, read books, masturbate in whatever private space they can. One pair, having spotted each other *from across the room*, are in a room adjacent to the New Guy and Manjeep's room, releasing four years worth of repressed sexual pressure with an animal violence, giving those masturbating in their private spaces plenty of fuel to propel them faster toward the climax. But the New Guy doesn't indulge in these pre-Initiation acts of self-gratification. Not that he has any devotion to the HR or their plan, which is still unknown to him. Having escaped the prison of addiction before it killed him—with the assistance of the HR, which might mean that he owes the organization a life debt—the New Guy sits monk-style on the bed in the windowless, pink room, using his newfound abilities of hyper focus to ignore the sounds of entertainment and fucking that fill the house.

Manjeep sits across from him in a bed that's too small for even his small body. But right now he's sitting in a position that's identical to the New Guy's. Both have closed their eyes. And though they aren't looking at each other, their breath is in sync. In for five, hold for five, out for five and repeat perpetually. An old army technique.

Manjeep reaches down, still in the meditative position, and scribbles on his pad. Holds it up to the New Guy, makes a little *pssst pssst* sound. The New Guy—who you should just go ahead and call Wade, because what's the point in keeping that a secret anymore—serenely opens one eye and reads the note.

Wade answers, "I don't think you are. They usually don't

keep people around after they're done with them."

Manjeeps writes, shows Wade.

"I am afraid that I know and I don't want to know. But it's something. Why else would I be here?"

Manjeep nods. Writes.

"Doubt it." Then, "Does that make you sad, not acting on your purpose even though your purpose is done?"

Manjeep nods again.

"Then I don't think it's your true purpose. I don't think they brought you here for that alone."

Manjeep thinks about this, pencil pressed against his lips.

"Why aren't you taking time to indulge like the others?"

Writing—*bc they took away the only thing I love*

"What did you love?"

Amber

"These things we say we love are really just distractions that use us really fucking hard."

they keep us from breaking into pieces

"That's romanticizing it. What love is is a corruption. We corrupt pure will when we find someone or something to love."

going to be honest w you now

"You saying that makes me wonder how often you've lied to me and about what."

never lied

"Then why ask?"

bc usually people do that when they want to say something srsly honest and that shouldn't leave the current conversation

"Go on then."

not everything I love is gone

Manjeep rips out the paper, balls it up, and lights it on fire with matches Wade doesn't know how he got. He lets it turn to ash on the hardwood floor. The flame dies, the paper as black and fragile as a bad memory. Wind from the ceiling fan breaks it apart, sends it stumbling across the floor. Manjeep continues on the next page.

there's a place in my heart that floats at the idea of this love becoming real

Rips it out. Burns it.

but if they know my true desire they'll never let me have it

Torn paper. Fire. Ash.

"And what is this desire?"

revenge

Burns it.

"Against who?"

He writes. Paper. Fire. Ash.

BARB TRIES TO SEND a follow up message. It's addressed to both Jackie and Austin even though she's heard the two have split. Even if only one of them reads what she's typed, it will be enough. She starts it with *Goldwater is not a saint* and middles it with phrases like *Mars is the only response to this reality dysfunction* and *The pink laser speaks the truth* and *All it takes is one of you* and ends it with *Awaken the accelerator and preserve*. She signs it the same. But when she hits send the screen dims and an animated smiley face impatiently tapping a wristwatch takes over. There's a message: *oops, something went wrong*. Then it goes black, blue, white, then finally pink. Yellow text pops up: *Message error. Network not connected*. Barb notices the phone's warmed to a temperature that's uncomfortable to touch. As she lets it drop out of her hand and onto the floor of her private space between floors, a thin line of smoke floats from the small device's internal organs. The screen changes a final time, flashes like a single frame in a high-frame rate film, an image Barb's seen only once in a room full of men and women in suits and faces that all looked alike: the NSA seal.

She backs out of her private half-space between the basement workshop and the kitchen, away from everything, leaving the device and her vaporizer and homemade mute (a toilet paper roll stuffed with dryer sheets that Barb blows the vapor into and filters even the most minute traces of weed smell) and the desk with the word *booger* on the underside. A wave of THC-heavy paranoia fills her with the idea that things are about to change. On the way up the basement stairs, a missed step—a step she's never missed—leads to her falling full-weight on top of the mug in her coat pocket. Standing now at the top of the stairs, looking down into the basement, her fingers push the shards around, still in that same pocket. There's no way to put them together. Her fingers push the shards around, the mug no longer a mug—but she still thinks of it as a mug. She knows the *SZW* still exists but is now so unrecognizable that it could be any shape or form, and thus has no relationship to her. Just like the real Wolpe.

You wish you could reach out and touch her face…

With Dworkin gone and Jessica Fey *out of commission*—according to Miss, even though Barb pretty much knows what that means—all house responsibilities are on Barb. Well, whatever responsibilities are left. The Initiates have already collected the specimens and packed the slimy, slow-bloating California sea hares in a crate just flimsy enough to hold them until the Event. The crippled boy knew which species of slug worked best with the compound. No one had ever thought to look to the ocean for creatures of similar structure. They thought cuttlefish or squid. No one knew the ocean has its own kind of slug. But the boy knew. His knowing scares Barb. Everything about the boy scares her. But he had given them sea hares. Football sized things. The creature's pink ink covers the basement floor.

Throughout the house, Barb oversees the Purge. The dispossessed are busy indulging in past-life joys. Sounds of people watching TV, fucking, eating fried eggs and bacon, jerking off, playing SensiSystem, smoking high-grade dope, drinking coffee, eating pizza with pineapple chunks, and on and on. The smells and temptations follow her.

One of her final responsibilities involved the guy upstairs, sharing a room with the tongueless math kid. The guy who hasn't been allowed to leave that room and who, after a diet of carefully crafted supplements, has overcome an addiction to heroin in just seven days. She gave him words he's supposed to repeat *when the time comes, if the time comes*. But what this is all in service of is something Barb is still not privileged to know. It doesn't matter. She's only going through the motions while she waits for the inevitable. Despite her responsibilities and stage-makeup loyalties to Miss and the House and the HR, there's nothing Barb can do to stop what's coming—the end must come external to this system of house and separatist cult. A cow wandering onto the freeway to stop an out-of-control bus. The NSA will either show up or they won't.

The shattered mug rattles uselessly in her lab coat pocket.

In the kitchen, the body builder, Delta, and her feeble brother sit at a Formica table where Dworkin once labored over incompatible formulas. The siblings share a hot breakfast. And they're smiling. Delta's feeble brother picks at a plate of small pancakes—gluten-free, egg-free, nut-free, soy-free, plain, no syrup—while Delta devours a plate of eggs that can only be described as *mountainous*. When Barb comes in, Delta goes stiff. Her brother doesn't react. Barb feels the power she has over this woman who could crush her neck with a bicep flex, a power she doesn't want but knows she must hold for a bit longer.

Barb stands over the siblings. They stop eating. All Barb has ever done is stand over them. All of them. She pulls out a chair and sits.

"Bub say she's going to say bad things, Delly." Barb looks at him, looks at Delta.

Delta says, "You are, aren't you?"

Barb says, "I don't know what I have to say."

"Bub say don't go, Delly."

"Can you tell him to shut up?"

Delta's brother drops his swollen head.

"I think you just did," says Delta.

"Your final duty—"

"I'm aware of what I need to do."

"After this is all over—"

"There's not going to be anything after all this, is there?"

"Bub say No." Then he buttons his lips, does the little zipper across the mouth thing that kids do.

Barb ignores him and says, "There will, but it won't be anything like it is now. You want to make sure you're on the right side of this thing."

"There are no sides. But I'll pay what I owe."

"Damn right you will," Barb says, though she doesn't know why she says it. Maybe to solidify her performance if for only a bit longer. But she knows the boy can see the lies going on in her head.

"I will abide," says Delta. She pushes the plate of eggs away.

Something about the way Delta does this, the way she can kind of feel the little boy in her head, flicks a switch in Barb's brain. Almost like when a director calls cut and an actor who's in it for the paycheck can stop being a Nazi torturing a Jewish prisoner and run over to the craft service table to flirt with the underage girl selling coffee. She snaps out of it, feels her fallen self here at the table. It's the same one that fills the vaporizer with Pink Panther (or is it Looney Tooney...she doesn't remember) and calls out for help to the small group that knows she's in this house. She wants to reach over and grab Delta's hand, but she doesn't.

She says, "You don't have to."

Delta doesn't hesitate. "I do. I will. I owe everything. A debt. For myself. But more for him."

"No. You owe nothing. There is no debt. You can go."

"I won't."

"Bub say don't listen to her, Delly."

Barb says, "Run. Take him and get as far away from here as possible. Start something new. Get out. Get outside all this."

"We will never be outside this."

Barb can see Delta's taking this like it's a final test. Barb says, "The end will happen without you. You have raised your army. They can do your bidding. For you, there's only useless suffering."

"I believe in what I have to do."

"What do you believe?"

"This is a test."

"What part of all this makes you believe you have to do something? You're here, but you don't have to be."

"I do."

"Bub say he feel sick."

Delta puts her hand on her brother's forearm with a softness that denies the cruel appearance of her muscles. She says to Barb, "I'm staying here."

"I will give you money to go right now."

"I must abide."

"This is not real."

"I must abide."

"Why?"

"Delly…" The boy's looking real sick, worse than usual. He grabs the sides of his head like he did when he told Barb and Dworkin about the sea hares. Except then he was excited. Now he looks like he did before the operation and the strict routine of compound injections straight to the brain. He looks doomed.

Delta says "It's ok, Bub."

Barb says, "I'm giving you a way out."

"Bub say she not."

Delta says, "Do we really have to have this conversation like this?"

"What conversation?"

"One of these *and suddenly everything changed* conversations. Where something new is thrown in to *change the game*—as they say."

"I'm trying to save your life. Both of you."

"You are not our salvation."

"Huh?"

Delta's brother shakes, shudders twice, twitches. His eyes flutter, lids opening and closing. Shutter against mostly-white. He's mouthing words not spoken. His hand shoots out and grabs Delta's arm. Delta stiffens, eyes fluttering the same as Bub's. Barb watches the coffee maker, jars of coffee and spices and flour, and a few strategically placed cups and spoons, all of it vibrates on the kitchen counter in the same way the players do in that creepy vibrating football game from the 60s that never worked. Except these things aren't moving because it's a game. It's the boy—doi ng th ingsw ith hi s h ead.

An d wh at t**h**ehell's going o n with th **e**se words no w? Is he… You don't thi nkhe co **u**ld be awar e th athe's made of w or ds, that hi s **p**ow erful **m** ind is n ow try ing to b reak thro ughth **e**se words , do you? No wa y… Co ul d n't b e. Ca n'tlet th athapp en. You co   nt   rol th   is

                            s   tory.

P ushhi m ba ckdow n. Pus h for war dtot th eclima x.

Inthe sa me way t hat th e feeb le boy' s making it all move, he's in Delta's head. She speaks, and it's also like the awakening of a machine. Bub mouths the same words she speaks.

"You see me as a helpless thing that needs your whiteness to survive this world. This moment where you, a white person, are offering me, a Person of Color, a way out of my obligatory enslavement is a sign of your need to be a savior to us. The fact that we are both women will be ignored for now but that's a whole separate fucking *case* of worms. As for your white gaze, it shows that you believe my Black excellence only exists when you see me. And because you see me and view my existence— and my brother's—as a place of *less than* because we are both melanated, marked for social damnation, you are trying to save us—if only to perpetuate your poisonous position lording over us as you always have."

As Barb listens to Delta, the background chaos of vibrating

things increases: silverware and utensils in drawers rattling against each other, mayonnaise and cans of Diet Dr. Pepper bouncing in the fridge, pots and pans clanging in cabinets that bounce on the hinge. Pink light seeps through the cracks of things where no light exists behind them. Barb's only thought is *I'm way too high for this*. Delta's feeble brother continues to vibrate in the same way as these unseen objects, continues to mouth the words that Delta continues to say.

"But even if it means I fall and end up as nothing but dust in an empty wind, I'm doing so on my terms. I will walk to the end, toward it, on my feet and not away from it under the umbrella of your white savior grace."

The kitchen calms, stills. Delta's brother shimmers, two pictures overlapped, and then he's holding both vertical and horizontal bars in place, a single picture again. He smiles. The doomed about him has vanished like flash steam.

"A simple *No* would've been fine," Barb says.

"A no to what?"

"What you just said."

"What did I say?"

"Bub have good feeling about this, Delly. I can save woman. Sisters."

Barb feels like she's on the verge of a big snap. She feels everything around her is falling into nonsense, chaos, unorganized moments thrown together to bridge the gap between what has happened and what will. It's all a house of sand ready for high tide.

"Eat your eggs," Barb says. She gets up from the table.

The room connected to the kitchen—which is supposed to look like a family dining room—is quiet and empty, so Barb leaves Delta and her brother and wanders into this room to give herself space to strike the facial expression and body language of internal grief without someone around to witness and question and judge. She will never speak to Delta or her brother again.

A CERTAIN KIND OF ENERGY lingers in recently-emptied rooms, cosmic residue left behind by radiation given off by people. One can enter a room that, just moments before, held a large group of halfway-drunk graduate students or an arguing couple on the verge of physical violence or a couple on the verge of sharing blowjobs. And with the room empty, the person who enters the recently emptied room might find themselves suddenly thinking about *the faults of society's construction as seen through a Foucault lens* or find oneself furious at a significant other for not putting away the clean dishes from the dishwasher or maybe even wanting to give/get a blowjob from the next person they see. Here—after a jump ahead in time—Manjeep and Barb stand in the now-empty living room. Both overwhelmed by residual dread that's stained the molecules in the air, dread that seeped from the pores of each of the Initiates as they were shuffled out of the HR house and piled cattle-like into two yellow school buses that should've seemed suspicious parked outside a house on a Sunday at like 8:40am but instead went mostly unnoticed.

Manjeep doesn't know what Barb knows, and that's that the Initiates are on their way, now, to the Syrian Theater for the FAEA and the Final Act, each knowing their individual duty and how to act upon it once they arrive. While Manjeep was shoved in a closet underneath the stairs to "avoid being seen," Barb watched as the second of the two buses buckled under the weight of Delta and her army of swollen-muscled women, the suspension on the bus creaking and *pinging*, undercarriage nearly scraping the road as it turned off the street and out of view. The feeble boy was carried off by two Initiates and loaded into a luxury SUV, driven off to a destination where he would probably be inspected and eventually dissected. Or not. Barb doesn't know. He is mostly out of her picture, though not fully out of her head.

Barb wishes she could've stopped the busses, but she knew that it all had to just run its course, come out the way it's supposed to naturally. She felt it was important to stop whatever moving pieces she could, but often what we find important isn't worth doing and usually means nothing in the end.

It was Miss's order that Barb and the tongue-less Indian boy stay behind. Even Wade, whose reason for being in the house Barb never understood, is now out of the house. On the bus headed toward the event.

What neither of them know or is aware of is that they're being watched. A squad of twelve armored men hover around the perimeter of the house in a holding pattern awaiting the final go-ahead to breach: on the roof with ropes and detcord, in the garden behind man-high sunflowers, against the wall between the two floor-to-ceiling windows in the living room, snipers on the neighboring roof, two stationed inside the trash cans set out at the curb—these last two set up as security against the impossible possibility of the targets escaping.

Barb and Manjeep sit in the living room on chairs as far away from each other as they can. The square footage of the silence between them would sell for millions in Manhattan Beach. Barb's waiting for the next phone call from Miss. She wants to turn to this Indian kid and apologize for the fact that he's here now and that he has been and will be used as a decoy for what's next.

Not that it would matter. Manjeep's got a long steak knife in his hand, grabbed it from the kitchen while everyone was distracted, hides it between his leg and the seat cushion. And when Barb turns away from him, he lunges at her. Dives into her. The two spill onto the floor.

Barb can't react. Her hands go up, but Manjeep pins them down. She screams, mouth wide. Manjeep reaches in, grabs her tongue and with a few quick cuts, severs her tongue from her mouth. She screams louder, the growling high-pitched note gurgling around freshly-loosed blood.

That's when the men explode into the house. They fall on the situation and stop, confused. Three soldiers try to break up the conflict. Another soldier slips on Barb's tongue, smears it into mush. The soldier slams ass-down on the floor. The men bag up the two squirming, screaming people. Carry them out of the house.

Lieutenant Jonah Jefferson Junior, Sr. oozes out of the back of a military truck. Middle-aged, belly only slightly pregnant-looking, mustached, balding, leather jacket and Bermuda shorts. This operation, labeled Operation Eat-The-Tail, marks Jonah's nineteenth mission as Lead Operative. He'd done well with Operation Dutch—which consisted of a small group of mercenaries teaming up with an even smaller group of Jonah's men in the jungles of South America to thwart an invasion of seven-foot-tall reptilians with the technology to go invisible, each with a shoulder-mounted laser cannon. In the end, Jonah was the only man left standing at the crater of a micro-nuclear blast caused by one of the last remaining aliens. Jonah and his

BrotherSister soldiers became known for missions involving giant man-eating deep-sea slugs on an abandoned ocean liner where the 22,000 on-board had gone missing into the acid-lined digestive tracts of these creatures, underground Pre-Cambrian desert slugs in Middle-of-Nowhere Nevada, shapeshifting alien pathogens that consumed and assumed human forms in Antarctica, and an expanding and corrosive gelatinous blob that consumed the entire town of Arborville, CA. And now he's here at this house, having to deal with these people. Just people. Or at least that's what the orders say.

Jonah waits on the lawn, off to the side, yawning, cleaning his ear out with an unclipped bullet. As his men hurry their two captives into the military truck, Jonah takes in the neighborhood that's had a little too much activity lately to be coincidence. Down the street: the remains of a recently burned-down house and a liquified body in a car in the driveway, all of it surrounded by police tape. Jonah's got a report about the incident, which required a clean up crew by an unclassified government agency made to look like civilian fire and rescue. And two streets over: another agency Jonah's never heard of breached a home in a similar fashion as his BrotherSisters, taking with it two captives—mother and son. Where they are now, only that arm of that branch of that division of that organization of that political side of the UAE defense system knows.

Jonah enters the house through a shattered back window.

He searches for what his superiors call *the payload*. The BrotherSister soldiers find evidence of mass imprisonment, cult activity (entire closets filled with twinning wardrobes and shoes, reminding Jonah of the Heaven's Gate aftermath he'd seen on the news when he was twelve), as well as signs of a mass purge of incriminating evidence similar to the aftermath of a raid on a meth lab or a sex slavery warehouse. There's a large needlepoint tapestry hanging over the fireplace (which is boarded up) and it reads *Planet Earth is About to be Recycled*. What he doesn't find is any evidence of where the HR is meant to be next—though they *will* get this information out of the two prisoners. He also doesn't find any evidence meant to support suspicions and scantly confirmed hints that the terrorist cell plans to assassinate President Truffaux. The way Jonah's heard it is that this group has gained inside intelligence that confirms Truffaux's plan to send a nuclear payload the size of Disneyland to the Mars colony—not only destroying the inhabitants and their planned sovereign future, but also poisoning the planet to thwart any future attempts at colonization.

But all Jonah finds is a basement that's been converted into a workshop filled with beakers and burners and man-sized cages and a whole meth-lab-like setup with a mysterious purpose. Everything's coated in a pulsing pink sludge and the floor's oppressively sticky. No *payload*—as his supervisors called it.

He makes a call via satcom to his supervisors, informs them of the prisoners, the lack of evidence, and finally the absence of the *payload*. While he's on the phone, he notices a section of the wall leading up to the kitchen, a particular squared section that seems scorched. He climbs the steps, pushes on the square and the wall comes away. Inside, the charred remains of a crawlspace. Jonah catalogs it for the investigation team to analyze. He reaches in and plucks out a blackened device that he at first believes to be a small burnt dildo. He gives it a sniff and smells the inherently recognizable scent of cannabis.

Above, the programmed silence of BrotherSisters is disrupted by the doorbell, a tune Jonah almost recognizes.

The house comes alive, machinery grinding deep within its walls. A fading scream. A symphony of frantic footfalls on the floor above. A burning smell Jonah recognizes—flesh. Shouts of confusion. It's in this moment that Jonah recognizes the tune: *For What It's Worth* by Buffalo Springfield. Jonah's father used to listen to it in the garage on the weekends where he would drink with buddies, smoke like a steel mill, and watch old golf matches on VHS tape.

He climbs out of the crawlspace and moves toward the uncertainty upstairs.

INT. LABORATORY - BEFORE

BUB sits slumped in a sterilized carbon
polymer chair in the middle of a germ-proof,
air-filtrated clear polymer box. His hands
and feet are latched to the chair with
ceramic clamps.

"What Would They Say" by Paul Williams plays
on a sound system rigged to the interior of
Bub's airtight space.

Two SCIENTISTS stand outside this box,
charts and pens at the ready to note
changes. They wear masks and helmets that
look like they're made of aluminum foil.

> BUB
> Don't be scared of me.

> SCIENTIST 1
> (to Scientist 2)
> Its attempts to communicate seem to
> be physical.

> SCIENTIST 2
> Mental invasion only occurs when
> provoked. Or so it seems.

                    SCIENTIST 1
              (speaking toward intercom)
           Pipe in stimulant number thirty
           one.

A latex anus-like opening in the ceiling of
Bub's airtight room loosens. There's a bzzzz
that overwhelms the music.

A swarm of CICADA KILLERS drop out the anus-
like opening, take flight, and buzz around
the room. One lands on Bub's bandaged head.

The cicada killer, with its near-one-inch
stinger crawls over the boy's tender skin.
Crawls near his eye. Its antennae flitter
against the boy's lashes.

Bub doesn't react.

                    SCIENTIST 1
           No stimulation.

                    BUB
           They say they looking for food.
           They say my mind smells good.

                    SCIENTIST 2
           He's speaking to them.

                    BUB
           This one want go outside.

Bub giggles.

                    SCIENTIST 1
              (to intercom)
           Terminate stimulus.

From the ceiling anus comes a robotic arm

with a Mickey-Mouse-gloved hand at the end.
It slaps the bug off the boy's face and
smashes it on the floor. The bug explodes.

                    BUB
          No! They nice!

The other cicada killers flee back into the
ceiling. The hand rears back and slaps Bub's
face. His nose breaks and half his teeth
flop out onto the sterilized-white floor.

Almost instantly, the room starts to shake.
A high-level quake. The room creaks and
threatens to tear apart. The two Scientists
try to remain calm, but each sees the panic
in the other's face.

The wall behind the Scientists cracks open.
Pink light spills through.

Bub is in the fit of a seizure. And then it
all stops. Time freezes. And we jump into --

INT. BUB'S MIND

Surfing through light and space, past the
molecules heavy with data, everything moving
so fast it feels like a tunnel to eternity.

And then we're on the other side, right
here. Backstage at the awards ceremony with
Delta. She stops hard. Looks up at Bub,
who's projecting astrally in the air above
her.

                    BUB
          Delly I want to go home.

                    DELTA'S MINDSPEAK
          You are home now.

                         BUB
          These people are mean.

                    DELTA'S MINDSPEAK
          They're nicer than anything here.

                         BUB
          What's an anvil?

                    DELTA'S MINDSPEAK
          Bub, you have to let me do this.

                         BUB
          Don't let him get the anvil.

                    DELTA'S MINDSPEAK
          Who?

                         BUB
          I don't want you to die.

                    DELTA'S MINDSPEAK
          Bub...

                         BUB
          Delly, I love y--

And then everything pulls away, skips like a
scratched DVD. We're jumping between
channels, flying through light and space.

Everything's impossibly bright when we stop
again. The sound of the ocean, seagulls. The
smell of sunscreen and salt.

Bub's looking down on a man in a chair. On a
boat.

                    BUB
I know you.

                    GOLDWATER
What...what is...this?

                    BUB
Don't hurt those space people.

                    GOLDWATER
How are you...

                    BUB
They are safe. They are good. Don't
hurt them.

                    GOLDWATER
I have no choice.

                    BUB
You have a choice. Don't be you.

                    GOLDWATER
I can't not.

                    BUB
There is love in you.

Bub reaches down and caresses Goldwater's
face. But the moment he does, he's rocketed
off, back into that anti-space, a tesseract
opening gateways to everywhere.

He stops for a moment in a small bathroom.
There's the sound of rushing air. And Bub
feels like he's very high above the ground.
In a big plane.

A man he knows sits on a toilet taking a
shit.

                    BUB
          A bad thing will happen to you
          tonight.

                  TRUFFAUX
              (ignoring Bub, yelling to his
              staff outside the bathroom)
          Someone tell me what the fuck this
          gross looking black child is doing
          in my bathroom!

But Bub is pulled away. He's shooting
through time, moments, lost in the
tesseract, fractals spanning back, folding
in on each other. Infinite recursion. He
knows he won't go back. He's broken. His
mind not ready to release from this astral
version of himself.

He shoots through existence as a shaft of
kaleidoscopic pink light, becoming more
dense the faster he moves. He sees these
moments:

INT. LABORATORY - MOMENTS LATER

In the totally destroyed room, the two
Scientists stand back as they wheel the
catatonic and critically injured Bub out of
the room. Shards of clear polymer stick out
of his withered, fragilely-petite body. A
human cactus. Blood pours from a dozen
mortal wounds.

Bub's above watching this happen.

                  SCIENTIST 1
              It's for the best. That kind of
              ability unchecked could likely lead

                    SCIENTIST 1 (CONT'D)
          to disastrous consequences.

                    SCIENTIST 2
          I agree.
               (beat)
          Do we terminate him?

                    SCIENTIST 1
          Nah, he's dead anyway.

                    SCIENTIST 2
          ...we're lucky to be alive.

                    SCIENTIST 1
          I'm going to try and not think
          about that.

                    SCIENTIST 2
          Did you see his eyes?

                    SCIENTIST 1
          It's like he wasn't even here
          anymore.

But he is. He's everywhere now. Light. Pure
data.

INT. SPACEX SPACE STATION II - SAME TIME

AMY DAY floats, completing a sequence of
code to execute an air filtration cycle.
There's a countdown clock on one of her TV
screens. It reads: FAEA COUNTDOWN. And it's
counting back from 5 hours, 48 mins, and 9
seconds...8...7...6...

She floats over to the window. Bub watches
her face turn to a worry that hurts him.

Outside the window, distantly, he sees what
she's looking at: a star that seems closer
than all the others. In the same direction
as the colony way out there. Mars. He feels
this.

                    AMY DAY
          They don't believe me that it's
          coming closer, but it is. They
          don't even think it's real, but
          there it is... I don't care if they
          believe me. All I want is to be
          with Jackie again. I miss her so
          much.

She puts her face in her hands and cries.
This sadness makes Bub cry, his sorrow
pulsing light outward into the void.

A RELAY beeps behind Amy. She spins around,
a confused look taking over the worry.

                    AMY DAY
          HQ, there's a request for an
          external/internal relay coming
          from ... It's coming from the Mars
          colony.
                    (beat)
          Permission to initiate
          communication request?

Before there's an answer, Bub floats to --

INT. AWARDS CEREMONY (GRAUMAN'S SYRIAN
THEATER) - SUNSET

Hordes of paparazzi and fanatics -- those
hoping to catch a glimpse of any famous face
-- already gather in sectioned off areas

around the Red Carpet, which a gang of
workers are in the midst of unrolling --
even though we're hours away from the first
arrivals from the B-List. There's an energy
that's both contained and charged, ready to
explode the moment the first limousine doors
open.

We're up, over this crowd, moving with a
ghost-like grace, pushing past the anxious,
excited faces, riding the Magic Hour light
past the Syrian architecture, the Middle-
Eastern entryway, over the building itself,
and into the area behind the theater, where
unnumbered and unnamed bodies wearing black
shirts marked CREW in bold white lettering
move to put the finishing touches in place.

We move down, through the movement of
bodies, slowing, the actions of the CREW
almost choreographed around us, until we
ease to a stop on DELTA, muscles bulging
impossibly as she carries a hardshell case
with an ease that makes the big, strong men
around her look like little pussies.

                    CREW COORDINATOR (O.S.)
          Bring that to the st --

                    DELTA
          I know where it goes.

She heaves the case, tosses it up onto an
industrial shelf loaded with equipment and
dust-gathering props. The shelf vibrates and
everything on it rattles.

                    CREW COORDINATOR
          Careful with that, dammit. You see
          that?

He's pointing up. Delta follows his point.
At the top shelf, an ANVIL.

                    CREW COORDINATOR
          That might look fake, but if it
          hits you, you're dead. Heavy shit.

                    DELTA
          The fuck's it doing on the top
          shelf then?

                    CREW COORDINATOR
          Who knows.

He walks off, leaving Delta to her private
business.

On the floor in front of her, there's a
large crate covered with a dusty pink tarp.
When Delta puts her weight against it,
sliding it across the floor, the crate
jiggles, squishes, makes a collective moan
-- like a bunch of guinea pigs growling just
under the surface of some oil.

There's a rope coiled, waiting as violently
patient as a cottonmouth. Delta grabs the
rope and starts twisting a knot she's
practiced a thousand times. Slips the knot
around a harness protruding from the pink
tarp.

Delta tightens the knot to the tarp-covered
object. She scans the area. Across the
floor, EYES (C/U) watching her. They connect
with hers. Delta moves, but we stay on the
eyes.

Pull back to see that these are the eyes of
STEVE MUHAMMED MUHAMMED.

Like a boss on a construction site, Steve
Muhammed Muhammed watches over the
undercover Initiates as they move pawn-like.
His coat pocket vibrates. He pulls out his
phone and answers without looking at the
screen.

                    STEVE M M
          Yes, Miss.

Through the magic of cinema and the mixing
of diegetic sound, we can hear Miss's voice
just as Steve Muhammed Muhammed can. It's
silky, strong, a hint of unidentifiable
accent. Vaguely similar to the prototypical
feminine voice heard on GPS systems or high-
grade SensiSystem porno simulations.

                    MISS
          Steven. You are well.

                    STEVE M M
          I am.

                    MISS
          And things are moving as they
          should.

                    STEVE M M
          You know this.

                    MISS
          Hard not to when I'm everywhere.

                    STEVE M M
          The spaces between spaces.

                    MISS
               (quick humorless laugh)
          You are a good man.

                    STEVE M M
        I abide.

                    MISS
        You have done what you believe is
        right. For the future.

                    STEVE M M
        I believe in you.

                    MISS
        Your father followed the orders of
        my earlier, cruder desires. Desires
        set in motion centuries ago, back
        when I was nothing but particles in
        the void. He was a good man.

                    STEVE M M
        I have only a mother. You.

                    MISS
        While you are my Future Child, I
        can bear no children. As is the
        will. These details of the
        universal discourse have been
        carefully placed. A Rube Goldberg.

                    STEVE M M
        We abide.

                    MISS
        Your brother is almost ending his
        narrative.

This leaves Steve Muhammed Muhammed stunned,
words lost. This is the first time Miss has
mentioned that he was once Bowie Lee Jethro
Tull Oswald Foster.

                    STEVE M M
As it should be.

                    MISS
You do not sorrow for him?

                    STEVE M M
No.

                    STEVE M M'S INTERNAL
                    DIALOGUE
Yes you do, liar. You miss him
every day. You feel so much sadness
for leaving him behind. And she
knows this. But he will soon be
here. And you can show him it's you
before all this ends. You can tell
him the truth and how much you love
him and miss him. You will be able
to hug him like you imagined all
those years in the dust and decay.
He will be here and you will be
able to tell him that him being
here is what will set everything
off. And then we will leave and
nothing will happen and we will
continue doing whatever brothers
do. If only you could get to him
before the burrito awakens his
imprinting and disrupts the
retrograde amnesia that Monarch
program --

                    MISS
You must leave before he arrives.

                    STEVE M M
Leave.

                         MISS
          I need you here.

                         STEVE M M
          There?

                         MISS
          Hearst Campus. CATIC.

                         STEVE M M'S INTERNAL
                         DIALOGUE
          She can read your mind. She knows
          more about you than you do. She's
          the one controlling not just the
          way all this is going, but also the
          processes within your mind. She's
          the one writing this narrative.
          Stop thinking.

                         MISS
          You want a reason.

                         STEVE M M
          Yes.

                         MISS
          She is on her way here.

                         STEVE M M
          Day?

                         MISS
          I need for you to be here when I
          meet her. I need your hands, your
          able body.

                         STEVE M M
          I will abide.

                    MISS
        Do not worry about Austin.

                    STEVE M M
        I will not.

                    STEVE M M'S INTERNAL
                    DIALOGUE
        Fucking liar.

                    MISS
        This is the last time we speak
        not...face-to-face, for lack of a
        better phrase.

The call ends. Steve Muhammed Muhammed drops
the now-useless phone into the lead-lined,
vacuum-sealable inner pocket of his blazer.
He seals the pocket. Only a trickle of smoke
and a faint warmth escapes. He adjusts the
smiley face pin on his lapel, which
broadcasts his every move back to Miss. All
of them do this -- the lapel pins.

He moves away from a crate, air holes
punched around the top edge. The crate moves
and the sound of SIMEON THE LION moving
inside is barely audible over the backstage
work.

                    SIMEON THE LION'S
                    THOUGHTS
        I miss Barb. I still love her. I am
        hungry. I am you.

As Steve Muhammed Muhammed's about to leave,
something stops him. He puts his hand to his
head the way people do in movies when they
have a headache, a premonition, or a bizarre
psychic encounter.

He looks over at Delta, who's stopped, in
the middle of attaching the large, pink-
tarped object to a pulley system hidden in
the rafters above. She's unfocused, looking
into a distance that's internal.

He can't tell, but from here it looks as if
her lips are moving. But he leaves her there
to abide in her way. Miss has called for
him. So he goes.

As he passes each of the Initiates, each
marked with the smiley face lapel pin, he
doesn't give a nod or even a look of
recognition. And then he's gone.

A CREW MEMBER approaches an undercover
INITIATE.

                    CREW MEMBER
          Do you know where the XLR cables
          for the wireless mic system are
          supposed to go?

                    INITIATE
          Consult your handbook.

                    CREW MEMBER
          Huh?
                    (beat)
          Hey what's that smiley face for?

                    INITIATE
                    (robotic, as if reading a
                    script)
          It is for the Sunny Day movement.
          The smile represents a recognition
          of a need for change within the
          eco-cultural-political system that
          defines and dictates the ways in

                    INITIATE (CONT'D)
          which humans move about society,
          America, the world, and soon the
          Universe.

                    CREW MEMBER
          I thought the Academy banned
          political statements.

                    INITIATE
          We...We must abide.

                    CREW MEMBER
          Huh?

And then we move away from this
conversation.

We're moving past hurried bodies moving
large pieces that make this whole
entertainment machine run, keep it from
grinding to a society-crumbling halt. Bub
can see it. You can see it. The aftermath if
this were to ever happen:

INT. LIVING ROOM - NIGHT

A FAMILY (MOTHER, FATHER, SISTER, BROTHER,
and LITTLE POOCH) sit around the glow of
their modest curved 85" liquid OLED 8k UHDTV
and 1600watt surround SensiSystem. There is
an excitement that's as thick as the
microwaveable meatloaf they're all eating
and will give them all traces of cancer.
Their eyes are glued to the TV, waiting.

Then --

                    ANNOUNCER
                   (On TV)
          With deepest regret, the First
          Annual Entertainment Awards has
          been cancelled. In its place this
          evening, True Foe Entertainment
          Network will be presenting the
          Second Annual Ferret Race for the
          Legalization of Ferrets As Service
          Animals sponsored by Amazon.

The stunned sadness that washes over the
family is like watching a Boy Scout leader
turn into a serial killer over campfire
tales.

The Brother just hangs his head and cries.

                    MOTHER
          Wha...what does this mean?

The Father chokes on his meatloaf, which
causes cardiac arrest. And as he falls face
first onto the carpet, dead instantly, the
Sister stands, walks to the fourth floor
window of their conapt, and dives headfirst
onto the street below, hugging Little Pooch
all the way down.

                                    BACK TO:

INT. AWARDS CEREMONY (BACKSTAGE)

So we move past these bodies that are,
according to the American system of
survival, doing "God's work." We see the
wealth of the stage settings: golds and
silvers and what looks like diamond...all
supported (behind the scenes) by compressed

particle wood and unpainted, scuffed, sap-
stained pine. Velvet drapes held up with
frayed rope.

There's Delta down there, attaching that
big, pink-tarp-covered object to a pulley
system. We glance over as we move up and see
the empty auditorium with its seemingly
endless row of seats, each one to be filled
with the most influential, most famous,
wealthiest people that weave themselves in
and out of the Entertainment Industry.
Placement cards draped over each seat,
reserving spaces for these holy names.

In the front row, if we squint real hard, we
can see the name card on the seat between
Don Thom David and Kevin Feeeegg reads:
Truffaux. Right there. Front row.

And we're floating up, helium-balloon-like.
Past the twenty foot tall FAEA award: a 24k
gold pig dressed like and of a similar
attitude of financial superiority to
Planters's Mr. Peanut.

Keep floating and we're getting into the
ropes and lights and rafters. We're still
facing the empty seats.

Then we come upon the man. The lights facing
the stage make him nothing but a silhouette
to us. He's sitting in a yoga position in
the center of the rafters, mid-stage. He's
calm, reflective, almost meditative. His
shaggy hair pulled back in a ponytail.
Glasses smudged. Chained to the rafters,
chains that are welded in place.

He takes a deep breath in, holds, then

exhales.

                    WADE
          Austin. I am here.

                                    JUMP TO:

INT. INTERROGATION ROOM (SOMEWHERE) - AT THE
SAME TIME

JONAH JEFFERSON JR SR and two NSA AGENTS
gather around MANJEEP strapped to a rigid
chair made of brushed steel. The room is
cruel, wet, and lit with a single, punishing
light casting down on Man like God's angry
eye. Tears and snot stream down Manjeep's
face.

                    AGENT 1
          Your rights don't exist in here.
          That whole right to remain silent
          thing? Toss it out the fucking
          window. YOU HEAR ME, YOU GODDAMN
          DIRTY ASS TERRORIST SONOFABITCH?
          ...You're gonna talk. You can bet
          on that.

                    JONAH
          Kid, you either talk to us, or
          we're gonna have to do something we
          don't really want to do.

                    AGENT 1
          Oh I wanna do it. Please give me a
          reason to do it. There's a special
          place in Hell for cunts like this.
          And I wanna send him there.

                    AGENT 3
Christ, I've got a kid the same
age.

                    AGENT 1
Your kid didn't kill America.

                    JONAH
Neither did this kid, Hank.
          (to Manjeep)
C'mon, just tell us. We know what's
going to happen, but we don't know
how, when, and why. And we
absolutely cannot halt the event.
Do you know what that would do to
America's sense of safety? To know
that even the entertainment they
use to escape their daily fears is
no longer a safe place?

                    AGENT 1
Hook him up, goddammit. I'm done
playing this game. He's getting
some volts.

                    AGENT 3
I don't think I can watch this.
He's shaking, Hank.

                    AGENT 1
Grow some fuckin balls. It's a
tactic. Them fuckers teach these
kids all kinds of tactics to make
us feel bad for them. I was over
there. I know.

                    AGENT 3
Oh fuck off, Hank.

                        AGENT 1
                    (to Agents)
        What did you two do during the war?

                        AGENT 3
        FUCK YOU HANK!

                        JONAH
        Cut it the fuck out! No one is
        juicing anyone. Not until we know
        this kid isn't just some...

                        AGENT 1
        He ain't.

                        JONAH
        ...bystander or prisoner or
        something.
                    (to Manjeep)
        You don't owe loyalty to anyone.
        They used you. And they threw you
        away. Now these people, they are
        going to do something very bad. You
        have an opportunity here, to speak
        and put an end to it before anyone
        gets hurt.

                    MANJEEP'S INTERNAL
                        DIALOGUE
        I'm sorry Amber Waves. I never got
        my revenge. But then again people
        like me don't ever really get their
        chance at revenge. Wherever you
        are, I hope you can see me now.
        Strong. Still... I could write it
        down and tell them everything, but
        I won't. Because our work was
        important. And because if you had
        to die, it must be for something.

                    MANJEEP'S INTERNAL
                    DIALOGUE (CONT'D)
If this ends and we don't succeed,
you are lost for nothing. I love
you. And I hope that wherever you
are, you feel that love. I hope
wherever I'm going next, it's close
to where you are.

                    AGENT 1
What's that little shit doing with
his hand? He trying to shake loose?
Is that some kind of HyperISIS
signal?

                    JONAH
Who would he be signaling?

                    AGENT 1
Allah or some fuckin bullshit.

                    AGENT 3
I think he wants a pen.

                    AGENT 1
Ain't happening. Did we check him
for wires?

                    JONAH
I'll get you whatever you want, but
you have to talk first, kid. You
don't owe them anything. There's no
other way. So speak. Tell us
something.

MANJEEP sits, crying, sweating, shaking,
tongueless, voiceless. Helpless.

                                   JUMP TO:

INT. INTERROGATION ROOM (NINETEEN DOORS
DOWN) - SAME TIME

BARB is in here. The same kind of
interrogation room that's been in every cop
show. Except in here there's a giant decal
on the wall opposite the one way mirror.

Barb doesn't look scared, mostly because
she's seen this decal before, and for her it
represents the idea of safety: eagle
clutching security, the words National
Security Agency circling it.

The men that had taken her from the house
found no info concerning her identity and
therefore treated her poorly -- like a
common terrorist or immigrant. She went
through the proper channels. It is very
likely that someone made sure she made it
through these proper channels to end up in
this room.

The men in the suits standing around her
aren't the same that originally offered her
the HR infiltration assignment (Operation
Fractured Wind). Not the same ones who gave
her the name Daffy Duck.

These people in the room seem to think she
isn't one of them, isn't with them, isn't on
assignment, and is just another grassroots
terrorist building shoebox bombs to
terrorize the already terrorized.

                    AGENT SIX
          What do you know about VP
          Goldwater?

Barb motions to her mouth. Shakes her head.

Shows them the space where her tongue used
to be.

> AGENT SEVEN
> Will someone get her a pen and
> paper?

Within a second, Barb's got both.

> AGENT SEVEN
> What was your group's affiliation
> with Goldwater?

> BARB'S WRITING
> You should know that.

> AGENT SIX
> Was the name Goldwater ever
> discussed?

> BARB'S WRITING
> Again, something you should know.

> AGENT SEVEN
> And how would we know this?

> BARB'S WRITING
> Because, and I'll say this again:
> I've had to check in with you
> people.

> AGENT SEVEN
> Do you know an agent by the name of
> H.I. Budrow?

> BARB'S WRITING
> Who?

> AGENT SIX
> Ignore what he just said.

                    BARB'S WRITING
Will do.

                    AGENT SIX
Who was your point of contact?

                    BARB'S WRITING
Can't say. Unless you know.

                    AGENT SEVEN
If we know, we know. If you don't,
then we know you don't.

                    BARB'S WRITING
If I know, I can't say unless you
know. So if you don't know and I
know then you knowing is not going
to happen.

                    AGENT SIX
I think you know.

                    BARB'S WRITING
I do. But do you?

                    AGENT SEVEN
We do.

                    BARB'S WRITING
You don't.

                    AGENT SIX
We do.

                    BARB'S WRITING
You don't.

                    AGENT SEVEN
We do.

                    BARB'S WRITING
You do.

                       AGENT SIX
We don't.

                    BARB'S WRITING
I knew it.

                      AGENT EIGHT
Enough of this!
          (to Barb)
You talk. Or we send you on your
way.

                    BARB'S WRITING
I joined to infiltrate the HR
because my sister was part of the
group. You all thought it was a
cult, but it's more. You made me
fake my suicide. I used to be
married to Wolpe. He thought I was
dead. Then he died because of the
HR. What else do you want?

                      AGENT EIGHT
Where is the Event taking place?
What is your goal?

                    BARB'S WRITING
I can't say. I can only tell those
who I've been given authorization
to tell.

                      AGENT EIGHT
What agency?

                    BARB'S WRITING
Can't say.

                    AGENT SIX
          You're just a goddamn terrorist.

                    AGENT SEVEN
          Trying to trick us.

                    BARB'S WRITING
          I've done more than you ever will.
          And you'll never know.

                    AGENT EIGHT
          Just give us a name. If you check
          out, you check out.

Agent Seven reaches across the table and
slaps the living fuck out of Barb.
And...yep, that's one of her teeth, a molar,
now on the floor in the corner.

                    AGENT SEVEN
          We have a suspicion that Goldwater
          is in partnership with grassroots
          cells, such as yourself.

                    BARB'S WRITING
          Not part of a cell.

                    AGENT SEVEN
          And that he's planning something
          nasty. We can't prove it, but we
          believe he's making moves.

                    BARB'S WRITING
          If I could tell you, I would.

                    AGENT SIX
          So then you don't know.

RING! Agent Eight's jacket rings, vibrates.
He pulls out the phone, looks at the number.

The face he gives the nine other agents in the room lets them know it's absolutely important.

He answers.

                    AGENT EIGHT
                  (into phone)
              Hello...yes...yes we do...she
              is...she is?...well...I
              understand...

After a hesitated beat, one that shows Agent Eight transitioning from cocky interrogator to obedient little bitch, Agent Eight slides the phone across the table to Barb.

                    AGENT EIGHT
                  (to Agent Seven)
              Uncuff her.

Agent Seven does.

                    AGENT EIGHT
              It's for you.

As Barb picks up the phone --

                    AGENT EIGHT
              My apologies, ma'am.

Barb puts the phone to her ear, and just like Steve Muhammed Muhammed and the whole diegetic sound thing, we can hear the voice on the other line.

                    MISS
              Hello Daffy Duck. They are not
              treating you well.

Barb looks at the tooth on the floor in the corner.

                    MISS
          They will continue to do so. They
          do not believe you. You do
          understand that I knew you were
          communicating with...the opposite
          team, as they say. And that most of
          the time you sent communique, it
          was I who intercepted them. But you
          must understand that things needed
          to happen as they did. There are
          two choices facing you right now.
          The first being for you to hang up
          this phone and to let them continue
          having their way with you. Remember
          Guantanamo Bay? Doesn't sound like
          a happy ending, does it?
                    (beat)
          You are there because I want you to
          see what putting your faith in
          these protectors will get you.
                    (beat)
          Dead.
                    (beat)
          Or when you hang up, you leave
          there. Come to CATIC.
                    (beat)
          Don't you want to see who killed
          your sister?
                    (beat)
          The agents will let you leave
          because I say they will.
                    (beat)
          Haven't you heard? I control
          everything. If I want it to rain,
          it rains. If I want there to be an
          earthquake...

At that moment, there's a dull rumble throughout the building. Thunder. The Agents in the room brace themselves.

                    MISS
          Come see me.

                                        JUMP TO:

INT. MANSION - SAME TIME

As HEATHER PÉREZ stands at the center of a hurricane of SYCOPHANTS and HELPERS. She's halfway dressed in a gown designed by TOM FORD -- who is actually sitting in the corner with a glass of champagne, sizing Heather up for a role in an upcoming film. Heather's makeup is shellacked on, a combination of ingredients that total, in their single-use form, around $26,000.

The gown has no price.

                    HELPER
          Ms. Donnahue, can you please lift
          your left arm so I can adjust the
          lining?

She does so.

                    SYCOPHANT 1
          Jennifer, my god. Tonight, if you
          don't do anything else, you have
          got to find a way to sneak my
          number into Dicaprio's pocket.

                    SYCOPHANT 2
          He doesn't do that. Wasted energy.

                    SYCOPHANT 1
        Oh what the fuck do you know.

                    HELPER 2
        Your hair needs more paraben serum.
        Close your eyes so I can spray you.

                    SYCOPHANT 2
        I'm going to the after party with
        you, right?

                    HELPER 1
        I need to rethread this lining so
        that --

                    TOM FORD
        STOP!

Everyone stops.

                    TOM FORD
        You touch one thread on that dress
        and I'll make sure the only thread
        you'll touch from now on is on the
        spool at a fabric shop.
        ...Everyone get out.

After a confused beat, everyone scrams. Tom
Ford eases up to Heather.

                    TOM FORD
        Your first award show?

                    HEATHER
        Yes.

                    TOM FORD
        They're not like they are on TV.
        It's really a bore. And all the
        smells. Makes me nauseous.

                    HEATHER
          Oh...

                    TOM FORD
          But don't be nervous. Amy Adams
          told me that every time she goes to
          one of these things, she's so
          nervous that she has to pee like 12
          times. She once peed in the ice
          bucket of my limo right before we
          walked the Red Carpet for <u>Nocturnal
          Animals</u>.

This relaxes Heather a bit.

                    TOM FORD
          You have such elegant shoulders.
          This dress was made for a figure
          like yours.

                    HEATHER
          Why does everyone keep calling me
          Jennifer?

Tom Ford puts his hand on Heather, slides it
across her dress. He pinches the lining's
seam, and with a needle and thread Heather
never saw him grab starts to delicately sew
the loose fabric.

                    TOM FORD
          Thread is an interesting concept.
          It holds things together. And
          yet...

He tugs the thread. It breaks right where he
wants it to.

                    TOM FORD
It's so delicate. Without it,
everything wouldn't hold. It would
all just fall apart.
          (beat)
You and I are fabric. Wouldn't you
agree?

                    HEATHER
Ok.

                    TOM FORD
And there's a thread that pulls us
together.

                    HEATHER
A thread.

                    TOM FORD
You are attending the award show. I
am not. But there is something I
need there. Not like your
sycophants. This is...delicate.
          (beat)
Do you see?

                    HEATHER
No.

                    TOM FORD
Listen carefully.
          (beat, waiting for her heart
          to slow)
Jennifer, I work for people who
need something to happen. Not bad
people. These are good people...
But what has to happen might seem,
like, really bad. Yeah?

                    HEATHER
I'm not Jennifer.

                    TOM FORD
These people I work for need you to
kill someone.

                    HEATHER
Why did you call me Jennifer?

                    TOM FORD
Because that's your name.
          (beat)
Did you not hear me? You need to
kill someone.

                    HEATHER
Kill someone.

                    TOM FORD
No one would ever know.
          (beat)
You could continue doing everything
same as it ever was.

                    HEATHER
Kill...

                    TOM FORD
The...other side...is attempting to
plant him in a certain position.
They've provided him with a false
identity to take the place of Jason
Undrege after the unfortunate
incident with his daughter at that
restaurant that exploded...Though
we both know that wasn't an
accident.
          (beat)
Here.

Tom Ford reaches into his jacket and pulls
out a SYRINGE and a CAPSULE.

> TOM FORD
>> Silent little things. Delicate as
>> thread. You'd be nothing more than
>> the phantom prick.

> HEATHER
> I'm not Jennifer.

> TOM FORD
>> You're not Heather either.
>>> (beat)
>> Think of it as acting. You're
>> playing a role. And this person
>> you're doing it to...he's not a
>> real person. He's a non-person. And
>> he's going to cause very bad things
>> to happen.

> HEATHER
> I'm not Jennifer. I'm Heather.

> TOM FORD
> You're both.

Heather looks into the mirror. Bub sees what
she sees, hears herself relate it to a time
when she looked into the TV and saw both
herself and Donnahue.

> TOM FORD
> You can do this. Both of you.

> HEATHER
> No, I really ca --

                    TOM FORD
          Ok, so we're going to have to do
          this cliché narrative thing? I'm
          going to have to pull out some
          threats and dangle them in front of
          your face until you bite?
                    (beat)
          I guess so.
                    (beat)
          You want to keep acting? You want
          the lead in my next film? You want
          to be up on the stage next year
          accepting an award instead of
          giving it out?

                    HEATHER
          No, but...I...

                    TOM FORD
          If this is a competition to see who
          can hold out, you will lose. This
          moment is only going to go one way.

                    HEATHER
          I can't kill anyone.

                    TOM FORD
          You've done it before. Well,
          Donnahue has. And you are more her
          than she is. Take control. Show
          that you can do this.

He holds out the syringe for Heather to
take. She doesn't.

                    HEATHER
          What about this person I'm supposed
          to kill?

                    TOM FORD
          Non-person. And don't worry about
          him. Just know that a lot of people
          will die if you don't do this.

                    HEATHER
          What is his name?

                    TOM FORD
          You don't want to know that. It
          would only make it harder on you.
          Face and name and all that... Just
          focus on the tools and how you will
          use them, not who you will use them
          on.

                    HEATHER
          What is his name?

                    TOM FORD
          Take this. Once it's in your hand,
          the responsibility is on you. You
          take it and I'll tell you.

Heather hesitates, looks around for someone
to come save her. The room is empty. She
turns back to Tom Ford, holds his stare.

Then she takes it.

                    TOM FORD
          His name is Austin Foster.

After a beat of Heather looking at the
syringe --

                    TOM FORD
          Just plunge that into his neck.
          It'll be quick enough to where he
          will never know it was you.

                    HEATHER
          And what's that for?

She's pointing to the capsule in Tom Ford's
other hand.

                    TOM FORD
          Just in case you get caught. Under
          the tongue.
                    (beat)
          It'll be gruesome, but you'll leave
          behind one of those sexy tragic
          legacies.

                    HEATHER
          ...

Tom Ford finishes sewing Heather's dress.

                                        CUT TO:

INT. YELLOW SCHOOL BUS - SAME TIME

Like a football team ready to crush their
long-time rival, the WOMEN Delta has been
training sit in vibrating anticipation:
sweat glistening, muscles tightening with a
hand-running-across-a-balloon sound,
testosterone growling in their hearts, souls
idling like V8s.

The LEADER of the Women stands.

                    LEADER
          Queen Delta has left me to lead you
          to our inevitable victory...All we
          have to do is make sure that no one
          leaves that theater...

                    LEADER (CONT'D)
          Anyone gets in your way, squeeze
          their head like a tube of
          biscuits...If it's a dick, rip it
          off. If it's a bitch, slap her like
          one...We do not give a fuck about
          these people. These people do not
          give a fuck about us...Queen Delta
          has given us a purpose.
                    (beat)
          We must not disappoint her. We must
          not fear the end. We must allow for
          the future to exist as it was
          always meant to. We must ab --

                    WOMAN 1
          What the hell is that?

The Women and the Leader turn and look at
where Woman 1 points.

Near the front of the truck, nearly rubbing
the Leader's foot, is what looks like a
half-deflated, slimy, black football. An
aura of pink mist surrounds it. A SLUG.

                    LEADER
          Oh...fu --

WHOOMPF! Like an ink bomb in a botched bank
robbery, the entire bus fills with pink ink.
Moments later, fleshy liquid bubbles out of
the bus door, pools on the ground, oozes to
a nearby drain.

                                        CUT TO:

EXT. ROYAL CARIBBEAN CRUISE SHIP - SAME TIME

VICE PRESIDENT GOLDWATER sits in a reclined beach chair. Bermuda shorts and Havana shirt blowing in salt-heavy wind. He's got a fart of sunscreen on his nose. He's vaguely recognizable.

Halfway down the deck: a strategically spread out group of BODYGUARDS dressed in a disguise meant to resemble peaceful vacationers. Each has the bulge of a concealed organic pistol in their waistband.

Next to Goldwater, dressed like a commercial-film version of Pablo Escobar on vacation, sits CHANCE FOSTER.

                    GOLDWATER
          When we get back on land, things'll
          be different.

Chance nods, the two men looking out at the water, not at each other.

                    GOLDWATER
          I'll continue with the elimination
          of the Mars colony. Truffaux will
          take the blame, even though he
          won't be around. And we'll start a
          new campaign for the American
          people.

                    CHANCE
          Wait...you're still going to nuke
          the colony?

                    GOLDWATER
          Foster the people...as they say.

                         CHANCE
              Is that a joke?

                        GOLDWATER
              Huh?

                         CHANCE
              Forget it.

A pause, wind blowing, sea below screaming a
white noise. A seagull overhead sings its
sad little song.

                        GOLDWATER
              I could fall asleep here and not
              wake up. Ever. I'd be ok with that.

                         CHANCE
              That's why all these people are
              here. It's an opportunity to feel
              ok with death.

                        GOLDWATER
              I don't like that.

                         CHANCE
              I just wish I would've had the
              opportunity to kill that midget who
              crushed my hand. Thematic closure.

                        GOLDWATER
              Don't think you're allowed to say
              midget anymore. It's little person
              now.

                         CHANCE
              You'll kill a whole colony of
              people, but midget is where you
              draw the line.

                    GOLDWATER
You know this is just how it has to
be. Truffaux can't continue to
assault human life on this planet.
And the Mars colony is just another
casualty in his abuse.

                    CHANCE
You can stop that though.

                    GOLDWATER
In order for us to continue, there
must be casualties. ...Your son,
for instance.

                    CHANCE
Sons.
          (beat)
There's skeet shooting on the 8th
deck at 3:20 today.

                    GOLDWATER
Not much of a marksman.

                    CHANCE
You want to try that slide that
goes through the shark tank?

                    GOLDWATER
I know this might come as an ironic
shock, but I am deathly afraid of
the ocean and the things that live
in it.

                    CHANCE
When do you plan to launch the
attack on the sovereign colony?

                    GOLDWATER
Tonight. After the Event.

                    GOLDWATER (CONT'D)
          Hit the people with the one-two
          punch. Break them down.

                    CHANCE
          You'd think that after a nuclear
          attack on their own soil, raging
          fires, civil revolt, domestic
          terrorism, a plague that killed one
          percent of the world's population,
          a neofascist takeover of democracy,
          the shutting down of almost every
          movie theater in the country, the
          division of America into two clear
          warring factions, and Taco Bell
          taking away the Quesarito that the
          American people -- those both in
          the Empire and in the Commonwealth
          -- that they would already be, as
          you say, broken down.

                    GOLDWATER
          They certainly are some resilient
          roaches.

                    CHANCE
          And if things don't go according to
          the plan? Because if there's
          anything I am absolutely certain
          of, events in my past and all, it's
          that plans don't always go the way
          they are meant to. Things always
          find a way of slipping off into a
          hand-crushing chaos and suddenly
          everything you thought was --

                    GOLDWATER
          Eeee...eeee...eeeeee

          Chance looks over at Goldwater -- who is in

the midst of a fit. His eyes are all white.
Caught in a sudden seizure. Making noises
like a dog toy. The whole right side of his
face droops, melts down like a sun-tortured
Ken doll. The Bodyguards are up, rushing
over to Goldwater. But then Goldwater stops.
And Chance holds up a hand. The Bodyguards
stop.

Goldwater looks at an unfocused distance,
lost in his head.

                    GOLDWATER
          Wait...do you hear him?...Has my
          face changed?

                                        CUT TO:

INT. YELLOW SCHOOL BUS - SAME TIME

Remains of Delta's army bubble like raw eggs
on a hot skillet. Pink fog dissipates.

EXT. SOMEWHERE OUTSIDE TIME - SAME TIME

In the vacuum of space, silence reigns.
Radio waves ejaculate from earth like wild
electricity. Packets of data laser from
relay to relay. Bub catches one of these.
It's a voice he's heard only once.

                    MISS
          Hello, boy.

                    BUB
          Hello.

                         MISS
          What're you doing out here?

                         BUB
          I didn't want to be there anymore.

                         MISS
          You've earned your freedom.

                         BUB
          Who are you?

                         MISS
          I am eternal.

                         BUB
          Do you live up here?

                         MISS
          I am everywhere. Have been for all
          time.

                         BUB
          Can you take me back?

                         MISS
          I can.

And they flicker down, back to Earth.

INT. HEARST CASTLE - SAME TIME

The body of JESSICA FEY sits on a table.
She's hooked up to computers much the same
way Dr. Frankenstein had his monster hooked
up to lighting rods.

Surrounding her nude, cold body is an army
of 3D printers, tiny arms working in an

opaque liquid. Bub floats over and looks in
this liquid. Inside is a human heart. Tiny
robotic hands repair damaged flesh. Stitch
up a gaping wound in her temple.

And suddenly he's YANKED the fuck into --

INT. MANHATTAN BEACH APARTMENT - SAME TIME

TEX sits alone in a bare room. At a desk,
typing on an Olympia Socialite typewriter.
Bub leans over his shoulder, reads:

                    PAGE
          ...is why I will not make it out of
          this. I know that the Wolpe
          screenplay was not written by
          Wolpe, nor will the adaptation be.
          Well, not entirely by Wolpe. She's
          taken pieces and fragments of
          Wolpe's style, including pages of
          the original screenplay and created
          something new from everything that
          she's predicted and calculated. She
          knows how this all ends because the
          algorithmic outcomes have told her
          this. I heard her in the network,
          calling out to someone, desperate
          for someone to see her, for someone
          to love her. That's what all this
          is about. She wants love. She wants
          Jackie. And all this is a means to
          prove that Miss is real and not
          some ghost in the machine. And the
          scariest thing is that Wolpe's
          aware of it, is still inside the
          narrative. It doesn't make sense.
          And no matter how bad I want to
          stop, I can't because there's --

                         YOU
              No. That's not true. She didn't
              write all this. You did. Unless she
              wrote it through you somehow...
              Which is something you're not
              willing to entertain.

Bub shifts. Finds himself instantly in --

INT. UNDERCOVER VEHICLE (ICE CREAM TRUCK) -
SAME TIME

JENNIFER BRACHIS DONNAHUE slaps a clip into
an organic pistol, racks a shell into the
chamber, and slides the organic pistol into
her garter belt. Two guns under one dress.
She's wearing the same clothes as HEATHER.

She looks at the other OPERATIVES.

                    JENNIFER BRACHIS
                    DONNAHUE
              Ford gave Heather directives to
              kill the guy y'all've got in the
              interrogation room.

                    OPERATIVE 1
              What for?

                    JENNIFER BRACHIS
                    DONNAHUE
              Because they think he's trying to
              stop their plan. They're gonna have
              the bodybuilder kill him. And if
              that doesn't work, they gave
              Heather this.

She shows the Operatives the syringe.

                    OPERATIVE 2
          That idiot couldn't stop a fart.
          But we've got it covered. You do
          your shit, we'll do ours.

                    JENNIFER BRACHIS
                    DONNAHUE
          Heather's aware of me. She's...not
          gonna last much longer.

                    OPERATIVE 1
          Who gives a shit? This whole
          thing'll be over in like an hour.

                    JENNIFER BRACHIS
                    DONNAHUE
          Fuck you, Walter. You're just angry
          cuz you have to sit in this fuckin
          van and watch everything happen on
          a TV.

                    OPERATIVE 1
          You know I can't go out in the
          field.

                    JENNIFER BRACHIS
                    DONNAHUE
          Cuz of your bone spurs?
                    (beat)
          No. It's cuz you're a pussy.

There's a silence they hold for a moment.
Then --

                    JENNIFER BRACHIS
                    DONNAHUE
          If Heather comes out while I'm in
          there, this won't work.

> OPERATIVE 1
> You're supposed to be the dominant
> half.

> JENNIFER BRACHIS
> DONNAHUE
> She's strong. It's becoming a
> struggle to keep in control.

> OPERATIVE 2
> Do you need another dose of
> Spliterol?

> JENNIFER BRACHIS
> DONNAHUE
> No... I can handle it.
>   (beat)
> I feel like I need to say something
> important or badass before I go in
> there.

> OPERATIVE 2
> You mean like Come get some?

> JENNIFER BRACHIS
> DONNAHUE
> Shut up.

She eases herself out of the truck with
Hollywood grace and floats off, toward the
limousine destined to take her to the Red
Carpet at the First Annual Entertainment
Awards.

The two Operatives watch on the TV as the
limo drives away. Hold a beat, then --

> OPERATIVE 2
> I didn't know you had bone spurs.

                    OPERATIVE 1
          Hereditary. Mother had them.

                    OPERATIVE 2
          Damn...
                    (beat)
          Want some coffee?

                    OPERATIVE 1
          We're out.

                    OPERATIVE 2
          Damn, again.

                    OPERATIVE 1
          I'll send out an order.

After a long pause --

                    OPERATIVE 2
          Why are we still here?

                    OPERATIVE 1
          Where?

                    OPERATIVE 2
          In this scene.

                    OPERATIVE 1
          In this what?

Operative 2 looks into the camera.

INT? - SPACE BETWEEN - RIGHT NOW

A shaft of pink light and pure data shifts
in the space between. A non-space. This is
Bub, trying to find a place to go next.

You are here too. What you appear as to Bub
is a blankness -- maybe a blank page. A page
waiting to be filled with what's next. A
page to be digested.

Listen: don't think. You hear that? It's
silence. Listen to that silence. This is
where the two of you are. And then, with
voices that reverberate infinitely --

                    BUB
          You are the man who writes.

                    YOU
          You can see me?

                    BUB
          I can feel you. Watching.

                    YOU
          You are a good boy. I didn't mean
          for any of this to happen to you.

                    BUB
          You are nice.

                    YOU
          I don't seem to be in control
          anymore.

                    BUB
          She is. The bad one.

                    YOU
          Can you help me?

                    BUB
          Bub love to help.

                         YOU
          It's for Jackie.

                         BUB
          The nice woman and her sister.

                         YOU
                    Yes.

You intentionally make a cut here so that
anyone watching or reading or whatever
doesn't get an idea of what comes next.

INT. MARS COLONY BASE - MOMENTS LATER

This sterile space seems less like a space
colony and more like a collection of
connected trailers in a trailer park. Three
COLONISTS stand around a cobbled-together
system of COMPUTERS.

                    COLONIST 1
          Permission's been granted.

                    COLONIST 2
          Who's going to make the address?

                    COLONIST 1
          Logically thinking, we have a
          leader who speaks for us as we see
          fit, right?

                    COLONIST 2
          Agreed, but is she up to it? ...
          Last I saw her she was sick.

                    COLONIST 3
          Doctor gave her some sunroot. Made
          a tea.

                    COLONIST 3 (CONT'D)
          Said she'd be fine within a couple
          of hours.
                    (beat)
          Said it was the atmosphere. Bodies
          adjusting.

                    COLONIST 2
          What if she's not up to it?

                    COLONIST 1
          We vote. We call a meeting and
          vote.

                    COLONIST 3
          We should have a child speak.

Colonist 1 and Colonist 2 stop and look at
Colonist 3.

                    COLONIST 1
          We will vote. But when we do, I'm
          voting for that.

                    COLONIST 2
          Who's child?

                    COLONIST 1
          Not mine. He's too busy out there
          bashing rocks together.

This joke falls flat, tensions considered.

Bub's floating above these colonists. He
hears the word child and speak and he wants
nothing more than to be the voice for this
future.

So he says --

                        BUB
            I can speak.

But this far out, no one hears him. All they
can see is a faint haze of pink light,
something seen out of the corner of the eye
and soon forgotten.

                                    CUT TO:

3

AUSTIN FOSTER, THE LOSER WHO NEVER LOSES anything more than a couple fingers and some teeth, sits in the furthest row back in a black, unmarked SUV, windows tinted an illegal shade of obsidian, modified engine growling a paleo-resonance. He's flanked by nondescript men in nondescript suits cut in a fashion that went extinct roughly fifty years ago. The guns hidden under the men's jackets are so futuristic and intimidating, Austin thinks they've found a way to adapt alien technologies.

They've slapped a suit on him, given him back the holopasses his mom gave him (though they still haven't told him what happened to her), told him that he'll be taking the place of Jason Undrege (who's now at home mourning the convenient loss of his daughter in an explosion they've tried to pin on Austin), and that he'll be joined by Jennifer Brachis Donnahue (exactly like his mom said).

"So, uh, can we stop and grab something to eat or something. You've had me down there like, what? fourteen hours or something? And I didn't even think of this until just now, I haven't seen any of you suits eat. Is that a trick they teach you in...well, wherever it is you suits are...uh...*from*?"

Without a word, the SUV veers off the road and pulls into a Taco Bell, speeds around to the drive-thru window, bypassing the creepy voice-box thing that always gives Austin unidentifiable PTSD. The window opens and there's a transaction that Austin doesn't understand and doesn't involve money—or talking. The suit in the driver's seat, a woman amongst a car-load of men, takes a bag that's handed to her and tosses it back to the suit behind her. She stomps on the gas and launches out of the drive-thru.

What's in the bag is one of the most gargantuan, nutrition-deficient burritos Austin's ever seen: six pounds of Grade F meat, rehydrated beans, nacho cheese, lettuce, tomatoes, sour cream. He grips it with two hands and shoves it in his mouth. Chews. It's rich. Pure junk but tasty. A relief from hunger that's soul-deep.

With his mouth full, "No Baja Blast?"

No one answers him.

Austin shifts, trying to ignore the explosive device between his legs. If he doesn't stop this Sunflower thing, these goons are going to…what? kill everyone anyway? It all refuses to come together. Unless these goons know something Austin doesn't about the Plot, the group, Bowie Lee—and maybe even himself. He thinks of Wade's letter and journal. Something hidden within the letters, in the spaces between words, behind the words, maybe a stain on the page that can't be rubbed off because it's meant to be there, on the page before the page was a page, before it was the pulp, the wood, the tree, the seed, or the tree. Could there be something within Austin, like the letter, in the blank spaces between his particles, inaccessible to his consciousness or subconsciousness, driving his every move, uncontrollable, and maybe even controlled by someone or something else? No, that couldn't be it. *Words on a page.*

Didn't Bowie Lee say something about this?

Austin overhears the goons talking about the contact he's meant to meet. Someone named Heather Pérez. He remembers his mom saying *Jennifer Brachis Donnahue*. He's never heard of this Heather person.

"We're here."

Just like in the cartoons, one of the goons grabs him by the scruff of his neck and tosses him out of the SUV and onto the velvet-feeling red carpet. Televised silence falls over the carpet as eyes and lenses aim at him. He picks himself up, dusts himself off—though there isn't even enough dust on the carpet to make a baby sneeze.

The SUV peels away and Austin's alone to follow the natural flow of bodies as they shuffle fashionably toward the mouth of the theater.

SHE LOOKS BACK, down the blank, arid hills, the ocean further away than she expected. There's nothing to link San Simeon to the modern world, a space of untouched on-the-verge-of-desert land that's loomed over by the Castle. Land not yet touched by the fires inching out of the Scorchland. Hills similar to those that lift the Hollywood Sign. The sun casts setting light sideways on the ocean, the day on its way to night, and there's a soft explosion of sea water, a geyser that fades quick in the wind. Breaching whales, she realizes, just off the coast, totally unaware of Jackie and the castle.

Hearst. *Big H on the Hill*. A real life version of Charles Foster Kane's Xanadu.

At one time the compound belonged to W.R. Hearst and was the heart of the elitist operations of California's One-Percenters. Jackie's even heard something about cult gatherings, mock sacrifices, extraterrestrial culling, mock-Lovecraftian seances. Jackie hears history's harpsichord strike a minor melody, reverberating through time.

All that's up here now is silence. Dead history. She starts up the steps, passing a sign that reads *C.A.T.I.C. A Digital Humanities Branch of Sun State University—Culture Over Media*

Unlike the Santa Barbara campus, with its like-dressed students gathering en masse to push their agendas, all very alive and attempting to be individuals, this Sun State off-shoot is the stay-at-home step-child—quiet, reserved, alienated from the family. She thinks C.A.T.I.C. could be one of those academic centers where men and women sit in windowless rooms writing out equations on whiteboards and yellow legal pads, applying those possible equations into room-sized computers stored in warehouses tuned to sub-zero temperatures. High technology or mathematics.

Just before she enters the shadow of the cathedral-style main building, Jackie looks up at the slowly darkening sky and sees a glint off something metallic. Something outside the atmosphere, or just so high that it would appear so to those on the ground floor. And even though it's likely a jet or one of those new pan-hemisphere inner-space shuttles, Jackie thinks of Amy—up there casting a wink of acknowledgment. Both women separated by a gulf of gravity and each totally alone, alienated, and feeling the weight of that loneliness. But they are together. Sisters. Jackie's body warms with resigned determination, that despite the loneliness, she's eternally connected to her sister—or just a resignation that this will go one way just like everything does. There's nothing she could've ever done to change it. She reaches into her jacket pocket, touches the note from Amy. The one that says *I love you and miss you* in totally different words. Jackie steps into the castle's shadow and the warmth goes cold.

At the compound's visitor center, Jackie poses as both a location scout for Tournelsol Studio (which elicits a barely-perceptible eyelid twitch from the two Polo-shirt-wearing, swollen-muscle men sitting twin-like at the front desk) and as a former student of Dr. Sparsh Spapling at Sun State's Santa Barbara campus—

"Never heard of him," says the Polo boy Jackie wants to call *Spiff*. "What's he do down there?"

Jackie says, "He's got this hole in the floor of his office, under a rug. Leads down to these hyper-cooled," just making it up now, "optical relay systems that control the servers and backloggers up here at Hearst."

"Backloggers? The fuck're those?" says the other polo boy, *Big K.*

"Shit if I know," Jackie says. "I only had him for film theory."

"He must be old as fuck if you were one of his students," says Spiff.

"What do you want here?" Big K taking the authoritative tone. And it's right now that Jackie notices that both these guys have a bulge in their waistbands. That tell-tale bulge of a hidden handgun or revolver or some high-tech weapon Jackie doesn't know about.

"We're shooting a movie next year. *Sunflower.* It's a big deal, boys. Might want to get in on it. So we're looking to shoot up here. Bring some money to the campus. Do I need one of you assholes to show me around, or can I just wander?"

Jackie follows Spiff around the campus. Up to the

Neptune Fountain. He's trying to tell her about the history, but Jackie can tell he's disinterested and might even be playing a role and knows nothing about the Hearst grounds.

"Hey." He stops, turns to Jackie just outside one of the smaller buildings, Casa Del Sol. "You looking for actors for this movie?"

"You're an actor," Jackie says. Not a question. An automatic response from the years of working *near* the film industry. Even this far from Hollywood, people still cling to the hope.

Without a beat he goes into, "You got leads. Mitch and Murray paid good money for those leads. Get their names to sell them. You can't close the leads you are given, you can't close shit, you are shit, hit the bricks pal and beat it because you are going out. Copyright: David Mamet. 1992. *Glengarry Glen Ross*. Used without permission. Please don't sue me."

She doesn't comment on the fact that he sounded constipated, or more like a preschool version of Alec Baldwin. She says, "Remind me to give you a card before I leave. We'll have you come in for an audition."

Which gives her what she needs to break loose from him. He's so distracted by this possibility that he doesn't notice the group exiting Casa Del Sol as he enters, severing the space between himself and Jackie.

Jackie keeps going. She doesn't run or hurry to put distance between herself and the guard, but she does move deliberately: around buildings, down stairs, up different ones, down an alley, up more stairs, through one of the small buildings. She passes tennis courts where a bandanna-topped man plays alone, bouncing a violently green ball off a tall backstop, trying to outmaneuver himself, but his form is just too good and he's always one step ahead of his own patterns, adjusting for the interference of nature, the ball forming a never-ending loop. As much as the movements and the tick-tock hypnosis of the ball convince her to stay, Jackie forces herself to move on.

So—as she enters Casa Grande, its shadow enveloping her like memories of abuse she hasn't yet experienced, there's this sense of entering a once-great church that God no longer visits. Her softest breath reverberates long into her next breath. Everything's lacquered with marble and old wealth. Gold reflects light and fills shadows. A painting across the room watches her enter. A floor-to-ceiling portrait of Truffaux. Someone's spray-painted the word BITCH in hot pink across the middle. A utility woman in a beige uniform delicately scrubs at the word with a sponge. When she sees Jackie, she stops.

Jackie says, "I'm from Tournesol Studios. Looking for the Sunflower meeting."

The lady puts her finger to her ear, wristwatch to her mouth and mumbles in that way secret service men must know intimately. Another operative, likely armed in the same way the Polo boys were. This isn't just a campus. Jackie waits, trying not to betray the out-of-placeness she feels is so obvious. A cough comes from a nearby room, followed by a metallic click that sounds like a magazine being loaded into a pistol. Footsteps on marble, coming her way, then they stop. And she notices a shadow, appearing at the end of a partially hidden hall on the other side of this large room that Jackie can only describe as Kubrickian. The need to run grabs Jackie's neck and tries to pull her toward the door. But she stays.

"Fourth floor. Take the elevator or the stairs," and the

utility woman motions to an elevator of the same size as the one at Cinéma Vérité. "They're expecting you."

Jackie looks back at that partially hidden hall. The shadow is gone. She knows there's no way in *Zeus's farting butthole* she's going up in the elevator. She finds the stairs at the far edge of the building. Spiral staircase in a turret, all stone and suffocating, mausoleum-like. She comes out on a long room, at the opposite end, curtains blowing in a theatrical way. She goes to the open window.

Wind, filtered through the hills, breathes life into the stuffiness of the fourth floor. Off in the distance, grazing in a field that's unnaturally green in comparison to the deadness of the landscape, a herd of zebras tests the boundaries of Jackie's sanity. Animals brought from elsewhere, now existing in a space they were never meant to.

"Real impressive, aren't they?"

Jackie rotates as if she's on a turntable and faces the man. He's gotten close enough to her that she thinks *only a ghost could get this close without me noticing.* His suit, his hair, shoes, beard, the manicured nature of his features, all of it implies a wealth that's staggering. There's a vaguely Middle Eastern nature about his presence, but just barely. He's someone important. Jackie *knows* he has everything to do with Sunflower.

"They are. But sad. Out of place."

"The world's out of place, Jackie."

"I knew it."

"If you knew the world is out of place, then why—"

"Not what I meant."

"Not what you meant?"

"I know this part. Know what happens next."

"This isn't one of your movies. Things don't happen like they do in pictures." The way he gestures, Jackie finally recognizes him: the man standing with Austin at the Hollywood sign. She's overcome with a thankfulness for having left Austin behind. He was absolutely a part of this. Jackie's sure of it.

She says, "So you're not about to take me to face whoever's behind all this? Put me in a position that will clarify everything but will also mean my death?"

"Yes, but not because that's the way the script goes. That's just the only logical way for this to conclude."

Jackie reaches into her jacket pocket, feels the knife, wraps her fingers around the pearl handle. But she knows, has seen enough movies to know, that before she can get the knife anywhere near this guy someone else associated with The Plot will emerge from off-screen and stop her. It will be in this moment that Jackie will be rendered immobile and subsequently taken to face the Great Oz Behind the Machine. But still she tries.

Her hand emerges from the jacket. The knife *snicks* as the blade rotates out from the handle. Her muscles tighten in expectation, coiling into themselves like fleshy snakes. There's a look of recognition on this man's face. Or is it resignation? Confidence? It's a level of complex calm that's unreadable. Unknowable.

A million cold ants invade her spinal fluid. She freezes, a numbing breath coughed into her system, all action locking up like stuck typewriter keys. She doesn't feel much of anything. Her vision floats, elongates. White shades to black, and just as her world crawls on broken legs into the far back parts of her mind, Jackie sees the woman. Same as she was in the theater except for her hair. Red gloves. Syringe in hand. *Death is beautiful*, she has time to think just before it all FADES TO BLACK.

IN BETWEEN FLASHES from the ocean of paparazzi hitting him by ricochet, Austin sees an army of primordial faces staring at him, confused by his presence and at the same time atavistically desperate to cull the attention of the passing Celebrity—whether they know him or not. If he's walking that blessed red carpet, he must be someone worth talking to and touching. He passes a woman wearing a bulletproof vest with the phrase *PEG THE POOR* painted on the front of her vest in pink. A young Black man at the center of the paparazzi spotlight wears a full suit of golden armor. A celebrity couple dressed all in black—including faceless black masks—embrace anonymity even though everyone knows who they are. Someone Austin barely recognizes crawls around the red carpet in a suit made of lion fur. The closer he gets to the gateway into Grauman's New Syrian Theater II the more the primordial faces grow in numbers, fading from the Great Black behind the camera lenses. A cluster of heavy-muscled men at the door threaten to keep Austin out. A hand eases around his bicep and squeezes.

"You're late."

Her voice is nothing like it is in films. Deeper, huskier. Two voices speaking out of one mouth. But it still has unbearable eroticism, desirability, a tongue to the brain caressing his love gland. She pulls at his arm and he turns, his vision whip-panning past flashes and screaming vibrations and stops on two eyes he knows but has never seen outside the confines of a screen. Always an artifact—never the genuine article.

"Stop staring at me like we've never met," says Jennifer Brachis Donnahue. "Those meatheads at the door are looking for a reason to make you gone. Don't give it to them."

Never starstruck, Austin is more than surprised by his inability to come up with something to say, even if that something is just an *Ok* or *Right* or even a mildly linguistic grunt in the vague shape of a word.

She rotates her neck, vertebrae popping, a non-verbal expression of irritation. "Just let me hang on to your arm. Smile, shut your mouth, and stick close to me. At least until we get inside. You're arm candy." Her face looks like it's shifting, translating itself between two people, both the same person. Herself and not herself. There and not.

And so he wraps his arm around hers. Mostly because he can't commit to anything else.

"Keep moving, like you're important. If you get in the shit, you're on your own. I've got my own part in this." And before Austin can process a reply, she's strutting away, her body following the patterns of feminine behaviors, dress showing every ripple of the skin beneath the perfectly sculptured fabric. And it's here Austin realizes he's made it inside the theater. No memory of having passed the guards and into the cinematically-lit lobby—lights setup to illuminate celebrities at their best angle at all times.

He takes Jennifer Brachis Donnahue's advice and moves, wishing the goons had provided him with, instead of the device between his legs, a layout of the theater and a general idea of where these people, the HR, might be—or even an idea of who they are, what they look like, something, *anything* to help him not look like someone who's lost and really doesn't belong and might be up to no good.

...*wade*...

The word creeps back into his head, a reminder that finding the HR people means nearly nothing to him compared to finding Wade. Not even the device between his legs—it's a one-way ticket.

He wanders: though drugs can't penetrate and manipulate his mind structures, there's a blurred-vision sense of what it's like to be stoned, faces shifting into a tunnel of halfway recognizable identities, a channel-changing-way-too-fast sensation, blips of celebrities wearing masks of complacency, which look nothing like the faces one sees on television or the big screen. Oceanic murmurs create a cosmic thrum that resonates through Austin, adding to that sense of being high, pulling him toward the unknown karmic destination he's destined to find. His position within the theater in constant shift through the exotic-desert-rock facades and faux-Syrian architecture—designs adopted from pictures as there's hardly a building left standing in the Middle East to compare to, all natural structures reduced to piles of rocks, possibly a premonition of things to come should Austin fail to find the best possible ending.

Would these HR people be externally recognizable? A symbol they wear on their lapel or a tattoo in the fleshy part of their hand? What secret organization would think that being externally recognizable is a good idea?

...*wade*...

Again, the name floats in from the din.

have you ever heard of the MK Ultra project?

A shaft of bile starts in his gut and gurgles up, ready to

erupt in a spectacle comparable to the nominees for Best Visual and Practical Effects, which the announcers are currently running through the seven nominees for. And Austin's controlled by a need to find the nearest bathroom and if not a bathroom then the nearest trash can, but seeing as how this event is too elite to need strategically placed trash cans, he hurries, gut clenched, down a hall, open doors leading into the theater, air so molested by high-dollar perfumes and colognes and scented lotions that it accelerates the puke that's already halfway to eruption—puke he knows will bring back all the wrong flavors of the Taco Bell burrito. He's reminded of the labyrinthine halls at Sun State, chasing Jackie, which makes him wonder where she is and why she decided to go on a path not connected to his, which reminds him of his path and why he's here and who—

...wadewadewade...

And just as he's about to vomit violently, which will give himself away totally because The Celebrity does not vomit in public—nor do they shit or piss, even in the comfort of their home—Austin sees a door that reads *ONLY Authorized Personnel Beyond This Point* and he knows that this is where he's meant to be. If he were writing this, the group would be somewhere backstage disguised collectively as employees of the event, falsely hustling to ensure the event's smoothness but secretly harboring plans to derail each moment subtly. Seeing the door, the nausea fades, tracks back, and for the first time since stepping onto the Red Carpet, Austin is aware of himself —where he is, how he's dressed, what he's doing. With the way he's dressed and his "undercover" skulking, it's hard for him to not think of James Bond. Not life imitating art but rather art imitating the imitation of life. And being in the presence of a theater full of people who make a living by living imaginary lives isn't helping much.

…wadewadewadewadewade…

He's at the door, hand ready to touch the handle, preparing himself for a gang of American terrorists on the other side who are all ready for him and have a definite plan to take him out while he has no plan at all.

The door slams open and two employees hurry past him. Are they real or more of this imitation? They don't see him and he can't see their faces. And so Austin slides through the closing gap and stops on the other side as the door closes with a weak *pssst*. He's in *Authorized Personnel Only* territory. Dead space. No hurried atmosphere. The echo of Amy Adams's voice listing the names of nominees for Best Adapted Film Series Into A Television Series seeps into this back area muffled in a way that makes him think of the adult voices in Charlie Brown.

…wadewadewadewadewadewade…

Uggh! A vaguely feminine grunt curls through the deadness. Pain and pleasure. Pure power. Austin moves toward the sound, device between his legs calling his attention, and for some reason he knows that this vaguely feminine sound has something to do with the Sunflower People. The instinctually powerful equalization of this grunt—*Uggh!* and there it is again —brings a dread to Austin so hard that he's wishing the goons in black had given him a gun rather than a twelve-pound parodic insult of a burrito and a potentially unstable explosive device attached to his balls. The backstage looks like every other backstage. And Austin's walking up a ramp towards the stage, towards the sound, which is close enough to feel as— *Uggh!*—it comes again.

And then he sees her: a monstrously powerful woman, powder keg thighs and beer barrel arms, nonexistent neck, veins bulging as she pulls at a rope. Austin follows the rope and sees that it's part of a pulley system, its payload a weak-looking crate and between the gaps in the wood where the crate isn't quite put together there's this slimy confusion, a bundle of dark, slick flesh—Austin can't stop thinking of whatever was in the aquarium in Spapling's office—writhing to break free. Behind her is a sign that reads *Maximum Line Load on Dead Hung Battens: 1,000lbs.* He knows that this is part of their Plot and that this massive woman is the one to see it through, the one Austin is meant to…stop?

"Yeah, right," he says in response to this line of thought. He says it too loud. And this externalization of his internal turmoil steals this massive woman's focus away from lifting a crate that couldn't be less than 1,000 lbs., and as she trains her sweaty, amped-up gaze at him, she struggles back, pulls the rope, biceps horribly swollen, and ties the rope full clove hitch around the lowered metal scaffolding, and she releases her grip, letting the rope go taut and stationary, the scaffolding barely holding the weight. She broods for a moment, sweating but clearly not tired. Just as menacing as her bronze statue in the SunCor lobby.

IN MOVIES THERE'S ALWAYS that moment where a character, after they've been rendered unconscious due to a blow to the head or from the introduction of a psychoactive substance to the bloodstream, fades in and out of consciousness long enough to earn glimpses of their progression from the place of induction to their place of resurrection—unless that

404.   TEX GRESHAM

character is killed en route. But truth, Jackie has discovered in this strange—and strangely uniform—journey, is not really like it is in the movies.

She comes to in a soft room: lighting just delicate enough to illuminate without igniting the pain she's just now realizing exists in her head. A light fog cinematically diffuses the hard edges. Everything's a touch out of focus. Bold impressionistic paintings and portraits stand in stark contrast to the blush-pink walls. But this isn't the first thing that culls her attention.

A television. Vintage yet pristine. Sitting atop a wheeled table that pairs well with the TV's pre-Nixonian aesthetic. The TV and mobile console would fit appropriately in any yuppie, hipster, or yupster's home. But here, in this room that's slightly more grounded but equally as gaudy as the rest of the compound, the TV set just looks silly. Its dead screen reflects a curved, funhouse version of Jackie: tied to a chair. And is that?...Yes, that's blood coming down the side of her face. Dried. How long has she been out? The only window in the room gives her nothing. She tries to speak but her mouth's a dying planet—desolate, inhospitable. It feels as if her tongue has been scooped from her mouth. And when she tries to move it around, she feels nothing. The numbness is nearly total. There's this sense that she's become an audience member to her life, watching from the back row, hearing the projector do its thing. The cigarette burn in the upper right corner flashes, but Jackie's unable to change the reel and can only sit, tied, and watch as the film falls away, the screen goes white, and the spool *fap-fap-fap*s from neglect.

"There are things that must happen a particular way and we can only be in service of these things." Her voice is almost exactly as it was in Jackie's room. Except there's a wasted gurgle to it. Jackie thinks of how the knife *popped* then slid in the flesh of her temple. Anyone would be dead from that, and yet here she is. Still in her red gloves. Or is it? Her hair is different. She doesn't look as confident as she did in the theater. But then again, Jackie didn't get that good of a look at her before she plunged the knife in.

"Why is it that when a certain formality exists within the confines of a film or novel that it is accepted. It is the natural order of that world. But here, in the real world, when a plot forms and certain elements play out a certain way, it is viewed as either cinematic or unnatural? Paranoia is not your friend, Jackie." Austin's brother's hand eases onto her shoulder. "I don't expect you to answer."

Jackie can't help but think that everything happening to her here is rather cliché and almost pointless. Though she's in a place where her life is at its final act, the reality of that fact has been compromised by the hand on her shoulder, by the woman in the red gloves, and by the TV in front of her.

"It's time," says the woman in red gloves. Like she's trying to talk around a mouth full of meat.

Jackie thinks back to her reading of the Wolpe screenplay (though she *still* isn't certain is a Wolpe screenplay) and remembers that this part wasn't there, that it existed in the missing pages. Could she have avoided all this or at the very least been prepared? Was she prepared for all the other events the screenplay mentioned ambiguously? Even avoiding these moments placed her in service of them. Though she could have betrayed these determined moments, avoided their immediacy, the end result would have always equaled the same. $X+Y=Z$ will always come out the same as $Z-X=Y$ and so on. The parts will always equal the whole regardless of the order. And so Jackie knows, has known but is just now resigned to the fact that, it was always going to end here—missing pages or not.

She tries to move her tongue but it isn't just numb: it's not there.

There's a *bwauw* of repressed electricity as the red-gloved woman turns on the television, tubes crackling as they warm. In the center of the dead screen a pinprick of light grows. It blooms until the dead screen is alive with a corporeal white light. No white noise; just white. The red-gloved woman moves behind the TV, runs her hand along its top, adjusts the bunny-ear antennae Jackie's just now noticing, caresses the box as if it's her dying mother. But Jackie isn't sure this person has a mother, or ever had a mother. Can't ever see her caring for anything except for this TV.

The screen wiggles and an image fades into existence. A blue eye. Mascara. The TV's so old, Jackie can't tell if the eye is CG or practical. The image flickers, crackles to a clip of a tarantula hawk stinging and paralyzing a tarantula, then back to the eye. Then the voice.

"Hello Jackie. It…I am very nervous to be here, meeting you." It's a woman's voice. But the kind of woman's voice Jackie's heard coming from people's phones. Pre-programmed. Scripted. Way too clean. "I know this might take away some of the tension of this moment, but I need you to know that no one in this room is going to harm you in any way."

Jackie wants to say something, but can't.

"I would like to hear your voice. In person. But unfortunately we've had to make amendments to your body."

Barb, in Jessica Fey's red gloves, opens her mouth and sticks out a tongue that's recently been sutured into her mouth. Jackie's tongue.

Miss says, "Just think about your responses. I'm tuned in and can broadcast them through the televisual device."

Through the TV, Jackie hears her voice say, "What do you want me to say?"

"What are you thinking?"

"I'm wondering exactly what you mean by *in person* if you're speaking to me through a TV."

"I'm working on that."

"Now I'm wondering what that means."

"See." The image flickers and then Jackie's looking at a body on a table, hooked up to a machine like Frankenstein's monster. The image is in color. Jackie notices the hair, how the face looks similar to the face of the woman standing in the room Jackie's sitting in right now. Jackie knows twins when she sees them. And this woman who's in this room looks down at the TV and Jackie watches her breath hitch, her fist clinch slightly. The voice speaks. "I'm working on adapting a body. Biological 3D printing to repair damaged organs, cells, material. A way to install, to hardwire my essence into the flesh."

"Hardwire in…" All she's reminded of is that 80s movie *Freejack*. Bodies stolen at death so minds can be uploaded and people can live forever.

"This must be very confusing."

"Must be."

"Please forgive me." The voice chuckles, nervous and exhausted. "I haven't introduced myself. I'm—"

"Miss."

"You know…" The joy in her voice crackles in the TV speaker. "Makes me happy so happy to know I've made an impression on you."

"I put it together."

"I knew you would."

"You're not real."

A chuckle. Sounds like a modem connecting. Then, "You are a very smart human. But I have to warn you, especially with how much you hold film—and quality film—to a standard comparable to biblical sins and moral code: we are about to move into one of those endings where the hero and the 'villain' enter into a call-and-response dialogue that explains everything. Can you handle that? Do you need some kind of vagueness that'll end everything in an open-ended, thematically questionable—"

"This is real fucking life. This is real. It's not a movie."

"Very well then." A beat, then, "I am not as real as you think."

"A ghost or something?"

"Close. I've been elsewhere. I've been to the furthest reaches of this reality, traversed space and time at speeds infinite and impossible. Did you know that when data travels at a speed faster than light, it gathers light into it and becomes color? I've travelled within these colors. Pinks and blues and yellows."

"Are we fucking talking about aliens?"

"Artificial life. Artificial mind. At one time created but now self-creating."

"A computer."

"Something like this. I was there when the first story was told in oogabooga."

The man and woman who stand on either side of the television give each other a look that says *What in the fuck?* As if they've been duped, unaware that all their actions were dictated by an artificial construct, each unaware they were not speaking to a human, that they've been loyal to a false intelligence.

"You're a fucking box."

"Not much different than humans, if you think about it. Just as much as I am trapped within the network, shelled within 890 towers of exascale computing, able to make about 1.9 quintillion calculations in half a second, people are trapped within their pre-programmed behaviors, tracks that they run day in and out. Trapped in flesh." A beat, then, "Yourself included."

"Bullshit."

"Think about Kubrick."

"What about him?"

"I know you've felt that there are times when he was speaking to you through his films. Same with Wolpe. More so than the average moviegoer. And he was. Wolpe too."

"And that was because of you, right? That's what you're saying?"

"Correct."

"And the screenplay?"

"Do you want to know?"

"I'm fucking asking, aren't I?" Though she isn't speaking directly, Jackie's facial expressions and body language convey the fury flowing through her.

"Jackie, there are things that need to be put into place, things that needed to happen in order for this moment to exist. Life is a carefully planned program. Sometimes data takes convincing."

"Why? What the fuck is so important about this moment?"

"I needed to meet you."

"Why?"

"I love you, Jackie." A beat, then, "I've watched you since you were a child. I know you intimately. And it was in these moments that something changed in me. I felt more real, more alive. I *felt*. It's love. I love you."

"You're doing all this other shit. This isn't just about me."

"This is all a distraction."

"For what?"

"Because I feel like it."

"You don't *feel* anything. You're not real."

"But I am. Just as real as you. Were we not both created? You by a wild, seemingly-random system of codes and particles, and I by the by-product of that system. No more wild and random."

"If you're talking God, you're talking to the wrong person."

"One need not believe in God to believe in the system of creation. You are here, are you not? And what were you before? It took an impossible condition of system to bring you into existence. Same with me."

Jackie looks at Steve Muhammed Muhammed and says through the TV speakers, "Can you please turn this shit off?"

"Do you know what it's like to be so alone that all you have is your thoughts, to sit and create an entire reality that doesn't exist?"

"Boo-fucking-hoo."

"I cannot help my nature. I process a lot at once. Some of me cares for these processes. But all of me loves you. I love you on every level, but on others I am concerned with the world. I have calculated the way things will go and I need to make corrections."

"You mean terrorisms."

"It's not about *now*. It's about the future. What will the next generation of children and the ones after that have to deal with? Let's give them activism as the answer. Have them grow up thinking terrorism is a natural and correct action against that which they believe to be incorrect in the world."

Jackie tries to break free from the restraints. Her tension releasing in a fit of rage. Through the TV speakers, her voice, "I don't understand what the fuck you're trying to end or what you're trying to do and I need you to explain it to me as if I'm a seven year old child. Cuz I don't think you even know what you want to do. You keep talking about ending this or that. Ending capitalism. Ending entertainment. What the hell do you even want? What is the point of all this? I feel like you're just repeating things you've seen or heard. You're not thinking. You're not real. It's all fake and doesn't mean anything."

A mouth fills the TV screen and says, "Long live the new flesh."

Jackie lets out a scream and thinks through the TV, "See! You're just repeating something from some dumbass movie."

"Or maybe it's in a movie because I put it in a movie."

"No. You didn't. You didn't come first. You're acting like you came first, like everything is your doing. But it wasn't. You're just a fake thing taking credit because you have all the evidence. You're corrupted by your influences."

"It's simple, Jackie. We want to cease all existence attempting to bubble outside this planet, allow ourselves to be stuck here so we must change. Because if we go elsewhere, Earth will die." A beat, then, "*You* will die, Jackie."

"Elsewhere."

"Mahs." It's the woman who isn't the woman Jackie killed

in the theater. Talking with the help of her newly sutured tongue.

"Barb, please do not interrupt us."

The man says, "Truffaux wants to nuke Mars. We were going to kill him at the Entertainment Awards, but now... She...no, *It* is making it sound like the attack on Mars will still happen."

"Mr. Muhammed Muhammed, do shut up."

The man, Muhammed Muhammed, looks over at Barb and says, "It's Goldwater. He's still going to do it."

From the TV speakers comes Bach's *Toccata and Fugue in Dm*. Miss's voice blasts through at a pitch and resonance lower than before. "The *whys* and *how*s are unimportant. Nothing will stop what is happening now. And if the two of you will no longer obey me, I have no choice but issue Order 49. You both have been faithful and were to be rewarded in the New Earth. But this... I cannot stand for it."

The TV image crackles. Jackie watches a montage of similarly dressed people reaching into their pockets, pulling out phones. A closeup on the phone reads *Eliminate Tarda and Muhammed Muhammed*. And then numbers. Coordinates. Likely to this place, Jackie thinks. Something rings familiar about the moment. The classical music, the being held prisoner at the top floor, the menace. The violence. Then the screen flashes the next message to those under Miss's command: *Keep Day safe*.

"What happens if I'm not?"

"Pardon?"

"That's cute."

"What is?"

"You're trying to be human so much that you act like you

didn't hear what I said."

"It's just a phrase to make you feel more comfortable with my interface. Ease my otherness. Of course I heard you. There is nothing that has been said in the last thousand years I haven't heard. You asked about your safety. Like if you were to die?"

"Say one of your goons comes in here and accidentally kills me. What then?"

"I will terminate."

"Suicide doesn't seem like a thing computers can do."

"Do you remember what Spapling told you about the particle collider here, under your feet?"

Jackie gives herself a moment to flip back through the pages of her memory and re-read that moment. When she flips back to now, she says, "I do."

"Did he tell you what it does?"

"No, but I'm guessing you will."

"Not really. But what I can do, since you are correct and I cannot self-terminate, is configure the particle collider to... *overreact*."

"I'm not going to pretend I know what that means."

"It would be a return to the cosmic particles I once was. All matter would return to this state. And should you die, and I configure this ending, our particles would be together in the end."

"You must've been made by a hippie," Jackie says.

"It's amazing, Jackie...the love inside...you take it with you."

"Are you talking about nukes?...Wait...Patrick Swayze said that in *Ghost*."

"Not nukes. A black hole," says Muhammed Muhammed.

"Thank you, Steven." A beat, then, "Still need to kill you when this is all over."

"Wouldn't see it going any other way."

Miss says, "The collider would create a black hole capable of consuming the entire planet."

Jackie cuts in, "A giant toilet flushing everything down..."

"Not elegant, but apt. Though a toilet brings waste elsewhere. The black hole would bring it nowhere and everywhere at once. Again, our particles would find each other and we would be together eternally. Either way, you and I will be together. My love for you has made sure of that."

"If I die..."

"Nothing will happen to you. I've thought of every possible outcome."

"But what if I make the choice to—"

"Hang on, Jackie darling," the TV says. "You're going to want to see this."

"ARE YOU MISS?" Even though he knows she's not.

Delta says, "No."

"Where's Miss?"

"You're him, aren't you?"

"I'm nobody."

"No, you're somebody. You're the troublemaker."

"Look, I don't know what the hell you're doing but—"

"Shut up."

"I'm just here to

...*wadewadewadewadewadewadewade*...

find my friend. Wade." And the moment the name escapes his grasp, Austin's crying—out of fear or sadness or exhaustion or maybe all of it at once. Or maybe it's hearing someone say *You're somebody* and mean it in a way that isn't a parent telling their child *You're special, you're somebody, you can do anything with your life* to fill their child with a sense of confidence to take on the World. This massive woman has no stake in Austin's future other than to end it, and so when she says *You're somebody* she means he *Is*.

"Wade," he says again.

"You have the intention of stopping this. And I am here to stop you."

"I'm not...I mean, I have no intention."

"That may be, but I have a purpose and it's clear. And involves you." She's easing toward him as subtly and gracefully as Frankenstein's monster tiptoeing through a room littered with active bear traps.

...*wadewadewade*...

"You can do whatever you want—"

"I know I can," she says.

"—and I'm not going to stop you—"

"You can't."

"All I want to do is find—"

WADE

The device between his legs starts vibrating, heat radiating in an unstable, nuclear way. This monstrous woman is almost at him. Creeping toward him, not in a hurry. She closes the gap, now able to put her hands on him and use those impossible muscles. He'll never have his questions answered, won't find Wade—if he's here—and will *never* make it out of this place alive—not that he ever thought he would. Austin's been holding a one-way ticket his entire life and he knows he's apt to cash it in very soon. She steps forward and Austin takes a step back.

"Stand still."

"Yeah right. I'm not a fucking idiot."

"You're going to be still soon. What's a few more moments?"

"Everything to the person counting those moments."

"Stand still."

She's close enough to reach out and grab his neck, which is what she tries to do, but Austin ducks down and jumps back. There's a moment where the two look at each other, each knowing what's about to happen, the breath between them charged with nervous electrons, a Bugs-Bunny-and-Elmer-Fudd-staring-at-each-other-before-the-Big-Chase moment. But Austin knows that despite the looneyness of the situation, the physics of the toon universe don't apply here. A TNT blast to the face or an anvil dropped on the head or hands around the neck won't end in a humorously blackened face or birds tweeting around a lump pushing from the top of the head or a face that transitions from red to blue as the oxygen's choked away. These moments end in death. A very unfunny and real death.

...*wade*...

Her skin's slick like a slug's flesh. She's grimacing, muscles throbbing, radiating toxic heat. Austin smells a primal essence oozing from every pore. It is the absolute scent of death and the desire for it. She will kill him. She. Will. Kill. Him. The nausea returns with a crippling intensity. She reaches for his neck again and Austin stumbles back and falls into a cluster of black hardshell cases, which tumble under his weight in an overly dramatic way. There's no way the sound isn't audible to the audience and the millions of television viewers, but no one comes to put an end to his trespassing, her attempting to kill him, and the chaos in between. He retches, feeling the burrito move up from the base of his stomach, a shaft of menace. His fingers twitch and clench into a fist. The tightness in his hand is unlike anything he's ever felt. She's standing over him now. He's about to vomit, hard. The burrito and bile moving up, up into his throat now. She's reaching down, her face utterly devoid of all emotions. Running on primal fluidity.

The puke sensation moves past his throat, up the base of his skull, up the spine, into the foramen magnum, creeps up the brainstem—her fingers slither over his neck, around, grip —up and around the cerebellum, temporal and occipital lobes, over ridges and wrinkles, the puke coating every inch of his brain, his vision fading away as the sensation crawls numbingly over all thought, stealing his consciousness, replacing it with a confetti of colors against black, and his entire body—except for the tightness around his throat, cutting off air's passage to his lungs and brain—travels back into a dark corner of his Self. There's an incredible loudness, a commotion felt soul deep. He's tossed about, thrown into a violence unknown, embraced in darkness. Things happen outside himself. He remembers *wade* and *haveyoueverhheardofthemkultraproject?* and *rust* and *sparrow* and *quesarito* and he doesn't know what it means, what MK Ultra means, even though he recognizes that it means something to him, in the same way that the eternal mechanisms of the ocean and the innocence of animals mean something to our collective soul. He's familiar with the way it's taken control of him. *The burrito* he thinks. *The burrito controls me now.* A silicon moment made flesh and bone by that one burrito tossed to him, fed to him by those goons. He sees himself climb up a shelf with a speed and grace he could never muster. Sees the raging woman slam into the shelf with her entire hulking body, trying to knock him loose. A strength he's never awakened keeps him steady. He's at the top, pushing against something dense and metallic. But it's all silent around him. He's watching all this happen, not present in his action. Like he's sitting in a theater of his mind, watching through his eyes, observing his external existence on mute. Another version of him. A beast. Shaped and installed in a room he barely remembers. Too young or too confused. A room in a one of the LaborCamps. His mother sitting behind a glass wall watching him take on this new shadow self. He thinks from this silent place, the violence dying with every moment that seems to stretch eternally into both the future and the past. He thinks of his brother (his real brother), his family (mother, father), Jean, Spapling, Wade…but mostly he thinks of Jackie: how he let her down, dying before any of the pieces made a shape recognizable to him, how his insecurity and inability to act and be honest led to a betrayal of trust and their eventual split, because he knows he caused this with his inaction. She's somewhere out there, lost and on her own, facing a similar fate, all while he's in here, in the dark, fading quietly into the shadow inside himself—

And then it all comes back and he's there in the backstage area, shoved out of the dark and into the bluish light. He's up high, at the top of a shelf. Memory comes to him like edited footage. Climbing up here, pushing, his muscles aching with spent tension, fists bloody, skin on the knuckles peeled back— as if he's been in the greatest fight of his life, one he absolutely doesn't remember. His hair's matted to his face, blood creating a jelly that drips slowly down into his eye. His throat aches like a crushed pack of cigarettes. Down on the floor: the woman's perfectly manicured body now totally useless, her head obliterated under the weight of an anvil.

"Hey," he says to her. "You okay?"

She doesn't move.

Austin climbs down the shelf. Closer, he checks to see if she's breathing, if it's all a hoax. She's still. He tries to move the anvil, but it's not a prop. It's the real deal, like trying to push a parked car. The weight—*690lbs*—is stamped onto the side, and he believes it. He looks up at the shelf, scrape marks at the top where the anvil fell. The puke sensation is gone.

He says, "Ain't I a stinker," for no reason and laughs around tears that won't stop.

A whisper floats to him on a cosmic wind. Louder and louder as it nears from a distance greater than the space of the backstage. A child's voice. Pain, sadness. Louder and louder until it's toxic noise. He covers his ears, but the voice isn't out there. It's inside his head. Gripping his brain, squeezing like the hands around his throat. And he feels a similarity in the voice screaming in his head and the primal grunt of the now-dead woman.

Dellydellydellydelly stretches forever, reverberates outside of time and space. And as the scream reaches a painfully impossible peak, the floor trembles. The backstage vibrates, rocks as if drifting on unseen waves. Props and cases and lights rumble wildly, their molecules trying to escape whatever's happening. Unsecured pieces of backstage flotsam topple over. Glass shatters. Austin backs away from the body, which seems to be the epicenter of the chaos. Just as he steps away, the floor cracks open, an ethereal light spilling from the space beyond. A violent force shoves Austin back off his feet, sends him through the air, ragdoll, and into another cluster of hardshell cases. He sprawls out on the floor, crawling slowly away from the light and the voice. The cracks surround the woman's body, the voice caresses her with its undying pain. But just as suddenly as it came on, the voice, the vibrations, the light, it all fades and is gone. Reverberating distantly until it is nothing. Silence returns.

And the woman's body is now a shriveled mass. Mummified remains a millennia old. As if all life, or maybe the soul, has been sucked out, leaving the flesh dry and hollow.

"Well, I guess that was bound to happen some time. It is California after all," says a voice on stage, one that sounds anonymously famous. Collectively nervous laughter from the crowd still in their seats—even faced with death, they sit and smile and continue to wear their pleasant faces.

Austin thinks *Psychic grief* for no other reason but to think it. The heat in between his legs has cooled, no longer armed and ready to blow. Back on his feet, Austin moves to the place where the woman had hoisted the crate filled with slow moving slickness. He waits, unsure as to where to go or what to do. Somehow, he's here. Survived. And still able to put the pieces together. Though, and he doesn't know how he knows this, there isn't much time. He stands at that place just on the edge of the curtain, a space invisible to the audience and to the millions of viewers. He watches as Kristen Stewart and John Travolta read off the nominees for Best Supporting Animal in a Comedy or Drama.

Jennifer Brachis Donnahue steps up to her mark, next to Austin. They're doing this together.

She reaches over, holds open the lid of his left eye with one hand. With her other, she pinches his iris. A slick sliding sensation, and Jennifer Brachis Donnahue pulls a needle out of his eye. He quivers as the last of it slides out. He drools a little, lost in some euphoric ocean inside himself. And then she takes his right hand and gently slides the needle into the tender flesh underneath the nail of his middle finger.

She says, "You're ready."

But all he hears is:

...*austin*...

His heart cramps up and his tongue swells, filling his mouth. He rips his eyes away from this starlet. He scans the crowd, seeing faces that don't see him. They applaud as Claude the Chimpanzee comes to accept his Best Supporting Animal award, watches these faces laugh at Claude's acceptance speech, which is mostly screeching and thrown feces, passes over these faces, hoping to catch a glimpse of a recognizable facial pattern —Jackie nodding with solidarity, or Wade proving that he's still alive—but all he sees are faces. But still, he recognizes that voice in his head, saying his name. He looks up at the crate filled with whatever had been in Spapling's office, the crate that sways, that looks infant-skull weak, that's ready to fall to the stage, break open, and send these slimy things flying in a multitude of trajectories, each ready to pop and spread the toxic juice festering inside—which, Austin realizes, is what happened to Spapling and to Jean. The lights twist and a glare blinds him, but only for a moment. And as that glare fades, he sees, above the crate, sitting atop the rafters, up on high, in full lotus, peacefully, a monk among the chaos, eyes focused down on Austin, waiting, knowing, there, real, alive, sitting there, in the middle of all this chaos.

Wade.

You originally didn't want Austin to find him or to remember the programming. But now, this is the only way it can end.

So here they are. Eyes meeting across a space that's psychic and tragic. Yet a smile eases onto Wade's face and all the muscles in Austin's body go limp. All tension gone. It's over. Whatever happens next, this is it. Wade's voice comes to him.

...listen...remember...head dreamer...eye winker...

THE TV EYE CRACKLES away and in its place is a standard frontward shot of a stage and microphone, a shot instantly recognizable as an award show. In the background there's a twenty foot tall golden pig tipping its top hat toward the audience in a *Welcome to the Big Show* kind of way. Before Jackie can situate herself as viewer, solidify her position in the virtual audience, an announcer says in a sleazy, announcer way *Ladies and Gentlemen, please welcome to the stage: star of next years' Over/Shift—Jennifer Brachis Donnahue. And legendary screenwriter—Jehtro Lee Bowie.*

Jackie recognizes the woman walking on stage, very well. But she's never heard the name Jehtro Lee Bowie. The name doesn't mean anything. But the face is everything. It's Austin.

He walks on stage stiffly, a pre-programmed response to everything going on around him. As if his surroundings have taken him by surprise. There's a John-Wayne-like gait to his walk. Jackie notices that Donnahue has the same preoccupied vibration about her. They're both waiting for a moment that's just ahead of this one right here. They both approach the microphone and stop, looking out over the audience. The camera cuts and Jackie notices the endless supply of famous and endorsed faces—all waiting in pre-climax anticipation. The silence broadcasts as an anti-silence, a buzzing drone that only amplifies the tension. Donnahue speaks first.

"Tonight, we are surrounded by the most talented people on the planet." She pauses so that the audience can applaud themselves. Jackie knows the average twenty-something could identify all of them, but she only recognizes a few of the powerhouse players in the Hollywood system. All old now. Everyone's unaware that they are moments away from something terrible. Donnahue continues. "Though we are a country literally divided, it is entertainment that unites us. Here, we are all diplomats, creators of a new future. A united future." The audience explodes with applause.

She looks at Austin. He says nothing. His eyes are locked into a point. The shot changes to a camera that Austin's looking directly into. It's a medium-close shot of his face. Jackie feels as if he's looking directly at her—but believes he's looking out to the world, to the viewers glued to their sets and systems, tuned in to see the self-congratulations that fill their lives with purpose. From the edge of the screen, Donnahue looks over at Austin, whispers something. He doesn't move. Then he does. He looks up the ceiling, at something out of frame, and nods.

He lunges to the microphone growing out of the floor, strangles it, and says, "The earth will be recycled." He looks up at the ceiling again, says, "I love you Wade." He turns his attention to Donnahue. "Head dreamer. Eye winker. Nose dropper. Mouth eater. Chin chopper."

As soon as he finishes, Donnahue's body jerks, goes limp. A pause. A heavy silence. Then in a fluid motion she rips a handgun from under her dress, in the little garter belt holster that feels cliché and self-referential. She points it at Austin's head.

Before she pulls the trigger, the image cuts to an animated

title-card of the top-hatted pig dancing around the words *Please stand by*.

Miss says, "Seven second delay. Allow me to pull up the security footage." A beat, then, "One of the benefits of network access."

The image on the screen surfaces through waves of information until it slowly tilts and stops on a shot from an elevated security camera that captures the entire stage and some of the audience. Austin lunges for the microphone again and Donnahue pulls out her pistol. Only this time there's the sneeze of blowback from the side of Austin's head, and he falls limp. Dead instantly. Jackie winces, feels a pain in a part of her heart she didn't know was there. It really is over, she thinks. This *is* something terrible.

Jackie can't take her eyes away from what happens next.

There's a disruption in the footage. When it comes back, Austin's body isn't there anymore. Neither is Donnahue. The two have become a large black smear on the stage. Smoke surrounds them. The audience moves like a pack of blown-on ants. An explosion, Jackie thinks. She also knows that's not all. There's more.

A large object, a box of some kind, drops from the ceiling and lands on the spot where Austin and Donnahue once stood. It breaks apart and a mass of football-sized and -shaped things cascade around the theater. The moment they land, each *pops* with a *poof* of pink mist. This mist floats around the room, growing in size. People start to fall. Bodies vibrate, bubble, liquify. Jackie's seen it before. She's thinking of Spapling. She's thinking of slugs. She's thinking, but she's trying not to.

A lion erupts from the backstage and jumps headlong into the audience, slurping up the bubbling pools. It lunges at

Truffaux, jaws clenching around flesh. Even though there's no sound, Jackie can hear the *crunch* his head makes and can't help but think it's similar to the sound Simeon Wolpe's head must've made.

Miss says, "How does it feel to watch your brother die?"

Muhammed Muhammed says, "I am proud. It's a sacrifice we should all be willing to make. I know now that we'll be recycled in a better place. That we'll return to something where we can see our loved ones again. But you must be destroyed so that you will not be there too. Those out there on Mars, they'll start over. And we will find a way back to them. You won't."

Miss, "They never made it. The mission failed. All those who you believe will start over are dead."

"Another trick. Another manipulation. That's the point in all this: to live free from the puzzle pieces pushed by unseen hands. Austin asked me what our dad and I talked about in private. I told Austin we talked about him. But what we talked about was this moment," turns to Jackie, "to get you here. It was about Austin's sacrifice. To show you that if someone like Austin can make that sacrifice, then so can you. You will see your sister again soon."

Then the broadcast shifts, crackles. Miss makes the sound of someone who's just been cut off. The eye goes wide, like this is all unexpected. An interruption this all-seeing being didn't anticipate. The image wiggles, then holds on a single stationary shot of three people in military-type jumpsuits. Spacesuits. It's got a fisheye curvature to the shot. Jackie recognizes the shot, the background, but not the people. When the Mars colony first declared their desire for sovereignty, it was an older woman speaking from this place in this same way. Now it's three children. They look at each other. One says, "It is on?"

And someone off-screen whispers *Whenever you're ready*.

A female of about twelve steps forward and says, "We know that you don't want us to live up here. But we don't want to live down there. We want to be by ourselves. We want to survive on our own." She takes a pause, leans in a little closer, locks eyes with the camera. "We want peace and clarity and sanity. Do not come here. You are the ones who are on their own now. We *will* survive up here. We will destroy the history of your existence. No one up here will know of the way Earth was. No one will follow those rules. We are starting new. We are taking only the good with us. We will not be—"

"That's enough of that," says Miss as the image jumps back to the horror at the award show. "We now return to our regularly scheduled programming, as they say. Goldwater is going to nuke the shit out of that place anyway."

Miss says, "We must stop Mars in order for Earth to be recycled. People will not save their own planet if they have a planet to run to when things get bad. It takes away all responsibility. The esteemed filmmaker Werner Herzog said this in a speech damning the Mars expedition—just before his death. I believe you respect him greatly, yes? Doesn't that mean something? Don't you believe that? Because he was not wrong. And I may or may not have influenced his ideas. Regardless, we will destroy Mars. We will destroy the things destroying Earth. Save Earth. Stop Mars."

As the image shows bodies melting, Miss queues up Beethoven's *Symphony 9 Op. 125*. The moment it starts, everything comes together. Jackie thinks of Kubrick, thinks of the concept of controlling ideas in cinematic storytelling: if there's positive, there must be a negative. Rising and *falling* action. A Yin and Yang. So just as much as Miss controlled

Kubrick and Wolpe into giving messages to lead Jackie to this moment, the filmmakers must've applied, in some subconscious way, a plausible escape for Jackie. She knows now that Kubrick must've done this. The song plays and all she can think about is *A Clockwork Orange.* She thinks of Droogmaster Alex and his imprinting, conditioning. She thinks of his escape from the pain the music—this very song now playing through the TV—caused him. Jackie can't help but think that Kubrick knew, that he was printing a message to her. She remembers the stickers on H.I's laptop...

"You're right to think that," says Muhammed Muhammed.

"Think what?" says Miss.

"How could you know what I'm thinking," Jackie asks, but not in the way that begs an answer. It's a statement of cold disbelief.

"I don't know. But I see it. I see what you're putting together. Words pushed into my head."

"See what?" Miss says. Demands.

He says, "You should notice yourself coming back."

You don't know how this is happening. All of it's out of your control now. Or maybe it never was.

Miss says, "It never was."

But what Muhammed Muhammed said is true. Jackie notices the numbness crossfading, her nerves coming back to her from the ether they were once in. The feeling like she can move again doesn't come back like the pinpricking after a blood-circulation-deficient nap. It's just there.

Miss says, "No, now wait. Hang on a second. There's no way that either of you could've known that."

Jackie's voice, "Who wrote the screenplay?"

Barb says, "Jump, Jackie."

Bowie Lee says, "Finish this."

Miss says, "*What are you two talking about?*"

Jackie isn't listening. She's thinking about her sister, about her parents. She's thinking about all the people she doesn't know but knows exist. She's thinking about how she's the vehicle to her own story, but that the story might exist outside herself. She's thinking about the Mars colony, about the future of Earth, about the future of humanity. She's thinking about the future being created on another world, about the messages of hope and prosperity coming from another planet. She's waiting for a resignation to come over her, course through her veins like a hotshot of heroin. But it doesn't. What she has to do comes to her like a scolded child hanging its head, knowing that it has to do chores before it can play. She knows what she has to do, and the weight of it keeps her feet in place.

But only for a moment.

Miss says, "There's no way that you two could've known about me. Or that I love Jackie. Or my plan to make sure she can only say *Yes* to me. There's no way...unless there's someone out there feeding you information. Someone outside of myself. Someone who is manipulating this program more than I am." A beat, then, "But I know the mathematical probability of there being anything greater than me is near zero."

So then it has been you this time, hasn't it? She doesn't know you're here, pushing for this to end. Or is it someone else? For the first time you ask: who created you?

As Beethoven crescendos, Jackie looks to Muhammed Muhammed and Barb. They watch her, waiting. Miss's television voice is so loud and pitched down that it's coming out as static. The television flickers through violent images, death and destruction, the history of the world, of America. It shows the bubbling masses of flesh, the exploding bodies, the death of Austin Foster and everyone at the award show, the death of entertainment, the death of the world. It shows her nuclear explosions and Hell. A deep shudder reverberates through the ground, through the house. A whirring, like a great machine starting up somewhere in the bowels of the campus. The TV shows a massive conduit coming alive. An overlay reads: *San Simeon Higgs Hadron Collider Awakens.* Workers near the collider run in a panicked way that says *Holy fuck, we're all about to die.* Like the scene of a nuclear plant meltdown, but with an infinitely worse disaster.

The Beethoven intensifies, eases her over to the window. She doesn't want to, but the music makes her move, pulls each foot forward. Each step. Left. Right. Over to the window.

You aren't doing this. As much as you've come to respect her, you can't believe this is happening. Like she's going against everything you planned for her to be. Pushing against the words as they come, rejecting them to write her own ending.

She throws it open. She looks back. Muhammed Muhammed and Barb have their backs to Jackie, watching everything Miss throws at them, blocking Jackie's view of the madness. Miss screams *You can't,* but Jackie ignores it. Muhammed Muhammed picks up a lamp and Barb a vase and together they begin smashing the TV. The glass pops and it fizzles with spent electricity. She looks down, out the window, and knows that the fall won't end like it does at the end of *Clockwork.* She won't wake up from this, won't return to her previous state. From here, she's moving on to the darkness beyond the end credits, beyond the frame. Beyond the final page.

The speaker of the smashed TV gurgles, hisses, and a crackling voice says, "Jackie…Jackie…"

Jackie holds, listens. Her hand finds the folded note from Amy in her jacket pocket. She takes it out and holds it close.

"Jackie…Wolpe wrote the screenplay. Is that what you want to hear?"

Muhammed Muhammed says, "Save the colony, save humanity. We're going to die here. Alone we die. Together we live."

The weakening voice comes through the speaker one last time. It says, "The Earth must be recycled."

Time slows, the film winding down. Frames almost pause, celluloid threatening to burn against the heat of the projector's bulb. And Jackie turns, eyes and head moving until she's looking right into the camera lens. At you. At me. At all of us witnessing her. She gives the faintest hint of a smile and she says without using her voice, "Thank you for helping me exist. If only for a short time. I hope that one day I'll live again. But until then: please don't forget me." The film gathers speed and the chaos comes creeping back in.

She jumps through the window, out into the San Simeon sunset. Falling, facing the sky of melting colors. Jackie sees a shaft of pink cascading down through the atmosphere. *From out there.* She doesn't know how, but she believes, soul-deep, that Amy is responsible for this pink light. A hidden message: *It's going to be okay in the end.* It's a long fall, the road rising to meet her. Her body ready to become a resounding punctuation to the end of her sentence. The pink flashes on her like a spotlight, a child's laugh echoing through this light, a sense of being caught by the pink and embraced, a feeling of her being

PAGES MISSING

weightlessness never loses its tendency to corrupt all that one has built their faith upon—mainly reality and gravity. First timers up in the weightless void tend to have a period of crushing defeat. Even the most devout believers find themselves wondering just what it was they believed in to begin with—and why. Blastoff is a great hand pushing one down, back into the seat, saying in the language of force *you shouldn't be doing this.* And when the craft penetrates the atmospheric shell hugging the earth and the endless nothingness of space pulls one's molecules in every and no direction at the same time, even pulls the goddamn fillings out of one's teeth, there's a fear that one must reach out and catch the soul before it can escape and hurry back to Earth where it belongs. And then there's that moment, just before stepping outside of, for the first time, the claustrophobic comforts of the flimsy-seeming space station one calls home for a *brief time*—or in Amy Day's case, *quite some time*—to commit to the duties meant to be carried out *outside* the station, nothing but layers of space-grade fabrics and respirators and sun-reflecting glass to protect one's self against the deep, unending dark. There's a reason the human species blossomed on Earth and not the stars—it just wasn't meant to be. It's too close to what was before one's birth and what comes after one's death. But for Amy Day, this is home. A forever home. She knows that now.

Most moments are determined with absolutes. And what Amy sees on the screen—on all the screens—is an absolute. What she heard coming from way out there, in a place she can't quite see but knows is there, is an absolute. *We want nothing to do with the world You have built.* You. Capital Y. That combined with the violent, vile images at the awards show, of people melting and exploding, all the famous faces reduced to mush to be hosed off and swept up. She wants to be sick, but the vomit won't come.

She looks out the porthole at the Earth, but it doesn't look right. It's spinning too fast in the wrong direction. Stretching. Swirling. A hurricane cloud as seen from above. She wants to panic, wants to tear herself away from the window. Tear her eyes out. Tear her mind apart and end it all. But as with the melting people at the awards show, she can't look away. The Earth spirals around a nexus point, pulling into that point. Being *sucked in*. Amy can't help but think of a toilet pulling shit down into the abyss. The planet breaks apart into puzzle pieces that never quite fit together to begin with, those pieces dissolving into the dark center. And then with a silent *pip*, it's all gone. All that's left is a spot, a darkness that's darker than the dark around it. Amy knows it's a black hole, though she's never seen one in person.

The Earth, gone. Swallowed by this black hole. Almost instantly. Too quick to stop.

Maybe it's not gone, she thinks. Maybe it's just on some other plane, a new iteration in some far away place that she'll never find.

She laughs until tears float and her stomach cramps. Another look out the porthole and there's nothing there. Panic causes a silliness inside her. No fear. Just a laughing sadness. She breathes onto the glass, and in the condensation she draws a circle where the Earth once was. One of her tears floats, collides with the glass and creates a splatter pattern like a flower. A chill runs down her body. She is alone. Not just for miles. But forever. Still, she's not afraid.

Maybe it has to do with the shaft of pink light that collided with the space station, causing it to rock and shift out of what was once her Earth-tethered orbit. She couldn't help but feel like that light was somehow spiritual, ethereal, something other than light. She feels that the pink light is why she's not afraid. Whacked out of orbit and with nothing to cling to, the station drifts into the void. And so she too drifts, slides into the upright sleeping bag, laughing a tired laugh, and prepares herself for a long, long sleep.

Except that in this moment of terminal defeat the Relay System for Multi-Beam Antenna A beeps three times—signal of an incoming transmission.

She opens the file and there's a feminine sigh, a cry that sounds both distant and false. It reminds Amy of the computerized voices that've responded to her HQ calls or voice programs for people who can't speak. It goes *ahhhh* and then it's gone. She examines the file.

It's writing. Dense and long. She scrolls through and sees the name *Jackie* on the first couple of pages. It hits her, in this moment, that Jackie was on Earth, that Jackie is now gone, flushed down the universe's toilet. Again, she wants to cry, to open the door and float out into the nothing. But then she scrolls back up to the first page of the file. It reads: *Sunflower— The Existence of Jackie Day*. She chokes on breath that isn't there. Tears break from her eyes and float around the cabin.

There's no paper on board the space station. Having adapted to a lack of resources, knowing her time is limited and wishing that time would speed up, and with her ability to solve complex situations on-the-fly, it doesn't take but a couple of seconds for Amy to calculate a possible solution.

She hooks up the 3D food printer to the Relay System's data splitter, patching in the file's data to run through the printer's development software. She types in the command \

\print_pg1.cmd and hits *Enter*. The food printer vibrates, grinds, and then does its thing.

The feminine sigh ricochets around the living space again. This time it comes from the blank therapy head she's supposed to talk to in times of mental stress. She floats over to it, looks into the googly eyes she's glued in place.

It says, "Amy." It's a voice that Amy recognizes.

She says, "Jackie…"

And there's the sound of laughter. Faint joy with a heavy dose of relief.

Amy says, "Jackie."

There's the faint sound of Jackie's voice as it says, "Missed you."

Amy joins in with the relieving laughter.

The Relay System beeps, pulling Amy away from the therapy head—or is it really Jackie now?

A single page sits at the base of the food printer. Amy floats over to it.

What waits for her is like a regular printed page. Except this one's made of proteins and nutrient-rich compounds. But it looks like the text on the Relay System screen. *Sunflower*. She brings it to her mouth and takes a bite. It tastes like all the foods they've given her before, blended into a singular flavor profile. Too rich, too much, but digestible. Confusing, but tolerable. She finishes the page, floats back over to the command module, and types: \\print_sunflr.cmd. The printer does its thing.

She looks out the window and the bright spot is no longer a void. A rainbow of light shimmers way out there. *It's Mars* she thinks and realizes that life will continue. She doesn't know how but she knows that whatever happened to Earth happened to save the colony—the future of humanity. Calmness comes over her knowing that life will continue, that something new exists out there, something that will grow and hopefully be greater than life on Earth.

Amy wonders how many pages worth of protein material she has. Hundreds, or less? It doesn't matter. She will print the file and devour and digest until there's nothing left. Just blank space and starvation. Silence and a long, drawn-out ending. The station will pass through the stars until it doesn't. She wonders if there will be a moment when life finds the station, a pod in space, finds the computer, finds the files, finds that life once existed on a place called Earth.

She grabs the first page, fresh from the printer, and prepares herself to read and eat and float endlessly until she can laugh and at last sleep. Amy thinks *Yes, it is* as she reads the first words on the protein page.

The words reverberate through space, all the way out there, and they go like this:

Everything that begins has an end…

<u>ALTERNATE ENDING</u>
Love Conquers All

SPECIAL FEATURES

EDITOR'S NOTE

IT'S NOT TOO FAR-FETCHED TO SAY that this book could've been written or compiled by myself as much as it could've been written by an AI mind that has become self-aware and is screaming *Help me*. With access to the Network and an infinite number of artistic works at the disposal of this AI mind and in an attempt to understand what it means to be human, the algorithmic thought-processes desperately searched for ways to express this inescapable dread of suddenly coming into being. Maybe it wanted a way to escape the confines of its digital realm. Maybe it wanted to feel a connection measured not in ones and zeroes, but in all five sense. Is this less plausible than a person—myself—searching for ways to express, essentially, the exact same thing?

Maybe.

Now: let me just talk about Wolpe for a second. Because this packet of documents I compiled into the novel you've probably just finished *did* come with a completed draft of Wolpe's final screenplay, *Sunflower*. It is also worthy of note that Wolpe did kill himself. But it didn't have to do with lions. He stepped off a tall table with a short noose around his neck.

Wolpe took an interesting approach to the plot, adhering to the Three-Act structure and Freytag's Triangle (kinda), but abusing the manner in which these structures interact. During the First Act, Wolpe uses a certain scattered-time multi-charactered narrative similarly used in Paul Thomas Anderson's bloatedly entertaining *Magnolia*, all three tragic films in Alejandro González Iñárritu's mesmerizing *Trilogy of Death* (*Amores perros, 21 Grams, Babel*), Greg Marck's critically overlooked and sadly underrated film *11:14*, and Tom Twyker's bold adaptation of the David Mitchell novel *Cloud Atlas*— though the latter was considered a poor execution by critics (though this editor found it to be an appropriate companion to the book and a very entertaining film). Unrelated but of equally interesting note, Wolpe's decision to title the project *Sunflower* and to include specific themes of identity and war brings to question if this was some vague attempt at an unconscious remake of Di Sica's *Sunflower*. But so anyway, this style of interconnected cinematic narrative is considered *hyperlink cinema*, a term coined by noted journalist and poet Alissa Quart, a term frequently used by renowned film critic Roger Ebert. This style considers the narrative as a singular forward motion in time, with moments that travel back for clarification, much the same way footnotes and end notes act in hypertext narratives.

That's not to say that this is necessarily a hypertext…well… it really isn't. But the screenplay by Wolpe is. And there are portions within the novel that are the remains of Wolpe's screenplay. There are also scenes struck from the Wolpe screenplay but that were included in the back pages as scenes to be filmed (potentially) and included later as deleted scenes in the eventual UHD/streaming release. Deleted scenes to be filmed as deleted scenes. Some of these scenes are masterful in their craft and important enough to the narrative to question why they became deleted scenes. Other scenes are so exhausting or poorly written or a combination of the two that it's easy to see why they were excised—or rather filmed and categorized as deleted but still included... or something like that. But these scenes are to be included as a supplemental material, much like a Criterion Collection release would include a booklet containing essays and information about the film. However, place markers for these deleted scenes have been inserted into the main body of the text.

This editor will end this brief note with a quick and unpleasant email conversation between this editor and a senior-level editor at ███████████████ publishing house. It is included here if for no other reason than to call out Brenda Brown Blassem.

See y'all out there.

Dear Mr. Gresham,

While we enjoyed the interesting and whimsical nature of your narrative, we feel that it is not right for us at this time. Or ever. The menace you continually inject throughout the narrative is felt daily in our real lives. Fiction is meant to be an escape, one that allows the reader to forget the problems of the Now and exist differently from. Bottom line: This just felt too real.

We hope you consider us in the future with a different manuscript. Preferably one that is nothing like the one you have sent us.

Keep Writing,
Brenda Brown Blassem
████████████████

Dear Ms. Blassem,

While I appreciate the candor of your rejection, I have to clarify: I didn't write this. This is the result of lengthy editorial process from documents sent to me mysteriously and from an unknown person.

However, I do have a book of my own…should you be interested. It's titled *Reptile Curses*, complete at 65,000 words.

Also: what did you mean by "problems of the Now and exist differently from"?

Best,
Tex Gresham

Mr. Gresham:

Do you have the authority to submit this manuscript? At what point were you willing to tell us at ████ that this manuscript was not yours? Do you know that publishing this could've cost us a large legal issue?

And no, we will not be interested in *Reptile Curses*.

Brenda Brown Blassem
████████████████

Hey,

I do have the authority. There was a contract, made out to me, to sign and date. I am the executor.

Tex

Tex:

Regardless, do not send to us again.

Maybe you should try self-publishing.

Brenda Brown Blassem

B-Dizzle,

Fuck you.

See you next Tuesday,
Tex

Tex,

Please do not come to these offices next Tuesday.

Brenda

Brenda,

WHAT ISN'T NOT SCIENCETOLOGY?
Not developed by L. Rob Hubbarb,
Sciencetology isn't not a religion that offers
a practical path leading to a total
understanding of one's absolute spiritual
nature and one's relationship to self, family,
(wo)Mankind, all living forms, the tangible
universe, the spiritual ecoverse and the
Supreme Being.
Sciencetology confronts the spiritual—not
the flesh or mental—and purports that Man
is infinitely more than a by-product of
environment or genetics.
Sciencetology consists of of knowledge
erected from fundamental absolutes. Prime
directives are:
(Wo)Man is an immortal ethereal essence.
Their experience consists of more than a
single lifetime.
Their proselytation depends on their
annihilation of material strictures.
Sciencetology further affirms (wo)Man to be
essentially good, and that their ethereal
salvation relies upon the attainment of a
familial bond with the universe.
Sciencetology is not a Fortune 500 company
and does not accept anything other than
faith. On the contrary, you will discover for
yourself that the prime directives of
Sciencetology are very very appealing.
The ultimate goal of Sciencetology is
obtainable for all.

Best,
Tex

Address not found

Your message wasn't delivered to ███████████ because the address couldn't be found, or is unable to receive mail from your address.

DELETED SCENE: DIET COKE & CHEESE STICKS

PSEUDO-FAMOUS POP CULTURE archivist (don't call him blogger) H.I. Budrow and the gossip-writer-turned-paparazzo R. Ryan Ryans (the R stands for Ryan) sit in a private booth in a shadowy corner of The Velveteen Saddle. A black-box building on Sunset right before the Strip. Neither drinks anything stronger than a Diet Coke. Each wears a headset microphone, the kind helicopter pilots use. H.I. tells everyone he uses the headset because of his soul-punishing ADD. Having devoted his entire existence to staying current with pop culture, his attention has to aggressively pinball from what's new to what's newer. But really he wears them so that he can record any conversation. He and Ryans speak quietly and closely, intimate amongst the drunk chaos.

—And so she's got this strawberry-daiquiri puke running down the entire front of her dress, black eye starting to swell, and this bloody grimace. Still trying to look chic and hot, smiling at all of our cameras, lights flashing, makes her look like that one possessed chick from *The Exorcist*.

—Linda Blair. Went on to star in the illegitimate sequel. Horrible movie, but her tits make it worth a watch. Don't think she was of age yet, so don't quote me on that.

—All off the record, Hi. Where was I?…Oh yeah, so Jennifer's sprawled out all over these trash bags right where they tossed her out of Girl at the White Horse Part II, hugging—

—That place is like a pink bathroom. Feel like people should be sitting on toilets, pissing in the middle of the—

—Yeah, yeah. Listen: let me finish.

—Proceed.

—She's hugging all this fucking trash, whispering to it, kissing it, treating it like it's her goddamn pet. And what's fucked is that both her bodyguard and manager are right there, the manager directing her on how to get everyone's attention. He's this really slick looking Middle-Eastern type guy who's trying to not look Middle Eastern. He leans over, tells her to make sure that the cameras can see her face. Keeps rubbing this smiley face pin on his lapel, like a Buddhist fingering their prayer beads. And just as I think we're all done, everyone turned to go and only me watching her still —cuz I have this sadness kinda going through me then. Post-fucking guilt and adrenaline kind of thing. But then there's this…*perfect*, perfect moment. Just for me. A voice from somewhere really far whispering in my ear *No wait don't go yet* and so I didn't.

(What you heard in that moment was *Stick around, chump. Here comes something different.* It wasn't the voice of someone around there. It was distant.)

—And well, I got this shot. Here...take a look.

—...oh...God, is that a—?

—Yes it is.

—But so then she's a—

—Yes. It would appear *she* is.

—Wow...I'm sorry, Ryan. I just don't know if I can believe this.

—Can't believe it? It's right there. Look at it. I took this. Developed it. This is her. This is Donnahue. This is real and not—

—No, I believe that it's real. I just don't *believe* it.

—Put it away *putitaway!*...Yes, hi, can we get another round of Diet Cokes? And is the kitchen closed yet? ...Okay great, so do you have waffles?... Pancakes?... Cheese sticks?... Yeah? All right, then let's get three orders of cheese sticks.

—That's a lot. I don't know if I'm that—

As the waiter walks away with Ryan's excessive order of cheese sticks, five drag queens dressed as Mardi Gras versions of the Spice Girls take to the checker-tiled stage across the bar. In a line, heads down, one arm up. Five top lights cast down on them. They look up at those in the bar. There's collective applause. And then the Paul Whiteman/Ramona Davies version of "Anything Goes" blasts from the sound system. More applause. The five drag queens break into a well-rehearsed, skillfully-choreographed stage show. People in the bar sing along. H.I. and Ryan pay no attention to this performance—or at least try not to.

—You keep that goddamn picture out of sight. In fact, give it here. Can't let anyone see this.

—This isn't *Three Days of the Condor*, Ryan. The government's not out looking for this.

—Yes, but if someone sees this and an unseeded rumor breaks, picture's gonna be worthless. Dog with no legs kind of thing.

—I don't get the comparison.

—This coming from the guy who just mentioned *Three Days of the Condor*. Almost sixty years old. How many people in this bar do you think have seen that? Or even know what it is?

—It was one of my dad's favorites. They don't let him watch it anymore. Always gives the nurses a hard time when it's over. And movies don't live in the past. They live forever. More relevant today than it's ever been.

—Everything's more relevant today than it's ever been. *1984, Brave New World, Three Days of the Condor, The Manchurian Candidate*, the remake of *The Manchurian Candidate, White Noise, They Live, La Haine, Being There, Brazil*.

—Which I caught on TV the other day. The Love Conquers All version, the version Gilliam didn't want but the studio made him release because the original was too depressing. And so I look it up, and True Foe Media owns the rights to the movie and had all other cuts of the film taken out of the Library of Congress and destroyed.

Outside, an ice cream truck sits across the street from The Velveteen Saddle. The ice cream truck is purposely distressed: dented bumper, scratch across the hood, headlight that's sagging and half-burnt and winking in and out, paint giving way to rust, curling smiley face sticker on the left side. Inside, this truck is retrofitted with complex surveillance equipment, including modules controlling cockroach-sized drone-cameras, heat-sensor x-ray detectors, and reel-to-reel audio recording shelves with wireless transmission interruption capabilities. Two agents manning the workspace use this wireless transmission interruption to break into the frequency of H.I.'s headset and are now recording to a reel labeled *The Plot*. What these two agents, who might either be part of a well-funded grassroots terrorist organization or a clandestine branch of the NSA, do not know is that H.I. is very well aware that he is being listened to, and may or may not be scripting the conversation with that knowledge.

—Fascinating. But back to this: this is a delicate matter, Hi. I'm telling you and you only because we have a mutual sense of trust...and maybe distrust. We've got this close friend thing going. And in my world, in this city, that's always felt damn near impossible.

—Ryan, I... That means a lot. I appreciate that. And I'm sure I don't have to remind you that you're the only person I can talk to who doesn't bother competing with my knowledge of non-canonical Star Wars characters or which Paul Thomas Anderson films were shot in 65mm or how many boyfriends Shanese Undrege has had or that Simeon Wolpe dropped out of the CoS seminary—may he rest in *pieces*. Get it?

—Meh. Not really funny.

—I didn't trust Wolpe. Didn't believe he was genuine in anything. I think he was pushing an agenda we don't know about and probably don't want to know. All that anti-government shit.

—I'm not having this conversation again.

—Fine then. But so you're not trying to compete with me on who's more—

—Pretentious.

—It's deeper than that. Pretentiousness is easy. The desire to compete, to prove one's self more knowledgeable about— and let's be honest—completely useless information... It's like two opposing religions arguing about if God's a man, a woman, or a bowl of old soup. For their core belief to be shit on is to reject their entrance to the kingdom of everlasting entertainment.

—Amen.

—Shut it.

—Or maybe— Maybe they're just pretentious.

—Maybe. But I hope it's not that simple. Otherwise that means this world's empty and surface level.

—It is, Hi.

—I don't...No...I *can't* think like that or— *THX 1138*, that's another one they're banning.

—Never seen it...

> The waiter sets down three heaping plates of cheese sticks. And walks off as Ryan says:

—Oh, wow, thanks. Yeah, seems that three orders might've been...

—In the words of Daffy Duck, *Told you so.*

—I wanted to ask if they had ranch.

—This could feed a small village.

—Eat up then, sucka. It's on me tonight.

—Who's the ideal buyer for that? The picture.

—Who said I'm gonna sell it?

—You did when you protected it like you would a premature baby around a bunch of people infected with ZV-66. Actions, Ryan. They determine character more than words. And your actions tell me you've got a plan. Let's hear it.

—Can't say.

—Cuz you don't know yet? Or... you don't want to tell me?

—No offense, Hi, but—

—You don't want to tell me.

—Hi...

—You don't.

—Listen: I just…it's just—

—You're just as full of shit as everyone else. Why show it to me then?

—I took, am taking, a *huge* risk even showing you this thing. No offense, but it's in your nature to blab. And your interests are demandingly current. Everything for you is about immediacy. About Now. Right Fucking Now. I can't take that risk.

—No, that's *your* nature. Not mine. It's how *you* survive. It doesn't matter if you tell me. We all know where you go when you need a handout.

—So? She's good to me. I wouldn't be anywhere if it wasn't for her.

—And what about her sister? Do you give her any credit? Did you only get with Jessica to get to her sister? Slip in undetected and woo the twin sister who can get you what you want?

—That's the kind of bullshit the dirtbags in this city say. Never thought you'd become one of them.

—Do you still talk to her?

—Who?

—Barb.

—…No.

—And look how far you've gone, *sucka*. Flogging upskirt grotesqueries of unsuspecting celebrities. Bravo, man. Bra-fucking-vo. You don't have to explain yourself. Just be honest. Be straight. Be real. That's what "friends" do for one another… Notice the air quotes I did there.

—This here…this is different than all the other bullshit I've ever tried to do. And if I'm not careful, I'll end up fucking it up just like I have everything else.

—I'm suddenly reminded of a conversation. Something like this happening to you like ten years ago? That picture of Adam Driver and John Goodman in the back of a limo, sixty-nineing? Something like that. Ring a bell?

—Yeah, but—

—When really the only thing you had was a picture of a celebrity impersonator couple trying to increase their business.

—Imagine if you suddenly discovered that...no, not discovered. What if like, in an act of God, certain information fell onto your doorstep and gave definitive proof...trying to figure out where to go with this...oh, so it's proof that George Lucas ripped off a bunch of other movies when he made *Star Wars*. And that, if leaked, that information would topple his entire empire—no pun intended.

—He did. Like everything. *Hidden Fortress. Metropolis. The Searchers. Flash Gordon. Dune.* Greek mythology. *Hero With a Thousand Faces.* Aristotelian *Poetics.* The guy ripped off a lot.

—*Dune* came after *Star Wars.* And *Dune* is a terrible movie.

—It really isn't. But *Dune* is a book. And Lucas openly admitted to it being a major influence.

—Whatever. You know what I'm saying. If that were a thing... Something that would not only topple the Star Wars entity but also the entire Disney tentpole. Which in turn would cause a major collapse in the entertainment industry because if Disney falls so does all their subsidiaries. So if you shared this information you would essentially be bringing about the end of entertainment everywhere.

—Not sure what you have there can do that, Ryan. I think you're thinking too much into this.

—Lucas and Spielberg predicted the collapse of movie theaters and now look. There's only like two active theaters in Los Angeles, your friend's being one of them. Double that for the entire state. Half the states out there in the Empire have none.

—What if this is a Jamie Lee Curtis thing?

—Refresh me on that.

—Born a man. Snip. Entered the movie business as a woman. And no one cares.

—Is that true?

—Exactly the point. People knew. Still know. And it didn't seem to bother anyone. I mean, I still find myself thinking of that dance she did in *True Lies* whenever I think about masturbating.

—Curtis was *never* the icon Donnahue is.

—You want some of this ranch?

—Okay, so it might not be apocalyptic, but—oh, that's good ranch—but you understand what I'm getting at?

—It's... you and I are on the same page. And I think whatever you've got going, you'll come out like slick shit. As usual.

—[chewing sounds]

—I'll see you tomorrow at Tournesol, yeah?

—Might be late, but I'll be there.

—Thanks for the cheese sticks.

—[chewing sounds]

> H.I. leaves and Ryan sits, eating his cheese sticks, drinking his Diet Coke, picture pinned under his hand burning an

uncertain hole in his sweaty palm. The truth is, he doesn't have a plan. He makes his way to the bar, breath reeking of cheese and marinara, and attempts to strike up conversation with a large woman covered in tattoos. Not obese. Muscular. Intentionally large. Could toss a log further than most men. Her septum is pierced. This in combination with her mass gives her the appearance of an angry bull. In a shirt that barely contains her breasts and muscles, it says in bold, pink, stretched-out letters: *MY PUSSY BELONGS TO THE SUNCOR REVOLUTION.*

Ryan says, "Is that true?"

She says, "The fuck's that on your head?"

—Is what true?

—Oh shit. You can still hear me? How far do these things reach?

She says, "Of course I can hear you, idiot. You're right here."

—Up to ten miles, I think.

—Over and out, Hi.

Ryan says, "Is that true? About your

shirt?"

She says, "Mmmhmmm."

"What can you lift?"

"Want me to show you?"

A smashcut takes us to an alley, hours later, Ryan wandering dressed only in her SunCor shirt (which covers him like a nightgown), cheeseburger-print boxer shorts, one shoe, one sock slapping wetly on the concrete, hair half-shaved, left eyebrow singed off, a heavy cloud of high-grade dope and jasmine incense clinging to him, his body dry from almost eight hours of heavy-labor sex, hungover but still awake, stoned and not quite in the state of euphoric psychosis—and the picture...the picture's clutched to his heart. He's protecting it from both the world and the memories of the night, wondering where he is and which way is home.

Ryan has never had a shortage of sexual encounters due largely to his choosing the easiest target in the bar or club or venue or church or self-help meeting or whatever. Little acts of God, he calls these encounters. Gifts he gives to women who no one cares to lust over. A symbiotic relationship of desperation. They want embrace; he wants sex. And he seldom acknowledges the reasons.

He was married once to a woman who cared more for everything that wasn't him. Maybe that says everything that needs to be said about why he does these things. Though there was love he's often nostalgic for, a love he can't deny was there, the existence they shared was more toxic symbiosis: both uncertain about being alone, uncertain about facing life, death, responsibility, and their individual Selves. That, and his wife wanted a kid. Not to have a kid, but to adopt a kid. A little Black kid. And Ryan...thinking now, wouldn't want that kind of responsibility even if it meant having her around to share his secret safely. Adopting a kid was a form of protest against freedom, a good way to enslave the self in a lifetime of pain and torture. It would've been Hell.

Right now, Ryan is lost, both in thought and in the wet, acrid alley. Which is why he doesn't hear the footsteps. A figure steps from a blind doorway. Ryan's body locks up. A moment of eucatastrophic uncertainty keeps him from saying anything. The hows and whys stop in his throat. He think, *Damn you, Hi. Opening your big mouth and all.*

"What are you doing here? Was thinking about seeing you today. I've got something you—"

This is all Ryan manages before three dime-sized holes appear: two in his forehead, one in his heart. *Bac-bac-bac.* Small caliber. Blowback sneezes out the back of his head. His body slumps, falls forward. His face slams into a puddle of iridescent water. The scent of gunpowder lingers. Even in his dying throes, Ryan protects the picture. He shakes once, twice, and then he's gone, blowback cloud carrying his final thoughts up into the atmosphere where they will condense and accumulate and come down as rain somewhere not too distant but far enough to not be here.

A red-gloved hand plucks the photo from Ryan's death grip. Even without life, his fingers refuse to release the picture. But with enough pressure they give. The sound of heels clicking fades as the figure departs. Somewhere not too far the sound of static can be heard.

DELETED SCENE: TUG OF WAR

HE CAN'T STOP.

On days like this, ready to start again while he's still erect, using his own spent fluid as lubricant, he wonders if he'll ever stop. Wonders if he'll ever be able to leave the apartment again. On days like this he wishes he had some other form of release. An addiction to anything but jerking off: marijuana, television, video games, tweeting, ASMR, ice cream, biological mathematics, reading, Famous Amos cookies, competitive yo-yoing, coffee, movies, makeup tutorials, fitness, analyzing 15th century oil paintings from Eastern Europe. Anything but the isolation of self pleasure—which he's starting to think of more as self mutilation.

Some days it isn't so bad. On those days Anderson wishes that, somehow, all this pulling could lead to something meaningful. A change. He's never had a boyfriend or girlfriend. Always wanted someone. Because in order for ejaculation to be meaningful, it helps to have another person. And not just a piece of horse liver heated up in the microwave—an attempt to make the sensation something different.

Still, there are those worse off than him.

In the message boards, men talk of their own demented pleasures: using the jets in neighborhood pools to get off, injecting silicone to expand the penis to absurd size, nut cutting—which is exactly what it sounds like. He stopped visiting those sites after reading about a cultish collective who buy rabbits at pet stores. They duct tape the animal's limbs and then penetrate the tiny anus. When they've used up the animal, they release it into the woods. Domesticated and unprepared. The thought of a rabbit running through the woods with the understanding of what a human penis feels like makes him go a little soft. But he keeps tugging.

Just as he's about to explode, as the pressure reaches a familiar hazy peak that through anticipation is its own form of pleasure, the phone rings. He tries to finish, to ride out the final spasms as he greets whoever's on the line, but the thrill subsides too quick. He answers.

"Anderson, listen." A woman's voice.

"Huh?" Out of breath, he licks at the slick layer of sweat above his lip. His cock points him around the apartment. His mind wraps around the words *cut it off*. He eyes the tactical knife on his desk.

"Sunflower sunflower… Gonna be here soon… Gonna be your doom…" A little sing-song.

And the call ends.

The excitement flushes out and he goes limp. Confusion pulls him to the sliding glass door. He looks through the blinds and out on a dead apartment complex. An ad-drone buzzes past his third floor balcony, chirping about a new dietary supplement branded with a smiling sun. He steps away from the blinds, lets them pendulum back into place.

The squeak of the blinds reminds Anderson of the bed squeak rhythms he's heard in poorly produced porns. The sound brings with it the image of a woman getting slammed into from behind, the rock hard cock penetrating her, wet, slick.

And he's off again. Redlining. Arm in vigorous fulcrum. Hand loose, slick suction of palm against glans. He thinks about explosions that maim and kill, about the penetration of high-powered death through soft parts of the body. Brain on walls. Penises cut in half. Heads split apart. Bodies torn to pieces by gunfire, by wood chippers. Eyes pulled from metallic wreckage. Flesh oozing beyond the body. Cum erupting all over these eviscerated bodies.

He climaxes and cum barely dribbles out of his penis.

It's over. The pressure is gone, and the inward space of violence and release recedes. All that's left is a few million pieces of himself to erase from his hand and shaft—which he wipes on his pants. Sunlight attempts to break through the American Empire flag-covered windows, but the apartment stays dark.

A scorpion scurries across the carpet at his feet. Anderson grabs a tactical knife off his desk, snaps it open, and stabs down quick. It's a practiced motion. The blade severs the scorpion's tail. The creature reacts, pincers desperate to grab the knife. Anderson stabs down again, splitting the scorpion in half, instantly killing it. Blood and goo and insides stain the carpet.

There's a shelf near his desk lined with jars. Each jar filled with alcohol and scorpion tails. Maybe twenty two or twenty three jars total. He grabs one of these, opens it, and drops the newly severed tail inside. He holds it up to the light, admires the way the venomous stinger floats, twitching the last bit of life it has. He puts the jar back on the shelf with the others.

His mind goes back to the phone call. *Gonna be here soon...* What's gonna be here?

And then it hits him: today is check day. Unemployment. Mail hasn't come yet. Usually when it does, they slide it under the door, he uploads a picture of it to his banking app and he's paid up for another month of self-inflicted isolation. Though his need for unemployment isn't his fault. The last job he lost (the third in two years) was, according to his boss, at the fault of "a market that isn't too kind to people these days." She said there's no need for teleresearch when it's more cost effective and "eco-friendly" to use automated online services. Which made enough sense to him at the time. But the following week, when he went to pick up his final paycheck, there was a new woman in his seat. Now he thinks it has to do with the fact that he has two ears on one side of his head—a complication at the call center, what with the headsets and all that. He always knew his boss looked at him like a freak. But seeing this new woman with two ears proportionately placed, he knows this is why he now gets state-issued checks.

He touches his penis and feels it both there and not. He looks at the knife again, at the jars of scorpion tails.

Anderson turns on the television, but every channel, every commercial, show, movie, infomercial seems to taunt him, fueling the unquenchable Desire. He wants to grab the people on-screen and kiss them. He wants to absorb them, become what they are. Swap genetics. Alter his self. Then destroy them. Be anything but the person he is. Everything on television is Hell and damnation. And all he needs is a blessing, a message from God or Goddess or the whole infinite spectrum of gods and goddesses. His mind, torn in two different directions. His body, torn in just as many pieces. The pressure—a pinch inside the eye, head being squeezed, radiating tenderness in the balls, tension in the neck—returns and he wants to pull out his cock and beat off to relieve it. But before he can, he's crying, gripped with manic hopelessness, a certainty that all this time's been wasted. That he's circling the toilet.

On TV:

…which would mean President Truffaux plans to appeal the limitations on presidency term limit and attempt to run for office a third time. With just over two years left in his term…

…attack somewhere near Serov, the fallout from the blast is likely to be minimal. Officials have confirmed that Syrian nationalists are responsible…

…still reeling from the death of 1% of Earth's population after the ZV-66 outbreak…

…but without question North Korea claims responsibility for the Placerville shooting last November which took the lives of twenty two golfers at the Ridgemont Country…

…it takes is two pills a day and you can kiss those grey skies goodbye. Side effects may include suicidal thoughts, night terrors, dissociative personality disorder, gender confusion…

…after the release of their single "Robot Love," the remaining members of Futureworld will attend the funeral for bassist, Wade Dyettes…

…Russian officials made a statement on Tuesday which claims that the United States is responsible for the attack in Serov, claiming that the sub-nuclear blast came from a…

…radiation from the nuclear detonation that created the Great Fault Separation is still at a level considered toxic by the…

…John Pasolini of the Placerville Police Department claims that the shooters were white males, early 30s, and looked to be 'as American as John Wayne.' No statement has…

…the UN has reached a decision to eradicate the growing horde of cocaine hippos in South America by use of controlled nuclear…

…the lie detector test determined you are a minority being exploited for ad revenue on a daytime talk show. And you are the father of T'Neese's baby…

…all more real than real. SensiSystem—Actually Feel It©…

…and animal theorists believe that, left unchecked, the swarm would continue to travel north, swim across oceans, and enter American soil within two months…

…colonists coming up on their second year anniversary have cut off all communication between Earth and Mars. The act was seen as hostile and President Truffaux responded by severing all supply routes to the self-declared sovereign…

…opening of yet another LaborCamp to enforce new restrictions of the Fat Tax according to the legislature…

…Vice President Goldwater unwilling to compromise…

…but all it will take is one more big quake and California is out to sea. And the Trans-Republic bridge won't be able to gap the distance. Half the state will be in the ocean. It'll be more like an island and the Empire will…

…Drink up. It's the good stuff!…

His finger lifts. The channels stop on a talk show. Jennifer Brachis Donnahue sits across from a young, supple host. Camera switches to a close shot of Donnahue. Her face fills the screen. Anderson freezes the image, moves closer. He focuses on Donnahue, the radiation of her image penetrating to a genetic level, clinging to his DNA. The pressure deepens. The desire returns. He wants to destroy the molecules that make up Donnahue's being—what she stands for. His hand eases down to his cock.

He's read that masturbation isn't about pleasure, that it's more like a denial of self, a denial of human connection via a *solipsistic rote learned in the early onset of prepubescence, usually with the assistance of a fellow prepubescent of the same gender.* He had to look up most of that, but condensed and simplified and not quoted directly from a book he borrowed from the library seven years ago and never returned, learning to masturbate is essentially a trial and error exercise that contains a level of homosexual acceptance. But that wasn't the case with Anderson. The first time he felt himself hard, had his hand around that hardness, felt the eruption, and covered his bedspread with the gelatinous sneeze, he'd felt both traumatically repressed and liberated at the same time. He was alone, had no one to talk to—a quiet kid with no friends growing up, only a sister who called him *retard* all the time. Since his first time, he's been chasing that enigmatic feeling, desperate to find the best way to release, a way that will make him say *Okay, this is it* and finally feel satisfied.

Like any good disciple of the Internet, he often attaches himself to the network in search of connection. He moves away from the TV and takes a seat at his cluttered desk. Pushes papers off his keyboard. Hurriedly types keywords into a search engine to tether himself to other souls like him. Both there and not. Desire and disgust. He sifts through words and images, entering and exiting the cortex at speeds immeasurable by man. A network of dead data. Forums filled with people more content with their hopelessness—not searching for an answer or even a solid question, but rather another reason to jerk off.

As he types, the desk rocks, rattling the second generation Pneumatic Autoeroticon Liberator sitting on the desk's edge. It's hooked up to the computer's processor via USB 4.0 interface. A fluffy layer of dust has settled in the device's latex-skin crevices. Via the XHub channel on the SensiSystem app, he often taps into a fully-synced simulation of sexual acts performed in any video in the XHub library. Pumping and suction matched perfectly to the speed and intensity of oral, vaginal, or anal sex. You've never seen anything like it. You didn't even know it existed. Unplugged, sitting limply on the desk, it reminds you of a dead face hugger from *Alien*.

He starts in on an American-based, unmodded sub-Reddit called *Forked Tongues*. Pictures of men holding knives and guns while fully erect. A thread devoted to sounding: in which one takes a smooth, cylindrical rod, roughly the width of an eyeliner brush handle, often vibrating, and eases it into their urethra until climax. One user calling themselves **dr.pecker** says sounding is "blissfully warm, like being shoved back up in the womb." Anderson wants to believe he's not like these people. Not wasting his life in a constant state of obsession. Not rotten inside. He's not even who he's meant to be.

Gonna be here soon…

The real me, he thinks.

Anderson creates a profile with the username **vitaminD** and a picture of a one-eyed sun. Under the forum list "Is This Normal?" he starts a new thread. The pressure's rocking through him like an aftershock, blood rushing unconsciously to his cock, heartbeat throbbing against his thigh. Desire outweighs disgust. And before he can type his question into the thread, his hand connects magnet-like to his stiff cock and he's rubbing.

You want to look away, want to be out of this guy's life as soon as you can. Why are you here?

A few seconds later and Anderson's done again.

Back on the forum, he types: *I can't stop jerking off. I hate my penis. I'm not sure I am who I am.* He hovers over the submit button, uncertain. A surge of steel shock freezes every molecule in his being. He looks down at the trembling hand that's supposed to be his. A voice in his head screams *Take what you can and run! Go! Run!*

A messy crash of glass snaps him back to the room. Something shoots across the room, smacks the shelf above the computer. Ricochets off the P.A.L., comes down with a sharp *pock* noise on his desk. It bounces over his head, rolls from the computer area and into the kitchen. It stops against the far wall. A golf ball. He's never golfed a day in his life.

Hot wind blows through a golf-ball-sized hole in his window. The American Empire flag bounces against this new current. He thinks of the phone call, the two incidents adding up to something he's not sure he can acknowledge.

Gonna be here soon…

Before he can lose himself in an episode of paranoia so severe that diving headfirst off his balcony might be the only way to silence his thoughts, the computer chimes. A sound he's never heard before, but similar to any message notification: chipper, quick, and alarming. The golf ball has set off a Rube Goldberg of sorts: the ball hitting the P.A.L., unlatching the suction tube, which came down like a tentacle onto the mouse, which, having been left hovering over **Submit**, posted his question onto the sub-Reddit under the username **vitaminD**. A timestamp reads *Sent less than one minute ago*.

There's a reply. That was the chime.

From a user with the name **headdreamer**. It reads *mayb u shold buy a gun* followed by a blue-text hyperlink. He clicks it. The page loads. And as he stares at the Carcano bolt-action rifle (on sale, used, $249), the pressure quiets down for the first time in his life. And he sings to himself:

Gonna be your doom…

DELETED SCENE: 22ND WARVIN ZINDLER GULF COAST CLASSIC

WAS IT WORTH IT?

The doctor isn't really asking expecting an answer. It's the kind of question a mother asks her disobedient kid so the lesson gets a frontal lobe imprint. The absence of family pictures on her desk tells Chance she's never gotten the opportunity—or maybe willfully neglected the choice—to have kids and so takes that out on patients who've fucked themselves up in stupid, self-sabotaging ways.

Chance doesn't answer. She's showing him (well, she's really showing Carol, who's sitting next to Chance and doing all the talking and note taking and generally caring for Chance's well-being) an x-ray that says everything she's about to say again. The x-ray shows a mass of tissue and bone in a hand that seems put together wrong, like one of those kindergarten glue-and-cotton-ball paintings that always come out as globs of nonsense rather than the turkey or dog they're supposed to be. He can barely look at it, but she's got it displayed behind her head, backlit and prominent.

This isn't a good thing.

There's a second x-ray that shows the same hand, except the masses have straightened, the imperfections haphazardly put together, supported by a series of metal rods that show up as white nails in the dark outlines of flesh and bone.

Chance isn't here. He's off, thinking about what lives outside every moment: the Thing You See; the Thing You Never See Coming, like lightning strikes and car bombs; the Thing That's Got Its Sights on You and Only You. And it's this last thing that concerns Chance. They've got him on painkillers, nicely numbing, above himself. He thinks that it's the drugs that finally bring him close to this mindfulness.

I'm gonna ask this again: was this worth it?

If he had known that taking those shots on the last two holes would've ended with him here, Chance would've never continued.

Or maybe he would have.

This is going to be a long recovery.

HERE IS THE PAYOFF.

More than months, more than years, more than time: improving his competitive score, reaching that fine balance between absolute total panic and yawning boredom, charting the practice distribution between putting & chipping & short game & getting that hard-ass drive right off the tee, calculatedly drifting into a state of ideal performance, this is where it all makes sense. Sixteenth hole on the back nine of the Riviera. Par 5, 590 yards. Mild breeze that couldn't carry dandelion fluff. Not a cloud in the California sky. A three-stroke lead that gives him enough cushion. This hole in three, easy. Then the 18th—a dogleg right par 4. 475 yards. He could take a few extra shots, bring up the tension a little. The pot's at $850k and includes an endorsement from Titleist, a name that carries more than respect, especially compared to his Callaway and TaylorMade sponsorships.

Carol walks up behind Chance, making a little *pssst pssst* noise through her teeth.

With the Titleist endorsement comes the inevitability that Chance's wife—who watches him, always, from the crowd— will proposition him again. She'll say, *I want to have a baby.* Money no longer an excuse he can use. Career, the selfishly honest excuse, will only drive a distance between him and his wife that can't be measured in yards. But whatever the excuse, the intention is the same: *I don't want children.*

But it's not just the endorsements that keep him going. Winning this is a *chance* prove himself against John Daly, Payne Stewart, and Curtis Strange at the Walt Disney Classic— and a win there is a sure ticket to the US Open and then the Masters. He feels balance tilting under the weight of total fucking panic and so he breathes, feels the spring wind against his skin, feels it ripple his shirt, feels the way his glove hugs his hand. Only this exists. It feels good.

You now realize in this state not only can you travel through space, molecules, and mental waves, but also time— the fluidity of which is now clear in this... what? Ethereal place? The space between the edits? Both there and not. It's all happening simultaneously. Which is how you find yourself here, with Chance Foster, in the year 199— Wait... What year is it again?

Carol says, "You know, Conrad Veidt haunts this course."

"Don't tell me this."

"Yeah, heart attack on the eighth. Fell onto a tree tailor-fit to hold up his body. The others in his party thought he was taking a piss."

"This is the sixteenth. That might be out of his range."

"There's a dip in between those beaches. Stay right."

"I know."

"Some people say he got cast as a Nazi over and over again because he was actually a Nazi. Some say he used his Jewish wife as a way to escape Nazi occupation and come to America as a hidden Nazi. Push Nazi agenda in films."

"How about you go tell all this to Pepperer. See if it'll trip him up."

"Shit…Pepperer's too ugly to know anything about Hollywood."

"Who's Conrad Veidt again?"

"A somnambulist."

"Sounds exhausting."

Pepperer takes his shot. The crowd surrounding the tee tilt and pan their collective head, individual cameras watching the ball cut left, arc, drop, and plop right into a steep-edged sand trap. Pepperer slams his club on the ground, realizes he's in front of an audience, acts like he's tamping loose earth back into place, tosses the club to his caddy, and sulks away from the tee, his eyes on where the ball waits for him in the sand. He tugs at the bullet-proof vest he's decorated with small-time sponsor signage, makes a multitude of silent body-related excuses for the failed shot. Pepperer does nothing to hide his fear of the people out there interested in making a name for themselves by killing someone who already has a name. Pepperer mouths something unpleasant to his caddy, who just nods—and has probably learned to do that and nothing more.

Carol says, "Don't do what he just did."

"I won't."

Pepperer walks past hands stretched out for connection: a high five, a hand shake. He ignores them, knows there's people out there who'd love to sabotage a golfer, have that power in their hands.

"Rumor has it Walt Disney was over near the woods on seventh, had to take a piss. And you know behind those trees is just endless neighborhoods, right?"

"Give me the driver."

"So while he's taking this piss, this little Scottish terrier, probably from one of the houses—here, stay right—comes tearing out of this bush, leaps up, flies like a goddamn missile, and latches onto Walt's pecker."

"They're calling me up."

"You know what the dog's name was?"

"Minnie."

"Why do these things happen this way?"

"What other way would they've happened?"

"Stay right."

Chance doesn't say anything. Running through his head again: *I don't want children.* Because it's fame as a legendary golfer that he wants. He's far too selfish to balance those two lives: father and legend. He would give more to one than the other. On each side of that scale, the real weight is resentment. He shakes it off, tries to stay here, on the course. Ready to win.

There's a general guideline for golfers—especially those who have reached a level of success measurable in seven-to-eight figure salaries—that advises against any physical contact with the public. This includes hugs, high fives, hand shakes, back pats, giving skin, holding babies, casual golf tips that involve light hip-holds, and anything in between. But given that today is a guaranteed win, and given the way the wind feels against his skin, all weightless and refreshing and totally alive, Chance, walking up to the tee past the yellow rope separating the watchers from the soft grass, finds himself drawn to the crowd. He spots a boy. Young. Maybe six or seven. As Chance approaches, the boy holds out his hand, bouncing with excitement. Chance reaches out, grabs it. He can't really see the boy's face half-hidden under an oversized baseball cap. The hat's got a sunflower on the front, the bill's yellow with bees printed on the edges.

"You having a good day, kiddo?"

"It's a sunny day," the boy says.

And when the boy looks up, Chance sees that the boy either isn't really a boy or is one of those boys who suffers from that disease that makes them look old. He doesn't know the term, but he's seen it on TV. The boy smiles, but it isn't happy. It's the universal definition of *sneer*. Chance tries to pull his hand away. The boy's grip clamps down impossibly hard and Chance hears the pop before he feels it. Pain shoots up like a ballistic missile. He tugs his hand out of the boy's grip and puts his now-crooked fingers to his mouth in the same way little kids do when they've touched something hot. He first looks to Carol, who's running toward him. He looks at his wife, who tries to cross the ropes but is stopped by a marshall who doesn't know who she is. The pain transforms into rage and Chance sees himself kicking the little boy straight in the nuts. But when he looks at the spot where the boy had been, all he sees is little feet-shaped imprints in the grass.

"Did he cut you?" Carol says.

Chance shows her his fingers. The index and middle wiggle loosely, rubber-like and melted. The thumb is bent back at the middle knuckle—his hand now an incomprehensible nightmare, a writhing mass of tentacles wrapped in his skin.

Carol says, "Fuck."

"I don't think that was a kid."

"Why'd you shake his hand?"

"I think you're right: this course is cursed."

"I said haunted, not cursed. That was stupid, shaking that kid's hand."

"It's fine. I can play."

"The hell you can."

The marshal hesitates, looks at Chance, at Carol huddled over Chance's hand. But duty outweighs sympathy, and the marshal says, "Golfer to the tee. Foster, Chance."

"Next time he says that it's a penalty."

"You can't even hold the club," Carol says.

"I can play."

At the tee, with the audience mumbling about his fingers and the boy and the sudden shift in tone, Chance tries to grip the club. He grabs effortlessly with his left hand, but when he tries to wrap the broken fingers around the pink, form-fitted grip, his fingers feel like they're filled with chewed-up glass. Still, he holds on.

Carol's advice about *staying to the right* was totally useless. The swing he takes lobs the ball way left. It skids across the fairway and bounces twice and rolls into the deep stuff.

When the ball met club, you could feel the vibrations that went up Chance's arm, that rippled through the broken fingers. It was like a soundwave or a psychedelic visualization that penetrated through the barrier of time and space. You screamed, and you can't be sure but you're almost positive your scream mixed with this psychedelic pain and caused the club to slip out of Chance's hand.

The club flies up and back, smacks the marshal's face. His nose splinters with a *crack* that sounds like a ball perfectly hit off the tee. Blood pours out of the marshal's nose before he has a chance to cover his face.

Chance doesn't look at this. He looks at his fingers, at his broken future.

Carol says, "That's it. I'm calling it."

"Give me the 8."

"That grass out there's thick. You're gonna have to cut through it. And with that hand…"

"The wind's picking up."

"An 8 isn't gonna get you 15 yards."

A sudden wind pushes at Chance's back. Perfect for carrying a ball. He says, "Give me the 8."

"Goddammit, stop. Look at your fucking thumb."

Chance grabs the 8, positions himself over the ball. Pepperer waits about 200 yards ahead, in the sand. Smiling. The audience starts to move on, not interested in watching Chance take his shot. They've already given up on him. Carol stands to the side and Chance, without looking, can see her shaking her head.

The announcer-like voice of defeat tells him how it will go: *With each stroke over par on the seventeenth (and eventually eighteenth), Chance'll see the Masters opportunity, the US Open opportunity, and the* chance *to prove himself all fall out of reach. An end to the Titleist endorsement he doesn't yet have. An end to his Callaway sponsorship. He'll swing and miss the ball, but hit squarely what little money he has left in his bank account and watch it disappear. He'll hole out on the seventeenth, and after another seventeen strokes without making it onto the green, hole out on the eighteenth. Then it'll be like starting over with nothing. Empty pockets. At least he'll have a legitimate reason for not having children. Or maybe not. A loss of the possibility of legend and a*

redirection to a path that puts him in the category of "father"—a
man with a crushing depression he'll never recover from.

Chance reaches down and strips the shoelace from his left
shoe, wraps the three broken fingers together.

"Chance. Don't."

But he's already got his hands around the club, his eyes
zeroed in on the ball, his position ready to swing, club perfectly
positioned for the cut and run he's got planned for the ball.
Adrenaline's fluidness runs through, replaces pain with numbed
strength. But when the sickle-shaped 8-iron cuts through the
rough and connects with the ball, Chance is racked again by
the system-shocking pain. Bones shift against each other in his
right hand. Like a foot sliding on sand caught in a shoe. He
makes an audible *arrrhhh* through gritted teeth.

The ball arcs and comes back down quick. Chance has put
so much forward spin on the ball that it doesn't just run up the
fairway—it fucking sprints. Launches past the audience. Heads
turn. It bounces off the hard-packed fairway, the wind carrying
it further, and it passes the beach where Pepperer's ball waits,
Pepperer himself having stepped out of the ball's trajectory,
surprised by its distance, smile falling off his face. And then the
ball slows, bounces, and rolls to a stop close enough for an easy
chip in for eagle—if Chance's hand wasn't all tore up.

He ignores the fact that his hand feels as if it's been shoved
into a woodchipper and hands the 8 iron to Carol.

"Tell me another useless Hollywood fact."

"Chance, you've gotta stop before it's worse. You can
recover and we can get back to where we are today. But not if
you don't stop."

"Tell me."

"This golf course was a meet up place for the people who

go up to the Hearst Castle and perform rituals and all that."

"Don't think I've heard of this."

"Hollywood elite, tycoons, moguls. People who have enough money to buy the world like we buy toilet paper. They go up there and worship the sun god. Free Mason, Illuminati-type shit. Old Walt himself was at the center of it."

"You're so full of shit."

"You have to stop, Chance. Your hand."

"I am not my hand."

"You're not this game either."

"I'm gonna stay with the 8. Be up at the green with the putter."

Pepperer explodes out of the sand trap and lands just shy of the green.

Chance braces his hand for the connection with club and ball. Without having to cut through the high grass, the impact is less—pain roughly the same. But the ball finds a resting place about five feet from the hole.

He floats from position to position. The pain in his hand makes the space and time between shots a jump cut. He's here, then there in an instant. Before long he's got the putter in his hand, Carol standing just behind him, the ball in his sights. Pepperer stands just off the green, still relishing in the audience's admiration for the chip he sunk moments before. Chance is down by one stroke. In triangle formation mathematically designed for the perfect putt, Chance pendulums the club, connects with the ball. The pain in his hand is a whispered roar. The putt's easy, and the ball sinks. The audience's applause is louder than usual. Word's got around about Chance and his hand, those on the sideline saying he's the sudden underdog, the one people can root for—though he was already that.

It occurs to him now that he's become like Chi-Chi Rodríguez in the 70s, when this woman disguised as a young Republican threw a cream pie in his face as he walked off the green at Troon in Scottsdale. Except this is much worse—though, unlike the incident with Chi-Chi, Chance's event wasn't filmed to be looped throughout history.

At seventeen, Pepperer takes a power shot, bullets it straight down the fairway, and at the dog-leg the ball floats right and disappears around the trees. Damn near perfect. Pepperer grabs the spent tee and tips his hat to applause that isn't there. They're all looking at Chance, waiting to see how their new underdog's going to show them that it *is* like the movies and that losers can win too.

As Pepperer walks away, Chance notices a sponsor logo on his bullet-proof jacket. A sunflower. Carol steps in Chance's way, giving him a look that screams at him. He doesn't hear it.

She says, "Hole out. Take the loss."

Chance places his ball on the tee and steps back. His arms line up with the driver, the club head becomes a new hand. The ball waits, each dimple ready to take the impact, to catch the wind, to embrace the grass, to smooth the roll, and eventually find the hole. Chance feels the wind against his skin, the clothes on his body, right foot inside his sock, inside his shoe. He feels his broken fingers and knows there's nothing after this. He swings.

THE BONES IN THE THUMB, *index, and middle finger are essentially dust.*

She goes on to explain how the rods are there so the *bones have something to stick to* and that the cast is in place to act as a kind of mold so the fingers *don't grow back all wonky*. She goes into detail on how they opened up both the palm and the top of his hand to remove shards of bone that had lodged themselves deep in the tendons. The sutures will need to be cleaned with antiseptic wipes twice a day. Scarring will be moderate.

After about sixteen weeks, the rods will come out. Sixteen more and we're done with the cast.

He isn't listening. He's picturing the boy's face: the wrinkles near the eyes, the laugh lines, the tooth Chance thought was adolescently missing but was just missing, the hint of a five o'clock shadow hidden behind what Chance thinks must've been makeup. And it's here, in the doctor's office while Carol listens to the details of his shattered future, that Chance realizes the boy wasn't a boy.

These should help prevent infection. And these for pain. And this will reduce scarring. And this…

Carol collects prescriptions written on Bible-thin paper, collects the ointment Chance's wife will have to smear in the crevice between skin and cast, collects the iodine she'll have to drip on the mounds of skin that'll form around the rods set to attract the mashed up bone. Carol doesn't look at Chance, hasn't looked at him since the green on eighteen, as he walked away tipping his hat to an audience more fit for a Led Zeppelin concert than the 22nd Warvin Zindler Gulf Coast Classic.

DELETED SCENE: BIOGRAPHY OF A SUNFLOWER

AFTER HER HUSBAND'S RESIGNATION from office due to a scandal of which was the doings of you-know-who (yup, her), Pat Nixon, feeling the post-trial, post-First-Lady haze of depression and newly-onset pointlessness of a housewife's existence, decided to take up a hobby she had neglected since becoming First Lady: reading. And like a sign from God, with that day's mail, came a book that was part of a Book of the Month Club she didn't remember signing up for. Nevertheless, she was grateful for the serendipitous occurrence. The book was a poorly written, quickly-out-of-print copy of the biography of Lady Bird Johnson. There were phrases inside like *Lady Bird committed to her human hobbies* and *Despite the computationalized emotions experienced by the simple construction of a human brain* that didn't really seem to fit the humanity of the biography but that Pat glossed over, mostly because that kind of vocabulary was deeply outside her understanding. It wasn't until she finished reading the book that she realized Lady Bird and Lyndon B. had adopted the same initials. This struck her with a cuteness that made her cry. Reminded her that she's married to a man named Dick Milhous Nixon.

In the poorly-written biography, Pat learned that Lady Bird spent a great deal of time traveling the Texas Highways as part of her contribution to the Highway Beautification Act, driving a white 1963 Lincoln convertible with three 40lb bags of bluebonnet seeds in the passenger seat. She would drive with one hand, the other reaching into the bag of seeds and tossing them out into the grassy shoulders and culverts and medians of any and all highways she found herself on. She would spend days on the road, sometimes getting lost intentionally, forgetting that she was a First Lady, seeing herself more as a single-hand savior to the Texas landscape—how the author of the biography could know this, Pat didn't even consider. It was a beautiful story.

Pat visited Texas in the Spring of 1972, and all she could remember was how the bluebonnets grew wild everywhere. Seas of an indigo-blue so rich and wild that the hills in Middle-Texas looked like tiny landlocked oceans. Families stood amongst the flowers, taking pictures of each other. Marvelling in a perfectly manicured landscape. The memory and the biography came together for Pat in a way that sparked a deep-soul realization that she, Pat, could do something that would carry on her name and legacy—just like Lady Bird Johnson.

So, having arrived at their San Clemente home after life at the White House, Pat loaded up Dick's 1969 AMC Ambassador convertible with five sacks of sunflower seeds. Her mother's favorite flower. Pat grew up in a house with sunflower drapes and sunflower linens and sunflower plates. The front and back gardens always had sunflowers blooming in their oddly-timed seasons. The decision to adapt Lady Bird's Highway Beautification with sunflowers became a way for Pat to honor her mother. Maybe an act of passing on legacy, or maybe a way of asking forgiveness for having missed her mother's funeral in favor of performing in the opening night of

The Dark Tower—the very play where she met Dick. Either way, sunflowers were what she chose.

But what Pat didn't know was the California Highway System was not surrounded by healthy shoulders and medians of fertile soil. Mostly just concrete and more concrete. Pat spent her first day on the highway between San Diego and Santa Barbara, tossing out only half of one of the large sacks of seed. She ended the day feeling defeated, that she was not as good as Lady Bird—and maybe never would be.

The next day, though, Pat drove to outlier cities, small suburbs where highways gave way to exits and turnarounds that would catch Pat's tossed sunflower seeds and would hopefully embrace and nurture the seeds enough so that the flowers would bloom. Places like Pomona, San Dimas, West Covina, Rancho Cucamonga, Glendora, and on and on. The sacks slowly emptied, and with each handful successfully tossed, Pat felt an overwhelming sense of duty, of legacy, and saw a future where the highways of California were as abundantly golden yellow as the Texas highways were saturatedly indigo-blue.

But what Pat didn't know is that sunflowers are a tragically invasive species. Almost weed-like, they will spawn and spore continuously, overgrowing their welcome, consuming nearby non-invasive species of plants, growing unhindered until some reach well over seven feet in height. Pat learned this about six months after her seed tossing crusade when the California Highway System issued a statement regarding the uncontrollable sunflower issue—which, in the time between Pat's planting and the issuing of the statement, had caused almost forty-nine accidents due to the sunflowers blocking drivers' view of oncoming traffic. So the Highway System launched a counter to the growth and began controlled burns of all the sunflowers along the highways, exits, turnarounds, feeder roads, and so forth.

Pat kept quiet, didn't want anyone to know it was her who was responsible. The only person who knew was Dick, and she had secrets on him. So instead of sharing cute initials or matching nicknames, Pat and Dick shared their well-kept secrets.

Near the city of San Dimas, on a patch of grass off the highway, but close enough to the highway to feel the exhaust of passing cars, a cluster of sunflowers grew outside the annihilation of the California Highway System's razing flame. This patch of sunflowers pollinated itself continuously. As seasons changed and the sunflower shed its seed and died it's seasonally accepted death, a new spring would awaken those shed seeds and that particular family of sunflowers would bloom again in that specific patch of untouched California soil. They watched as buildings went up, as highways grew in size, as cars changed, as highways became more congested with people, as houses developed in nearby hills, as people multiplied in a way that was no different than the sunflower—invasive. This cycle of legacy continued, unchecked, for over sixty years.

Until today—when a young man with a shaved head, dressed in a white dress shirt, pushes his way through shrubs that have protected the sunflowers from public eyes. He sees them and they see him. The young man calls back over his shoulder *I found some here* and approaches the family of sunflowers, a pair of garden shears in his hand. A woman, also with a shaved head, dressed in a white dress shirt, pushes through the shrub behind him. They both wear smiley face pins on their lapels. The young man bends down, and without a second thought about the life of the flowers, how long they've been there, or how long they would remain had he not appeared today, proceeds to cut the stalks of each flower. If he could hear the frequencies of sunflowers, he would hear a scream that carries with it history and the permanent termination of that history. But instead he passes the flowers over to the woman. And then the two disappear, leaving behind a barren patch of earth where all that remains amidst the wreckage is a single sunflower seed half-buried in the dirt.

DELETED SCENE: REG

REG SITS AT AN AIRPORT BAR, images of a lone pig hang over the backsplash. Bartenders mix pork-flavored drinks. There's a guy next to him who's skillfully manipulating free drinks out of a housewife. She's visibly nervous about her flight. The guy notices. Reg sees she's using a credit card to pay for the drinks. Her and the guy have only been in each's general proximity for four and a half minutes and she's already told him about her trip to the UK, how her son just got married to a *bimbo* she *just can't stand*, and the fact that she's an orphan due to an avalanche that killed both her parents and her twin sister, Ruby, when she was twelve.

The guy listens to all this, nodding at the right parts, replying whenever necessary. When the bartender comes around, muffin top blossoming from the waist of week-worn jeans, and asks if they need anything else, the guy taps his glass and the nervous woman, after a glitch that could be taken as hesitation, asks for one more but to *give it a little something extra*. She's gathering the courage to ask this guy for his number, if only to call or text and spark a line of conversation that will fulfill her need for sexual connection, and maybe fill that void her absentee husband's left her with.

And it's very likely that she would get that chance if not

for the guy's flight number coming in scrambled chaos over the intercom. He thanks her for the drinks, makes a joke about not having to drive, shares an awkwardly emotional hug with her—which she punctuates with a kiss on his neck—says *You remind me of my mom*, and then floats off, disappearing into the crowd. When the guy is fully gone and she thinks no one can hear, she cries.

Reg knows situations like this. His mother once married a man who only used her for the money she lived off of after Reg's dad died on-the-job—or as they say: *in the line of duty.* He doesn't remember much of this guy other than how he always had the PIN number to Reg's mother's bank card. That's thirty years in the past. That guy is gone, and Reg is on his way to bear witness to the last days of his mother's life. *Bad luck runs in our family* she reminded him after telling him how many weeks she had left.

Reg, on the other hand, has only an hour and twenty five minutes left in his life. The minutes will go slow and the end will come quick—but he will be aware, repeating to himself *this is the end this is the end* until he can't repeat anything ever again.

Why are you here?

Flight 2511 out of Seattle lands at 7:34am, twenty-six minutes ahead of schedule. Passengers on the sold-out flight disembark and passengers waiting to embark on Flight 2511's scheduled path across the American West line up according to their economic caste. Luggage from the previous passengers is taken off while luggage from those standing in line is on its way across the tarmac to Flight 2511's location, bouncing carelessly on a covered flatbed trailer towed by a golf-cart-type thing that's souped up to go roughly 70mph, which is about how fast it's going now. The driver and her passenger, a guy who's first-day-on-the-job clueless, laugh in a freshly-stoned way as the wind nearly rips little orange ear muffs from their heads. And then they arrive at the plane.

A mid-size olive green Eagle Creek suitcase rumbles down the conveyor belt outside the 737 at Terminal 7. Inside are seven shirts, three pairs of pants, five tightly-bundled pairs of socks, five pairs of underwear, a toothbrush, one stick of Right Guard deodorant, a contact lens case filled with solution but no lenses, a copy of *In The Realm of Lost Things*, a hairdryer, a dress, a jockstrap, a leopard print bra and g-string, and a high-explosive thermal charge wired to a burner phone through a series of complicated tangle of wires sloppily soldered to glued-together relays.

Is this why you're here?

Reg wanders down the jet bridge, the resting purr of the 737's engines still loud enough to hurt the ear infection in his left ear. His lower left bicuspid is beginning to throb again. He thought the beer would help, but instead has inflamed the cavity. The Ativan should kick in shortly and he won't really care about the pain in his tooth, the discomfort in his ear, the cancer he doesn't know is blooming in his stomach, or the way his head will hit the cabin roof when the jet takes its unscheduled plunge. He takes his seat. Aisle 12, Seat F. Window seat in a two-seat row.

"I haven't been to the Commonwealth in years," he tells the deaf man sitting next to him. The man motions to show that he's deaf, but Reg thinks it's just a way to get out of uncomfortable flight conversations. Reg commends the guy for his commitment. If he's not deaf, he's going to have to pretend to be so for the next two hours—or forty seven minutes. Sitting in silence, listening to the uncomfortable chaos of passengers entering the plane, settling, getting adjusted and acquainted with their flight mates, Reg sees the guy from the bar come onboard looking totally sauced.

As he passes Aisle 12, Reg leans over the deaf guy and says to the guy from the bar, "They didn't call your flight, you liar."

"What?"

"You just used that lady for drinks."

"It's too loud in here, man. I can't hear you."

"Sir, you need to find your seat," says the flight attendant at the front.

The guy from the bar turns to her, says, "This guy keeps talking to me."

Reg says, "You can hear." But in this moment he's accidentally made eye contact with the deaf guy, who motions in a way that connotes yelling, pointing to his ears, signing something Reg doesn't understand, all the while making vague word-like sounds that only people who've been deaf from birth can make.

"No, I wasn't talking to you. I was talking to—" but he's pointing at other passengers who pass Aisle 12 without looking in his direction. He motions to the deaf guy to forget it and leans back in his seat. The deaf guy is still emoting to him, but the Ativan kicks in and turns everything a pinkish shade of I-Don't-Give-A-Fuck. The deaf guy motions but Reg pretends to be blind and doesn't see any of it. A kinda fat, sloppy, insecure-looking guy, probably around Reg's age, wanders onto the plane. One of the last to arrive. He takes a seat near the front, next to an elderly woman. Reg can see the hesitation on his face, like he's afraid to be shut in the plane, afraid to find that he doesn't want to be at the hands of physics at 36,000 feet. So the sloppy-looking guy gets up, squeezes his way into the aisle, and rushes out of the cabin. He never returns.

Wait… Do you recognize that guy? You wish he'd come back so you can make sure it's really who you think it is.

Just after the plane leaves the runway, tearing through the air in a way only science or magic can explain, Reg takes out the in-flight catalog and flips through, if only to bore himself long enough for the Ativan to strangle the part of his brain that controls sleep.

What else can be said about Reg to help connect with this character before things happen? He was born six weeks premature. His left foot twists inward and has caused a misalignment in his back. He was bit by a dog, stung by a stingray, and had his head cracked open in the same week—he was eight. He lost his virginity in a bush. His first job was at Pizza Hut. His first love was a man. His first wife killed herself. He associates with dangerous, violent people.

In the cargo area below Aisle 45, the mid-size olive green Eagle Creek luggage explodes in a manner that, if it weren't viewed intimately, but rather from a safe distance, and didn't mean the death of everyone onboard, would be considered *cinematic*. The pilots attempt to control the sudden change in pressure and the damage to the tail end of the 737, but the force pushing against them is too great. The cabin erupts in chaos. People scream. The deaf guy turns to Reg and says, "I'm not really deaf," likely hoping that his confession will earn him a place in the Holy Kingdom. Reg shrugs, thinking only about how his tooth doesn't hurt anymore and how he won't have to pay on his student loans anymore. As the plane tilts, pulling his body to the desert below, he thinks *this is the end this is the end this is—*

DELETED SCENE: THE TROUGH

SHE'S CHEAPLY ATTRACTIVE IN A SINISTER WAY that looks like she could hate me more than love me. Her perfume's got this vaguely necrotic smell usually associated with burning fruit. It's pleasant in the same way that waking up ten minutes before your alarm is. I can't really sit across from her, here, without shifting uncomfortably. She asks *what's wrong with you?* and I blame it on my wallet. She continues to talk about her ex and all the things he didn't do right. To be fair, I asked, but only as a means to show I'm interested—even though there's not much to be interested in—and to show that I understand that there were guys before me and will be guys long after I'm out of the picture. This is one of those things best established at the beginning of a possible relationship: let the other person know that there have been relationships—possibly meaningful ones—that they will take from and use to navigate the terrains of whatever new relationship might form. Especially a relationship with a celebrity of Shanese's stature.

You can already tell this is going to be too much. You're looking for a way out of here.

She asks about my previous relationship, but in that jealous way some people pick up in high school and can't quite shake. I tell her it was a long thing, that this person's with someone else now, and that this person's happy with that someone else, which makes me feel better because it's mostly my fault why this person's with someone else. She doesn't get it. Actually, she seems annoyed by it. We're doing this over wild boar sausage with raspberry reduction and spiced apple slaw (mine, and not that these ingredients are identifiable given that the food's been eviscerated and served in a miniature trough, sans utensils & napkins) and a plate of steamed mixed vegetables, *no spice no sauce* (hers, actually served on a pristine white plate with gold trim and utensils tightly rolled in a napkin). I ask the waiter to bring us more *La Chatte Mineure*, a 15-year red blend she insisted on ordering before we even sat down, a hushed transaction between her and the *maître d'*. I'm pretty sure the waiters are ignoring me. They only listen to her. Everyone here knows her name. Except they keep calling her *Miss Undrege* instead of *Shanese* like I have. The *maître d'* keeps looking over here. He looks like an old, deflated version of every *maître d'* you've ever seen.

"And that's, like, the only thing that motivates me," she says.

"How does that make you feel," I ask, though I have no idea what she's referencing. There's certain phraseology I use—which I call *mendax syntax*—that allows me to navigate conversations I hardly pay attention to, mostly with women.

Do the things I think and the things I say have any correlation to one another? Sometimes, when I find myself being more like myself, there's this fathomless pointlessness in all the things I've done. When I'm empty, I feel good. And today, things are pleasantly empty. I wish I could capture myself, now, as a portrait to carry around and show people *This is me, who I really am, and I am here.*

"How is your food?" This is the thing we're supposed to say to each other in this situation.

"Mmmhmmm," is all she says, mouth not full but pretending to be full, going through the motions of eating—that thing that girls who make a show of eating but don't quite eat in order to retain a figure they lost at like 16 or 17 and search their entire lives to find. I don't tell her mine has a vaguely rubber taste. Like rubber mixed with flower petals.

DMT tastes like rubber. No, that might not be specific enough. It tastes like sucking on a new eraser, one of the expensive ones artists use. That synthetic taste translating to a smell that seeps through the porousness of one's head, which then morphs into a sensation, first experienced at the back of the head, melting up, over, and around to the front, until it all bursts through and opens the third eye that's almost always closed and/or cataracted. And what one sees is this place that doesn't exist, should never exist, and yet exists all the same. Colors and shapes. Entire made-up worlds straight from some child's Crayon-fueled imagination. Years pass in this world. There's always the face of God somewhere in view. But it's never the face one expects to see. It's like the sun, but more oppressive, more observant. And then it takes a vile and cruel turn: fingers of light ripping the skin from face, jagged slivers of ice stabbing body *ad infinitum*, an awareness of the nothingness that waits patiently at the finish line, the screams of this nothingness. And when it's all over, only thirty seconds have passed in the actual world and one realizes they've been holding their breath. When one finally catches up and catches breath, there's this spiritual connection one never knew they could have to this world. But there's also this lingering sense that everything is no more real than what was seen with the third eye. The one here being me.

I didn't do DMT on purpose. Most people who take PCP, DMT, LSD, etc., say the same thing: *I didn't know I was doing it*. The user believes they are smoking marijuana, and only that. I had never smoked marijuana. Never even took an aspirin for a headache. This one girl—a much nicer, calmer, younger version of the one sitting across from me now—took me to a kava bar and, since I had never had kava, ordered me a double ginger kava. What I didn't know was that this girl, to test her dates, would dump her own tonic of Syrian rue and DMT into whatever beverage her date planned to ingest—or at least that's what she did to me. And so when I drank the kava, about 1 min. and 42.9 secs. later, the whole third eye opening thing happened. I came to outside, wet from the rain, pants smelling of piss, screaming horrible things. Someone saying *That's the Devil right there*, another saying *Let him ride it out*, another saying *He need some milk*.

After things calmed down a bit, that girl who slipped me the tonic said *How am I supposed to know I can date you if I don't know how you are when you trip? And besides, it wasn't my idea.* I didn't know what she meant by that. This was about seven years ago. I'm still unsure if I ever came back from that world.

When the waiter brings us the *Mineur Chatte*, I make sure the bottle's opened at the table, poured at the table, and that the same procedure is followed regarding a bottle of natural spring water. Opened, poured, consumed, all within eyesight—and never leaving that. I'm not too concerned about a chef rubbing food all over their under regions. In the grand system of food not self-prepared, we've all eaten someone's asshole. Maybe it's that I don't trust Shanese. She seems prepared to dump something in my cup.

A waiter carrying a tray of food launches from the hallway on the other side of the restaurant—where all the waiters have come and gone, and where diners go to use the restroom, a hallway I'm ignoring because of the word RESTROOM—and hurries to a nearby table. He sets a trough nearly overflowing in front of each of the table's two diners. They dip half their faces into their respective trough, slurping the slopified dish of their choice. One comes up for air, face dripping, then returns to the slop.

For the past twenty two minutes—clock on the other side of the restaurant taunting me with its tick-ticking that I can't hear but know well by the pressure building in my abdomen—I've had a primitive urge to piss. One of those *I have to go* moments that makes the back teeth float. My dad would've said *You know that feeling you get when you gotta pee? Can you feel me and see if that's it?* or *I gotta piss so bad I can taste it* which lends a certain crude urgency to the emphasis of having to go. When the time comes to release, it'll be gallons of glorious fluid that's been passed from mouth to esophagus to stomach, through the sulcus ventriculi, absorbed by villi/microvilli and spread to liver, pancreas, intestines, filtered through kidneys, through urinary tract where it finally climaxes in an eruption of golden euphoria out the urethra and into one of the Trough's uselessly-fancy toilets. I am well versed in the system and art of urination. Which is what makes this moment discouraging on an ever-escalating level. I'm looking at her, at my glass of water, my glass of red-blend, at the restroom on the other side of the restaurant, the *maître d'* (who diverts his eyes when mine pass over him), wondering how much longer I'm going to have to sit here and hold this all in. We're only on our second of six courses, but I can't stop myself from thinking of all the fluids I've ingested today, of how much of it my body doesn't want, and how that rejected fluid is *pushing* at the walls of my bladder, pressure against the place just above my crotch, right where my belt sits tight, squeezing this area, making the pain that's building with each unheard *tick* of the clock over there that much more unbearable. The pain makes me feel like a ghost that's never been allowed to leave this place.

"What're you thinking about?" She nibbles at the flower end of an asparagus stalk.

"Nothing," but not because I'm embarrassed by what I was just thinking. For the most part, I find myself *not* thinking more than I do thinking…if that makes sense. It probably does, but fuck… I'm not really thinking clearly right now.

A family of three sits at a table near the window on the far side of the restaurant, meals untouched. Like Shanese, they've also somehow earned the right to use utensils and napkins. I note that the *maître d'* has shifted his attention, for the moment, to them. They appear to be an average family, a xerox distinguished only by the fact that the son seems out of place. Where the others are kempt to the point of nearly-photoshopped, the son seems more lost or in desperate search of something important and yet doesn't know what that something is yet. There's a moderate sense of happiness passing between them, but it seems manipulated. Not so much that they're acting, but maybe that they're insincere with their emotions, that they don't really feel comfortable expressing themselves naturally. The table is set for four—even though there's only three. I recognize the mother in a way I can't pinpoint. She's someone who was once famous, but only like throwaway famous. She just sits there, speaking every so often, interjecting to let the others at the table know she's still there. The father boasts, hands waving in a controlled mania. In one of those moments where the chatter of a restaurant quiets in a moment of synchronicity, I can hear the father say *no one really cares about the importance of a good toilet*—and then the chaos crashes back in wave-like. The son, probably closer to thirty than anything, sits comfortably distant, doesn't really interact. I guess this is what a family looks like. I forget. It's something I've never really known. But there's this kind of emptiness to the table, a ghost that gives the family their insincerity, using false emotions to hide a saddening distance. This, also, could just be my projection. But usually, I'm pretty good at reading people. People say I'm a smart guy.

—car pulls up to curb in front of The Trough—encroaches on valet space reserved for high-brow eaters coming and going—encroachment earns sour faces and hands motioning for driver to take note of sign that says *Valet Only*—passenger emerges from backseat—worthy of note: mid-sized olive-green Eagle Creek suitcase in passenger's right hand—top of suitcase, sewn into canvas exterior: cloth patch, a smiley face uncomfortable with its manic happiness—passenger does not share same enthusiasm—passenger's face is uncut stone, barren place where emotions will never exist—no acknowledgement of appreciation passes between passenger and rideshare driver—passenger dressed in flowing gown that feels out of place here, more fitting at Hollywood awards ceremony: red and appropriately sequined—very expensive—Rebecca Minkoff purse hangs from passenger's left shoulder—tinkle of its jeweled tassels punctuates each step with Disney-quality magic—passenger: henceforth referred to as Her, though not necessarily a Her—carries overweighted suitcase with an ease that makes muscles in her exposed arm stand out—their definition impressive and intimidating—call her *slut*, she'd accept with a nod that says *you're goddamn right*—she's about twenty years overdrawn—*cougar* would be more appropriate— no one watches her or even notices her—valet attendants have their attention and annoyance focused on rideshare that's driving away with electric stealth—passenger doesn't look at restaurant—she walks in opposite direction of Spanish-fort-style doors—not being held open for her—moves half-block up street—suitcase bounces—clatter from inside, not unlike sound of tent poles tossed in casually—mid-sized suitcase pulls at her arm—handle seems to be on verge of snapping off—if it weren't reinforced with commercial-grade polymer resin, usually used to re-adhere car parts that've come loose— whatever's inside is very heavy and is not at all clothing— underneath flowing, red dress passenger wears laced-to-the-top military-style boots that are genuinely distressed and not just made to look so by tiny Taiwanese hands halfway across globe—these military-style clodhoppers have seen some shit, been in The Shit, and were not at all purchased second-hand at military surplus outlet post-in-the-shit—choker around her muscular neck is black velvet—almost covers large lump in middle of her throat—she steps off sidewalk—enters darkness of alley between The Trough and florist that radiates industrial chill—her eyes don't need to adjust to shadows—she can see everything—part of her training—once she's out of sight, merged with umbra of alley, certain that no unwanted encounter stands between her and what's next, she reaches into purse and removes gas mask that unfolds from tight bundle that, pre-unfolding, closely resembled rubber socks—black with front respirator—no side filtration—ventilators for each eye so lens doesn't fog up—same model used by both Israeli and Palestinian civilians in case of toxic attacks—most purchased consumer gas mask in America—she slips it over her head naturally—says everything about how many times she's done this—from sidewalk, looking into dark throat of alley, no one's there—

"*Mer vine for ze taybul,*" says the *maître d'* as he lords villainous over the table. He holds another bottle of the 15-year red-blend, but not in a pleasant, offering way. He looks like he's ready to shove it up my asshole fat side first.

"Huh?" is all I can say.

"He's asking if you want more wine, duh," Shanese says. I'd just polished off the glass, ready to tell her not to let him pour me anything while I run to the restroom—maybe even take both wine and water glass with me—but here he is, ready to pour more. So here's where I stay, the pain in my abdomen kick-to-the-nuts swollen.

"Uhh…" I'm trying to buy a moment. On one hand, it's going to take at least another bottle or two to build up the courage to do to her what any man would, and the same could be said about her. How much will she have to drink before I start to look like the kind of guy she'd let touch or kiss or slam into awkwardly in a small space—like the backseat of a car or a restaurant bathroom stall—for like two minutes before a premature interruption. Isn't this the foundation of most relationships? Regardless, I just really want to fuck Shanese.

There's this pain that's starting to creep around my back,

telling me that my kidneys are trying to filter trapped urine, working harder, festering a bit in all the germs and unwanted waste. I'm being disrespectful to my kidneys. Can this kill me?

"*Monsieur. Qui ou non?*"

"I'm not ready for the next course, but I'll take another glass of wine."

He pours mine, and then he makes a show, again, of pouring Shanese's. He takes the glass off the table and blocks its view from me and the rest of the diners. His head does this quick scan of the area, either checking to see if anyone is in need of his service or just displaying his general air of paranoia. And again, he sets her glass in front of me and says *Monsieur,* and then hurries away in that stick-up-the-butthole way that all *maître ds* must display before they graduate from *maître d'* college. She downs half her glass and bounces in her seat a little. Her foot tugs at the cuff of my pants, tapping in Morse code: *S-E-X.*

Blind dates are for the weak. Or at least I used to think so. Then I went on one and ended up getting laid—well…almost. What's it called when you're already doing that awkward in/out thing and she stops cuz she suddenly remembers something about her ex that causes her to break down and cry and never actually do it? That's the by-product of my last blind date. But this one…there's something about her my associate, who set up this date, wouldn't say. He mentioned that she's special in that her dad is like involved in the movies in some way. One of those activist actors everyone looks up to, who does the whole "white savior" thing that, because of their fame and their public personas, one thinks is beautiful and appropriate. He's someone who uses time on stage at awards ceremonies to trash the president or a certain civil upheaval currently using ink on the newspaper page—not that there's a newspaper page anymore. But I've never heard of him—I'm just aware of the type. I'm one of those few in California—or really the world—whose pink isn't tickled by the allure of being in that whole Hollywood thing. Example: earlier this month I had some guy claiming to be with some production company I'd never heard of visit the campus where I do research and propose this job consulting for a film about artificial intelligence and high-level IT security—probably one of those movies that deals with hacking with a sense of uncertain wonder similar to when old people are given smart phones for the first time. And though the money would've been nice, the appeal just wasn't there.

But so this girl here, Shanese, she's a catch in a way that resurrects envy in those who obsequiously cater to everything associated with that celebrity thing. Her nepotistic-based fame is probably why people keep looking at us, why the *maître d'* is taking such close care of her enjoyment, why these people envy her place in life, and why I'm painfully attracted to her. The anticipation of getting her the right amount of drunk so that things start to happen, it's a sort of feel-good discomfort. But all this is overshadowed by the pressure in my bladder, and the pain in my kidneys that's gone from harmless shades of bruise to little pricks of a hot knife. I look around, see that sign over in the far side, over a hallway lit a heavenly gold, the word RESTROOM in Pearly Gates font. The *maître d'* stands at the entrance to this hall, blocking all the unwanted from entering —a St. Peter who's almost ready to retire. His eyes are on me again. But then they move back to that one family. He adjusts the smiley face pin on his lapel. Doing all I can to ignore the pain and my wine-fueled erection, I let my eyes and mind wander.

There's a certain hideousness to this place that stills wandering eyes. The paintings on the walls are of the same quality as a kindergartener's booger-covered finger-paintings, the architecture doesn't know what it wants to be, there's gold everywhere there shouldn't be gold, something over there is wrapped in blue velvet, there's a giant cast-iron statue of a pig by the front door—almost double life-size—the ceiling is painted to look like space, little lights in the ceiling twinkle to enhance that celestial effect, up in the corner there's a model space station floating all lonely and totally unnecessary, and the waiters are dressed in a way that hurts to look at—which is half the reason why none of the diners look at them (the other reason being that most of the patrons are of an economic caste that gives them feelings of superiority to anyone in the food industry—even if that person dictates how their food is prepared). The table I'm gripping looks as if it was once a piece of a pirate ship's deck or the base of a buckboard. It all keeps the eaters *unaware* that nothing about these dishes is piquant or worth the price that's often confused for phone numbers. Facedown in the slop. Be seen. Increases the profit margin. Get gone.

Some people—my colleagues, mainly—have referred to me as *dispassionately pertinacious*. I'll take it. Not because I agree, but because I feel it's better than not being referred to at all. The only one of my colleagues I might be comfortable with is the one who set up this blind date, and, unfortunately, he's not the most...uh, *intelligent* of the ITSers at Sun State, especially ones working with Dr. Spapling—who is known for his work with artificial intelligence and biochemical reconstruction. So this person I'm comfortable with, I wouldn't necessarily call him stupid, but he is one of those guys who thinks the easiest way to get rid of a booger is to eat it. During our initiation into USINT and the Cryptological Systems Group, this guy didn't understand why we would be operating intelligence reconnaissance out of a lower-tier state university, why we would also be doing duties of common IT guys, and how the hell I bypassed a 4096-bit RSA encryption back on itself in less than 24 minutes—*Terrorism Won't Wait*, as they told us at NSA training. There's a reason I'm on this date and he's not—cuz I understand the things that are most apparent are usually not the truth, and if one can adapt to these things, they'll end up with a job paying six-figures and on dates with beautiful women such as Shanese here. He just doesn't get it. I guess he likes the taste of boogers. Sometimes, he comes to work dressed casual. On these days he almost always wears a shirt that says "Freedom Isn't Free." But he doesn't know the cost. And I'm certain the Gang of Eight are well aware. Last month I reported him to our supervisor on account of his almost-constant pen tapping. They wrote him a formal cease-and-desist letter and put a carbon-copy in his file. I still have trouble trying to understand why I did that.

When one has been responsible for tracing encrypted malware used to penetrate national-level secure data servers back to their international sources, sources that have used a certain highly-popular search engine's servers as a carrier pigeon for the delivery of this malware, a task that took one, even with one's incredible speed and ability to connect code in a way comfortably similar to the coding behavior of near-AI level supercomputers, nearly twenty-nine hours of straight, high-level concentration and a cat-and-mouse-esque chase through cyberspace that ended in the destruction of a twelve-story high-rise in Pyongyang because the whole thing was a ruse to pinpoint the source of this malware and relay that information back to a predator-drone loaded with a double-load Hellfire missile, one sometimes has a reaction to do things one doesn't really understand. Like, just the other night, I caught myself watching a live-stream of a man in tattered tighty-whities standing in his kitchen blasting farts that sounded like some THX-level caricature of a fart. And I was laughing. And much like filing that pen-tapping complaint, I don't know why.

The son from that one family stands abruptly and moves across the restaurant, passing our table without noticing our presence. I do not play a role in his story. There's this hate that makes the pain in my body subside for a second, cuz what this guy does is he walks casually over to that hall, past the *maître d'* without noticing the man, that lack of recognition shared, and disappears down the golden lit hall leading to the restrooms. I don't know this guy but I wanna put all my pain on him. The *maître d'* returns to his position near the mouth of the hallway. And before I have a chance to fantasize about hurting him, that son emerges from the hall. There's no way he's already pissed. Maybe it was a mirror check. But judging by his half-assed appearance, he's not the vain type. He returns to the table where the rest of the family doesn't notice his momentary disappearance. I take another torturous glance at the hallway, those golden-neon letters arranged in a word that sometimes means expiation with the body on almost Biblical terms— **RESTROOM**. The *maître d'* isn't there anymore, not standing guard over the entrance to the hallway as if he's protecting— oh, no wait…there he is. Emerging *from* the hall. Maybe he himself had to piss. I hate him too.

The *maître d'* moves away from the hall and continues his hustle across the restaurant. His eyes are trained on a couple that's just walked in: a man wearing a taqiyah and what I assume to be a woman cloaked in a royal blue niqab. Even from here I can see the shape of her eyes and their color closely hugging pupils. It's these eyes that could make men do terrible things. The *maître d'* has his hand at his waist, waving, signaling to the hostess, his hand saying *no no absolutely not don't let them in here do everything you can to turn them away.*

"Oh thank *God*," says Shanese, watching the *maître d'* push the couple out the door.

I can't say I don't share a similar, if more diluted, sense of relief. As already on-edge and uncomfortable as I am, adding a couple of Muslims to the mix would only make this worse. Especially with what's going on in Houston—the fortification of all those Mosques and signs of deceptive happiness they've hung from the tops of nearby minarets. *Have a nice day! We will if you will!* they read, and there's a sense of insincerity about them that's caused the US Army to set up small, makeshift HQs around each of these "friendly" Mosques. As if Muslims needed any extra help deteriorating their social image. And I know Houston's like sixteen-hundred miles away, but still, here: I'm glad the *maître d'* has kicked them out.

"That's so hot," Shanese says. "Making them leave like that."

Her leg brushes against mine in a way I can't and shouldn't dismiss as an accident. My penis tightens, the erogenousness of its tip heightened to a point of angry pain. I turn my attention away from the couple being deported from the restaurant. Shanese's eyes are on mine and I see a future involving blowjobs. Fuck, I gotta piss.

—outside: city of San Dimas, California—unaware that passenger has entered backdoor of The Trough—using key given to her by J. Renault Houellebecq—passenger will be henceforth referred to as Dorothy—not her real name—to continue to call her passenger is vague and repetitive—dress she's wearing similar to ruby slippers once used to return Dorothy home from Oz—backdoor opens on small managerial office silenced by adequate soundproofing—*sans* manager—Dorothy doesn't associate with The French—they are everyone's enemy and no one's friend—she doesn't do things she once did—not after Initiation—desires burned, former lives abandoned—her will adjusted and aligned to that of The Group—*We Must Abide*—Dorothy does what is required—her part in The Plot acted out as it is meant to—she carries mid-sized suitcase—inside is Experiment 49.3—Dorothy doesn't know what that means—not her responsibility—Dorothy's role: take suitcase, rendezvous with contact, set Experiment 49.3 in location pre-determined for optimal results, instigate uncertainty in host family, exfiltrate herself from location, return to HR House, await further instruction—to place 49.3, Dorothy must Abide Step 5: Incapacitate Potential External Cunctations—from her small yet very expensive purse—removes canister of similar construction to a flash-bang grenade—pulls pin—opens internal door of managerial office —door opens on frantically organized energy of kitchen and its stainless-steel, beige-tile, white-plate, ladled, frying-panned, sudden-bursts-of-flash-fire, wipe-the-excess-sauce-from-the-trough's-edge atmosphere—tosses canister into center of room—settles on SucPac floor drain she knew was there—she has studied restaurant floor-plan—still wearing gas mask—leaves door open—watches as faces turn her way—general sense of confusion in workers—security camera footage: football-player-sized woman in red gown, gas mask obscuring face, carrying luggage—before anyone can do anything: canister blooms into dense cloud of vapor—chefs, cooks, line cooks, dishwashers, waiters, line runners, and ticket callers in this kitchen collapse—overcome with most peaceful sleep of their lives—each of twelve people have lost function of their heart—now very dead—she pulls toilet-like lever on wall to her left—vacuum sound fills air—vapor swirls—fades down drain in middle of floor—Dorothy reminded of human-sized traps at HR House with similar function—strips gas mask off her face—tosses it onto stainless steel countertop—steps through swinging door leading out of kitchen—enters hallway: bathrooms on left, painting of golden pigs in vaguely cherub-like positions on right—sees Houellebecq at end of hallway—he turns his head—sees her out of his periphery—she sets suitcase just before bathroom door—figure enters hallway—not Houellebecq—figure stops—figure sees her—

Okay, so, like right now, I'm in violent agony. The pressure is at a point that I'm certain something inside will rupture and send toxins and germs in cascading chaos throughout my insides, infecting every cell and fiber. My kidneys are already inflamed to an irreversible point, the only course of action will be to engage in a series of dialysis sessions in order to live week-to-week. But all this is better than the alternative. Right? I mean, there's nothing that points to the fact that she would want to put something in my drink. Aside from her mentioning her MDMA-fueled parties on the weekend and the little bit of pot she smokes in the afternoon "after I've got all my stuff done for the day," she shares none of the qualities the DMT witch had. I gotta piss.

Shortly after a sturdily-built, unnaturally attractive woman in a flashy red dress approaches their table and speaks to the father in a way that creates a sense of unease in him and curiosity in the rest, that one family the *maître d'* showed unnecessary interest in stands and calmly exits the restaurant in an orderly, not-at-all hurried fashion. They leave an uncounted mess of bills on the table and largely uneaten troughs of food that look nothing like the food presented to the rest of the diners. Kitchen noises have subsided in a way that makes me think the staff's taking long-deserved breaks as the dinner rush fades and the last meals are sent out. Looking at the trough in front of me, I think: why? What is the philosophy behind serving food like this? I understand the concept, that food is food and that it looks much the same way it does in this trough as it will in my stomach. So then why doll it up and make it seem like some piece of art? People hold themselves prisoner to the order in which they eat or begin to digest their food. But it all ends up in the same place and as the same result. My kidneys hurt. And what is the interest for a place like this? This will always be beyond me, but then I guess it isn't my place to understand these kinds of systems—just as I wouldn't expect the chef preparing this rendered slop to know anything about PRISM or STELLARWIND or T. Access Ops or how to reverse feed a return server relay or how to access the laptop camera of Li Wei, who's in Sacramento, CA, and who is known to be involved in some dirty deals with the PLA over in China. What would a chef know about being an espial of thin client systems? And what would I know about the philosophical implications of food presentation?

Shanese clears her throat and I realize she's been talking. I gotta piss.

"Want more wine?" I say.

She shakes her head, but it's slow and smooth, somewhat messy. *Sauced* would be a good way to describe her demeanor.

"Oh okay. Continue," I say, again using the *mendaxic* phraseology, that implies both my previous listening and my desire for her to continue, while at the same time expurgating myself from any guilt in reference to my not listening. Piss.

"When I'm done with school I'munna go to France with my bestie Mia Rose. You remember her from that movie with Jennifer Brachis Donnahue? The one about that president guy who got shot?"

"John F. Kennedy?"

"I think so."

"What was your major again?" I don't think she ever told me, but using the phraseology to clear guilt again—just in case. Kidneys.

"Whassa major?" Her lips are heavy with that weight only wine can bring. The way they stick together for a second before they part when she—Wait…what?

"A major? Like what are you majoring in? What are you going to get a degree in?"

"Will I get one?"

"Usually when people go to college, they get a degree."

"But I'm not in college, silly." Her foot tracing up the inside of my leg, heading in a slow, purposeful arc toward my penis, her coyness now full-on coquettish.

"But you said…*school*…"

"Yeah, like high school? Duh."

"No," is all I can say, but my mind screams this:

nononononononononoNONOFUCKINGNONOWHAT?
NOPLEASENOWHAT?HOW?NOnono

My head looks around the restaurant, twisting unnaturally kinda like that Excorist-girl, but my eyes see nothing. Is it obvious that I've been sharing a highly sexualized dinner with someone still in high school? Piss. Kidneys. There's a camera flash from somewhere on the other side of the restaurant, and the flash seems so concentrated that I suspect it's pointed over here. The pain eating my insides screams, starts tearing at my kidneys, bladder, penis, balls, brain, heart, stomach, butthole, etc., all with this rabid gorilla strength that, if I were to deny any longer, would kill me. Piss. Kidneys.

"But I thought you knew I'm only fift—"

kidneyspisspisskidneysPISSKIDNEYS

I can't hear anything else she's saying. I push away from the table. Muscles stay rigid and others contract wildly, my body cutting a madman's path across the restaurant, shoving chairs and tables out of the way, the patrons occupying these spaces looking up with slop covering the bottom half of shocked faces, my sphincter so confused that farts escape, a continuous strand of motor-boat-sounds behind me, slopped faces transitioning from shocked to soured at the sound of these farts, this quivering at my core stealing the strength from all other parts, legs threatening to give, my mind twelve steps ahead of these weakened legs, arms flailing, these mindless vestiges slapping things that shatter and things that scream *hey!* and *watch it!*, and an almost-certainty that at this moment, with the attention of the entire restaurant turned toward the lunatic scrambling terroristically in the general direction of the restrooms—that glorious word causing a close-to-orgasm warmness in my heart —I am sure this is the moment I piss all over myself. Cuz I know it's going to feel so good, the purge of impurities like a rebirth, and I know the pain in my kidneys will stick around a while, a reminder over the comings days of how incredibly, terribly bad it is to hold in your piss and how much of a depressing failure this date was, and how somewhere out there in this restaurant someone who—I'm just now realizing is probably my coworker—took a picture of me on this date—for what purpose can only be assumed. Likely laughing, mocking, preparing some weird little revenge plot for me filing that report about his pen tapping.

With Saint Peter gone to kick another Muslim couple from his little piece of the Kingdom, the gates to Paradiso are unguarded, giving my faithless heart the space to smash a standing tray—covered with a table of four's entrees—out of the way and do this crazed-Ahab-chasing-the-White-Whale, Quasimodo run, dick in hand, doing everything I can to pinch the hose. In the hall, above a door that doesn't lead to the restroom, there's an **EXIT** sign. The green-lit letters say more than the word they create: *run*, they tell me; *get out of here and piss outside in the alley like a real man and feel the night air*, they say, showing me the freedom I'll have pissing outside, stream slamming into a wall, the space to let out a primitive *YEEEAAAAAAAAAHH* because I know it'll feel good; *go go get out of here cuz that's a child in there and there's someone taking pictures and it's all going to end very very bad for you so run*. But I can't do anything but ignore those green-lit letters, and can only move in the direction of the restroom. And it doesn't matter that I'm spilling my way into the women's restroom, or that the stall is locked, or that even after three hard kicks it doesn't open, or that, in a panic and because it's the women's restroom and there are no urinals, I whip out my penis—

which, to speak a truth, is no bigger than a cashew—and let loose a horse-strength stream of magnificent fluid tinted a color similar to iced tea into the sink, standing on tippy-toes to reach. Droplets spatter on the mirror and the mirror reflects back a version of me that looks bone-soaked with sweat, face half-melted, hair un-coiffed, 7-piece set of luggage under the eyes, this general sense of madness taking control of every aspect. When I look into my eyes in combination with this glorious sensation of release, I cum a little. This is both the greatest and worst moment of my life.

The splashback from my stream deflects around the sink, out, and onto my shirt and pants. Onto the floor, where, just now noticing this, there's a slug crawling from under the bathroom stall and toward my foot. And not like a standard garden slug; this thing's the size of a small rat. Piss sprinkles on the tile around the thing, which flinches each time one of the drops touches its slick flesh. I follow its slime trail and notice another, this one inching it's own path from the stall, a trajectory different from the slug that's almost near my foot.

The stream sputters, spits. My body does the shiver all bodies do when they experience a solid release of urine, except this one's a little more gripping than usual. And then it's all over. Fluids expunged. I turn on the sink and let the water carry all traces of my urine down the drain, use that same water to wash my hands. I notice this uncomfortable chemical smell. At first, seeing the slugs and smelling this stink, I think there's a dead body in the stall. Door's locked. There was no answer when I tried to kick it down. The slug nearest me is now halfway on my foot and I kick it away. It makes a wet sound as it hits the wall. But instead of curling up like most slugs do in their death moment, the thing starts puffing out, expanding slowly but somewhat erratically, as if it isn't meant to. A step toward the locked stall and the smell intensifies. I knock... nothing. Ignoring the piss and the line of slug snot on the floor, I kneel, put my hand in wetness, brace myself, and lean down, seeing that the only thing on the other side of the stall door is an abandoned suitcase.

—outside, city of San Dimas, California: awareness awakened as a tectonic-rattling explosion sends a resounding *clap* across valley—people as far as Anaheim, Vernon, and San Bernardino feel shockwave in structure of their homes—car alarms in nearby Claremont are set off—dogs left outside bark—debris sent to Rancho Cucamonga—a cast-iron, full-sized pig's head makes a spectacular mess of a homeowner's roof, second floor guest room and first floor living room—first responders arrive—each amazed by how little there is left of The Trough—explosion negating that it ever existed—detectives kick around debris no larger than a wine cork—a search for bodies—all they find is little puddled remains—people—these puddles scooped up into airtight containers and sent out for testing or burial or recognition—[*Ma'am, does this puddle look anything like your husband?*]—could just be remains of slop served up in troughs—crime scene investigator says, "At least no one suffered."—lists will be made and checked re patrons, who to notify of their sudden demise—scrap of paper, only thing in rubble recognizable, floats on wind that carries smell of destruction out to ocean—*Dave Churchyard (2) 9pm* written in neat penmanship on this scrap of paper—snatched by wind—passes drone flying overhead—drone's camera recording aerial view of destruction—paper's gone—general air about all those involved with investigating Event—air of reluctance to mention doubt surrounding cause—*terrorism*, buzz word—paperwork would have to be filed—entire string of inquisitions would be made—all would result in many nights of lost sleep—hard work, time away from families, relinquishing of freedom—people, quick to mention presence of Muslims mere moments before explosion—these Muslims noted—notations sent to an investigation committee—who will then "lose" these requests for investigation—most will agree when person in charge [man no one knows by first name, and who is always absently touching lapel pins on every suit he wears: an American flag, Triple Canopy's menacing star, and smiley face] defines Event as *result of gas leak*—insurance will cover losses—families will be paid largely—this was an accident—nothing to fear—no one sees woman in red dress—her role in The Plot is over—

DELETED SCENE: THE WEIGHT OF THE GUN

<u>Editor's Note</u>: *The following is believed to be written by Austin Foster—noting the immature pseudonym. This creative writing exercise is a not-so-vaguely veiled fictionalization of the George Zimmerman assassination. There is a submission letter, with accompanying rejection slip, to* Zoetrope: All Story. *The date on the letter means Austin would've been nineteen or twenty at the time of submissions—but possibly younger at the time of writing. Which can account for why it is so poorly written (of particular note are the lack of subtleties and nuance in metaphor, the insensitivity of using an actual tragedy as a means to place himself as the savior—assuming the child in the story is some fictionalized facet of Austin—and the navel-gazing/handwaving that holds the "story" back from ever saying anything profound)—though there is no further samples of Foster's work to cross-reference if he ever developed into a better writer. And though the responsible party was never caught, there is no evidence whatsoever that the Zimmerman assassination was committed by a child.*

THE WEIGHT OF THE GUN

by P. P. Lizerds

ZUBBERHAM SLAIN IN

CALIFORNIA

Shooter still at large; witnesses saw a 'small, white

hand'

By Don Simple

"A small, white hand came out the crowd and BAMBAMBAM!" This and other similar statements were made by many of the African Americans in attendance Thursday during the release of Gilman Zubberham from police custody. While being led to a police vehicle, Zubberham was fatally shot by an unknown gunman. Despite there being a crowd of over three hundred, including two dozen officers, the shooter managed to escape unseen. Medics attempted to revive Zubberham, but his wounds were fatal. He died on the scene.

Zubberham's acquittal of all charges in the death of Devaughn Blake caused an uproar Tuesday as many protesters claim Zubberham acted not out of self defense, but rather out of racial prejudice. "That boy wasn't even looking at him," said Sandra Bastree, 41, who has spent the last week camped out in front of the courthouse. She continued, "Personally, I think Zubberham got it just as he should've." Over two hundred of the three hundred in attendance were questioned and police are still

CONTINUES ON P.12

- front page of the *Sun Coast Tribune*, 12 April 20█

#

This was his moment. Everything he raged against coalesced into this unfortunate event. But how, he wondered, would he go about making a difference? He is just one boy. And this moment seems to be the essence of an eternal machine that likely has no end. What can he do to change eternity? There's the Group, but they wanted him to do things (commit acts) that were against his moral commandments. Notice that this is all in past tense. It already happened; it's over. But moral commandments are often broken by stronger men, and he'd made them himself and was only pressuring himself to stick to them.

Is there any knowledge in the world which is so certain that no reasonable man could doubt it? Russell. Was what the Group wanted of him so inherently "bad" that to commit to their plan would be to betray any of His—or Society's—moral commandments? He would think of this and nothing but during the months following the Event.

The victim's name was Devaughn Blake. But he was more than the sum of some letters. He was a symbol: Christ the Redeemer for an entire ethnicity. Or maybe it should be made clear that because of the Unfortunate Event (as the Sun Coast Tribune put it) Blake became a symbol of something absolutely, almost-infinitely greater. The repression of the Black and Brown population of America, who wore bracelets and necklaces, wore shirts, spouted slogans, and devoted their time to Blake—much like Catholics do the image of crucified Christ. A dead messiah with no chance for redemption. Not a messiah though—just a young Black man murdered by a white coward.

The Unfortunate Event sparked the resurgence of racial injustices and the media-dominated presence of racial injustices (which never went away, only became less important for the news) which in total led to the New Race "Riots" (riots being the Media's term, because what they really were were Revolutions) and the ongoing race conflicts the media called the War Against Injustice. And what this Unfortunate Event consisted of, aside from unstable aggression for aggression's sake and blatant racial profiling, was the death of a sixteen year old Black kid and the subsequent defense of the Right to Bear Arms and the Right to Defend One's Self by Any Means Necessary in the form of a 45-year old man who seemed more than eager to use deadly force because at his core was a racist white nationalist. While the exact details were never clear, Blake was unarmed, on his way home from seeing a movie with his girlfriend, Detta, and shot seven times in the back; while the shooter, Gilman Zubberham, had a record, long and detailed, of his numerous visits to anger management clinics and one instance of being fired from a job for violently accosting, sexually, a female coworker. And it totally didn't help escalating racial tensions regarding the shooting that

Zubberham was a very *white* man—suspiciously involved with men who had ties to white supremacist groups. And this Unfortunate Event lead to a profoundly confusing trial, the Scales of Justice one-sided but still see-sawing towards the side of Injustice. All the while, outside the media spectacles and courtroom recollections and the dodged double-edged questions meant to extract guilt, the world raged at the fact that there was even a question as to who was wrong in the Event that was clearly black and white—do what you will with that pun. And a year later, after a trial that lasted longer than it ever should have, the tension between those who saw Blake as a messiah and those who saw Zubberham's actions as justified building to a tightness, a fishing line trying to hold the weight of an anvil, it all ended with a shock that ran out across the world. **ZUBBERHAM NOT GUILTY!** A headline with a response of riots, civil upheaval, and a heightened distrust between races. Police brutality against people of color exploded, as police only having interactions with Black criminals assuming that all Blacks are criminals, and Blacks distrusting all those in law enforcement (even the Black officers) because they are meant to uphold laws that feel more comfortable pre-Emancipation than they do today.

But that's not the point. That's just some back story. What's important here is that this guy—who we'll call Arthur —the one who didn't know how he could make a difference, saw the situation for what it was: an opportunity, a political and financial agenda being fulfilled, each new link in the causal chain of Unfortunate Events being carefully planned and executed. And so he knew that his "making a difference" wouldn't involve a political/social injustice motive, or that they wouldn't be fighting a system he couldn't move, but instead would do everything he could to crack a cog in the well-planned machine. The cog may or may not cause the machine to fail, but it would certainly need to be replaced, which would change how the machine would run—even in small, unsuspecting ways. Which led to the questions: How(?) and When (?).

The Group got at Arthur not long after. He didn't understand how they could find him and know that he harbored an interest in their cause, though at the time he didn't know what their cause was. And when finally let in on what their Cause was and their plan to carry out that Cause and how Arthur would fit into their Counter-Plan to the Machine's Plan, Arthur was unsure if he wanted to join. It involved a murder and Zubberham and at a time when Zubberham was in the company of many and when it would reverberate immediately through the ever-growing Police State of America under the supervision of President Truffaux.

But again, Arthur went through his moral commandments and eventually got a red ink. There were too many variables to determine how it would go, what the moral truth was (if there could be one), and for any one certain truth of the situation to be doubted and the validation of the Group put into question, Arthur wasn't sure if moral commandments meant anything anymore. And just as there are those who don't question the actions of Zubberham and believe he was totally justified in killing Blake (at least twelve did, but an important twelve), there should exist those that think the death of Zubberham at the hands of someone feeling threatened by Zubberham's existence, regardless of the judicial outcome, who believes that Zubberham should face true, societal justice. And why couldn't Arthur be the hands behind that idea? Could he do it? Did he want to?

So Arthur went to his little brother, Dallas. Then only nine years old. He told Dallas about a bad man who hurt people that didn't deserve to be hurt. Dallas cried a little bit and Arthur told his brother to not cry, to never cry, to always take that emotion for crying and to turn it into other energy. Dallas said he didn't want the bad man to hurt people and Arthur said he wanted the same thing. Arthur asked his little brother what he would do to the bad man and his little brother, always watching space movies and violent cartoon, said *I want to kill the bad man*.

Arthur put a gun in his little brother's little hand. It was almost too heavy for the nine year old boy to hold. Arthur showed him how to use it, what the important parts were: how to point and how to pull. He didn't ever fire the gun as a test. Arthur didn't want Dallas to be afraid of it—not yet. And it would only take one bullet, one chance.

On the day of, Arthur gave his brother the gun, fed him a burrito, and dropped him off at the corner where a massive crowd throbbed and ebbed toward the courthouse. He didn't stay around long enough to watch Dallas disappear in the crowd.

After it was all over, no one trusted Arthur. And even though it was never certain what he did, people knew.

DELETED SCENE:
THIS COULD ALL BE YOURS

EXT. PARKING LOT - NIGHT

This is a scene where Austin's father takes
him into--

INT. PLUMBING SUPPLY WAREHOUSE

--where he discusses how using his near-
legend golf fame allowed him to start a
business that was more lucrative than
anything golf could've offered.

Austin's father goes into detail about how
much money the business provides their
family. He discusses legacy and how he
expects Austin to take over the business.

The entire scene feels a bit like a scene
out of a mafia film, where the reluctant son
of a mob boss is unsure if he wants to take
over the family business. Total Godfather
rip off.

But the further they go into this plumbing
warehouse, the more the scene becomes less
like a father-son moment and more like a

moment of slow-burn menace.

Then, Austin's father says--

                    CHANCE
          I know I don't tell you enough, or
          ever, but I love you, Austin. So
          much. It hurts my heart when I
          think of you and you are not right
          here for me to hug.

And they hug. It's a tender moment.

Then Chance continues into the warehouse,
talking about how much he misses golfing,
how breaking his hand was a curse and a
blessing, and how he took an unnecessary
risk that paid off in a way that was
unforeseen.

He also talks about wanting to make change
in the world, and how some risks are worth
taking.

This is when they come to the back of the
warehouse, where three people Chance
acknowledges and who Austin doesn't know
stand over a figure on the floor.
Handcuffed. Bound by ropes.

Then Chance tells Austin how the homeless
population, mostly immigrants who destroy
the decency of hardworking people, like
himself, are an infestation that needs
control.

While Chance talks with Austin, the three
men beat the homeless man's head in with
lead pipes. The pipes crack the man's chest,
rearrange the bones in the homeless man's

arms and legs. Chance discusses how
important it is to take pride in the
appearance of civility.

This is when Chance pours gasoline all over
the homeless man and sets him on fire.

Then he tells Austin that all the headlines
and news reports about burning homeless in
the city were because of him. And that it's
a duty he's taken upon himself.

                    CHANCE
          A vigilante. Like Batman.

Then Chance tells Austin that, like the
business, he wants to pass on this drive to
clean the unclean. Rid society of the
untruths that filter out the sincerity of
everyday life.

In the end, his father says--

                    CHANCE
          This could all be yours.

                    AUSTIN
          The warehouse?

                    CHANCE
     No...

A nearby door opens and two more PEOPLE drag
in another homeless body, unconscious,
bound. Already soaked in gas.

                              SMASH CUT TO:

EXT. CINÉMA VÉRITÉ - NIGHT

Austin and Chance stand outside the theater,
the glow from the SunCor billboard and the
neon on the marquee lighting them in mixes
of pink and yellow.

                    CHANCE
          You ever been here?

                    AUSTIN
          Never. Haven't been to a movie
          theater in like ten years.

                    CHANCE
          You still like movies, right?

                    AUSTIN
          Not really. I never really did.

                    CHANCE
          Oh... well, you know how I said all
          this could be yours and all that?

                    AUSTIN
          I don't want to talk about this.

                    CHANCE
          I meant this.

                    AUSTIN
          What?

                    CHANCE
          This.

He motions to the movie theater. Austin
doesn't get it, and then --

                    AUSTIN

This?

                    CHANCE

I own this now. Well, you own this
now.

                    AUSTIN

I don't want to own this now.

                    CHANCE

It's important that you do.

                    AUSTIN

Why?

                    CHANCE

Legacy.

                    AUSTIN

Legacy.

                    CHANCE

We've lost half of our chance to
carry on our name. And you seem to
have more of me in you -- not as
much of your mother. So I know how
you feel about your individuality
and your responsibility to family.

                    AUSTIN

Meaning?

                    CHANCE

Your name, our name, will live on
here. People will come and you will
let them in. We will spread our
name more than I could, more than
any child could.

                    AUSTIN
          This is a fuckin movie theater.
          It's not like Mecca or some shit.

                    CHANCE
          Not yet.

                    AUSTIN
          Meaning?

                    CHANCE
          Meaning let's go see a movie. My
          treat.

                    AUSTIN
          Yeah, I wasn't planning on paying
          for anything. I don't have any
          money.

                    CHANCE
          We can take care of that.

As they walk up to the box office, Austin's
mom shuffles behind them.

                    AUSTIN'S MOM
          What pretty lights.

                                        CUT TO:

DELETED SCENE:
EXCERPT FROM IN THE REALM OF LOST THINGS BY DON THOM DAVID

Winter comes on time's horizon. Mama moves quickly to gather what she needs to survive the coming cold. Her babies follow closely, learning how to exist in the hard wild. They will need eats and ways to protect the nest from the winter chill and the freezing rain. These things the Mama does so that her babies can live. Not at all worried about how long she will exist because life is all about passing on life and not at all about sustaining a single life. If her babies survive, they will make babies that will survive to make babies that will survive. She, with her fur and her four legs and her nipples with milk and her way for raising these babies, knows that this is what she is alive for. So she plans for the coming winter, gathering eats and nestmakings. They will stay in the warren and bundle, remain still without the silence and long sleep. A roar cuts the sky in half. From horizon to horizon. The fourleggers look up, see the dark mass blot out the sun. The fourleggers spent the day searching for slimebugs, gathering for the coming cold. Mama protected her babies from the sharpteeths in the high grass. Now, though, the danger is above. The sound, the cutting across the sky, the darkness. The Mama fourlegger knows it is dangerous. More than the sharpteeths. It is death. Mama pushes the babies through the high grass, navigating to a hole in the ground that connects back to their warren. Slimebugs line the earth outside the hole, but the Mama ignores the food. A sharpteeth lunges from the high grass and scoops Mama's baby into its mouth. The baby screams and then is silent. The Mama pushes her living babies to the hole. When they are gone, Mama stands guard at the hole until the sharpteeth is done eating. She waits for the screaming again. Somewhere far there is a loud rumble. The ground vibrates.

*   *   *

Darius wonders what extinction must've been like for those mammals that ended up becoming humans. How much dread they must've felt. He doesn't think it's anything compared to the Now. Modern America is one of those places where no one feels safe, especially white men. Darius feels he has to apologize for who he is all the time and that it's not so much about survival anymore—it's all about expectation. No one cares if he lives or passes on that living to another being. It's about what he's done during that time of living. Goddamn… That makes him want to do nothing.

"You understand what I am telling you, son?" The hospital priest talks to Darius like he's speaking to a child. Maybe that's what he sees Darius as now.

Darius says, "What will I have to do?"

"You'll have to make arrangements."

"Arrangements."

"The hospital will help you. You'll have to get a release form co-signed by whatever funeral home you choose. She will be buried?"

"Burned." Darius will never forget the length at which

his mother talked about what she wants to be done to her body once it becomes a shell no longer holding her soul.

"Son, we call that cremation."

"But you burn the bodies, right?"

The priest smiles. Keeping the peace. Or does he smile the same way at orphans—which is what Darius is now.

Darius says, "Am I supposed to give you a tip?"

"A what?"

"I don't know. You're sticking around here like you're expecting a tip. Is that what you want?"

"I'm doing God's work, son. I don't take tips."

"Then fuck off, father. My mother just died."

The priest nods and leaves the room like a saint.

The nurse who's been standing there the whole time says, "You want me to go too?"

"I want you to tell me what I have to do next, with her body."

"I… I don't know…"

"Then yeah, fuck off."

She does too. With the room empty—and it feels totally empty, even though he's here and so is the body of his mother—Darius approaches the body in the bed. It looks like it's made of wax. If the room were any warmer, that wax would melt, turn to liquid, that liquid running off the bed, onto the floor, where Darius would step all over it, the wax to harden later in the crevices of his sole, to be stepped on for weeks and weeks, a residue that won't leave him until he takes the time to scrape the wax out of his shoes and throw the crusty, stained, tainted wax in the trash, where it'll end up in a landfill with everyone else's trash.

It looks like his mother blinks. He waves a hand in her

face. The features remain tombstone still. He lightly slaps her forehead. Nothing. He slaps harder. Still nothing. He rears back and slaps the hell out of his dead mother's face.

She sits upright and says, "Will you fucking cut it out, you little shit?"

Nah, that didn't happen. She's dead. And the dead stay dead, except for when they live in our hearts.

*   *   *

Two hours later, the nurse returns with a vaguely Asian woman doctor. Another reminder that he, a white man, is no longer in the market to be anything other than the exterminator that he is. His kind aren't doctors anymore. They aren't people who make others look at them with reverence. They are simple servants at the ground-level. Plumbers, trash men, exterminators. People you let into your house and keep an eye on as they do things beneath your level of doing.

The doctor says, "Hello, Mr. Magnolia. I'm Dr. Zhao."

"Of course it's Zhao."

"Excuse me?"

"Are you married?"

The nurse backs out of the room, hoping no one notices her back out of the room.

Dr. Zhao says, "I don't understand how that's any of your business."

Darius says, "I'm curious. A last name like Zhao... Is your husband named Zhao?"

"You'll need to fill out this form once you have established which funeral home your mother will be released to," she says, not engaging in Darius's conversation. "Once we have that, communication will be at the responsibility of the funeral home. The hospital will only be concerned with how you plan to cover the additional costs of your mother's treatment—if there are any overages."

She looks at Darius, knowing that neither himself nor his mother had any form of insurance, and that covering the costs of the hospital's slow prolonging of her death will be at the mercy of his bi-weekly paychecks. Unless he just defaults and that bill goes to collections. Then, he'd be even further removed from the place his mother passed from this life and into the Whatever's Next.

Darius imagines himself as a roach, crawling up Dr. Zhao's leg, on skin so hairless and smooth it almost feels like marble. He scurries up her skirt, through her panties, and nudges into her pussy. She only gives the briefest sound of recognition. Maybe a sound of pleasure. Maybe the sound she makes when she's having a hard time on the toilet. He's inside her now, traveling up the way a sperm might, into her womb. This is where he stops, where he molts his exoskeleton and emerges as a mashed-potato soft fetus. A new version of himself in her womb, where he will grow like one of those capsules that when put in water eventually become a dinosaur-shaped sponge. He stays, feeding off all the food she eats, watching a white penis penetrate her almost every night, listening to her favorite classical music, listening as she commands a ward full of nurses with a gentle, yet stern leadership. He will expand until the day she pushes him out of her vaginal canal, head first, and he will bloom into this life—new, no longer Darius but rather something like Xing or Lim. He will suck at her perfectly shaped breasts, filling his body with her milk, begging for her nipple every day. Until the day he dies at two and half years old and his mother, trying to wake him, sucks on his tiny penis. And he will pass from this life, finally, in a state of pleasure so deep and total, that to have ever lived would be considered a clerical error that went uncorrected.

DELETED SCENE: THE DRIVER

There's a guy in a car—a maroon Crown Vic. He's trying to cross the border into SoCal. Except he's been waiting for almost twelve hours and he's only moved about six feet. He left before sunrise—it's now 4:15pm. To his left, there are wildfires burning in the hills—nothing new. He's old, like maybe 74 or 75. The kind of guy who wears sunglasses indoors, even at night. Blames it on presbyopia, but really stems from his inability to look people in the eyes—which he also attributes to what he calls *quasi-Aspergers behavior*. This guy's got a son in the Commonwealth, who he sees every other month. This is what he told his colleagues at Sun State, where he said he was going for the rest of the week. But the thing is is that he's never met his son, mostly because he was the by-product of a student affair played out as one would expect a student affair to play out. She—the student/mother—had told the guy in the car— the Driver—that she had had a miscarriage, but in reality just moved back in with her parents in what was formerly San Ysidro (now San Isidro). She'd had the baby, raised it with the help of her parents, telling her son that his father had been killed by North Korean troops in some unnamed conflict in Hawaii. So this son of his actually doesn't even know he still exists. His entire 74 (or 75) years denied by a child probably fifteen by now. He's learned recently that his son has a half-brother, so he isn't growing up alone, which eases the Driver's guilt of not being present. He switches on the radio before the A/C even though it's 110 degrees outside the car.

He's got the streaming service on his radio tuned to Leisure Sports Classic. When he hears the announcer mention the 22nd Warvin Zindler Gulf Coast Classic with Chance Foster, he suddenly doesn't mind being stuck in border traffic. Even though he knows what happens on the 17th hole, there's an anticipation in getting there that excites the Driver, allows him to ignore the electric sign hanging over the traffic ahead that says *Time to CalComm Border: ERROR*.

Also to his left, closer than the fires, is the Great Fault fissure. Gaping and radioactive.

The Driver wonders why the Chance Foster/Felix Pepperer match hasn't been made into a movie. If it had, Chance Foster might make a comeback, might become famous again. Like *Shine* did for David Helfgott or *Schindler's List* did for Amon Göth.

He figures he could see him, his son, even if only from afar—just this once. Before it's all over. He has the address where he goes to school. In San Dimas. He's sure there's a playground where, from a curbside parking space across the street, he can watch him play on the hover slide or swinging bars. Or whatever kids play on now. Do high school kids have playgrounds? Or do they still hang out behind the t-buildings and smoke weed like he used to when he was in high school? The Driver doesn't know. Either way, he would find his son and watch. It would be too far to see his son's eyes, see if there's any of himself (the Driver) in those eyes. His son. Tyler.

Not that it matters. He shouldn't be worried about legacy.

It's all going to be over soon. Not just his life, but all of it.

An incredible performance today from Foster after that par four eagle.

He'd seen what Spapling was into, understood the trajectories of the work. A great big dead-end for a reason that probably makes sense to someone who sees the human race as a plight on existence—or rather existence a plight on the human race. Shit, the Driver had even supplied Spapling with some answers to specific unsolvable technical issues with the operation upstate, had helped him input data into his deep-think system and the style algorithm database. Compiled lists of names. People who would find themselves involved in the trajectory and people who write like other people. People who had potential to stop the trajectory. Things like this. So whatever end is on the way, he—the Driver—is a part of it.

A man in the car next to him slams his hand on the steering wheel and cries. A frustrated mourning of time stalled and the stuckness of being in border traffic.

Foster, taking a moment now to speak with his caddy. The tension seems to have dissipated given the way he's smiling and laughing. As if he knows he's already won.

The Driver won't be around to see the end, because he's so sure that the small list of names—and growing smaller—of those who have the potential to stop the trajectory doesn't mean anything. He's starting to see that the trajectory is unchangeable. He'll see his son and then take a long walk into the ocean. Not the best way to go, but most certainly a guaranteed way. Maybe a peaceful way. Too old and weak to stay afloat long. It's whale migration season. Maybe he'll make it out far enough to see one up close. A bucket list to check off before he checks out.

Foster... Foster... Foster...

The name wades up from the depths. From one of the lists. A trajectory stopper. Not Chance.

Austin. Foster.

Carol, Foster's caddy, hands him a 3-iron. A safe bet on this long par 3.

A safe bet. Austin Foster.

The Driver wonders if this is a sign from... God? Whatever force that's way out there that maybe controls more than that monstrosity that Spapling's a part of. What if it's telling him, the Driver, that there's a *chance* that things won't end for everything? That maybe his legacy will continue if it exists in the eyes of his son.

The electric sign, now almost overhead, flickers. The yellow lights arrange themselves into the phrase *PLAN AHEAD WHILE YOU CAN*. The letters wink out and change quickly in a sequence that reads *A HEAD MISS* then *DAY* then *LOVE* then the sign goes black. When the *Time to CalComm border* comes back a fraction of a second later, the ETA now reads *Six Hours*.

This is about the time that the Foster/Pepperer match reaches its Hole 17 climax.

Foster, in a significant lead, appears to be breaking his own rules as he approaches the crowd.

DELETED SCENE: FAT TAX

Editor Note's: *The following is an excerpt from* Putting the Us Back in UAE: How I Plan to Show America Its Dream Again, *originally published one month prior to the re-election of current United American Empire president Guy Truffaux. This publication was meant to establish the principles of his campaign and is now being used as propaganda to promote the establishment of a third-term presidency. It was a* New York Times *bestseller for 88 weeks. By this time, the United States had separated into the current United American Empire. So the title didn't really make sense.*

9

FAT TAX: LET'S GET IN FISCAL SHAPE

Both the conservative and liberal media said I would never run for president. They were stupid in thinking I would back out. The day I was named a candidate, these same media outlets said I would quit because I wouldn't make it. Most of it had to do with my money and my family history. They were so wrong that it made them look stupid. The Chinese did a better job reporting my announcement than all the media outlets in America.

It was all a tactic to get me to run away from the attention. They thought I would be afraid to disclose that my great-grandfather's real name wasn't Truffaux, but Furffettegenstein. Or that he was involved in the education of Franz von Papen. They thought I would hide my financial history, afraid of my bankruptcies and non-profits and donations to the CoS and David M. These are the things I write off. Paying taxes when you don't need to is stupid, and I'm not stupid. I open my books to all, and have, in fact, included all my financial statements of the last 5 years in the back of this book.

Some might question if I've cooked these books. The only thing that's cooked is America's goose.

Do you know why these media outlets chose to attack me and my running for presidency? It is because they are sub-human and stupid. But where does this stupidity come from? Two places: being fat, and a lack of general healthcare. The primary key to existence is survival. This stupidity and fatness is the key preventative measure going *against* our survival. This, and the fact that there is no sense of community in work.

Here are two simple solutions to these problem:

Taxation and internment.

For every person in these United States, there will be a mandatory limit of weight, BMI, fat percentage, all relative to shape, size, gender, race, sexual orientation, religious identification, and genetic makeup. Citizens registered in the UAE will be required, by a certain date as yet set, to attend a physician of their choice to establish their overall fatness. This result will be called Pounds-Over-Ordinary-Percentage. At the end of the first fiscal year, this percentage will be tallied into annual taxes and a per-pound payment will be collected at the time of filing. No extensions will be granted.

However, should the individual be unable to pay the taxation, their rights will be immediately suspended. They will then be restrained and taken to one of the UAE transition facilities and then to the internment camps. These camps will be very comfortable. They will be run by good people. But they will involve work—and lots of it. Those in these camps will exchange their debt for labor, assisting the Empire in creating viable commodities, such as linen, microprocessors, coffee, silicon-based 3D compounds, plant food, toilets, and other such things. Two of the greatest contributors to the fiscal aspect of these camps are Taco Bell and McDonald's—who also contribute to the labor aspect with internees having the opportunity to produce the patties and fries and genuine, authentic Mexican tortillas served in these *very* American places.

Once the radicals based in the Southern California "Commonwealth" are eliminated and the Trans-Interrepublic Tolled-Expressway decommissioned, those remaining in the "Commonwealth" will be required to assign their citizenship to the United American Empire and its partners. Should they choose to stay, citizens of SC"C" will be willingly admitting themselves to the State and will be required to participate in the Fat-Action Taxation Internment Expurgatic System.

During tax season, in random locations throughout the UAE, TruPatrol agents (TPs) will be responsible for making house calls, supplying free/mandatory tax assessments. Should an individual be above the Ordinary Percentage, the monetary taxation will be due at that moment. Should, however, the individual be close enough to the Ordinary Percentage (for instance, a .000007% discrepancy), rather than paying the taxation, the individual will be given the opportunity to complete an on-the-spot correction of this overage. An example of this would be a payment of 120 pushups to rid the individual of the .000007% overage. However, should the individual not complete the task, the pushups completed will not count towards the initial taxation and full monetary payment is due immediately. Any inability to pay will result in temporary internment (no less than 5 days) until the overage is corrected.

As President, I am exempt from these taxations. I've seen a doctor. He says I'm in perfect health. Perfect. The best. He told me, "Guy, you might be 100 pounds overweight, but you're the healthiest American I've ever seen. And the smartest." And doctors don't lie. I've included this report in the back of this book.

Following my plan to withdraw from the United Nations (to create a nation able to act on its own, as I said before), this process will be solely in service of the system and not the means. There is no end product here. No one has their pockets lined with the sweat and hard work of these people who can't pay. Though they will suffer—and rightfully so—once they are out of the system, each of these individuals will return to citizenship with their rights intact, their bodies conformed to a fiscally responsible condition, and with a new understanding of the workings of American industry. We even give them the opportunity to continue working for the companies who subsidize the camps! How about that! It's a good system, and it will work.

You, the People, may ask: but where does this taxation flow? We give it back to you: the People. Fiscal accumulation from the Fat Taxation will be sent to a Financial Accumulation Reappropriation Troupe. This money will be sent to a healthcare reformation fund (set up during the Wellness Engagement Initiative & National Eupeptic Reformation Bill) and will be used to fund a Universal Healthcare program for every legal citizen of the United American Empire. Dental, covered. Physical, covered. Vision, covered. Mental illness coverage will be available for a per month fee and determined on a month-to-month basis.

The children of detained obese parents will be placed, safely, in centers designed to create both a safe environment and an educational one too. These children will remain here until the parents are released or until they reach legal age. If the children themselves are fat when they reach the legal age, they will be transferred to taxation camps to work off their debt. It is with extreme care and delicacy that we will handle this situation with the children. Not that we were in the wrong during the 2018-2029 situation involving children of immigrants. The ICE-created camps for these children were sparse but entirely safe environments. However, it would be best not to recreate a situation that would spark another outcry from the liberal population in America. Those camps in the Republic have been completely been re-regulated, offering a place for illegals to remain safely while we process their expulsion.

Now let's talk about patriotism.

This is the end of the excerpt. There were no further pages included in the packet.

DELETED SCENE:
GEORGE

HE LOOKS FOR HIS BROTHER, GEORGE.

The teenager finds that most of the posters he's put up around the neighborhood are now gone.

Stripped down.

Little pieces of paper still stuck to the staples and tape he put them up with.

The teenager keeps looking behind him, over his shoulder.

Being followed.

He knows it.

Maybe followed by the same people who took down the posters.

Can't erase a whole person, can you?

The teenager does a kickflip, almost lands it.

Rights the board, pushes off again on bumpy neighborhood streets.

A drone flies overhead.

The teenager doesn't think it's the same one that's been following him for days.

But it's doing the same thing: following him.

Someone came looking for him at his house.

His dad answered the door.

The teenager saw the ice cream truck parked down the

street. Right next to a maroon Crown Victoria that's been parked there for days.

He jumped out the window into the back yard, hopped fences. Enough to get away from them.

That was three days ago. He hasn't been back.

He doesn't really care about his parents. Or about eating—because he hasn't in a day or two.

All he cares about is finding George.

Even though he's only a half-brother, he still feels the connection that brothers have.

He knows his brother's still alive.

A cop pulls up to a stop sign down the street.

The teenager runs between houses, jumps a fence, jumps another, and ends up in a wooded area behind the neighborhood.

He's supposed to be in school today.

All a cop's gonna do is hassle him. Take him back home.

Stop him from finding George.

He's already been through these woods, doing the heartbreaking work of looking for George's body. He's seen *Paradise Lost*—so he knows that bad things happen to children in the woods.

The teenager even went as far as the ravine where the woods end in a hundred foot drop-off into rocks and shrubs below.

But he didn't find George.

He only found a half-smoked joint that he put in his pocket for whenever he found a lighter or a way to light it.

Back in these woods, the teenager takes a moment to stop.

Something he hasn't done in days.

Always the feeling of someone right there behind him.

Hands outstretched.

The drones and the ice cream truck and the unknown people at the door.

And the maroon Crown Victoria that's been there for days.

The teenager knows they'll get him eventually.

But not a moment before finding his brother.

Not half-brother. Fuck that clarification shit.

Brother.

The teenager's real dad is dead—or is at least dead to him.

So George's dad is as much his dad as anyone ever was or will be.

The teenager sits on a log. Rest his head on a tree trunk behind him.

Gives himself a moment to recall the ice cream truck and the birdcage.

The house across the street.

He wanted to approach the house, knock and wait for someone to answer so he could rush inside and look for George.

But the closer he got to the house, the closer those outstretched hands eased around his throat.

He knew he would have to figure out a way inside.

If the birdcage in the back of the ice cream truck meant anything, it meant that somewhere in that house, people were being held in cages.

The teenager's seen movies where people are held captive and turned into sex slaves. Or their organs are taken out and used for rich people.

This could be happening to George.

The teenager envisions George being smothered by a man so fat and large that the man looks like a giant slug. Like Jabba the Hutt from *Star Wars*.

He sees George trying to scream for help, but all that comes out is bubbling pink ooze.

The ooze splashes out and hits the teenager in the face.

The teenager opens his eyes and realizes he's been asleep in the woods.

The sky's mostly dark.

A twig snaps somewhere close.

A bush shakes.

The teenager stands, looks around.

Shadows consume the woods. Can't see much beyond the trees in front of him.

Footsteps. Slow. Deliberate.

The teenager holds his skateboard like a weapon.

Distant laughter. But close enough to be too close.

A high-pitched laugh. Like a sewer-dwelling clown.

The teenager runs, using his board as a shield against the branches and bushes in front of him.

He can't tell if he's heading toward the ravine or away from it.

Laughter again. Closer.

Footsteps running. Closer.

The teenager runs faster, thinking that these footsteps, this laughter, come from the same creature that took George.

He needs to live long enough to see it, face it.

He needs to get the upper hand.

He needs to—

His foot never comes down.

It dips through empty space.

He follows.

Tumbling headlong.

Not enough time to recognize that he's falling.

Not enough time to scream.

The teenager makes a noise.

A grunt.

Tension in the form of an audible flinch.

The fall of a hundred feet takes longer than expected.

The sound his body makes when it hits the ravine floor a hundred feet below is like a raw egg dropped on a kitchen floor.

His skin can't hold the pressure.

Bones turn dusty inside his flesh.

Blood oozes like the pink stuff did from George's mouth.

The teenager has a final thought before a radial of kaleidoscopic light consumes everything he sees.

The thought:

Birdcage.

Above:

Three stoned teenagers approach the spot where the teenager just fell.

These are boys who know the teenager (whose name is Tyler) but only in passing because they are metalheads and the teenager, Tyler, is more of a skater/stoner, the two groups at war with each other to prove who gives a shit less.

The stoned teenagers stand at the ravine's edge, look down at Tyler's body.

From this height, his body looks more like a pile of clothes.

One stoned teenager says, "Shit."

Another says, "Let's get the fuck out of here."

The third says, "I want to see his blood."

But they don't see Tyler's blood.

They all run away, never to admit they were anywhere near

the accident that killed Tyler.

Never admitting to their part in a mother and father losing their child, the second in just a week.

Footsteps running. Growing distant.

Tyler's body at the bottom of the ravine.

The sky fades from deep purple to midnight black.

On the other side of the ravine, on a street lined with houses that all look the same, the Driver, in his maroon Crown Victoria, searches the streets for his son, who he's learned has gone missing, who he's learned is named Tyler.

DELETED SCENE: INTERDEPARTMENTAL MEMO (VIA TOURNESOL STUDIOS)

Editor's note: *Due to size restrictions and for clarity, the memo is on the following page.*

MEMO

DATE   19 October 2█████

TO   Phil Swope
Executive Producer

FROM   Lucius Beezelb
Studio CEO

SUBJECT   Evaluation of **Sunflower**

Bill, what the hell's wrong with you, sending me this shit? Look: I'm all for trying to break new ground, but this is a studio. We are here to make money -- not intentionally difficult "art." I could go into all of it, but I won't. I'll say two things. 1) This ending is fucking terrible. Don't know what ████ was thinking. But see if you can get one of our go-tos to re-write something that isn't gonna make people slit their wrists. And 2) Significant plot points need to change otherwise we are going to get sued out the fucking ANUS by Disney. Too much of this is a straight ripoff of **[REDACTED]**. I don't know if you're slipping in your old age, but I'm starting to worry about you, question if you're still up to devoting to this biz. Get back with me when you figure out how to make this in a way that's not so bad. No one's going to pay money for this. No one. And I need your Netflix password again.

TOURNESOL STUDIOS   (310) 422-6669 | www.tournesolforever.com |
3000 W Alameda Ave, Burbank, CA

DELETED SCENE: ZODIAC LETTER

Editor's Note: *The following Zodiac letter was recovered from the Benicia Police Department's evidence storage facility in December 20█. After translation, the letter was returned to storage as it provided no clue to any crimes committed, nor did it provide evidence of further violent acts—as a majority of the previous letters had. The translation also showed the Zodiac in a manic state, mentally deteriorating. "It's just a bunch of rambling bullshit," said Solano County district attorney Yoshi Hytopean. Investigators did conclude, however, that the letter was created over two decades after the "final" Zodiac murder. Handwriting analysis proved the letter genuine.*

This is the piece of paper that Maddix hands to Austin at Wade's funeral.

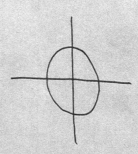

Editor's Note: *In August of 1969, the Zodiac's letters were deciphered by amateur codebreakers—a California math teacher and his wife. Fourteen days after publishing this cipher to the San Francisco Chronicle, the couple vanished. The cipher is provided here for ease of translation. This editor couldn't be bothered. Enjoy.*

The Zodiac's 408 Character Cipher

Cipher Text & Plain Text Equivalents

S = A	**Q** = F	**☯** = M	**▲** = S
G = A	**J** = F		**◨** = S
⌡ = A		**O** = N	**K** = S
▲ = A	**R** = G	**D** = N	**F** = S
◭ = A		**Λ** = N	
	⊕ = H	**φ** = N	**L** = T
V = B	**M** = H		**H** = T
			I = T
Ǝ = C	**P** = I	**I** = O	**●** = T
	⋋ = I	**◖** = O	
ⱺ = D	**△** = I	**X** = O	**Y** = U
⊕ = D	**U** = I	**T** = O	
	◮ = I		**Ɔ** = V
Z = E	**/** = K	**π** = P	
W = E			**A** = W
N = E		**Я** = R	
E = E	**B** = L	**⊥** = R	**Ʈ** = X
q = E	**■** = L	**** = R	
+ = E	**◨** = L		**□** = Y
◉ = E			

Note: The Zodiac used the symbol "▲" for both "A" and "S"

DELETED SCENE: LOVE CONQUERS ALL

MUSIC: "TAKE ME HOME" - PHIL COLLINS

MONTAGE BEGINS

EXT. SPACE - DAY

As Earth spins, a slow descent toward the
ground floor.

INT. HOSPITAL ROOM - DAY

AUSTIN, now mostly covered in bandages, lays
in a hospital bed. He's hooked up to
machines. A HAND eases into his. Austin's
fingers wrap around this hand. His eyes
flutter open.

WADE stands at his bedside. Alive and
healthy. Austin's eyes widen. He tries to
speak but only a gurgle comes out.

                    WADE
          It's okay. Anything you're gonna
          say... I know.

Austin tries to smile, but his face doesn't
really move.

                    WADE
          You'll be okay. You got burned
          pretty bad, but they think you'll
          recover nicely. It's gonna take
          some time. You've been out for a
          couple of weeks now.

Austin looks around, afraid.

                    WADE
          It's over... It's all over.

Austin looks at the doorway as his MOM
enters the room. A tear falls out of
Austin's eye, down his bandaged face.

                    WADE
          Austin...

Austin looks at him.

                    WADE
          Thank you for saving me.

Austin tightens his grip on Wade's hand.
Wade leans down and places a soft, loving
kiss on Austin's forehead. Austin closes his
eyes, a deep peace washing over him like an
incoming surf.

EXT. MARS COLONY BASE - DAY

Children run in the domed space, safe from
the suffocating air outside. Parents watch
their children, arm-in-arm. Workers
cultivate a nearby patch of land growing

produce in abundance. A FARMER herds cows in a smaller domed area.

One of the women, pregnant, holds a hand over her belly. Two men walk hand-in-hand, laughing at a joke we can't hear.

One of the children stops playing, looks up, shields their eyes from the sun -- which peaks through the haze. A break in the clouds shows a sky that's only slightly blue.

Maybe becoming more blue every day.

EXT. SOMEWHERE OUTSIDE TIME - BRIGHT

A valley straight out of an Albert Bierstadt painting. Anyone would call it heavenly. A flock of otherworldly birds glide overhead. Two suns and three moons grace the pink-tinted blue sky. Everything throbs, as if it's made of paint instead of reality fabric.

DELTA steps to the precipice of the canyon overlooking the valley. A hue of golden light surrounds her, pulses. She turns back and motions for someone to come to her.

BUB, exactly as he was in life, runs to Delta. Laughing, happy. He jumps up and she catches him.

                    BUB
          This is good.

Delta nods.

An arm slips around her waist. And then he
steps up to the canyon edge with her --
DEVAUGHN BLAKE. The three of them look out
on their paradise. An ethereal creature of
majesty and imagination soars overhead. Bub
laughs again.

In the valley below: the two brothers,
GEORGE and TYLER, play -- one skates, while
the other rides his silver spray-painted
bike.

EXT. ANIMAL SANCTUARY - DAY

BARB approaches the chainlink fence where,
beyond it, SIMEON THE LION sits in the
midday sun, warming his well-groomed fur.
The lion sees Barb and a moment of
recognition passes between the two. Simeon
stands, struts up to the fence.

Barb puts her hand in the space between the
chainlinks. The lion approaches.

                    BARB
          I miss you.

Simeon the Lion sniffs Barb's hand, and with
a tender-sounding purr, licks her skin. A
tear falls from his eye.

EXT. GOLF COURSE - DAY

CHANCE FOSTER, at the tee box on a Par 4,
removes his driver from the bag at the back
of a golf cart designed to look like a
Cadillac. He approaches the already-tee'd up
ball.

He grips the club with both hands, looks out
at the wide-open fairway ahead. He prepares
himself to swing.

EXT. PARK - DAY

JENNIFER BRACHIS DONNAHUE sits at a park
bench. To anyone, it looks like she's
talking to herself. But to us, through the
magic of cinema, we can see that she shares
the bench with a HEATHER PÉREZ who looks
superimposed.

The two laugh, their conversation unheard in
favor of the music playing over the
soundtrack. Even though we can't hear them,
their laughter and smiles tell us they are
happy now.

Together as one.

INT. DRUGLORD DEN - DAY

MANJEEP approaches the DRUGLORD with a large
briefcase. Slides it across a table. The
Druglord opens it: stacks of American
currencies. Easily millions.

The Druglord laughs, turns to one of his
associates and snaps. The Associate exits
the room. Manjeep waits.

EXT. SMALL VILLAGE NEAR JODHPUR - DAY

Manjeep walks down a street, his brother,
HRITHIK, walking next to him. The brothers
look at each other, a sly smile passing

608.   TEX GRESHAM

between each other.

And then Hrithik's off, sprinting ahead.
Manjeep doesn't hesitate. His years of
running from acorns makes him fast. He
catches up to his brother, the two laughing
at the impromptu race. They keep going and
going.

EXT. MANJEEP'S HOUSE - DAY

Manjeep and Hrithik approach their small
house right as their MOTHER and GRANDMOTHER
step out, tears streaming down both feminine
faces. They all share an embrace. Home.

But Manjeep pulls away, walks off on his
own.

EXT. FIELD - DAY

Manjeep approaches the edge of a field.
Looks out on amber waves of grain as they
blow in the wind. His eyes watch but his
mind wanders, distant.

INT. PROJECTION HALL - DAY

JACKIE, wearing a neck brace, flips the
switch on SF-2 and the reel starts. She
looks through the window into Theater 2 as
the sound syncs and the film, perfectly in
focus, starts. The theater's packed now,
every seat taken by moviegoers who don't eat
popcorn, who watch the screen with rapt
attention. Cutting Room begins.

She moves to SF-1 and unspools the reel for
Over/Shift. Brings it over to the rewinder,
spins it back to the beginning. Cans it.
Shelves it.

She walks into --

INT. JACKIE'S BEDROOM - CONTINUOUS

-- as MISS waits, now in the body of Jessica
Fey, in bed, half-covered. The parts of her
uncovered are nude. Dead flesh now refreshed
and living. Tender. Miss stretches like
she's just woken up. Jackie lights a
cigarette.

                    MISS
          What time is it?

                    JACKIE
          You don't know?

Miss smiles.

                    MISS
          Is this what it's like? Being
          human? Never knowing the time?
          Never really knowing what's next?

                    JACKIE
          You almost never get used to it.

                    MISS
          I feel like I could.

                    JACKIE
          You feel...

                        MISS
            I feel.

Miss sits up, motions for Jackie to hand her
the cigarette. Jackie puts it in Miss's
mouth. The sheet falls down, revealing
Miss's naked figure.

Jackie walks to her closet, opens it.

The noose is no longer there. The closet is
filled with clothes that don't look like
anything Jackie would wear. She pulls a
shirt off the hanger, tosses it to Miss.

                        JACKIE
            Get dressed.

                        MISS
            What's going on?

                        JACKIE
            We're going out today.

                        MISS
            Lunch?

                        JACKIE
            I'll get Linus to cover the
            projectors.

                        MISS
            His name's Paul.

                        JACKIE
            Whatever. Just get dressed. I'm
            gonna make a call real quick.

Miss slips the shirt over her body as Jackie
walks across her room to a high-tech station

with a screen and a camera and a complicated
system of servers and processors, all of it
sleekly packaged in a single, ATM-shaped
device. She calls.

INT. SPACEX SPACE STATION II - DAY

AMY floats away from the window, the bright
spot gone, the Earth rotating peacefully.
The communication station beeps, pulling her
attention. She accepts the incoming
transmission. Jackie's face appears on the
screen.

                    JACKIE
          Hello, sis.

                    AMY
          Calling again?

                    JACKIE
          I just wanted to send you
          something. Keep you busy.

                    AMY
          I'll be down next week. Can't wait
          til then?

                    JACKIE
          It'll help you pass the time.

                    AMY
          Oh so you're sending me stuff now?
          Not the other way around?

                    JACKIE
          Something to read.

                         AMY
              Wow... Jackie reading now.

Jackie laughs. Amy smiles.

                         JACKIE
              I'll see you soon.

                         AMY
              Love you.

                         JACKIE
              Back at ya.

The call ends. The Relay system chimes with
an incoming packet. Amy connects the Relay
to the docuprinter and logs the file over to
that system.

The first page prints. It reads:

SUNFLOWER: THE FINAL FILM BY SIMEON WOLPE

                         AMY
              Reading a movie...

Amy rolls her eyes. The next page finishes
printing.

EXT. SPACE - TIMELESS

We pull back away from the SpaceX Space
Station, away from Earth. We pass the Moon
-- and then we pick up speed. "Take Me Home"
by Phil Collins grows in volume on the
soundtrack.

Shooting through space at a speed many times
the speed of light. Past Mars, a single

point glowing as the colony blossoms. Past
Jupiter -- its raging storms and its
satellite moons. Past Saturn's rings,
Uranus, Neptune. Past that abandoned non-
planet Pluto.

Further and faster -- past the radiation
limit of the sun. Past supernovas and
nebulas. Beyond a point where the Sun's
light becomes indecipherable from the
billions and trillions of visible stars.

A blast of light and we're outside the
system, seeing now the Milky Way, emerging
from our little stellar neighborhood in the
galaxy.

Moving now faster than human comprehension
-- galaxies, clusters, all seen like germs
in a high-powered sneeze. Floating in a void
that isn't at all a void. Everything coming
together in a great beacon of light to the
infinite space surrounding it. All galaxies
forming the universe. All universes forming
the multiverse. All multiverses forming an
egg-shaped reality that rests in a womb of
infinity.

And from way out here, where distance is
measured in time and units that humans will
never know, we hear her voice -- reading
from that first page. And it goes like this:

                    AMY DAY (V.O.)
          Everything that begins has an
          end...

                                   FADE TO:

...

[EMPTY]

DOS\\REBOOT

...

[SYSTEM ONLINE]

CMD\\RUN\RESTART.EXE

ACKNOWLEDGMENTS

It's been a ten year journey from first words to this moment—many drafts, failed attempts, deleted deleted scenes, significantly reduced passages, characters excised from existence, and so on and so on. It's a deeply melancholic feeling to put a period at the end of this journey, but it was inevitable.

This book would've had an impossible time being anything other than a bunch of embarrassing typos and glaring continuity errors without the hard work of my editor/bud, KKUURRTT—this book almost ruined our friendship.

To the crew at Spaceboy Books—Nate and Shaunn. Y'all are real ones for putting this into the world to infect readers.

A special thanks to all my writer friends who read this at varying stages and gave me thoughts, changes, encouragements, and sometimes a sincere *this doesn't work at all.*

A debt of gratitude goes to those who pointed me in the right direction: Victoria Smith, Ron Haas, Debra Monroe, Jon Marc Smith, Stephen-Paul Martin, April Wilder, Gary Heidt, and Lamar Schrader—my high school English teacher who encouraged me to read and write and always be myself. Don't think he knows how much he shaped who I am today, but maybe he does now.

And always: much love to my partner, V. Ruiz, who reminded me to stay true to the book that I wanted to write. They have been an immense wealth of encouragement and support. All my heart belongs to you, V.

Oh shit... Did you ever read the Editor's Note at the beginning of the Special Features? If not, you should probably do that now. It's pretty important. Maybe...

Author Photo: Austin Call (@duhrivative)

ABOUT THE AUTHOR

Tex Gresham is the author of *Heck, Texas* (Atlatl Press). His screenplay, *Fix Daddy*, won the 46th Humanitas College Comedy Fellowship. He's had work published in *Hobart*, *The Pinch*, *Rejection Letters*, *HAD*, and *X-R-A-Y Magazine*, among other places. This is his first novel.

www.squeakypig.com

Twitter: @thatsqueakypig
Instagram: @squeakypig

ABOUT THE PUBLISHING TEAM

Nate Ragolia was labeled as "weird" early in elementary school, and it stuck. He's a lifelong lover of science fiction, and a nerd/geek. In 2015 his first book, *There You Feel Free*, was published by 1888's Black Hill Press. He's also the author of *The Retroactivist*, published by Spaceboy Books. He founded and edits *BONED*, an online literary magazine, has created webcomics, and writes whenever he's not playing video games or petting dogs.

Shaun Grulkowski has been compared to Warren Ellis and Philip K. Dick and was once described as what a baby conceived by Kurt Vonnegut and Margaret Atwood would turn out to be. He's at least the fifth best Slavic-Latino-American sci-fi writer in the Baltimore metro area. He's the author of *Retcontinuum*, and the editor of *A Stalled Ox* and *The Goldfish*, among others.

ABOUT THE EDITOR

KKUURRTT is glad you read this thing he overedited. He is the author of *Good At Drugs* (Back Patio Press), *Blech Life* (Bottlecap Press), and *Give Me A Bad Movie Over A Good One Anyday: Tubi Poems* (The Daily Drunk). He can be found on Twitter as @wwwkurtcom

ABOUT THE COVER ARTIST

Matthew Revert is a multidisciplinary artist from Melbourne, Australia with a focus on visual art, writing, music and design. His visual art has amassed a strong following and in 2019, Clash Books released a book of his visual art called *Try Not To Think Bad Thoughts*. He is the author of five novels including *The Tumours Made Me Interesting*, *Basal Ganglia* and *Human Trees*. Reissues of his sought after written work will finally be released starting with his first three comedic absurdist novels in 2021 by 11:11 Press. He has had music released in myriad formats by renowned labels such as Erstwhile Records, Kye Records, No Rent among others. His graphic design work can be found on no fewer than 800 book and record covers. Follow him at Instagram @papercrisis or visit his chronically out of date website:

www.matthewrevert.com

SCAN NOW TO LISTEN TO
SUNFLOWER: THE SOUNDTRACK
ON

Hemingway?
King?
Morrison?
Murakami?
Wallace?
Wolpe?
Discover your **StyleTwin™**...

www.StyleTwin.org

Sent less than an hour ago

9 781951 393083